Zeke Cooper

Justice at Agua Caliente

Ray Adkins

To!
Chuck
Best wishes
Ray Adkins
4-24-2010

ISBN: 1449996086
ISBN-13: 9781449996086

Chapter One
1878

It was mid-morning and a stagecoach pulled by a well-matched six-horse team raced its way up the side of the Sierra Nevada Mountains. It was bitter cold outside and almost as cold inside. Zeke was wearing a sheepskin coat that came down to mid-thigh. There had been a heavy rain the day before and the stage stopped early and stayed overnight at the last stage station before starting up the mountain. The driver had said, "I don't hanker on being on that mountain in a rainstorm, the trail across is kinda narrow in most places, narrower in others. It's a trail that's treacherous in the best o' weather."

As the six passengers boarded the coach at sunrise the driver commented, "This will be our last run through the mountain on this route until spring. It'll probably be snowing by nightfall, but we should be through the pass and on the other side of the mountain afore it hits. We'll be running with a strong six-horse team and ought to make good time."

The trail was indeed narrow, the higher up the mountain they got, the skinnier the trail became. It narrowed to about seven feet in some places and no more than ten feet wide in others. It clung to the side of the mountain, the left side against the steep rise of the mountain and the right side giving way to nothing more than air and a very long drop.

The team was galloping hard as they came around a left-hand curve. Suddenly the driver saw a ditch that someone had dug from the middle of the road to the edge of the cliff. On the other side of the ditch, several men were sitting on their horses. They had bandanas pulled up over their faces as they watched the stagecoach come around the bend and hit the ditch.

The driver swerved as far left as he could and tried his best to stop the coach but it was too late. When the right front wheel hit the ditch, the coach flipped over the edge of the cliff dragging the team of horses with it. As it went over the side, the door sprang open and Zeke jumped. When the coach hit the bottom of the cliff, it rolled over several times.

After the stagecoach went over the cliff's edge, the outlaws dismounted and approached the edge on foot. As they surveyed their handiwork, one of them swore and said, "I sure didn't reckon on that coach going over the cliff." Then he added, with a slight lisp to his voice, "Everybody what's on it is probably dead. I was looking forward to putting a hole through Zeke Cooper's head, but it ain't worth climbing down there to shoot a dead man and I don't reckon that it'd be worthwhile to climb down there to get their valuables."

"Yeah, you're more-n-likely right," answered one of the other outlaws. "Don't matter though, if they ain't dead now they soon will be. Look at those storm clouds to the west. That's a blizzard coming this way and it won't be long before it gets here. When that storm hits it'll finish killing anyone that might have survived the fall. We've done what we came to do and we didn't have to fire a single shot. Let's skedaddle out o' here whilst we can and get off this mountain afore that storm hits."

The outlaws turned away from the cliff and started back to their horses.

Zeke slowly regained consciousness, bewildered he wondered what had happened. He was laying on his back and staring upward at a cloud-laden sky. Looking around, he discovered that he was at the bottom of a cliff about fifty feet high. The ground sloped from the bottom of the cliff to a river about eight hundred feet away. Looking to the top of the cliff, he saw the backs of seven men walking away. Then he saw them ride in the direction from which he had come. One of the riders was riding a large white stallion.

Zeke sat up and took stock of himself ... outside of a few scratches, small cuts, some bruises, a headache and a sizeable lump on the side of his head he appeared to be okay. Further down the slope the stagecoach lay in a flat area about two hundred fifty feet from him.

Zeke got to his feet and started towards the remains of the stagecoach. About seventy-five feet down the slope were the dead bodies of the driver and guard. After checking the two bodies and being sure that they were dead, he went on down the slope. The slope was steep and he slipped and slid his way on down to the coach. It had come to rest tilted at about a forty-five degree angle against a large tree, which had kept it from rolling farther down the hill. The coach had lost its wheels and all that remained in one piece was the passenger compartment. The area by the tree was flat, about one hundred fifty feet in one direction and sixty to seventy feet in the other. Several boulders and five large trees were scattered in the flat area. Past the flat area, the hill sloped a little more gently another five hundred feet. At the bottom of the slope was a river about seventy feet wide.

Zeke pushed the coach away from the tree and it thudded onto its bottom. Looking inside what was left of the coach, he saw five people all tangled together. When he checked them, he found that they were all dead. The six horses that had pulled the stage were another hundred feet down the slope … all of them dead.

Still wondering what had happened he looked to the top of the cliff. He surmised that the seven men he saw riding away were somehow responsible. The cliff was almost vertical and it would be impossible to climb back to the road from here.

Zeke searched through the wreckage, found a shovel tied to the side of the coach and started digging the first of seven graves. As he dug the graves, he wondered what the names of the dead passengers were. He paused his digging and looked up the slope. He saw articles of clothing, torn apart luggage and personal belongings strewn down the slope from the bottom of the cliff to the coach and beyond. There was a small leather satchel laying just down hill from the coach. The satchel looked to be intact. Apart from possibly the contents of the satchel, it would be hopeless to try to match what remained of the luggage to its owners.

After Zeke finished digging the graves, he removed the bodies from the coach and carried them to their final resting place. Before burying them, he unsuccessfully searched each body in an attempt to find out who they were. He buried each of them not knowing any of their names. Then he climbed up the slope to the bodies of the driver and guard. It was getting close to dusk by the time he finished burying everyone.

The exertion of digging the graves had kept him warm but now he was getting cold. He gathered some deadwood from beneath the trees and built a fire next to a large flat-topped boulder about twenty feet from the coach. He knew that the boulder would absorb heat from the fire then radiate it back out. After he warmed himself a little, he retrieved the leather satchel and brought it to the fire. There was a smaller boulder by the large one, Zeke sat on it and opened the satchel.

When Zeke opened the satchel, the contents seemed familiar to him and with sudden realization he exclaimed, "Who am I? … I don't know who I am. … What am I doing here? … Why was I on that stagecoach? … Who were those men I saw at the top of the cliff? … Are they going to get help? … Probably not … if they were going to help they wouldn't have left."

Zeke searched through the satchel and found two changes of clothing, a bar of soap, shaving mug, shaving brush, razor and leather razor strop. He thought, 'This must be mine, the clothes look to be the right size for me and it feels like it belongs to me.'

What Zeke did not find, was the hidden compartment in the bottom of the satchel. The compartment contained a letter of credit from the Territorial Bank in Tucson. The letter, made out to Zeke Cooper, was for an unlimited amount. The hidden compartment also contained a telegram from Bob Douglas, two hundred dollars in bills and a deputy United States Marshal's badge.

Zeke sat by the fire and contemplated on what he knew. 'I was on a stage coach but I don't know where I was going,' he thought 'and I don't know where I've been either.' He reasoned, 'When the stage doesn't show up at the next station they will send a search party out. The best thing for me to do is sit tight right here and wait for them. Of course those men might be working their way down here, but I ain't going to count on them … they probably caused the wreck.'

A few snowflakes fell and Zeke realized that he would not be able to stay by the fire all night. He built the fire up, then went to the coach and got inside. He lifted one of the seats and found six lap robes in the compartment beneath it. Wondering how he knew the robes were there, he made himself a bed of sorts.

Cold, tired and very hungry, Zeke finally fell into a fitful sleep. His last thoughts were, 'Maybe tomorrow I'll remember who I am.'

He awoke several times during the night. Each time he woke up, it was after the same dream. A wolf standing on top of a bluff turned his head one way then back the other way and howled. After he howled, the wolf stood very still as if he was listening for something. Three times, he repeated the sequence of looking and howling. The first time the wolf howled he was facing west. The next time he faced east, then south and then north. A large blue roan stallion ran in the same direction that the wolf faced. Each time the wolf howled the horse reared up on its hind legs and with his fore hooves pawing at the air he whistled loudly through his nostrils. After the wolf howled and stood still four times, the horse came and stood beside him.

Each time Zeke woke up, he instinctively put his hand on the talisman that hung from around his neck. 'I know that wolf and horse' he thought. 'But what does it mean?'

The talisman, round and made of bone, had the shape of a wolf head carved in the center, with blue turquoise inlaid as its eyes. In a circle around the head were several symbols. There was the shape of four paw prints, one at each corner of the compass. Between each paw print was an eagle, a lightning bolt and a shield. In a circle between the symbols and the edge of the talisman were twelve arrows. The talisman, strung on a piece of catgut, had two wolf claws on each side.

Morning was a long time coming but it finally arrived. When Zeke poked his head out the door, he saw that about two inches of snow had fell during the night. He went to the boulder and started building a fire. As he was placing the wood for the fire, he heard a twig snap. With his six-gun in hand, he turned towards the sound with the muzzle of his gun leading the way. He saw a large elk grazing beneath a tree about fifty feet from him. His gun barked once and the elk collapsed to the ground.

Zeke replaced the spent cartridge in his gun with a fresh one before returning it to his holster. Then he went to the dead horses, retrieved the leather reins and tied the two together. He went to the elk and tied one end of the long leather strap around its hind legs. He threw the other end over a branch twenty feet above the ground and hoisted the elk up about five feet. He cut the elks throat to drain its blood and then went back to continue building his fire while waiting for the elk to bleed out.

After he got the fire going, Zeke went to a tree and looked for a forked branch. The first tree he looked at did not have what he was looking for so he went to another. The third tree had two forked branches that would work very well. They were the right size to place on either side of the fire to hold a spit, on which he could cook the elk meat. Zeke looked at his pocketknife and thought, 'I need a knife heavier than this to cut those branches off.'

He somehow knew that the stagecoach carried an axe for clearing a roadway of any fallen trees. Zeke went to the coach and found the box that formed the drivers' seat was still intact. The box was about five feet long two feet wide and just over two feet deep. Zeke flipped the two latches down and lifted the hinged lid.

Inside the box, he found an axe, a length of rope about twenty-five feet long, a large hunting knife, a cast iron pot, a metal spit rod and two metal forks to hold the rod. The box also contained a coffeepot, a package of coffee, salt, several tin cups, some metal plates, eight forks and four cans of peaches.

Elated with what he found in the box, Zeke gathered what he would need and carried them to the fire. He pushed the metal forks into the ground on opposite sides of the fire. Then he filled the cast iron pot with snow and hung it over the fire on the spit rod. It wasn't long before the snow melted and Zeke filled the coffee pot with some of the water. He threw a handful of coffee grounds in the pot and placed it on the fire.

While waiting for the coffee to boil, Zeke went back to the elk and started dressing it out. After he skinned and dressed the elk Zeke cut the right front forequarter off and carried it to the fire. He placed the meat on top of the large boulder and went back to the hanging elk. He hoisted the elk higher until it was hanging about ten feet above his head.

The coffee was ready when he got back to the fire. Zeke filled a cup and while sipping on the coffee, he started cutting some of the meat into small chunks. He put the chunks of meat into the now boiling water in the cast-iron pot and added a little salt. He cut up all of the meat, some into thin strips and the rest into cubes about two inches thick.

While working on the meat Zeke looked up at the road on top of the cliff. He thought, 'A search party will probably show up sometime this afternoon. After I eat

I'll search the debris scattered down the hill for anything that's salvageable.'

As Zeke ate, he pondered on his situation, 'I seem to know what to do and I'm apparently good with a gun. I dropped that elk with one shot between its eyes without even thinking about it. Maybe I'm a gunfighter … Do I make a living with my gun? … No, I don't think so … I know that I don't make a living with my gun. … How is it that I know these things and yet can't remember who I am or where I'm going?'

After Zeke ate and drank more coffee, he checked the trail of debris. He started at the top and worked his way down the slope. He found the guard's rifle, a box of cartridges and two canteens, but nothing else of any use.

Through the day, Zeke cooked the rest of the meat that he had cut up. He skewered the strips of meat onto the spit-rod and cooked the chunks in the pot.

He kept the fire under the cooking meat hot, without any smoke. Late morning Zeke built another large fire and fed it with green wood so it would produce a lot of smoke. With satisfaction, he watched the column of smoke rise into the air and thought, 'No way can a search party miss that.'

As he kept busy cooking the meat and keeping the smoky fire going, Zeke had flashes of memory. He recalled that the stage he was on would be the last one using this route until spring. He had been a bit dubious about taking it but he was in a hurry to get to … get to … get to where? About an hour before dusk Zeke muttered to himself, 'If anyone was coming they should have been here by now.'

Zeke was unaware that there was no search party. The light snow that fell during the night was from the edge of a snowstorm that had raged on the other side of the mountain from late afternoon until around three in the morning. The mountain pass that the stage road ran through, will not be usable until the spring thaw. The people on the easterly side figured that the stage had made it through the pass and the ones on the other side assumed that they had not tried. Both stations closed for the winter and they each moved their stock to another station farther from the mountain.

Once again, Zeke spent a fitful night in the remains of the stagecoach. As he lay there, trying to get to sleep he thought, 'There'll be more snow coming soon and I can't stay here. Tomorrow I'll gather what I figure I'll need and get out of here. I can't get back up onto the road from here, but if I follow the river downstream it'll take me out of these mountains and away from the snow.'

He awoke several times through the night. Each time was after having the same dream about a wolf and a stallion. The wolf and the stallion did the same as in the dreams of last night.

Zeke knew that the wolf and horse both meant something to him, but he just could not recall what it was.

Chapter Two

It snowed heavy during the night and was still snowing lightly when morning finally came. When Zeke stepped out of the stage, he sank into the snow. The snow was about two feet deep.

Zeke trudged through mid-calf deep snow to where his fire had been. He pushed the snow out of the fire ring with his hands and built a fire. After filling the cook pot with snow, he set it on the fire and waited for the snow to melt. It didn't take long for the snow to turn to water and he used it to make coffee.

He ate some of the meat he had already cooked and washed it down with coffee. As he ate, he took stock of his situation. 'The sooner I get off of this mountain the better off I'll be,' he thought. 'I don't know how long that will take in this snow. I best prepare what I'll need today and leave when it quits snowing. Trying to walk through this snow will tire me pretty quick. The first thing I need to do is make a pair of snowshoes.'

Zeke trudged through the snow to the tree where the elk hung. He cut two boughs off the tree. They were about three-quarters of an inch in diameter and six feet long. Then he cut several long, half-inch boughs from the tree. After cutting off a length of the leather strap that the elk hung from, he returned to the fire. He put more wood on the fire, sat down and began making the snowshoes.

He bent the three-quarter inch boughs into an oval shape and tied them with a piece of the leather strap. Then he weaved the half-inch boughs into the oval opening. When he finished he had two snowshoes about eighteen inches long and twelve inches wide. Using pieces of the leather strap, he tied them to the bottom of his boots.

Zeke stood and took a few tentative steps. Satisfied that they would serve their purpose he sat back down. While sipping on a hot cup of coffee he mentally made a list of what he should take when he left.

He figured that the meat he had already cooked would last him several days. He would take the coffee, coffeepot and spit rods with him. 'Maybe,' he thought, 'I can get everything I'll need in that satchel.' With that thought in mind, he went to the coach to get the satchel. He looked at it and thought, 'it ain't big enough to hold everything I need.'

Zeke went back to the fire poured himself a cup of coffee and pondered on what he could do. He mentally checked off what he would not need to take with him. While deep in thought, his eyes wondered around the area, coming to rest on the hanging elk.

"Of course," he exclaimed, "I can use the elk skin to make a pack."

He hurried to the tree and searched under the snow with his hands until he found the skin. He pulled it from the snow and went back to the fire. The skin was cold and stiff. He added snow to the cast iron pot and while waiting for it to warm, he pushed the snow from the top of the boulder. He laid the skin on the boulder, hair side down. When the water was almost boiling, he poured some on a section of the skin. Using the hunting knife, he began scraping the inside of the skin.

After scraping an area clean, he rubbed it with salt then poured more hot water on another area. About four and a half hours later, he had the skin in a usable condition.

The snow had stopped, but looking at the clouds slowly moving across the sky, he knew that it would soon be snowing again. He placed what he was going to take, except for the meat, onto the skin. He folded two sides over what he was taking and then rolled the skin into a tight bundle. He went to the elk, dropped it to the ground and retrieved the rest of the leather reins. He used the leather strap to tie the bundle. He tied it in such a fashion that he had a loop on each side for the purpose of putting his arms through. He cut off the excess leather and made a sling for the rifle.

He stood, put his arms through the loops on the pack and pulled it onto his back. He shrugged his shoulders a couple of times to get it comfortable and walked to the coach. When he got there, he removed the pack and placed it inside the coach.

Zeke had left the coffeepot out of the pack … it was setting at the edge of the fire. He went back to the fire, put more wood on it and poured a cup of coffee before sitting down. It was just before dusk and as he ate a piece of meat and sipped on the hot coffee, a light snow began falling. Zeke poured the coffee that was in the coffeepot into one of the canteens. Then he stood and carrying the coffee and a couple pieces of meat went to the coach.

Zeke spent the night in much the same way as the two previous nights. He awoke several times after having the same dream of the wolf and horse. Each time he awoke, he lifted one of the flaps over the windows and looked out into the darkness. He wasn't sure but each time he looked out, he thought it might be snowing harder than it was the time before.

Morning finally arrived and when Zeke looked out all he could see was white. The snow was silently falling so heavily that he could not see the flat-topped boulder by the fire ring twenty feet away.

The snow continued falling all day without letting up. Zeke sat in the coach, wrapped in the lap robes and tried to remember who he was and why he was on the stagecoach.

'Who am I? … Where was I going? … Where'd I come from?' Zeke pondered. 'Maybe if I go over what I do know, I'll remember more. I know that I was on the stage because I was in a hurry to get somewhere. I know that at least seven men are probably responsible for the stagecoach wrecking. I know I am good with a gun. It appears that I know how to survive. I feel that the horse in my dreams is my horse. … What about the wolf? … I feel like there is a connection of some kind between the wolf and me. … What does this talisman around my neck mean? If that horse is mine, why wasn't I riding him instead of the stage? Wait a minute … I remember why. I decided to ride the stage instead of the horse because of the weather and it is urgent that I get to … to … to where?'

Zeke dozed several times throughout the day. Each time he awoke he looked out the window … the snow was still coming down heavy.

Each time Zeke dozed, he remembered a little more. In that twilight zone between being awake and being asleep, he recalled some of the gunfights he had been in.

'I seem to be recalling more about myself,' Zeke thought. 'I must be a gun slinger … but which side of the law am I on? Am I a gun for hire? That doesn't seem right ... But what about the gun-fights that I recall?'

About mid-afternoon Zeke had to get out of the coach to stretch his legs and relieve himself. He strapped his snowshoes onto his boots and pushed on the door to the coach ... it would not open. He lifted the curtain and looked out. Snow was half way up the door, blocking it from opening.

Zeke pushed on the door harder ... it moved about two inches. He braced his back on the opposite side of the coach and pushed on the door with his feet. He opened it another four inches. He pulled his feet back and kicked the door with the bottom of both feet. The door opened two more inches. He repeatedly pulled the door shut then slammed it open against the piled up snow. He finally got the door open enough to get out of the coach.

The snow had eased up a little but it was still falling heavy and Zeke could only see about three feet. Zeke took care of what he so desperately needed to get out for. Then he got the shovel and moved the snow away from the door before getting back into the coach.

He spent the rest of the day and that night inside the coach. Zeke had dozed many times during the day and was unable to sleep that night. However, he did doze off several times and each time he dreamed the same dream of the wolf and the horse.

Zeke looked out the window shortly before dawn. The snow had quit falling and he could see a few stars here and there. At the first glimmer of light, he pushed the door open and got out of the coach. The sun was peeking over the eastern horizon and it was eerily quiet.

Zeke got the shovel and went to the snow-covered fire-ring. Luckily, the fire ring was on the leeward side of the boulder and there was less than a foot of snow covering it. He soon had a fire going. He melted snow and used the water for coffee. While waiting for the coffee to boil he went back to the coach and dumped the contents of the leather satchel onto one of the seats. When he returned to the boulder, with the empty satchel, he brushed through the snow on top of it. He retrieved the cooked meat from the top of the boulder. He put some of the meat in the cast iron pot along with some snow and placed it on the fire. The rest he put in the satchel.

As he ate Zeke studied the sky … there was not a cloud in sight. 'Hope I get off of this mountain before it snows again,' he mused. Then he went to the coach and brought the pack back to the boulder. He laid the pack on top of the boulder and opened it.

The coffee was ready and he poured himself a cup. He fished a piece of meat out of the now simmering pot and ate it. When he had his fill of the meat, he fished the rest of it from the pot, shredded it and returned it to the pot. After he finished eating, he filled one of the canteens with coffee. The other he filled with the shredded meat and broth.

He retrieved the articles that he had dumped from the satchel and put them in the pack. He cooled the pots in the snow and placed them in the pack. Then he placed the satchel filled with meat on the top of everything and rolled the pack as tight as he could and tied it.

He tied the two canteens to the back of his pack then stuck his arms through the loops and shrugged it onto his back. He slung the rifle on his left shoulder and started down the hill.

When Zeke reached the bottom of the hill, he turned and walked down stream alongside the river. He soon got the hang of walking with the snow shoes tied to his boots and had little trouble with them.

Close to mid-day Zeke came to a spot where he could go no farther. The mountain came to the edge of the river and ended with a bluff. There was no way to get around it and it was too steep to climb over.

Zeke turned around and started back upriver. It was just after dusk when he got back to the point where he had come down the hill. He slowly made his way back to the wrecked stagecoach, where he spent another night.

The next morning he headed upstream alongside the river. He stopped periodically to rest. Shortly after mid afternoon, he started watching for a likely place to camp for the night. It was about an hour before dusk when he came upon an area that would do. It was at the base of a bluff, there were a few boulders and not a whole lot of snow. Zeke quickly made camp and soon had a fire going.

Suddenly Zeke heard a noise … he stood still and listened intently. There it was again … it sounded like a baby crying. 'It could be a cougar,' he thought, 'they sometimes sound a little like a baby crying.' Then he heard it again … 'no mistaking it, it is a baby crying.'

It sounded like it was coming from a little farther upriver. Zeke shrugged his pack back on, kicked snow onto the fire and headed upriver to investigate. He followed the sound. The baby cried for a while then stopped for a short period and then cried again. Then it sounded like it was coming from his left.

Zeke listened to the cry as he studied the side of the mountain. He saw two very large boulders and a couple of smaller ones. One of the boulders was on one side of a large tree and the other two were on the other side. The crying baby was on the other side of the boulders. Zeke cautiously made his way to the boulders.

Chapter Three

There was a cave in the side of the mountain about thirty feet from the boulders and tree. The ground between the boulders and the cave had very little snow. Apparently, the tree canopy along with the position of the boulders acted like a shelter and prevented the snow from accumulating there. A very large pot, about three feet in diameter and three feet deep, sat on four small boulders over a fire ring. A wooden bucket and large supply of firewood was nearby. The entrance to the cave was about ten feet wide and seven feet high. Zeke went to the cave and entered. It opened into a cavern about thirty feet wide and around a hundred feet deep.

In the dim light, he saw a woman lying on a bed of twigs covered with a bearskin. She had a baby cradled in her arm and another bearskin covered them. He shrugged his pack off as he hurried to them.

The woman's eyes were open and she vacantly stared at the roof of the cave. Zeke knelt beside her … she was dead. He gently took the baby from the dead woman's arms and wrapped it in the bearskin. The baby was very thin and didn't weigh more than eight to ten pounds. He got his canteen of broth and dribbled some on the baby's mouth. The baby licked at its lips and swallowed.

Zeke held the baby and fed it broth till it went to sleep. He gently laid the baby down and decided the first thing to do is get a fire going.

While feeding the baby Zeke had spotted a fire ring about five feet from the makeshift bed. It was directly below a small natural chimney. The ashes in the fire ring were cold. There was firewood stacked beside the ring. There were also two enameled pots and a large enameled coffeepot. One of the cooking pots was fairly large and the other was of medium size. Both of them had food matter crusted in them.

Zeke soon had a fire going and it began warming the cave. He got the cast iron pot and the coffeepot from his pack and left the cave to fill them with snow. He placed the snow-filled pots on the fire and when the snow melted, he moved the cast iron pot to the edge of the fire. He threw a handful of coffee grounds in the coffeepot and set it on the fire. Then he took both enameled pots out and filled them with snow, brought them back in and set them on the fire. He did the same with the enameled coffeepot.

While waiting for the coffee to boil he checked the cave. Several piles of pelts lay at the far end of the cave. Zeke examined the skins and determined that the skins were mostly badger and otter along with four cougar, three bear and one wolf.

Several traps of varying size lay in one corner. Someone had placed a large piece of tree trunk about ten feet from the fire ring. The trunk was two and a half to three feet high and about three feet in diameter. At the base of the make shift table were two fairly large boulders. On top of the table were two tin plates, two tin cups and some eating utensils.

Close by the bed were two bundles of some sort. Zeke opened one of the bundles and found diapers made of sackcloth and three cans of condensed milk. When he saw the milk he thought, 'There must be a bottle here too.' But the only thing in the bundle was diapers and the three cans of milk. He opened the other bundle. It contained a few items of women's clothing … also made of sackcloth.

Zeke checked the bed that the woman's body was on and found the bottle. It was empty … and dirty.

Zeke poured himself a cup of coffee and sat at the table. While he sipped on the coffee he thought, 'I reckon this is a trapper's cave and that woman and baby are his. I wonder where he is. Something must have happened to him. From the looks of things, that woman hasn't been dead more than a day or two at the most. The baby appears to be about two, maybe three months old. I could survive the winter here … but what about the baby? There are only three cans of milk. Guess I could feed it broth and give it some stringy meat to suck on.'

The baby's crying pulled Zeke out of his reverie. He picked the baby up and cradled it with one arm. Then he stepped to the fire and picked up the cast iron pot full of warm water with the other hand. He went to the table and laid the baby, still wrapped in the bearskin on it. He sat the pot of water on one of the boulders. He opened the bearskin and removed the baby's fouled diaper. He started washing the baby with the warm water. The baby stopped crying and made a gurgling sound while waving its arms and legs.

"Well," Zeke said to the baby, "now we know you're a girl. You sure are skinny though, but then I don't suppose you've had anything to eat for a while. Sure, wish I knew your name. But I don't even know my own name so I don't reckon names really matter. However, I'll probably remember who I am … I keep remembering more as the days pass. We'll just have to figure out a name that fits you."

Zeke finished bathing the baby and put a fresh diaper on her. He went to his pack, got one of the lap robes that he had brought from the stage and wrapped her in it. He laid the baby near the fire, picked up the cast iron pot and went out of the cave. He also took the smaller of the enameled pots. He dumped the water from both of them and noted with satisfaction that the crud in the enameled pot had boiled loose and was now clean. He filled both pots with snow brought them back in and set them on the fire.

When the snow melted in the enameled pot, he set it to the edge of the fire to keep it warm. He left the cast iron pot on the fire to boil. He dipped some of the warm water from the smaller pot and washed the bottle with it. Then he opened one of the cans of milk and poured enough into the bottle to make it half-full. He filled it the rest of the way with warm water that he dipped from the pot.

As Zeke was preparing the bottle, an image of a woman and a baby flashed into his mind. He tried to remember who they were, but could not. He did feel that they were important in his life.

He picked the baby up and cradled her in the crook of his left arm as he held the bottle for her. She sucked about a fourth of the milk from the bottle and fell asleep. Zeke laid her down by the fire and placed the bottle in the small pan of warm water to keep the milk warm. Then he went to the body on the bed. He rolled her in the bearskin that she was lying on. As he wrapped her in the skin, he discovered that both her left leg and right arm were broken. He scrutinized her body and discovered many bruises on her. Her swollen and badly bruised face also had a few minor cuts.

'I wonder what happened to her,' Zeke thought. 'It looks as though someone beat her. She doesn't appear to be more than fifteen maybe sixteen years old.'

With a heavy heart and a feeling of sadness for the girl, Zeke finished wrapping her in the bearskin and carried her outside. Night had fallen but a new moon gave him plenty of light to work by. With the moonlight reflecting off the snow it was almost as light as day.

He didn't have a shovel to dig a grave. He found a deep snowdrift and buried her there, in the snow. As he buried her Zeke said, "I know this isn't much of a grave, but it is the best I can do for now." Then he fashioned a small cross from two pieces of deadwood that lay beneath the tree by the cave entrance. He pushed the cross into the snow above her head and returned to the cave.

When he returned to the cave, he went to the fire, picked up the cast iron pot and the large enamel pot. He carried them outside the cave and dumped the boiling water onto the ground. Then he filled both pots with snow and returned to the cave. After he set the two pots on the fire, he went to the skins at the rear of the cave. He picked up one of the bearskins and laid it out on the bed. Then he picked the sleeping baby up and laid her in the middle of it.

It was warm in the cave and Zeke had removed his coat when he came in the last time. He got the spit rod and the two forks to hold it. He pushed the forks into the ground on opposite sides of the fire. Then using the spit rod he hung the large enamel pot and the cast iron pot above the fire. He brought the satchel to the fire, opened it, took some of the chunks of meat and put them into the enameled pot.

When the meat was hot, he ate a couple of pieces and drank the rest of the coffee that was in the pot.

The baby made a short crying sound about the time Zeke finished eating. He picked her up and felt her diaper … it was dry. He removed the bottle from the warm water. After making sure that the milk was not too hot, he held the bottle to her lips.

After the baby drank her fill, she once again went to sleep. Zeke laid her back on the bed and fed the fire some more wood. He got the lap robes from his pack and lay down on the bed. He covered himself with two of the robes and thought about events of the day.

'How is it that I know how to care for a baby,' Zeke wondered. 'Why can't I remember who I am? Where did I come from and where was I going?' These thoughts were in his mind as he fell asleep.

About four hours later the baby woke him with a soft cry. He changed the baby's diaper and held the bottle of milk for her to suck on. As he cared for the baby he thought, 'I dreamed about that wolf and horse again, but I didn't wake up afterward. Maybe it's because it is warm in here. This is the warmest I've been since I left … since I left … where?'

When Zeke awoke again, it was getting light. He sat up and looked down at the baby. Her eyes were open and she was staring at Zeke. When she saw Zeke look at her, her face lit up and she made a gurgling sound as she waved her arms in the air.

"You look like a little angel lying there," Zeke said. "Reckon that that's what I'll call you … Angel."

Angel waved her arms, cooing and gurgling as though she approved.

Zeke added firewood to the fire then tended to Angel. When he fed her, she drank almost half of the milk that was in the bottle before falling asleep again.

As he laid her on the bed, Zeke thought, 'The milk will be gone before long. We are going to have to leave here and find a settlement somewhere. It will be several days before she is strong enough for us to travel. I need to start feeding her something more than milk. I can make meat broth for her, but she needs more than that. I have those cans of peaches … I can boil them down and make mush out of them.'

Zeke went to his pack and picked up a can of peaches. He sat the can on the table and used his knife to cut the lid off. He emptied the can into the enameled coffeepot and set it on the fire to boil. He prepared a pot of coffee in the other pot and set it on the fire. Then he put some meat into the cast iron pot and hung it above the fire.

The coffee came to a boil and he let it boil for a few minutes then poured himself a cup and set the pot at the edge of the fire to stay hot. Zeke fished a chunk of meat out of the cast iron pot and ate it as he drank his coffee.

After eating, Zeke went outside the cave to check the surrounding area. First, he scrutinized the area between the boulders and the cave. He saw a large box made of rough-hewn wood pushed against the largest of the boulders. The box measured approximately six feet long three feet wide and two feet deep.

Inside the box, he discovered two large bags of rock salt, a shovel, an axe, several small animal snares and a fishing line with a dozen hooks fastened to it. Zeke took the shovel out of the box thinking, 'Now I can give that poor woman a proper burial.'

Zeke picked a spot to bury the woman. He removed the snow from an area large enough for a gravesite. When he stepped on the shovel, he discovered that the ground was frozen. 'Probably ain't frozen more'n a foot,' he thought. 'I'll just build a fire here. That ought to thaw it enough to dig a grave.'

Zeke gathered some wood and placed it on the gravesite. When he had a thick pile of wood covering an area of about six feet by four feet he set it on fire. Figuring that it would be at least an hour before he would be able to dig, Zeke returned to the cave.

Angel was sleeping when he checked her. He went to the fire and noted with satisfaction that the peaches were cooking into a mush. Zeke removed the meat from the cast iron pot one piece at a time. He took each piece in turn and cut it into the tiniest pieces possible. Then he put the almost pulverized meat back into the pot. He let the meat boil down to a thick, gravy like consistency. Then he removed the pot from the spit rod and set it at the edge of the fire. After he finished preparing the meat and peaches, he went back to the gravesite.

The fire had burned out, but the ashes were hot and contained a few hot coals. Zeke shoveled the ashes out of the way and started digging. When the hole was deep enough, he retrieved the woman's body from the snow bank and placed her in the bottom of the hole.

Zeke had shoveled about half the dirt back into the hole when he heard a noise behind him. He twisted around just as the sound of a rifle shot filled the air. He felt the heat from the slug as it whizzed past his head.

Zeke's gun found his fist and it roared a reply. The rifle flew from the would-be back shooter's hands as he clutched his belly and fell to the ground.

Zeke cautiously approached the figure on the ground with his six-shooter pointing the way. When he got there, he removed the pistol strapped to the man's right side and a large hunting knife strapped to his left.

Zeke emptied the spent cartridge from his gun and replaced it with a fresh one before re-holstering it. "Who are you mister? Why did you try to back shoot me?"

"Who I am ain't any o' your damn business."

"Okay, why'd you try to shoot me in the back?"

"Cause you was there."

With a cold chill running up his back, Zeke realized that the man's tracks came from the direction of the cave.

Zeke demanded, "Have you been in that cave over there?"

"It's my cave."

"What about the baby? Is she alright?"

"I took care o' that whelp," the man replied. Then he emitted an evil laugh that ended when he started coughing and spitting blood.

Zeke hurried to the cave to check on Angel. When he came around the boulder towards the entrance to the cave, he stopped in his tracks. Angel was lying on the snow-covered ground in front of and to one side of the cave entrance. She was naked, very still and there was a bluish tinge to her skin.

Zeke rushed to her and picked her up. He put his ear to her chest and heard a very feeble heart beat. He hurriedly carried her inside. He wrapped her in a lap robe and laid her on the bed. He fed more wood to the fire then he stripped off his coat and shirt. He took the robe from Angel's body, held her to his warm chest and wrapped the robe around both of them.

He sat by the fire rubbing her body through the lap robe. As Angel warmed, he could feel life coming back into her. Her heartbeat became strong once again and she let out a wail.

Zeke gently rocked her as he said, "Shh, you're okay now … I have you, every thing will be alright."

When Angel heard Zeke's voice, she stopped wailing, opened her eyes and looked at his face. She took a deep breath and with a soft murmur, her face took on a contented look.

Zeke held her for another ten minutes or so then laid her on the table. He put a diaper on Angel then wrapped her in the lap robe and laid her on the bed. He took an empty tin plate to the fire, spooned some of the hot meat paste onto it and did the same with the peaches. He set the plate on the table then filled her bottle with meat broth.

He picked up Angel and cradled her in his left arm as he sat down at the table. He stirred the meat paste to cool it. When he was satisfied that it was cool enough he put a little bit on the spoon and held it to Angel's mouth. She opened her mouth and Zeke put the meat on her tongue.

Angel made a smacking sound with her lips, as she tasted the meat. She swallowed it and Zeke gave her a little more. Thinking that she would not be able to handle very much in the way of solid food, he gave her meat twice more. Then he did the same with the peaches.

Zeke held the bottle of broth to her lips and she readily started sucking the liquid into her mouth and swallowing it. He held the bottle as she greedily sucked a little more than a fourth of the contents from it before falling asleep. He gently laid her on the bed and left the cave.

Chapter Four

It had been a little over an hour since Zeke had shot the man who had tried to shoot him in the back. When he got to him, he saw that the man was still alive and in great agony, as he lay curled on the ground clutching his belly and moaning. When Zeke's shadow fell across his face, he looked up at Zeke and said, "Shoot me, put me out of this agony."

"Don't reckon that I'll do that," Zeke replied. "You're gut shot and I figure that you'll be dead in another hour or two. If I thought that it would put you in more agony than what you are in already, I'd skin you while you're still alive for what you did to that baby."

"You can't let me die like this, shoot me and get it over with."

"Maybe if you gave me some answers to my questions I might do as you ask. Where is the closest settlement?"

"That'd be Agua Caliente."

"Where is it?"

"It's about a day and a half upriver."

"Is there any sort of shelter between here and there?"

"Are you going to shoot me and put an end to my misery if I tell you?"

"Maybe … I haven't decided yet."

"I got another cave almost a days trek upriver … it ain't as big as the one here but it'll keep you warm."

Zeke asked, "What was that girl to you?"

"I took her and made her my woman, but she got to be useless after that squalling young'un was born so I left."

"What happened to her? How did her leg and arm get busted?"

"She couldn't keep that baby from crying so I whacked her a few times and left. Figured that she and that whelp of hers would be dead by the time I got back."

Zeke turned away in disgust as he contemptuously said, "I've had about all of you that I can take."

"You can't leave me like this," the man whined. "You promised you would shoot me if I answered your questions."

Zeke turned around and with a cold, hard edge to his voice said, "I did no such thing. I said that I might shoot you and put you out of your misery. You'll be dead soon enough and shooting you now would just be a waste of a perfectly good cartridge."

The dying man pleaded, "Will you at least bury me after I'm gone?"

"No," Zeke answered, "you're not worth the effort. What I will do is leave you lay right where you are and let the critters take care of you."

The man let out an ear-piercing wail as Zeke turned and headed to the woman's grave.

Zeke shoveled the remaining dirt into the grave. Then he got the cross he had fashioned and placed it at the head of the grave.

After Zeke finished with the grave, he returned to the cave. He filled the large pot in front of the cave with snow and then built a fire under it. After the snow melted, he filled the wooden bucket with some of the hot water and carried it into the cave. He set the bucket on the table and then checked on Angel … she was sleeping peacefully.

Zeke got the bar of soap from his pack and stripped off his clothes. He bathed, shaved and put on a clean set of clothing. Then he carried the clothes he had been wearing to the pot outside and put them in the now boiling water. He then went to where the would-be backshooter was lying in the snow. When he got there, he found that the man was dead.

Zeke squatted beside him and searched through his clothing in an attempt to learn who the man was. All he found in his pockets were two flyers. One flyer had a picture of the now dead man. Above the picture, it read one thousand dollar reward. Below the picture it read; Trapper Bart McHune wanted dead or alive for murder and robbery.

The other flyer had a likeness of Angel's dead mother. Above her picture, it read; five hundred dollar reward. Below the picture it read; Marjorie Catesby kidnapped from her home in Carson City Nevada, at the age of fourteen in April of eighteen seventy-seven.

'This is November eighteen seventy-eight,' Zeke mused, 'which means Marjorie has been gone from Carson City two years come April. At least now that I know her name I can put a proper marker at her grave.'

Zeke folded the fliers and put them in his shirt pocket, then went back to the cave. He checked on Angel and found her still sleeping. He went back outside the cave and used a stick to remove his clothing from the boiling water. He laid them across the woodpile then went inside the cave. He gathered Angel's dirty diapers and put them in the pot to boil clean.

Zeke picked up his wet shirt from the woodpile and wrapped it around a low branch of the tree. He twisted it, wringing most of the water from it and laid it on the boulder. He did the same with the rest of the clothing. With some of his laundry laid on the boulder and some across the woodpile, he went back inside the cave. After the diapers had boiled for a while, he did the same with them as he had with his clothes.

By the time, Zeke finished with the laundry it was dusk. He dumped the water from the pot and re-filled it with snow. Then he built the fire back up and went back inside the cave.

He tended to Angel, fed her and then sat at the table holding her in his arms talking to her.

"Well Angel, we now know that your mama's name was Marjorie Catesby and she has family at Carson City. There is a settlement up river about a day and a half from here. When you get a little stronger, we'll go there. You should be strong enough to travel in about ten days or so."

That night Zeke awoke twice after dreaming of the wolf. The dream was different now. The wolf and horse were running towards something and Zeke sensed that they were running towards him.

The next morning Zeke cared for Angel and had breakfast. After eating and Angel had fallen asleep, he went out of the cave and got the axe from the box.

He located a small tree about five inches in diameter and ten feet tall. He chopped the tree down and cleaned the branches from it. Then he carried the tree trunk and axe to the mouth of the cave. Using the axe Zeke hewed the trunk into a square board almost four inches by four inches. Then he cut two pieces … one about four feet long and the other two feet.

Zeke carried the two pieces into the cave and laid the shorter one on the table. Using his knife, he carved Marjorie Catesby … 1862 - 1878 on the board. Then he cut a narrow strip off one of the bearskins and used it to fasten the two boards together in the shape of a cross.

Zeke stopped work on the cross several times through the day to tend to Angel and prepare food. It was close to dusk by the time he finished the cross.

The next morning, he built a fire to thaw the ground at the head of Marjorie's grave … when the fire burned itself out, Zeke dug a hole and planted the cross. Then he went back to the cave and waited for Angel to awaken.

About an hour, later Angel awoke and he wrapped her in a lap robe. The two of them went to the grave.

When they got there Zeke stood by the cross overlooking the grave. He removed his hat and said, "Lord this young woman buried here was known as Marjorie Catesby. I imagine that she is already with you. Will you let her know that her baby is with me and I'll not let anything bad happen to her? I did not know her baby's name so I named her Angel … I hope that is okay. Bart McHune stole Marjorie and made her his woman. She was only fourteen at the time. Bart was wanted for many crimes and he was just plain no good. His dead carcass is lying in the snow over there. The only good thing I can think of to say about him is that his carcass will provide food for some critters. I reckon that he'll burn in hell for the life he led, but of course, that's up to you. Amen."

Zeke took Angel back to the warmth of the cave. He laid her on the bed and started thinking about what he needed to do before they went up river to Agua Caliente.

As the days passed, Zeke noted with satisfaction that Angel was gaining weight and starting to sleep less. During the time he was waiting for Angel to get stronger he used one of the bearskins and made a sling with a pouch. After he finished making the sling, he slung it over his left shoulder and under his right arm. He picked up Angel and put her in the pouch … she snuggled down into the warm hair of the bearskin.

Zeke put Angel in the pouch and walked around the surrounding area twice each day. He stayed outside a little longer each time. Angel seemed to like their outings … when she saw Zeke put the sling on she would wave her arms and gurgle her happiness.

The night of the fifteenth day after finding Angel, Zeke decided that she was strong enough to travel. She had gained considerable weight and her eyes were now bright blue instead of the flat dullness that they were when he found her.

Before turning in for the night Zeke prepared the pack and readied what they would need to make the trip to Agua Caliente. He had rationed the milk for Angel by diluting it with meat broth and there was enough left for one more feeding. The peaches would last for about two more feedings and there was enough meat for about two more days. He wasn't overly concerned about the meat as he could always kill another elk. But Angel was going to need milk and the nearest place to get that was Agua Caliente.

That night Zeke dreamed about the wolf and horse. The horse and wolf were running towards him and getting close. Zeke awoke and clutched the talisman hanging around his neck as he wondered, 'What does this mean? … What is that wolf to me? … What about the horse?' He fell back asleep as he pondered these questions.

Zeke awoke shortly before daybreak. He got up and added wood to the fire then started to prepare coffee and something to eat. Angel woke up and he tended to her. He fed her the last of the milk and refilled her bottle with the rest of the peach mixture. He filled one canteen with the remaining meat broth and the other with coffee.

He bundled everything that they were taking into the pack. Zeke sat down and strapped the snowshoes to his boots then stood and slung the pack onto his back. He put the sling for Angel across his chest and placed her in it. He slung the rifle over his left shoulder … they left the cave and started upriver towards Agua Caliente.

As he trudged up the mountain, the lay of the land forced him to veer away from the river. Zeke stopped for about fifteen minutes every couple of hours. About midday, he found shelter among some trees and boulders. He stopped, built a fire and warmed some broth for Angel and some meat and coffee for himself. As he ate, he looked at the sky and thought, 'By the looks of those clouds it'll be snowing again before the day is out. McHune said that the other cave was about a days trek upriver. Reckon we best get going and hopefully we'll find that cave before the snow starts.'

As the afternoon progressed, the snow started falling in the form of light, intermittent flurries. Zeke searched the surrounding terrain for signs of a cave as they made their way up the mountain. About an hour and a half before dusk, a light snow started falling and steadily got heavier.

Zeke started wondering if McHune had lied to him about the cave or if he had missed it. He desperately started searching for shelter as the snowfall became heavier.

Chapter Five

Zeke spotted three large trees … their position to each other formed a triangle of about twenty-five feet each direction. Between two of the trees and on the windward side was a very large boulder.

It was not a cave but the canopy of the trees would give shelter. A heavy layer of snow caked on the canopy formed a roof of sorts. The ground was frozen but void of any snow. Zeke removed the sling holding Angle and leaving her in the warm pouch laid her at the base of the boulder. Then he gathered some deadwood and built a fire.

After Zeke got the fire going, he put what food he had left on the fire to warm and made a pot of coffee. He also filled a pot with snow and placed it over the fire to melt. While waiting for the food to warm and the coffee to boil he used the knife he had taken from McHune to hack some of the smaller branches off the trees. He piled the cut branches next to the boulder making a pile about a foot and a half thick, three to four feet wide and a little over six feet long. He spread two of the lap robes on top of the makeshift bed then picked up Angel and placed her on the bed.

The fire soon had the area reasonably warm and Zeke removed Angel from the pouch and removed her soiled diaper. He cleaned her, put a fresh diaper on her, placed her back in the pouch and fed her. After caring for her, he gathered a large pile of deadwood placed it close to the fire then sat on the bed and ate as he sipped hot coffee.

Zeke slept restlessly and dreamed that the wolf and horse were getting very close to him. He awoke about every two hours and built the fire back up. The boulder absorbed some of the heat from the fire and radiated it back onto them. The heat of the fire melted some of the snow caked on the canopy and it dripped onto the fire making sizzling sounds.

Each time Zeke got out of bed to feed the fire, he noticed that the snowfall was heavier than the time before. Daybreak finally arrived and the snowfall was still heavy. He put a pot of coffee on to boil and warmed the broth for Angel. As he fed her the broth he noted that there was just enough for one more feeding.

He had two chunks of meat left … he cut them into small pieces and made more broth for Angel. As he waited for the broth to cook, he sipped on his coffee and watched the snowfall as it decreased and stopped.

Zeke broke camp after extinguishing the fire, stepped out from among the trees and headed towards Agua Caliente. About two hours later the clouds were gone and the sun was shining brightly. The lay of the land caused them to drift back towards the river. When they got close to the river, he discovered that they were at the top of a gorge and the river was some seventy-five feet below them.

Looking upriver Zeke saw several columns of smoke curling into the sky. They were about five miles upriver and on the other side of the gorge.

With a sinking feeling Zeke wondered, 'Did I pass a place to cross to the other side? … Maybe instead of veering away from the river I should have found a way to stay beside it. … Maybe there is a way to cross farther up. … I can be opposite that smoke in about two hours.'

When Zeke got to the point opposite the smoke, he looked up river and saw that the gorge narrowed about a half-mile farther up. It looked like something stretched from one side to the other. When he got to it, he found that it was a rope suspension bridge crossing to the other side about fifty feet away.

The rope of the bridge was about two inches in diameter. Each side of the gorge had two poles spaced about six feet apart. The ropes, tied to the poles spanned the gorge. There was a length of rope strung across from each pole and on top of them were wooden planks. Two more ropes swung across three feet above the bottom ropes. At about five foot intervals, a smaller rope stretched between the upper and lower ropes.

The bridge appeared to be in good repair, but it also had about a foot of snow on the walkway and icicles hanging from the ropes. As Zeke contemplated the bridge, he heard a noise behind him. He spun around with his right hand hovering above his six-gun, expecting to see an animal. What he saw was a man with two mules emerging from the tree line about seventy-five feet from him. He was riding one and leading the other. The led mule had an empty canvas pack strapped to its back.

As they approached where he was, Zeke studied the man. He looked to be about six feet tall and would probably weigh around one hundred seventy-five pounds. He was lean, muscular and wore a short beard. His hair was brown, down to his shoulders and he had a grey floppy hat on his head. His britches and shirt were made of buckskin and he wore moccasins on his feet. He held a rifle, in a soft leather sheath, crossways across the saddle with his left hand.

The man on the mule stopped when he got to where Zeke was standing.

He dismounted as he said, "Howdy, name's O'Hallahan … Shawn O'Hallahan. Don't rightly know the why of it, but most folks call me Gabby. Reckon you may as well do the same. This here mule I'm riding on is Metilda and that ornery cuss I'm leading doesn't have a name. If you're wondering if that bridge is safe to cross, I'm here to tell you that it is. Built it myself, I did. Saves me three days travel time when I go to Agua Caliente for supplies. Have me a place a little more than a half days ride from here. Got to get me some supplies to get through the winter … there's a hard snow coming. It'll be here in a few more days. Say, do my eyes deceive me or is that a baby you got in that pouch? Sure looks a might young to be out here in this weather."

"Yes Gabby, it's a baby, her name's Angel," Zeke replied. "We ain't out here by choice, but I need to get to Agua Caliente in order to get her some milk. I'd tell you my name but I seem to have forgotten it. I don't remember where I was going or where I came from either. I was on a stagecoach and it went over a cliff … I'm the only survivor."

Zeke told Gabby what he remembered about the stage and how he found Angel and her dead mother in a cave.

"Only cave I know of around here that someone lives in," Gabby stated, "is the one that a trapper by the name of Bart something or other has. It's back down the mountain a ways. Saw him not long ago, a mean cuss he is."

"He's a dead cuss now," Zeke replied. "He tried to back shoot me and I killed him. His name was Bart McHune … turns out that he kidnapped Angel's mother in Carson City about a year and a half ago. Her name was Marjorie Catesby. After Angel was born, he beat Marjorie bad enough to break one of her legs and an arm. Then he left them both, hoping that they would die before he got back. By the time I found them Marjorie was dead and Angel was close to it."

"There's a doc in Agua Caliente, maybe he can help you remember who you are. Seeing as how you're toting that young'un you climb up on Matilda here, she's gentle as a lamb. I'll ride that ornery cuss back there. She takes a bit of handling, rolls her eyeballs around whenever she doesn't like something. Being rode is one of them things. She saw me shoot an elk one day and whenever she acts ornery I just stick the end of my gun barrel against her head … straightens her right out it does. If we stand around here a palavering all day, we ain't ever gonna get across that bridge."

Zeke knelt down and removed his snowshoes before mounting Matilda. When Gabby started to mount the other mule, it rolled its eyes around and sidestepped as she shied away. Gabby removed the sheath from his rifle and held the muzzle end of it against the mule's head saying, "Listen here you ornery cuss, stop shying away from me, else I'll be leaving your dead carcass here for that wolf we saw on the ridge yesterday."

The mule snorted and rolled her eyeballs a couple more times, but stood still as Gabby mounted her.

When Zeke heard what Gabby said about seeing a wolf, his hand went to the talisman around his neck as he said, "Did you say you saw a wolf yesterday? I've been having dreams every night about a wolf … a wolf and a horse. They must mean something to me but I just can't remember."

Gabby took the lead and they crossed the bridge in silence as Zeke pondered on the wolf and horse, wondering what they meant to him.

Chapter Six

After they crossed the bridge, they rode alongside each other in silence for a ways. The trail was steep and twisted around boulders and very large trees as it snaked its way down the side of the mountain. About a half mile from the bridge, the trail became too narrow to ride alongside each other.

Gabby stopped and broke the silence saying, "The trail gets pretty narrow and a whole lot steeper from here to most of the way down. Being as how I know the trail I reckon I should take the lead." Then he continued, "I've been thinking on it and that wolf I seen on the ridge was a silver wolf. The biggest dang wolf I ever did see and there was a horse with him too. I recollect thinking, now that's the darndest thing I ever did see, a wolf and a horse traveling together … seems to me that that horse was a blue roan, a big 'un too. I've heard tell of a fella down around Tucson that rides a big blue roan stallion and travels with a large silver wolf."

Zeke blurted out, "That wolfs name is Spirit and the name of the horse is Blaze. I don't know how I know their names, but I'm sure that they are trying to get to me." Then he added with frustration in his voice, "I still can't remember who I am."

"Don't know whether or not you're the same fella that I'm a thinking of," Gabby replied. "The one I got in mind has a passel of books written about his exploits.

Maybe you've read some of them and that's how you believe to know the name of that wolf and horse."

"Maybe so," Zeke replied, "but why do I have several dreams about them every night? I somehow know that they are trying to get to me. In the beginning, I dreamed that they were looking for me. Then the dream changed to where they are running and getting closer to me."

Gabby looked intently at Zeke as he asked, "Does the name Zeke Cooper mean anything to you?"

Zeke was silent as flashes of memory started flooding his mind. 'That name should mean something to me,' he thought. Then he said, "It seems familiar but I can't hang anything on it."

"If'n you are this fella we're talking about, there's something you should know afore we get into Agua Caliente," Gabby said. "It was a mining town once but the mines played out and most of the folks left, but a few of them stayed on because of the hot springs. There are seven springs in total on the west and north sides of the town. Folks from hereabouts come to Agua Caliente to trade and make use of the springs. The heat from the springs keeps the snow melted and it is a whole lot warmer there. But to get back to what I want to warn you about, Agua Caliente has become a haven of sorts for outlaws."

"Are you saying that the town is an outlaw sanctuary," Zeke asked.

"Not exactly, it is and it ain't, a lot of the folks are a decent sort but what law that is there looks the other way for a price. Someone running from the law can stay there providing he pays the town's sheriff and cause's no trouble as long as he's there. I would say that at any one time there are at least twenty-five to thirty outlaws there. Especially so at this time of year, though I haven't seen him, I understand that the outlaw called the Lisping Bandit and his gang is here quite a lot."

When Gabby mentioned the Lisping Bandit, Zeke had a flash of memory that didn't seem to make sense. He saw himself and another man facing each other as if they were dueling, but their weapons were slingshots.

"When you mentioned the Lisping Bandit it jarred a flash of memory that doesn't make sense to me," Zeke said. "What else do you know about this Lisping Bandit?"

"Not much, excepting that he was a major in the army until he had a run in with Zeke Cooper three or four years ago. He turned to outlawing after he was cashiered out of the army."

Angel woke up, stretched herself in the pouch and smacked her lips indicating that she was hungry. The bottle of broth was in the pouch where it stayed warm. Zeke held the bottle as she greedily sucked on it.

"We can worry about all that later," Zeke said. "Right now the important thing is to get some milk for Angel and then get her to her kin in Carson City."

"We best be going then, but mind you we need to keep a watchful eye," Gabby stated as he took the lead and started down the much steeper trail.

The trail emerged from the tree line and took a sharp turn to the north as it widened and dropped down into the hollow that held Agua Caliente. Zeke and Gabby once again rode side by side. The air started getting warmer as they dropped down the side of the mountain. When they reached the hollow, the trail once again turned, this time to the east. About a half mile after the trail turned east, another trail from the northwest joined it. Zeke looked at the trail and saw that it snacked its way up the steep westerly side of the mountain.

As the town grew closer Gabby said, "The mercantile is on the way to the doc's place, reckon that we should stop there and get some milk for Angel, the doc can probably warm it for her."

As they rode into town, Zeke saw a livery stable, two saloons … the sign above one of them read, Elkhorn Saloon and Gambling Emporium … beer, distilled spirits, food and lodging. The sign above the other saloon read … Big Reds Top Hat Saloon and Brothel, drinks, eats, gaming tables, rooms, girls. There was also a small hotel, a bank and a mercantile along with several other buildings. Some of them were businesses along with several residences. In the main part of town, there was a covered boardwalk along each side of the roadway, connecting the buildings. A few of the townspeople were walking along the boardwalk … none of them were wearing heavy coats. Most were in their shirtsleeves and wearing a vest, but a couple of them wore a light waist jacket.

They stopped in front of the mercantile and dismounted. Gabby pointed to the east as he said, "The doc's place is four doors that way, if you would like I'll go in here and get some milk and bring it there."

"Thanks, that's a good idea Gabby, here let me give you some money." Zeke dug into his pants pocket, brought out two silver dollars, and handed them to Gabby. "If you get how ever much you can with these two dollars, I can get more later on."

Zeke started up the street as Gabby went into the mercantile.

As Zeke walked up the street, he came to a doorway that had a sign swinging over the boardwalk. The sign read Able Roberts, Medical Practitioner.

Zeke shrugged the pack off his back and placed it beside the door. Then he opened the door and stepped inside.

Chapter Seven
Silver Wolf headquarters
November 25th 1878

~

Tom Hampton, the Deputy United States Marshal in Tucson, rode into the ranch yard. He proceeded to the stable, where Lance and Lefty were watching him approach.

As Tom stopped in front of them, Lance said, "Howdy Tom, what brings you out this way?"

Tom stepped down from his saddle and removed a telegram from his shirt pocket as he said, "Glad I caught the two of you out here. This telegram came this morning … it's from Bob Douglas. I think you should read it."

Lefty was the nearest to Tom and he reached out, took the telegram and read it aloud. "Received telegram from Zeke stating that he was leaving Tucson on stage … has not arrived … is there a problem … advise soonest possible."

The three of them silently looked at each other for a minute as they contemplated the message.

Lefty was first to break the silence, "Dang he left near a month ago. Tom, you saw him get on that stage didn't you?"

"Yes, I did," Tom, replied. "It was around midday on the fifth of November. He certainly should have been to Sacramento by now. I sent telegrams to every telegraph station along the route he was taking, inquiring if they have seen him. I should be getting some answers by the time I get back to town."

"Lefty and I will get some gear together and go look for him." Lance stated, as Lefty handed the telegram back to Tom. "We'll go to Tucson with you to see what kind of answers you get back. But first we need to go in the house and tell Little Doe."

"I'll go with you to tell her," Tom stated.

On the way to the house, Lefty stated, "Looks like you rode that horse pretty hard getting here, cut one of ours out of the corral and the next time someone goes to Tucson they'll bring your horse along."

They found Little Doe in the great room with Zachry. Zachry White Wolf Cooper born on May twelve eighteen seventy-five was named after Zeke's father and White Wolf, Little Doe's grandfather.

As the three of them entered the room, Little Doe smiled and said, "Hello Tom, I don't see Eunice with you. How are she and the kids doing?"

"They are doing just fine. I'm afraid that I have some unsettling news," Tom replied.

"Is it about Zeke," Little Doe asked.

"Yes, this telegram came from Bob this morning. Seems as though Zeke hasn't got to Sacramento yet," Tom stated as he handed the telegram to Little Doe.

Little Doe took the telegram, read it and handed it back to Tom saying, "I knew something was wrong, but he is okay now. Since a few days after he left I have been having visions of Zeke in a dark place. He was lost and wondering towards a light. Each time I had the vision he was closer to the light. He has a baby with him now and will soon meet a man that will help him. Also Spirit and Blaze are close to where he is."

Tom, Lance and Lefty looked at each other. Tom stated, “Little Doe I don’t think I will ever get used to you knowing these kinds of things. But I do know that you have always been right. Do you know just where he is?”

“That I do not know,” Little Doe replied. “I do know that wherever it is, he is in snow-covered mountains and close to a place that is warmer than the surrounding area.”

“Why didn’t you tell us,” Lefty asked.

“There was no need to worry you,” Little Doe replied. “There was nothing you could have done, he is okay now and we will hear from him soon.”

“You still should have told us,” Lefty grumbled. Then he looked at Lance saying, “Come to think of it I haven’t seen Blaze or Spirit for some time now.”

Lance stated, “I haven’t either, I just figured that Blaze was in the mares pasture. That’s where he usually is when Zeke is gone without him. We don’t normally see much of Spirit when Zeke is gone.”

“All the same, I am going to Tucson with Tom when he goes back,” Lefty stated. “What about you Lance, are you coming along?”

“Reckon so,” Lance replied. “Ain’t a whole lot that requires our attention around here for now. I saw Aaron at the sawmill this morning and he said that everything was going well. I also saw C.C. there with three wagons … they loaded them with timber for the McClury mine.”

“That’s it,” Lefty suddenly exclaimed. “I knew that I had heard of a warm spot in the mountains. One of the miners that hired on at the McClury mine, said he had worked at a mine a few years ago that was south of Carson City. He said there were several hot springs in the hollow where the mine was located. The springs kept the hollow warmer than the surrounding area. He said that even in the hardest snow storms that the snow didn't stick to the ground more'n a day."

Lance stated, "That settles it, Zeke may not need us but he might, so I reckon that we should go up there just the same."

"Reckon I'll be heading back to town, I've done what I came here for," Tom stated.

Lefty replied, "It'll be getting dark soon Tom, you might want to stay the night and we'll all get a start first thing come light."

"Thanks for the invite, but I need to get back. My mind's resting a lot easier, after what you said Little Doe. I now know that Zeke is okay, but I agree that he may need a little help."

"Seeing that you're set on going back tonight I'll saddle you a fresh horse," Lance stated. "Lefty and I'll bring yours with us in the morning."

After Tom left on a fresh horse, Lance and Lefty went to the tack room and got a pack tarp. The tarp itself was about eight feet square and had pockets of various sizes sewn onto it. They laid it out on the floor and inspected its contents. It had a cooking pot, a coffeepot and a set of spit rods. The spit rod set consisted of two metal rods with a u shape on one end of each of them and a steel rod with a crank handle forged on one end. Steve Thomas, the ranch blacksmith, had made several sets of them for use on the trail.

Lefty and Lance then went to the larder that was off of the main kitchen and gathered provisions. They took coffee, dried beans, flour, salt, dried beef and a box of matches. As they were securing the provisions in the tarp Lance said, "I reckon it'd be a good idea to take the saddle and bridle for Blaze."

"Yeah, I think you're right," Lefty replied. "Spirit and Blaze have probably found Zeke by now. Little Doe said that he's okay but just the same I'll feel a heap better after we catch up to him."

Just before daybreak the next morning, Lance and Lefty rode towards Tucson leading Tom's horse and the buckskin that Zeke always used as a packhorse. The buckskin was just under seventeen hands tall and was a good match for Blaze's even seventeen hands. Lefty and Lances horses also stood right at seventeen hands.

Chapter Eight

When Zeke entered the doctor's office, he saw an examination table near the far wall. There was a cot along side the wall to his left, with a chair beside it. By the wall to the right, near the far wall was a cabinet that held bottles of varying sizes the contents of which were presumably different medicines. There was a doorway, with the door closed beside the cabinet. A desk occupied the space at the corner of the room formed by the wall to the right and the outside wall. A man seated at the desk got to his feet as Zeke stepped through the doorway.

"Doctor Roberts," Zeke asked as he came into the office.

"Yes I am doctor Roberts, what can I do for you?"

"I have a couple of problems," Zeke replied. "First I would like for you to check this baby, I found her and her dead mother a little over two weeks ago."

Doctor Roberts studied Zeke as he took Angel from him. He thought, 'I know this man from somewhere. He wears his gun tied down and probably knows how to use it. Could be he is one of the desperados I've treated in the past. But what on earth is he doing with a baby?'

Roberts walked to the door, opened it and called out, "Wings, could you come out here, I need your assistance."

A woman appeared … she took an apron off as she neared the doorway and hung it on a hook on the other side of the wall. She was just over five feet tall, slender and wore her black hair in a single braid down her back.

Roberts handed Angel to Wings saying, "We need to get her ready to examine."

As Wings took Angel to the examination table, Doctor Roberts turned back to Zeke saying, "You said you had a couple of problems, what other problem do you have?"

As he removed the pouch and took his coat off, Zeke replied, "I can't remember who I am." Then he told Roberts about the stagecoach wreck and later finding Angel and her dead mother.

Roberts cleared his throat and said, "You have what is called amnesia. We don't know a whole lot about it … it can be caused by a blow to the head or a catastrophic event. From what you have told me, I would say that a blow to your head caused yours. Memory returns in different ways, sometimes it is a little bit at a time. Other times something or someone familiar will trigger total recall of memory. I also must tell you that some people never regain their memory. I do not believe that is so in your case, as you are having flashes of memory returning."

Wings had Angel ready for examination and Roberts checked her over using his stethoscope, as he carefully poked and prodded her body. When he finished he said, "She appears to be about two maybe three months old. Healthy too, what have you been feeding her?"

"There were two cans of evaporated milk in the cave where I found her," Zeke replied. I made meat broth from some elk meat and I had four cans of peaches that I boiled until they were syrupy, then I added water to that."

"You said that she was pretty frail when you found her. Probably the sugar in the peaches put the weight back on her."

Gabby came into the office carrying a whiskey bottle filled with milk. "Howdy Doc, howdy Wings I got some milk here for Angel. The mercantile didn't have any cans of milk, but I remembered that Big Red keeps a cow behind her place so as her girls can have milk. We washed the bottle out real good afore putting the milk into it."

"Thanks Gabby," Zeke said, "I surely do appreciate all you have done."

"Shucks it weren't anything, I was headed this way anyhow," Gabby replied. Then added, "Reckon I'll go over to the saloon and get me a drink of whiskey," as he turned and went out the door.

Wings took the milk saying, "I'll go warm some of this milk and fill the bottle that I found in her pouch."

After Wings disappeared into the back Roberts said, "Wings is my wife, I call her Wings but her full name is White Wing … she is Paiute. I had a practice in Carson City but after I took Wings as my wife, most of the town folks turned their backs on me. When I opened a practice here, the people hereabouts accepted her."

"I know what you mean Doc … my wife is of the Zuni nation. Little Doe's grandfather is White Wolf, chief of the Zuni," Zeke stated. Then with a note of astonishment said, "Doc I'm starting to remember all kinds of thing now … but I still can't recollect who I am."

"You are doing good … you will probably recover your full memory anytime now. I would say within the next twenty-four hours at the most. I know who you are.

My father is a doctor in Tucson … Wings and I met you and Little Doe while we were visiting him there a couple of years ago. We were at the Wagon Wheel for dinner when you and Little Doe came in. My father introduced us and you sat at our table with us. Your name is Zeke Cooper."

"Doc I reckon that you may be right, Gabby said much the same thing to me. But I don't rightly know who Zeke Cooper is."

"I know without a doubt that you are Zeke Cooper, I thought I recognized you when you came in, but I couldn't place you until you mentioned Little Doe. She and Wings became quite good friends during the short time we were in Tucson. In fact, we visited you at the ranch that you and your partners Lance and Lefty own. The name of the ranch is Silver Wolf."

Gabby came into the office before Zeke could say anything … there was another man with him.

Zeke looked at the man with Gabby and said, "Howdy Thom it's good to see you again. What are you doing in these parts?"

Roberts asked, "Zeke do you know who this man is?"

"Yes, of course I do," replied Zeke. "This is Thom Langely, he's a writer and sometimes he writes about some of the things that I do."

"Then you recall who you are?"

An astonished Zeke replied, "Yes I do Doc. I've got all kinds of memories flooding my mind."

"Hot diggity-damn I knew that he was Zeke Cooper," Gabby exclaimed. "Good thing I run into Thom here, boy do we have a lot to tell you. When I went back to the Top Hat to get a whiskey, six men were standing with their backs to the bar. Thom was standing in front of them and talking to them. I stopped at the end of the bar and ordered a whiskey. I recognized the six that were together as some of the outlaws that comes here. Whilst I were watching them, one of them raised his glass and says, 'Here's to the death of Zeke Cooper.' That's when Thom walked away from them and came over to where I was standing."

Gabby continued, "He asked me if I knew you and I told him I weren't sure if'n I did or not. Then when he told me who he is, I said we needed to go where we could talk without anybody hearing us. We left the saloon and come here."

"It sure is good to see you Zeke," Thom said, "I heard that you was dead. I ran into a man in Carson City that said you died in a stagecoach wreck. When I asked him where the wreck happened, he said he wasn't sure, but that he heard about it here in Agua Caliente. So I came here to learn more."

"Well I was in a stagecoach that went over the side of a cliff, but as you can see I'm alive. The driver, shotgun rider and the five other passengers are all dead," Zeke replied.

"That wreck was no accident," Thom stated. "The men that Gabby saw me talking to are part of the Lisping Bandit's gang. They caused the wreck, but from what they told me, they did not intend for the coach to go over the cliff. They had two things in mind. First, they wanted you and secondary to that they were going to rob the coach and passengers. Whoever that Lisping Bandit is, he sure has a hate for you. One of the men that I was talking to was with him when they wrecked the stage … the other five were here at the time waiting for them. After his men told me what happened I asked where he was, so I could talk to him. They told me that he wouldn't be here for another four or five days … that's when I walked over to Gabby and asked him if he knew you."

"You said that there are six men here waiting for Cameron, that's the Lisping Bandit's name … Ryan Cameron," Zeke said. "He was a major in the army until he got himself kicked out four or five years ago. I saw the backs of seven men right after the wreck … counting the five men that were waiting for him, that makes it twelve men in that gang."

Zeke turned to Roberts saying, "Gabby tells me that the sheriff here is in cahoots with the outlaws that come here. Just how crooked is he? If I put those six men in his jail what do you believe he'd do?"

"I don't rightly know," Roberts replied. "Every sheriff we had before him quit and left town or they were gunned down. This town was pretty wide open and it wasn't safe for decent law-abiding folks to be out after sundown. When Tucker took on the job of sheriff, just about all of the violence stopped and you see the town's people out and about after dark now. Some people … including me, believe that he is taking money from the outlaws that come here and he lets them stay as long as they don't cause any trouble."

Zeke asked, "Do you know where Tucker came from or what he did before becoming sheriff here?"

"No, I know nothing about him prior to his becoming sheriff here," Roberts said. "Wings and I were in Carson City for three days and when we got back here, he was the sheriff."

Gabby spoke up saying, "I saw him around here off and on for five or six months before he became the sheriff. He had just killed a man when the town committee asked him to take the job."

"Who did he kill?" Zeke asked.

"Don't know his rightful name, far as I know he was just another two-bit outlaw that called himself Tex, he hung around here quite a bit. He had been hoorah-ing the town and feeling good about his self when he made the mistake of challenging Tucker," Gabby said. "I was in town that day and saw it all. It happened on the road in front of the Top Hat. Tucker's right fast with a gun. Tex started his draw first but Tucker shot and killed him before he cleared leather."

Zeke went to the door and got his pack that was setting just outside. He brought the pack into the room and opened it. He removed the satchel from the pack and opened the false bottom ... he took the marshal's badge but left the letter of credit, cash and telegram where they were.

As Zeke pinned the badge to his shirt he said, "Reckon I need to have a talk with your sheriff. Doc I would appreciate it if I could leave Angel here in your care for a little while."

"Yes of course," Roberts replied.

As Zeke turned and started out the door Gabby said, "Hold on a second, I'm right handy with this here rifle and I'll just mosey along with you, if'n you don't mind. I'll sit myself down on that bench outside the sheriff's office and make sure that you're not interrupt-ed while you talk to him."

"I'm coming too," Thom said. "I'm not as handy with a gun as some people are but I do carry one as a just in case."

"Okay," Zeke said, "but there shouldn't be any gun play. All I plan on doing is talk to him and learn where his loyalties are."

When they got to the sheriff's office, Gabby and Thom stayed outside while Zeke went in.

When Zeke entered the office, he instantly recognized the man sitting behind a desk near the far wall. He was wearing a sheriff's badge but his name was not Tucker. It was Sam Forrester … wanted for killing three people while robbing the bank in Prescott. There were four robbers that day … a posse gave chase and caught three of them. The three captured outlaws had a swift trial the next day and hanged at sunrise the following day. Sam Forrester got away with all the money from the robbery, which was just over two thousand dollars.

Chapter Nine

The sheriff's office was about twenty-five feet in each direction. A desk was in the right-hand corner of the room. The position of the desk was such that the background light would not blind a person sitting behind it when someone came through the doorway. A door leading to the back was about center of the far wall. A gun rack was to the left of the door, it had five rifles and two shotguns in it ... with room for more. A potbelly stove with a coffeepot setting on it was in the center of the room. A bucket three quarters full with water sat on the floor beside the stove. There was a large cabinet, with its doors closed along the right-hand wall near the corner of the far wall. A table about six feet long and half as wide was close to the cabinet and three or four feet from the wall. Six tin cups hung from hooks attached to the wall behind the table.

As Zeke stepped through the doorway, Forrester looked up from the desk and instantly recognized him. Forrester's gun-belt with his gun in the holster lay on top of his desk. Forrester scrambled to his feet as he reached for his gun with his right hand.

Zeke stepped sideways to the left of the door ... his gun roared to life and spit lead, hitting Forrester in his right shoulder.

The slug hit Forrester just as his he was pulling the trigger of his six-gun. He shot the floor as the gun dropped from his hand.

As Zeke stepped closer to him, Forrester blurted, "You're supposed to be dead."

"I've heard that too," Zeke stated, "but as you can see the reports of my death have been nothing more than wishful thinking. It's the end of the trail for you Forrester … you have a date with a rope."

"My name ain't Forrester … you've got me confused with someone else. My name is Tucker … Sheriff Alonzo Tucker."

Gabby and Thom rushed into the office when they heard the gunfire. Zeke said, "Thom, we need Roberts to come and dig that slug out of Forrester's shoulder … wouldn't want him to die from lead poisoning before he gets hanged."

Thom replied, "I'll get him here right away," as he turned and hurried off.

"Thought you said you were only gonna talk to him," Gabby stated. "Sure would hate to see what you'd do if'n you had something besides talk in mind."

With a slight chuckle Zeke replied, "Actually he gave me no choice. His name ain't Tucker, it's Sam Forrester and he's wanted for robbing the bank in Prescott and killing three people while doing so."

"Okay Forrester get on back there and into a cell. The Doc will be here soon and take that slug out of your shoulder. Then you and I will have a little talk."

As Forrester started towards the back he said, "I tell you I ain't Forrester, my name is Alonzo Tucker. I am the sheriff here and I ain't telling you a damn thing."

A ring of keys hung on a hook beside the doorway leading back to the jail cells. There were four cells along one wall … the cells on each end were occupied, leaving two empty cells between them. Zeke locked Forrester in one of the empty ones and then asked him, "What are these two locked up for."

"What they're locked up for ain't no concern of yours," Forrester snarled.

Zeke went back to the office and hung the ring of keys back on the hook as Roberts came in carrying his medical bag.

Outside the office, about twenty men were milling around in the street. Gabby was holding his rifle at hip level holding them back. Thom had picked up a shotgun from the gun rack in the sheriff's office and was standing beside Gabby … he held the shotgun at hip level, pointed at the crowd.

Zeke stepped outside and raised his voice so they all could hear, "I am a United States Marshal and I have arrested your sheriff. He attempted to draw on me and I had to shoot him. The Doc is patching him up … he'll live till he's hanged. His name is not Tucker, it's Sam Forrester. Forrester is wanted for robbery and murder. Now all of you go on about your business."

The crowd started breaking up and Zeke turned to Gabby and Thom, "Thanks for keeping them out here. Gabby two men are locked up in the back, why don't you take a look and see if you know who they are?"

Zeke, Gabby and Thom went inside and back to the cells. Doctor Roberts had already removed the slug from Forrester and was in the process of pulling bone fragments from the wound.

Zeke asked, "How's his shoulder Doc?"

"The slug busted up his shoulder joint," Roberts replied. "The wound will heal, but the way the bone is shattered he'll never be able to use his arm again. His gun fighting days are over"

"Doesn't matter much Doc," Zeke said. "He will be hanged before he has a chance to miss it. You know this man as Tucker but his real name is Sam Forrester. He along with three others robbed the bank in Prescott and killed three people while doing so. His three partners were caught, tried in the federal court in Prescott and hanged. Sam Forrester was tried in absentia, found guilty and is sentenced to hang. A death warrant on Forrester was issued by the same judge."

Roberts paused in pulling bone fragments from Forrester's shoulder saying, "I see … then there isn't much need in getting all of the shattered bone fragments cleaned from his shoulder. I'll just bandage him to stop the bleeding. When are you going to hang him?"

"I don't have a copy of his death warrant with me … I'd hang him right here and now if I did." Zeke responded. "Carson City is the nearest town with a federal marshal's office … I'll have to take him there to be hanged."

Roberts finished bandaging the shoulder, put his instruments back in his bag and picked it up saying, "I'll be going to my office, if you need me I'll be there."

"Thanks Doc, I'll see you there as soon as I get things cleared up here," Zeke replied.

Gabby knew the two men that were locked up. They are brothers and work a low yield mine a half days ride west of Agua Caliente … they also do some trapping. "Howdy Mike, howdy Andy, what're you two locked up for?" Without waiting for an answer, he turned to Zeke saying, "Zeke I know these two jaspers. They are the Ballard brothers, Mike and Andy. They got themselves a claim over west o' here. They got another brother too, his name's Billy he ain't here … maybe he's over to the saloon. I didn't see him when I was there though. Don't know what these two are in here for, but I'd be willing to bet you that it ain't much."

"Well Gabby," Zeke said with a slight smile, "maybe we could ask them why they are in here."

Turning to the cell that Andy was in Zeke asked, "What are you in here for?"

"Like Gabby said, it wasn't much. In fact, we shouldn't even be in here. We came into town to supply ourselves for the winter and stopped over to the Top Hat. Big Red has a new girl there and we had us a fist-fight to see which one of us would get her first. I guess we broke a couple of chairs and a table or two, but we paid Big Red for them. Then the sheriff came in, said we was being disorderly and arrested us. Told us we had to pay twenty-five dollars each or spend thirty days in jail."

"What about your brother Billy, is he in town," Zeke asked.

"He came here with us but he went on to Carson City. He's kind of sweet on a little gal over there," Andy replied. "He should be coming back here in a few more days … maybe he'll have enough money to pay our fine, but I doubt it."

Zeke replied, "If all you two did was have a fistfight that fine seems a bit unreasonable. Doesn't this town have a judge?"

"There use to be a judge here, but he disappeared shortly after Forrester became the sheriff," Andy replied.

"It appears as though I am the only law in this town right now," Zeke said. "I am going to let you and your brother out of them cells, but you stay in town until I check with Big Red and make sure that all the damage you caused is paid for."

With a big grin on his face Andy said, "We sure do thank you Marshal, we got us a room already paid for over at the Top Hat. You can find us there if the need comes up."

Zeke turned and went to the doorway, got the key ring and tossed it to Gabby saying, "Unlock their cells Gabby and let them out of there."

When they all got into the office Zeke said, "Did Forrester take any property from the two of you?"

Mike responded, "Just our six-guns and I had seven dollars and six-bits. Andy had eight dollars even, he put the money in that tin box in the bottom drawer of the desk, but I reckon that that is going to go t'wards our fine."

"How long have you two been in jail," Zeke asked.

"This is the second day … unless you count the night he locked us up," Mike said.

"I'd say that you spent enough time in the calaboose to pay your fine," Zeke said as he went to the desk and pulled the large bottom drawer open. He got the box and set it on the desktop. The box was twelve inches square and as deep.

When Zeke opened the box, he was somewhat surprised at the amount of money it contained. He later counted it and found the amount to be five thousand two hundred twenty six dollars in bills and gold pieces. There was also another six dollars and seventy-one cents in small coin.

Zeke gave Mike and Andy their money and they found their guns in the cabinet by the table.

"We sure do thank you again Marshal, we're going to the Top Hat and get us a beer. Maybe later we'll decide who gets that gal first," Andy said as they started towards the door.

"Hold on a second," Gabby exclaimed. "Reckon I'll go along with you, if'n Zeke doesn't need me for awhile."

"No you go ahead and go with them, I'll find you later," Zeke said.

After the three of them left, Zeke looked through the papers on the desk then pulled the drawers open one at a time and examined their contents. One of the drawers held a stack of wanted posters. Looking through the stack, he discovered one that read reward five hundred dollars above a picture … below the picture it read Sam Forrester, wanted dead or alive for robbery and murder.

"Look at this Thom," Zeke said as he handed the flyer to him, "must have been mighty sure of his self to keep this around. Forrester was doing pretty good for himself here, there's over five thousand dollars in that cashbox."

"What do you intend on doing with all that money," Thom asked.

"Well, two thousand three hundred will go to the bank in Prescott," Zeke said. "That's the amount that was stolen during the robbery. The rest of it I don't know yet, I reckon it should go to the town. Speaking of money, there's that five hundred dollar reward for the capture of Forrester … I suppose that you and Gabby can divide that between the two of you."

"We aren't the ones that caught him … you are," Thom protested.

"The two of you were a big help by keeping that crowd outside," Zeke replied. "I don't keep reward money for myself, it goes to whoever is helping me at the time and this time it was you and Gabby."

"Give it all to Gabby," Thom said, "I really don't need it and he can probably use it. I am nowhere near as wealthy as you are, but writing about you has made me pretty comfortable in that department."

"Okay I'll give it to Gabby. That five hundred will come out of the money being returned to Prescott ... they are the ones that put up the reward money."

The door to the outside flew open and a man full of self-importance strutted in. "I demand to know what is going on here. I hear that you shot our sheriff and locked him up. I am telling you, you turn him loose right now," he said as he came into the office.

Zeke looked at the man who stood about five feet seven inches tall, and wore a pinstripe suit. While not being fat, he was quite portly ... most of his head was bald with a fringe of brown hair around the sides.

"You don't come in here and demand a damn thing from me," Zeke icily replied. "Just who are you besides an arrogant ass?"

"I am Jared Witherspoon," the man said with great pomposity. "I am a member of the town committee and that makes it my business to know what is going on."

"I am Zeke Cooper, United States Marshall. You may well be a member of the town committee," Zeke replied. "But to me you are nothing more than a pompous twit that is full of your own self-importance. The best thing for you to do is go gather the rest of your town committee and I will meet you here in this office in two hours. At that time I will tell all of you just what is happening and why."

"You can't be Zeke Cooper," Witherspoon snapped. "He died in a stagecoach wreck awhile back. Whoever you are, you can't just dismiss me like that and I demand that you release our sheriff."

Zeke's eyes narrowed and with a cold, flat voice said, "I am not going to stand here and argue with you about who I am … or anything else. Now get out of here and go do what you were told."

Witherspoon opened his mouth to say something, but seeing the look on Zeke's face wisely changed his mind. He snapped his mouth shut, turned around and strutted out the door.

Thom busted out laughing after Witherspoon left. After regaining control of himself he said, "You certainly sent him on his way. I don't think that he's used to being talked to in that manner."

With a wry smile, Zeke replied, "I usually just ignore people like him, but when they start demanding, about the only thing you can do is what I did … otherwise you'll be explaining yourself till dooms day."

Zeke took five hundred dollars from the cashbox, put it in his pocket and then put the box back in the desk drawer. He then walked to the cells in back, stopping in front of the one occupied by Forrester.

"Take off your boots and toss them out here Forrester," Zeke commanded.

"What for, I ain't going anywhere," a surly Forrester replied.

Zeke drew his gun saying, "Get them off before I shoot you in your other shoulder."

Forrester complied … after some difficulty he got his left boot off and tossed it out of the cell.

"Now the other one," Zeke demanded.

With a sigh of resignation, he managed to get the other boot off. As he slipped it off of his foot, a two shot forty-four pistol fell from its holster sewn inside the boot. When the pistol clattered to the floor, Forrester hung his head and stared at it.

"Slide that gun across the floor to this side of the bars," Zeke demanded. "What else do you have hid on you?"

Forrester looked up at Zeke as he stood and pushed the gun out of the cell with his foot. His eyes darted both directions and then with a look of defiance quietly said, "Nothing, that's it."

"I don't believe you," Zeke stated with a hard, flat voice. "Get your pants off and slip them out here."

"I ain't taking my pants off," Forrester stated.

The gun in Zeke's hand barked once and sent a lead slug between Forrester's legs. "Get them pants off," Zeke once again stated. "The next shot will be higher and you'll be sitting down to pee."

With a look of total resignation, Forrester fumbled one-handed with his belt buckle. He finally got it unbuckled, unbuttoned his pants and let them fall to the floor. He pushed his pants to the outside of the cell.

Zeke picked the pants up and felt the pockets. He found that which he suspected in the right hand pocket … it was a set of keys to the cell doors.

"Turn around Forrester so I can see if you have anything else on you," Zeke ordered as he slipped the keys into his pocket.

Forrester complied and slowly turned until he was facing Zeke once again.

"Okay," Zeke said as he tossed Forrester's britches into the cell and kicked his boots back in as well. "You can put your clothes back on now. I'll be back later to talk to you, I am going to want to know about the outlaws that you have been protecting. You think on that while I am gone and keep one thing in mind, I already know quite a bit and I don't take kindly to liars."

Zeke picked up the hideout gun and turned to leave. Thom, who had been watching, left the room with him.

When they got into the office and shut the door Thom asked, "How did you know that he had that gun and a set of keys?"

"I didn't," Zeke replied as he locked the door leading to the jail cells. "But there was one time that I wished that I had searched a prisoner."

Zeke took all the keys he could find and as he and Thom left, he locked the door leading from the street into the sheriff's office. They turned up the street and started walking towards Roberts' office.

Chapter Ten

As they were walking Zeke commented, "I need to get both Angel and Forrester to Carson City … Angel to her kin there and Forrester to be hanged. You just came from there Thom, how long do you reckon it would take to get there using a team and buggy?"

"I left there yesterday morning about an hour after daybreak and arrived here late afternoon," Thom replied. "I rented a horse and small buggy there, the horse is a strong gelding he stands right at sixteen hands. We moved along pretty good, I stopped about every three hours to give him a breather … but he never seemed to tire between rest stops. When I first left Carson City, I tried holding him at a trot but he kept breaking into a canter so I finally just gave him his head and let him set his own pace."

"Some horses are like that, you learn to just let them have their head and they will move you along at a faster pace than what you would have set," Zeke commented. "When do you figure on going back to Carson City?"

"My business is done here now. The purpose that I came for no longer exists. We can leave anytime you're ready to go."

"Maybe we can leave in the morning … I hate to leave this town without any protection." Zeke replied,

"It depends a lot on whether Cameron's men are still in town. They probably took off when they heard about Forrester's arrest."

They arrived at Doctor Roberts' office and just before going inside Zeke said, "After I talk to Roberts, I'm going to the saloon and see if I can learn anything. After I meet with the town committee, I'll have a better handle on what I need to do."

As they stepped into the office Doctor Roberts greeted them saying, "I heard another gunshot, am I needed to patch someone up?"

"No Doc," Zeke replied with a wry grin, "what you heard was a request shot."

"A request shot?" Roberts said, "I don't believe that I ever heard of that."

"Well, I asked Forrester to take his pants off so I could search them and he refused. So I punctuated my request with a slug between his legs and told him the next one would be a bit higher."

"I see," Roberts replied with a slight laugh, "did it work?"

"Every time Doc," Zeke replied. Then he asked, "What can you tell me about Jared Witherspoon?"

"Not a whole lot, I don't particularly care to be around the man. He showed up here about three or four years ago and bought the hotel down the street. He is on the town committee and was the loudest voice for hiring Forrester as sheriff. Forrester got here about six months or so after Witherspoon. I kind of feel that they knew each other before they came here and I believe that if you dig deep enough you will find that they are in cahoots."

"Do you know where Witherspoon came from?"

"He claims he is from St. Louis. He hardly ever talks of anything worth hearing and I have come to disbelieve anything that he says," Roberts replied.

Zeke said, "I sort of got the same opinion of him myself. He came into the sheriff's office after you left and demanded that I turn Forrester loose. I told him to gather the town committee and that I will meet with them in a couple of hours."

"I am on the town committee and except for Witherspoon the others are a pretty decent sort," Roberts said. "I believe that they all have the best interest of the town at heart. I have to admit that Forrester quieted the town by controlling the outlaws. There are many of us here that would rather see them put in jail instead of given safe haven. Overall, the town has prospered from what the outlaws spend here … but at what cost to our self-worth?"

"That's something that each man has to decide for himself," Zeke responded. "Regrettably when it comes to money, there are too many that choose what they believe to be riches over the value of self worth."

"Doc," Zeke continued, "I want to kind of check out the town before I meet with that committee, but I need someone to watch over Angel while I am doing it."

"Zeke you are more than welcome to leave Angel here with Wings and myself while you do what you have to do. Don't worry about her … you can leave her in our care until you leave for Carson City."

With a, "Thanks Doc," Zeke turned and headed out the door with Thom right behind him.

It was just after dusk when they got outside. Zeke said, "Reckon we can start at the Top Hat, that's where Gabby was headed with Mike and Andy."

They crossed the street and headed to the Top Hat. When they got there, they pushed through the batwing doors and entered a large room. Zeke stepped sideways to the left as he entered. The doorway was located about center of the outside wall. The room was seventy-five feet deep and one hundred feet wide. A bar starting ten feet from the street-side wall and connected to the left-hand wall came out about twelve feet, turned and ran forty feet towards the rear wall. A very ornately carved back-bar ran the full length of the bar along the wall. A mirror about four feet wide and made of several sections covered the wall above the back-bar. A top hat was mounted on top of the back bar about halfway down. A stage was in the center of the far wall, a piano was to the left of the stage. A wide stairway in the far right corner led to the rooms on the second floor. Between the stairway and the stage, a doorway with the door closed led to an office and storage area.

Several tables filled the room and they had anywhere from two to six people sitting at them. There were men sitting at two different tables' playing cards … one table with six men and the other with four. The other occupied tables had two to five men sitting at each, drinking and talking. Eight scantily clad young women were mingling among the occupants at the tables. Some were delivering drinks while others wandered among the patrons talking to them … except for one table, which had four men sitting at it. The table that the four were sitting at was by the right-hand wall and well away from any other occupied table. None of the girls went near that table unless called to it.

The corner of the bar had two men standing on each side of it … eleven more men were scattered down the rest of the bar in groups of two and three. Gabby,

Mike and Andy were standing at the far end of the bar. A man wearing a red and white striped shirt and a bowler hat cocked to the back of his head, sat on a three-legged stool at the piano, playing it. Except for the music coming from the piano, the room fell silent when Zeke and Thom entered. Three young women were on the stage doing a cancan dance. The center dancer wore a black cancan dress trimmed with red and the other two each wore a red one trimmed with black.

Zeke said, "Thom, go on down to the end of the bar where Gabby and the Ballard brothers are … I'll join you there shortly."

Zeke watched the room carefully as Thom walked to the end of the bar. After Thom got to where he was going, Zeke turned his attention to the four men at the corner of the bar. He stepped closer to them, as he looked each man in the eye. Each of the four averted their eyes from him.

Zeke continued slowly down the bar, scrutinizing each man in turn. He also watched the room with the aid of the mirror behind the bar … he noted that the room was rapidly emptying. The dancers quit dancing as the piano tinkled to a stop.

When he got to where Thom and the other three were standing, Zeke slowly turned and faced the room. There were considerably fewer people in the room than there had been when he entered. Except for Thom, Gabby and the Ballard brothers the bar had no one left standing at it. The only table that remained occupied was the one where four men sat playing cards.

"You sure do know how to empty out a place," Gabby stated. "Except for that one fella sitting there playing cards with them other three, everyone in here is one o' the regular townsfolk."

Zeke asked, "Which one is that Gabby and what do you know about him?"

"The one that's facing us, he comes here pretty often. He's a gunsmith … goes by the handle o' Curly. Pretty fair gunsmith too, had him repair my rifle a while back and he done a right good job on it. Has a shop in Carson City he says."

"I see the one that you mean. He looks a bit familiar to me, but I can't place him. Reckon it'll come to me in a little while," Zeke replied.

The door between the stage and stairway opened and a woman entered the bar area. She was five feet seven inches tall, big boned, well-proportioned and long flowing red hair cascaded over her shoulders. She wore a full-length dark green gown, with a low cut bodice, that clung to her body and accented all of her curves.

She stood just inside the doorway as she surveyed the almost empty room. Her eyes came to rest on Zeke and she walked to him. With fire in her eyes she demanded, "Do I have you to thank for running all of my customers off? Ten minutes ago this place was bustling with business … look at it now. Just who are you anyway?"

With a wry grin tugging at the corner of his lips, Zeke calmly looked at her and replied, "My name is Zeke Cooper, Deputy United States Marshal. I take it that you are Big Red. Do you always greet people in this manner, or is it just when your Irish temper gets the best of you?"

Big Red looked at Zeke in silence for about thirty seconds and then busted out laughing. When she finally got her laughter under control she said, "You got me there, I do have a quick temper and I am Irish. Name's Barbra McIntyre, but most folks call me Big Red. I own this establishment and I don't think that you are going to be good for my business."

"If the majority of your customers are like the ones that just left," Zeke replied, "your business is definitely going to get worse. This town has become a haven for outlaws. After I take care of what I need to do in Carson City, I'm coming back here and do something about it."

"Yeah, right," Big Red responded, "and what are you going to do about Witherspoon and our crooked sheriff?"

"Your ex-sheriff is in jail and I'll be taking him to Carson City … he has a date with the hangman," Zeke said. "Aside from knowing that Witherspoon is a self important pompous ass, I know nothing about him … yet."

"I can tell you a few things about him," Big Red replied, "I first knew him in Virginia City … him and our sheriff. I don't know when Tucker changed his name from Forrester. That was his name in Virginia City … he was Witherspoon's man then and still is. Both of them left Virginia City about six years ago. Forrester left first, then a few days later Witherspoon left. During the two years that they were there, every large silver shipment going out of Virginia City was held-up. The sheriff at that time thought that Witherspoon was the leader of the gang that was doing the hold-ups, but could never prove it."

"You said the sheriff at that time, what happened to him," Zeke asked. "And why did Witherspoon and Forrester leave?"

"The sheriff secretly switched the shipment of two wagons of silver, to two wagons loaded with six men in each wagon. The outlaws stopped the wagons about a half day out of Virginia City. There were eight of them and instead of getting the silver they were expecting, they got lead. When the shooting stopped, seven of the outlaws lay on the ground dead. The eighth outlaw had only a slight wound to his arm. That outlaw was Forrester."

Big Red continued, "The sheriff brought Forrester back to town and locked him in the jail. That night someone, some believe it to be Witherspoon, killed the sheriff and broke Forrester out of jail. Forrester disappeared that night and turned up here a couple of years ago. Witherspoon stayed around Virginia City for a few more days, then one night he just disappeared. The next time I saw him was when he came here."

"How long have you been here," Zeke asked.

Big Red answered, "I came here about five and a half years ago and bought this place." She held up her hand saying, "Before you ask, I came across the money to do so honestly."

Zeke asked, "How did you do that?"

"I was working in Virginia City and I grub-stacked a down on his luck prospector several times. After he struck it rich, he showed up where I was working. I didn't recognize him at first … he was all gussied up in new duds and wearing a top hat. He asked me to marry him but I told him no. Then he asked me why and I told him that I am a whore and enjoy what I do too much to settle down with just one man. He left after some more discussion and the next afternoon I received a package. When I opened the package, I found his top hat, a bank draft for fifty thousand dollars and a note. The note said that if it hadn't been for me he never would have struck it rich. And that if I wanted to remain a whore, he would respect my wishes but I should at least have my own place. When I heard that the owner of this place wanted to sell I came here, liked the potential of what I saw and bought it cheap. It was just a bare bones two-bit whorehouse at that time. I closed it down and remodeled it to what it is now … an elegant brothel."

"A very elegant brothel indeed," Zeke replied. "Big Red I want to thank you for the milk that you gave Gabby for the baby. I would like to purchase some more in the morning, if you're of a mind to sell me some."

"I should have known that you're the man that wondered into town with a baby under his arm. You can have all the milk you need for that baby as long as you're here … and there'll be no charge for it," Big Red stated. Then she continued, "If you're really going to clean up this town, you can have a room here while you are doing it. I want to see those outlaws gone just as much as anyone else does. Just about every business in town has been paying the sheriff just to stay open … he calls it a tax but I call it robbery. I can't prove it but I am certain that the money winds up in Witherspoon's pocket."

"How do you figure that," Zeke asked.

"He told me that if he didn't receive free service here, he would see to it that my so-called taxes were doubled. He also threatened that great harm would come to me if I revealed Tucker's name to actually be Forrester."

"That's enough to put Witherspoon behind bars, while we learn more about him," Zeke replied.

Chapter Eleven

One of the girls came down from upstairs and had a surprised look on her face when she saw that the place was almost empty. Big Red went and met her as she reached the bottom of the stairway.

"Look at her Marshal," Mike said. "Ain't she purty?"

Zeke looked at the woman and said, "Is she the one that you two are fighting over?"

"Yeah," Mike said, "but we ain't gonna fight to see who gets her first. We have both drank four beers since we come in here and after we drink four more, we are gonna have a pissing contest instead."

"I see," Zeke replied, "and just how does that work?"

"The one that can piss the farthest wins," Andy replied as he and Mike continued drinking.

Zeke turned towards Gabby saying, "Gabby there is a five hundred dollar reward on Forrester and I reckon it to be yours."

Gabby protested, "But I ain't the one that got him, you are … and Thom was there too."

"I don't keep reward money," Zeke replied, "and Thom will make plenty off the story he writes about what happened here."

Gabby accepted the money saying, "That's a lot of money to me. I reckon that I'll stay here in town through the winter … it'll sure be a lot warmer than that cabin I got. Yes sir, when that snow starts coming down it gets fearsomely cold up there. Why I've seen drifts up there higher than my cabin. There was this one time a couple years ago I got snowed in up there and couldn't get outside the cabin for near onto three weeks. I knew that storm was a coming and got prepared for it. I brought Matilda and that ornery cuss into the cabin with me and we all stayed there till the storm blowed itself out."

"That cabin must have smelled pretty ripe by then," Zeke wryly commented. Then he continued, "I'm heading over to the Elkhorn and take a look see at who is in there, then I'll meet the town committee at the sheriffs office."

As Zeke turned to leave Thom said, "I'm coming with you."

"I'm coming along too," Gabby said. "Reckon them two Ballard boys can get along without me for awhile."

When the three of them left the Top Hat, they observed several riders leaving town in a hurry. They also heard the sound of distant hoof beats running hard echoing in the distance.

"Kind of late to be setting out for somewhere else," Thom commented to Zeke. "I would say that news of you not being dead has gotten around a bit."

Zeke answered, "It does appear that way. But I'd wager that there's at least one or two of the Lisping Bandit's men still in town."

As they listened to the distant hoof beats, they heard a wolf howl three times.

"That wolf sounds mighty close," Gabby said. "If'n it's the same one I seen on the ridge, he sure has moved fast."

"That's Spirit doing the howling," Zeke replied. "Reckon he and Blaze will show up here most anytime now."

When they got to the Elkhorn, Zeke stepped through the doorway first. The place was similar in size to the Top Hat … but not nearly as gaudy. A staircase in the far corner led to several rooms on the second floor. There was no stage but a piano was at the back wall.

Seven men stood at the bar in three different groups. A faro table was in the center of the room and there were five men at the table plus the dealer. Four of the tables scattered through the room had six men each playing poker and a fifth table had four men doing the same.

Zeke entered the saloon and stepped to the side of the doorway. He quickly scrutinized the room before slowly walking towards the bar with Thom and Gabby close behind him.

When they got to the far end of the bar, Zeke stopped and turned sideways so he could watch the room as well as the door.

The bartender came to where they were standing and asked, "What'll it be gents?"

Zeke ordered tequila, Thom and Gabby each got a whiskey. As they sipped their drinks Zeke asked Gabby, "Do you recognize the people in here?"

"Near as I can tell they're all regular town folks. I don't rightly know all of them but I've seen the most of them around town nearly every time I come here." Gabby nodded his head at a man that had left one of the tables and was walking towards them. "That feller there coming our way is the owner of this place."

Zeke observed the man approaching them. He was about six feet tall and probably weighed around two hundred pounds. The man was well dressed and walked with the self-assurance of one who knows his capabilities. He wore a six-gun strapped to his right leg.

When he got to Zeke, he stopped and with a soft southern drawl said, "Howdy, I reckon you to be Zeke Cooper. I am Bret Stevens and this is my establishment."

"Yes, I am Zeke Cooper, pleased to make your acquaintance. Do I detect a Virginia accent in your speech?"

"That you do sir … I come from outside of Charleston. I have heard of you and often wondered if you are one of the Richmond Coopers."

"That I am," Zeke replied. "My Pa and I left there in sixty-six … we had a plantation south of Richmond."

Zeke continued, "You seem to be doing a fairly good business this evening. The Top Hat kind of emptied out when I entered there."

"I'm not surprised," Bret replied. "Most of her customers are of the outlaw variety and mine are mainly locals. I allow the outlaws to come in here as long as they don't cause any trouble. But I would just as soon not have them around at all. There were seven of them in here when word spread that you were in town … they left in a big hurry. I understand that you are going to meet the town committee at the sheriff's office. Before you do that I believe that you and I should go to my office and have a conversation about what is going on in this town."

Bret led the way to his office and closed the door after they entered. He motioned Zeke to a chair as he sat down behind his desk.

"I am a member of the town committee," Bret began. "With the exception of Witherspoon the members of the committee are good honest people. Clive Baxter the blacksmith and Doctor Roberts are both straight shooters and as honest as they come. Then there's Jake

Quigley he's honest to a point but a bit too greedy for my taste. Witherspoon and his sheriff have the majority of the town cowed. Tucker collects what they call taxes, but it's nothing more than robbery, from all of the business people … except for me. Some of the outlaws would wreck the place of anyone that objected to their tax. When they complained to Tucker, he would make a big show of arresting the ones that did it. But he would turn them loose within an hour claiming that he didn't have enough evidence to keep them in jail."

"You said all the business people paid except for you," Zeke stated. Then asked, "Why not you?"

"When Tucker came in here to collect their tribute from me, I brought him here to the office. I took his gun away from him, pistol whipped him with it and threw him out. Then I went to Witherspoon and explained exactly what would happen to him if he sent anyone else to collect, or damage my property."

"I see," Zeke responded with a chuckle. "Why don't the rest of the business owners in town stand up to them?"

"I tried to get them to, but they just don't have what it takes to do so. Don't get me wrong, they're not cowards they just do not know how to handle people like Witherspoon … that and they like the money the outlaws spend. I reckon that besides me, Doc Roberts is the only one that has stood up to them. They need the Doc now and then, so they don't bother him."

Zeke asked, "Why haven't you done something about Witherspoon and Forrester?"

"Forrester?" Bret asked with a puzzled voice.

"Yes, that's Tucker's real name," Zeke replied. "He is wanted for bank robbery and murder. I'll be taking him to Carson City in the morning. As for Witherspoon, I'm not sure yet. I do know from what I have already learned about him that he has a cell waiting for him at the jail."

"What are you going to do about the outlaws? I could have taken care of Witherspoon and Tucker a long time ago. But I was here, and I know what it was like before Witherspoon and Tuck … Forrester showed up here. The town was wild and the outlaws did pretty much as they wanted. They ambushed and killed every Sheriff we had. I tried to get the townspeople to stand up to them, but they would not."

"As I said, Witherspoon will be put in jail tonight. Most if not all of the outlaws have left, but I suspect that one or two of the Lisping Bandit's gang are still here," Zeke said. "They expect the Lisping Bandit to get here in another four or five days and I don't believe that they will do anything till he gets here. I can be to Carson City and back by then."

"If you're of a mind to take them on here in town you can count on me to give a hand," Bret stated.

"I'll keep that in mind," Zeke replied. "But for now I reckon that the rest of the town committee is waiting at the sheriff's office."

Chapter Twelve

Thom and Gabby followed Zeke and Bret as they started to the sheriff's office. They stepped through the doorway to the street and Zeke suddenly stopped, there in the street in front of him stood Blaze and Spirit.

Blaze reared onto his hind legs, forelegs pawing at the air as he whinnied a greeting. Spirit bounded to Zeke and stopped right in front of him.

"Blaze … Spirit," Zeke shouted with joy, "it sure is good to see you."

Blaze came back down onto all four legs and nodded his up and down while nickering softly. Spirit sat on his haunches at Zeke's feet. Blaze laid his head on Zeke's shoulder and gently nuzzled him. Zeke patted Blaze along the side of his neck with one hand as he scratched Spirit behind his ears with the other.

Thom, Gabby and Bret watched as Zeke, Spirit and Blaze greeted each other. Thom briefly explained the bond that the three of them had to Gabby and Bret.

"I've never seen the likes of that," Bret said. "I'd swear that the three of them are talking to each other."

"I wouldn't bet that they aren't," Thom replied. "The three of them work together as though they are of a single mind. Spirit and Blaze always seem to know what needs done … and they do it. Spirit is a silver wolf and according to legend, there is only one of his kind on all the earth at any one time. Blaze is a one-man horse and Zeke is the only one that can ride him. Zeke has never tied or tethered Blaze to anything since the night he woke him up holding the tether pin in his mouth."

After a few minutes of greeting each other, Zeke turned and started walking toward the sheriff's office. Blaze walked to one side of him and Spirit on the other. Thom, Gabby and Bret hurried to catch up to them.

When they got to the sheriff's office, Gabby, Thom, Spirit and Blaze stayed outside as Zeke and Bret went in.

There were four men in the office and Witherspoon was their self-appointed spokesman.

Witherspoon loudly exclaimed, "It's about time you got here. We demand that you let our sheriff out of that cell back there."

Zeke looked at each of the other three men in turn. They all averted their eyes away from him. Zeke looked at Witherspoon and with a calm, flat voice said, "That is not going to happen. Just how did you get in here? I left that door locked."

"I happen to have a door key," Witherspoon blustered, "and I once again demand that you release our sheriff."

Zeke removed the keys from his pocket and started toward the door leading to the cells. As he unlocked the door, Zeke said, "Come with me Witherspoon."

With a triumphant look on his face, Witherspoon looked at the others gathered in the office and then strutted after Zeke. When they got to the cells, Zeke went to the one furthest from Forrester. As he opened the door he said, "Get in here Witherspoon, this will be your new home for awhile."

The blood drained from Witherspoon's face and he stammered, "Wha ... What are you talking about?

I am head of the town committee and I've done nothing wrong. You can't put me in there."

"I can and I am, now get your carcass in there before I loose my patience with you," Zeke sharply retorted.

A dejected Witherspoon entered the cell and sat down on the bunk. With a fearful voice he asked, "Just what is it that you think I've done?"

"You are going to be tried for robbery and murder," Zeke replied.

"But I haven't robbed anyone and I certainly haven't killed anyone," Witherspoon feebly protested.

Zeke didn't bother answering him. He went to the cell containing Forrester and unlocked it. "Okay Forrester go out to the office, you have some talking to do."

Bret and the other three men had gathered at the door and were silently watching. When Zeke and Forrester came towards the door, they stepped back into the office.

Zeke pushed Forrester towards the chair next to the desk saying, "Sit on that chair Forrester."

As Forrester sat down Zeke said, "Gentlemen you know this man as Alonzo Tucker, his real name is Sam Forrester. Tomorrow I am taking him to Carson City ... he has a date with the hangman. This evening he is going to tell us all about Witherspoon."

"Why should I tell you anything," Forrester stated. "You're gonna hang me no matter what anyway."

"You're right about that, you are going to hang. I'll give you a little incentive to tell us what you know," Zeke said as he turned away and walked to the door leading outside.

Zeke stood in the open doorway and snapped his fingers. He stepped out of the doorway as Spirit rushed into the office. Thom and Gabby came in behind him as Thom said, "This we got to see."

"Don't be alarmed gentlemen he won't hurt you," Zeke said as Spirit circled the room sniffing each man.

Spirit stopped at Forrester, sniffed at him and sat on his haunches about a foot from him. Then he licked his chops, opened his mouth and snapped it shut as he snarled, laid his ears back and emitted a low growl.

With a cold, flat voice Zeke said, "There's why you should tell us what you know. If you don't want to talk or if I believe you to be lying I'll let him have you. The way I see it is that you are going to die anyway and if I let him eat you it'll save me the bother of taking you to Carson City to hang."

An ashen faced Forrester stared with bulging eyes at Spirit. A wet spot appeared at the crotch off his pants, a puddle formed on the chair and dribbled onto the floor as a foul odor permeated the room.

A very frightened Forrester licked his lips and hoarsely croaked, "I … I … I'll te … te … tell you wh … wh … what you want to know, ju … ju … just don't let that wolf eat me."

"Okay Spirit lay down," Zeke said.

Spirit cocked his head sideways as he quizzically looked at the puddle forming on the floor. He stood and backed away about three feet, licked his chops once more, snarled and then laid down facing Forrester.

"Start talking Forrester … tell us what you know about Witherspoon. Did he have any thing to do with that bank robbery in Prescott?"

Forrester kept his eyes fixed on Spirit as he answered Zeke, "Yes, he planned the whole thing and helped me to get away. He hid me in town and while the posse was chasing after the others we left in the opposite direction."

Zeke asked, "Who killed the sheriff when you broke out of jail in Virginia City?"

"That was Witherspoon, he killed him," Forrester replied.

"Who killed the last sheriff that was here," Zeke asked.

"I don't know who did ... I just know that it was one of the outlaws. After the sheriff got killed Witherspoon figured that we could take over and control the town. He liquored up a two-bit Texas gunman and got him to hoorah the town. After I forced him to draw on me, I shot and killed him. Then Witherspoon got the town committee to appoint me as sheriff."

Forrester continued, "After I became sheriff we made a deal with the outlaws that come here. For a price, they can stay as long as they want if they cause no trouble. Then Witherspoon figured that the business owners should pay for our protection too."

Zeke asked, "What happened to the money you collected?"

"My cut is in that box in my desk drawer ... Witherspoon has the rest, most likely in his safe," Forrester answered.

Zeke said, "That should be enough to convict Witherspoon." Then he snapped his fingers and Spirit stood up.

Spirit walked to Forrester and sniffed his leg. Forrester yelled, "AAIYEEEEE," and fainted as Spirit hoisted his hind leg and marked him. Then Spirit turned, walked outside and joined Blaze.

With a slight chuckle Bret asked, "How did you train that wolf to do that?"

"The wolf's name is Spirit," Zeke replied. "I didn't train him to do anything. He has a mind of his own and does what he wants to."

Zeke went to the stove and picked up the bucket of water, then went to Forrester and dumped it on his head.

Forrester spluttered back to consciousness and looked around the room with terror-filled eyes. With a voice filled with fear he stammered, "Wh … Wh … Where is th … tha … that wolf?"

"On your feet Forrester and get on back to your cell," Zeke commanded.

With his eyes darting around the room, Forrester uneasily rose to his feet. He tentatively started towards the cells in the back.

After Zeke locked Forrester back in his cell, he went to the cell that held Witherspoon.

Witherspoon blustered, "You can't keep me in here. I demand that you unlock this door and let me out of here."

"You just don't get it do you? You are under arrest for murder and robbery. More than likely you're going to hang alongside of Forrester," Zeke replied.

"Murder," Witherspoon exclaimed, "you can't prove that I killed anyone."

"Yes I can," Zeke replied. "Take your clothes off and toss them out here."

Furtively darting his eyes around the cell Witherspoon said, "I ain't taking my clothes off."

"Yes you are, if I have to come in there and convince you, you'll wish that I hadn't. Now get them off."

With a sigh of resignation, Witherspoon undressed and dropped his clothes outside of the cell.

As Zeke searched Witherspoon's clothing he said, "The boots too, get them out here."

Zeke finished searching the clothing and examined the boots … the only items he found were some change, sixty-two dollars in bills, two cigars and a packet of matches.

"I figure you for a ladies hide-out gun. Where is it?"

Witherspoon's eyes darted to the bunk as he said, "Looks like you're wrong, as you can see I have no place to hide anything let alone a gun."

Zeke unlocked the cell door saying, "You're right … it has to be in your cell, get your carcass out here while I take a look."

As Witherspoon came out of the cell, he lunged at Zeke.

Zeke stepped back, his six-gun appeared in his hand and he whacked Witherspoon alongside the head with it.

Witherspoon crumbled to the floor … out cold.

Zeke entered the cell and went to the bunk. He flipped the thin pad that served as a mattress onto the floor. Laying beneath the mattress he found a small two-shot forty-four, a key to the outside door of the sheriff's office and a knife about six inches long. Searching further in the cell, he found nothing more.

Stepping outside the cell, Zeke took hold of Witherspoon's left leg and dragged him inside. Then he picked up the weapons and key, left the cell and locked the door. Leaving Witherspoon's boots and clothing on the floor outside of the cell, he went back to the office.

When he entered the office one of the men there asked, "What are we going to do now?"

"Just who are you, and what do you mean by that," Zeke asked.

"I'm Jake Quigley," the man responded, "I own the mercantile. What I mean is that now we don't have a sheriff and the outlaws will run wild again."

"Well Jake, perhaps you should hire another sheriff," Zeke replied.

"We've had other sheriffs and they were either killed or ran off by the outlaws."

With a hint of sarcasm in his voice Zeke replied, "This is your town Jake and just maybe if you stood behind your sheriff you'd have a peaceful town."

"The outlaws will be coming back," Jake persisted. "Where are we going to get a sheriff and what do we do in the meantime?"

"I am going to Carson City tomorrow," Zeke replied, "while I'm there I'll inquire about a sheriff for you. I don't believe that the outlaws will be back for four or five days, maybe longer. My business there won't take very long and I should be back in two days … no more than three."

Bret asked, "Will you be taking Forrester and Witherspoon with you?"

"I had planned on taking Forrester with me," Zeke said, "a death warrant has been issued on him and he will hang. But after what we have learned this evening, we need to put off his hanging so he can testify at Witherspoon's trial. I can take them both with me to be tried in Carson City … however I reckon it would be best if he was tried and hanged here."

"I for one agree with you Zeke," Bret said. "Problem is we don't have a judge here. While you are in Carson City can you get a circuit judge to come here?"

"I don't know how long it will take for one to get here, but when I tell them who we have in jail I don't reckon that it'll take long," Zeke replied.

"Hold on a minute," a worried Jake protested, "I don't understand why it would be best to try them here. Won't it make all the outlaws mad at us ... and they'll seek revenge?"

With a pitying tone to his voice Bret replied, "Jake if we try Witherspoon here and hang both him and Forrester, it will have the opposite effect. It will put the outlaws on notice that we hold no brook with their kind."

"Well maybe so," Jake replied dubiously, "I'll go along with what the rest of the committee decides."

After a short but heated discussion, they all agreed that it would be best to have Witherspoon's trial in Agua Caliente.

As the members of the town committee left the sheriff's office, Bret turned to Zeke saying, "If you need a place to stay, I have a room you can use."

Chapter Thirteen

Zeke locked the door between the office and cells. He locked the out-side door as he, Thom and Gabby stepped outside.

Blaze was standing in the street waiting for him but Spirit was not there. Zeke went to Blaze, reached up and rubbed his hand along side of his neck and head. Blaze lightly laid his head on Zeke's shoulder and softly nickered.

After a minute or so Zeke said, "Reckon we need to go to the stable and arrange for a stall."

As they walked to the stable, Thom asked, "Does Spirit always just disappear like that?"

"He normally doesn't show himself in a town," Zeke replied. "Spirit must be scouting the area around here and will show up at Blaze's stall after the town settles in for the night."

After arranging with the liveryman for a stall and grain for Blaze, Zeke said, "No need to close the door to the stall. Blaze will come back here later. He always comes and goes, as he wants. Later after the town quiets down, Spirit will probably show up here and spend the night with Blaze in his stall."

They left the stable with Blaze following along. Zeke turned towards Witherspoon's hotel as he said, "We need to search Witherspoon's office for any records he may have kept."

The hotel was a large two-story building. The entryway had a double door that opened into a short vestibule that led to a large lobby. A receiving counter about three and a half feet high and ten feet long was at the right-hand corner of the far wall. A guest registration book with a small bell beside it was open on top of the counter. About mid-way between the vestibule and the counter on the right-hand side of the lobby, a doorway opened into a dining room. Directly across from that doorway was another leading to a small saloon.

Zeke walked to the counter, which was unattended and struck the small bell. A man appeared from the saloon and hurried behind the desk asking, “Do you need a room?”

“No,” Zeke replied, “where is Witherspoon's office?”

“Mister Witherspoon isn't in,” the desk clerk replied. “He's at a town meeting and should be back soon. You can wait for him in the saloon, I'll tell him you're here soon as he gets back.”

Zeke's voice hardened as he said, “I did not ask you where Witherspoon is, I asked where his office is.”

“Mister Witherspoon isn't … is …,” the clerk started to say.

Zeke's right hand shot out and grabbed the front of the clerk's shirt. He jerked him against and partially over the counter. The blood drained from the clerk's face and his feet dangled in the air behind him.

“Where is the office,” Zeke demanded.

With an ashen face, the clerk stammered, “I … I … It's upstairs, the first door on the right.”

“That's better,” Zeke said as he released the clerk and gave him a slight shove backwards. “Now give me the key!”

The clerk stumbled backwards and hit the wall, which prevented him from falling onto his backside. With shaking hands, he got the key and handed it to Zeke. Then he stupidly reached for the forty-four revolver that lay on a shelf under the top of the desk.

Zeke had turned to go upstairs when he heard the clerk cock the hammer of his gun.

Zeke's six-gun appeared in his hand as he spun around facing the clerk. The clerk's right hand was above the desk, holding the forty-four pointed at Zeke.

The acrid smell of gun smoke filled the air as Zeke's gun roared a fraction of a second before the clerk's did. The clerk's right elbow shattered as the slug found its mark. The slug from the clerk's shot went wild as his gun clattered to the floor.

Zeke stepped back to the desk, with his gun pointed at the clerk, "Get out from behind that desk before this gun goes off again."

The clerk came from behind the desk whimpering, "You shot me."

"That's what happens when you point a gun at someone," Zeke sardonically replied.

Before re-holstering his gun, Zeke ejected the spent cartridge and replaced it with a fresh one. Then he tore the shirtsleeve from the clerks arm and used it as a tourniquet, tying it just above the shattered elbow.

Men gathered in the doorways leading to the saloon and dining room to see what the shooting was about.

Zeke turned to the gathering crowd and said, "I am a deputy United States Marshal, one of you men go and fetch Doc Roberts."

One of the men at the saloon door said, "I'll get him Marshal."

Zeke turned to Thom and Gabby saying, "I'm going to take the clerk up to Witherspoon's office. I'd appreciate it if you can keep this crowd down here and send Roberts on up when he gets here."

Zeke pushed the clerk ahead of him as they mounted the stairs. When they got to the office, he handed the door key to the clerk saying, "Open that door and get inside."

The office was not a very large room, measuring about fifteen feet in each direction. There was a large safe in the far right-hand corner and a desk beside it. A table about five feet long and three feet wide was in the center of the room. There were two large maps on the table. A closed door was at the left-hand corner. A window about center of the left hand wall overlooked the street below. A stove centered along the right-hand wall had hot coals in it.

Zeke indicated one of the five chairs at the table as he said, "Sit down on that chair there."

The clerk sat down as he surly responded, "You're going to be sorry when Mister Witherspoon gets back here."

"Witherspoon won't be back," Zeke responded. "Now suppose you tell me who you are and what you do for him. You are not just a desk clerk."

"People call me Blackie," the clerk sullenly replied. Then with false bravado demanded, "What do you mean Witherspoon won't be back? He'll be here most any time now and you'll get your comeuppance."

"Witherspoon is in jail along with your so called sheriff and you'll soon be joining them. Now answer my questions. What do you do for Witherspoon?"

Blackie's eyes darted to the large maps on the tabletop as he sullenly said, "I ain't telling you nothing."

Zeke walked to the desk and sat down on the chair behind it. He drew his gun from its holster and held it in his fist on top of the desk. As he pointed it at Blackie, he said, "This gun has a habit of going off now and then. I'll ask you once more, what do you do for Witherspoon?"

"I ain't te...," Blackie started to say.

Zeke's gun roared as it spit a slug towards Blackie. It creased his left shoulder and buried itself in the wall behind him.

Blackie's face blanched to a much lighter shade, his eyes opened wide with a blank expression. "Yo ... Yo ... You shot me again," he stammered.

"Blackie I'll shoot you again if you don't start answering my questions. The next shot will crease you where your neck joins your shoulder. If I have to shoot you again the third shot will shatter your left shoulder."

The door suddenly burst open as Thom and Roberts came into the room. "We heard a shot, what happened?" Thom exclaimed.

"Just persuading Blackie here to answer my questions," Zeke replied.

"He ... He's crazy," Blackie stammered, "Said he's going to shoot me again if I don't tell him what he wants to know."

"Well," Roberts said as he looked at Blackie's elbow, "if I were you I believe I'd answer his questions."

"You can't just let him shoot me," Blackie whined.

"I can and I will," Roberts replied. "I recall that I have patched up more than one man which you shot. You had no sympathy for them and I certainly have none for you."

Roberts finished with Blackie's shattered elbow and wrapped it with some gauze. Then he tore a bigger hole at the shoulder of the shirt. He examined the shallow wound on his shoulder and stated, "That's going to be pretty sore for awhile but it'll heal in time."

"Ain't you gonna put something on it to stop the pain," Blackie asked.

"No, I'll not waste any of my soothing salves on the likes of you," Roberts replied. Then he turned to Zeke saying, "Blackie here has shot several men since he has been here. He killed two of them without a reason … it was just plain cold blooded murder."

Roberts reached into his bag, took out a roll of gauze and set it on the table. "I'm going back to my office … if you have to shoot him again don't bother with fetching me. Just plug the hole with some of this gauze the bleeding will eventually stop."

Thom stayed in the office when Roberts left.

Zeke asked Thom, "Any problems downstairs?"

"Not really, a couple of men that were in the saloon had a notion to follow you up here, but they changed their minds."

Zeke turned his attention back to Blackie, "It's the end of the road for you Blackie. With Roberts's testimony you most likely will hang alongside of your boss."

Blackie sullenly replied, "You'll have to catch him first. You ain't gonna be able to keep me in no hoosegow when the Major hears of this."

"The Major," Zeke stated, "that means you're part of the Lisping Bandit's gang."

With some of his bravado returning Blackie responded, "He doesn't like that moniker and I ain't telling you no more. You can shoot me all you want, but he'll kill me if'n I tell you anything else."

Zeke rose to his feet still holding his six-gun in his hand. He studied Blackie as he ejected the spent cartridge from his gun and replaced it with a fresh one.

'He probably won't talk any more just yet,' he thought. 'I may get more information out of him after he's locked up for awhile.'

Zeke holstered his gun turned to Thom saying, "Keep an eye on him Thom, I'm going to search this office before we take him down to the jail. If he tries to get up from that chair, whack him over the head with your gun."

Zeke went to the safe and pulled on the door … it didn't budge. He went back to the desk and searched through each of the four drawers. Finding nothing of interest he pulled the top drawer all the way out and turned it over on top of the desk, dumping its meager contents. He found what he was looking for … the safe's combination written on the bottom side of the drawer.

Armed with the combination, Zeke returned to the safe and opened it. Inside he found stacks of paper money, gold coins, and nine bars of gold bullion. The gold coin and paper money, when counted later, amounted to twenty-one thousand, six hundred and ten dollars. There also were three ledgers.

Carrying the ledgers, Zeke went back to the desk. He sat the ledgers on the desk, picked up the drawer and started to return it to its rightful place. But he thought about the combination to the safe on the bottom of the drawer and sat it back down. He picked up a pencil that he had spilled from the drawer earlier, opened one of the ledgers to a blank page and copied the combination onto it. Then he took his knife and scraped all sign of the combination from the bottom of the drawer. He tore the page with the combination from the ledger and folded it before putting it in his pocket. Then he put the drawer back into place.

Zeke sat down behind the desk once again and opened the ledgers one by one. He discovered that one of the ledgers contained the name of each business owner in town along with the date and amount paid by each. The next one that he looked at was the amount of money paid by each outlaw along with their names … most of which had multiple entries. It also listed the date they arrived and the date they left. The third ledger listed dates, various landmarks and a few towns. Each entry also had two numerical amounts listed, one considerably larger than the other.

Zeke closed the ledgers and leaned back in the chair that he was sitting on as he thought about the meaning of the entries. The first two were pretty well self-explanatory. The third one was a bit puzzling as to what the dates, places and dollar amounts referred to.

As he pondered on the third ledger, his eyes drifted around the room. Then he focused on the maps on the table. Zeke arose from where he was sitting and walked to the table. One map was of the state of Nevada and the other was The Territory of Arizona. Each map had a line drawn on it at various locations with a date, one or two letters and a monetary amount written on the line. Turning back to the desk, he picked up the third ledger and stepped back to the table.

As he studied the maps and the ledger, he began to understand the entries. The dates written on the map coincided with the dates entered in the ledger. The letters matched up to the names of some of the outlaws entered in the ledger that Zeke thought of as 'the outlaw ledger.' There was one place on the Arizona map that had an X inside a circle, on the line beside it was the letter M and a question mark. The location did not match any of the entries in the journal.

Zeke broke the silence in the room saying, "Thom it seems that our friend Witherspoon has kept records of his thieving ways. It looks like he's in cahoots with the Lisping Bandit ... and a few other outlaws."

Zeke picked up the maps, laid one on top of the other, rolled them into a cylinder and placed them in the safe. Then he put the ledgers back into the safe before he closed and locked it.

Zeke said, "Reckon it's time for you to join your friends Blackie. Get up off of that chair and head out the door."

Thom turned to the door, opened it and stepped into the hallway. Blackie came out next followed closely by Zeke. They turned and proceeded down the stairs with Thom leading the way and Zeke still behind Blackie.

When they got to the bottom of the stairs Zeke said, "Thom I been thinking that someone else may possibly know the combination to that safe up there. It would set my mind at ease if you and Gabby stayed here for a little bit to keep anyone from going into that room."

"We'll guard it till you get back Zeke," Thom replied.

Chapter Fourteen

Blaze was in the street outside the hotel when Zeke came out and he walked alongside him to the jail. Spirit was nowhere in sight.

They arrived at the jail without incident, outside of a few stares and whispers from the people they met on the way. When they got to the jail, Zeke pulled the keys from his pocket, unlocked the door and pushed Blackie inside ahead of him. After unlocking the door between the sheriff's office and the cells, he once again pushed Blackie through the doorway ahead of him.

Witherspoon was sitting on the edge of the bunk in his cell. His head hung down, his arms folded tightly across his chest, as he seemed to be studying his still naked body. His arms had a few scratches on them, as did his legs from his attempts to retrieve his clothing lying on the floor just out of reach from his cell.

Zeke put Blackie in one of the empty cells and locked the door. Then he went to the cell that held Witherspoon. Sardonically Zeke asked, "Witherspoon why are you sitting there naked as a jaybird? You look ridiculous. Get your clothes back on."

"I can't reach them," Witherspoon whispered.

"What's that? I couldn't hear you … you'll have to speak a bit louder."

In a louder voice and with all of his pomposity gone, Witherspoon replied, "I can't reach them."

"Oh … yes …. Well I guess they are a bit out of your reach aren't they?" Zeke replied. "I'll just leave the three of you here alone. I'll be back in the morning."

Zeke turned towards the door as if to leave.

"Wa … Wai … Wait," Witherspoon yelled. "You can't just leave me here like this. Give me my clothes."

Turning back to Witherspoon Zeke said, "What did you say? You are in no position to be demanding anything."

A totally deflated Witherspoon subserviently whined, "Will you please give me my clothes?" … at least my britches?"

"I suppose I could," Zeke replied. "Before I do I am going to ask you some questions. I'll give you one piece of clothing for each answer that I believe."

Zeke continued, "I've been to your office and opened your safe. You have quite a stash of money and gold bullion. I also looked through the ledgers that were in the safe. What do the entries in the ledgers represent?"

Witherspoon's eyes furtively darted around the room and came to rest on his clothing, piled on the floor. Then in a barely audible voice said, "They are business transactions that I've conducted with the good people of this town."

"That's not good enough," Zeke responded. "One ledger is a record of the amounts that you extorted from the people of this town. I'm going to give you one more chance. If I don't like your answer, I'll leave and you can sit there in your all together till morning. Now tell me about the ledgers."

With an audible sigh Witherspoon replied, "You're right about that ledger, it contains the amount of taxes paid by each business. The other …"

"You're still not telling me the truth," Zeke interrupted, "reckon you might be more willing to talk in the morning." Then he turned and started towards the door.

"Wait … Wait," Witherspoon yelled as Zeke stepped through the doorway, closed and locked the door.

Zeke left the sheriff's office, locked the door and then headed to the Elkhorn. Blaze had been waiting in the street and pranced alongside of him. When he got to the Elkhorn, Zeke stopped and Blaze came to him.

As Zeke reached up and rubbed Blaze alongside his neck, Blaze nuzzled him on his shoulder. Then as Zeke turned to go into the Elkhorn, Blaze reared up onto his hindquarters and whinnied as he pawed at the air. When he came back down on all four legs, he turned and trotted towards the stable.

'Reckon that he's going to go eat,' Zeke thought as he entered the Elkhorn.

Bret was standing at the bar talking to the bartender. When he saw Zeke enter, he waved him over to where he was.

When Zeke stopped beside Bret, the bartender asked, "What can I get you?"

"Tequila," Zeke responded.

"Give us a bottle of the good stuff and two glasses," Bret said.

They picked up the bottle and glasses, went to a table and sat down. As they sipped the tequila, Zeke narrated what he had learned and found since he last saw Bret. Ending with, "We need to get the contents of that safe somewhere else. Thom and Gabby are guarding it for now."

"We can put it in my safe here," Bret said. "I'll round up a couple of good men and meet you there."

Then as an afterthought he said, "I think that I might be able to get hold of a cart at the freight office to haul it all on."

"If you get hold of a cart," Zeke replied, "the four of us should be able to handle it without involving any one else."

"Yes of course," Bret responded, "the less number of people that know about it, the better it will be. At any rate I'll meet you at Witherspoon's in fifteen to twenty minutes."

They finished their drink and left, Zeke back to Witherspoon's and Bret to the freight office.

Thom and Gabby had moved two chairs from Witherspoon's office to the hallway and were sitting on them guarding the door.

Zeke asked, "Have any trouble while I was gone?"

"Nary a bit," Gabby replied. "Except for that gunsmith feller everybody's stayed clear of us. He was being a might too nosey if you ask me. Wanting to know what was going on and where Witherspoon was at. I'm starting to believe that he is something more than a gunsmith."

"I still don't recollect where I know him from," Zeke replied. Then he continued, "He might be one of the Lisping Bandit's men. We'll keep an eye on him and see what he does. Bret is on his way to help us move the contents of the safe to the one in his office. He's trying to get a cart at the freight office. While we're waiting I'm going to take a look in the room behind the office."

Thom and Gabby remained in the hallway as Zeke entered the office and walked to the closed door.

Zeke opened the unlocked door and stepped through the doorway into a large room. The room was about twice the size as the office and opulently furnished. There were several oil paintings mounted on the walls. A settee upholstered with gold and red colored brocade was to one side of the room. Two large wing chairs matching the settee were in the room, one by the window overlooking the street and the other by the far corner of the room. An arched doorway without a door was in the center of the far wall of the room. A highly polished mahogany wood cabinet was next to the wall beside the window. A silver pitcher, silver tray and six crystal glasses sat on top of the cabinet. The cabinet had two doors made of several small panes of glass. Inside the cabinet were four bottles of brandy, one bottle of whiskey and two bottles of wine.

The room on the other side of the arched doorway turned out to be Witherspoon's bedroom. It was as opulently furnished as the sitting room. It too had a window overlooking the street. There was a large four-poster bed against the far wall, complete with canopy. A large stand with a ceramic washbasin, pitcher and tray on top of it stood in the far corner of the inside wall.

There was a wardrobe measuring about six feet wide, three feet deep and eight feet high along the wall opposite the window. It was made of mahogany and had two ornately carved doors reaching from top to bottom. Opening the doors revealed three drawers mounted along the bottom about two feet above the floor. Trousers, shirts, vest and jackets hung in the cabinet. Three pairs of boots sat on the bottom of the wardrobe above the drawers.

Zeke knelt down and opened the drawers of the cabinet one at a time. The first drawer held socks and handkerchiefs, the middle drawer held ties and a few pieces of jewelry. The third drawer was empty.

Zeke closed the drawers and stood up with a puzzled expression on his face. 'I'm missing something,' he thought. He stood back away from the wardrobe and studied it. 'There's something not right about that cabinet, but what is it? The clothes are hanging where they should be … the drawers are … are … wait a minute there's something wrong with the drawers.'

As he studied the drawers, Zeke realized what was wrong. The drawers were mounted two feet above the floor but they were only about eight inches deep.

Zeke went to the wardrobe, pulled the drawers out and set them on the floor. He found that they concealed a false bottom. In the space beneath the drawers and the floor, he discovered sixteen gold bullion bars. He also found a bankbook for an account at the Bank of California in Sacramento. There were several pages of entries. The last entry showed a balance of one hundred eighty six thousand dollars.

Zeke walked back to the office pondering on what he had found. 'Counting what is here and what is in the bank he has over two hundred thousand dollars. Twenty-five gold bars weighing about ten pounds each is roughly another eighty thousand. He should have quit while he was ahead. But then I reckon greed has no bounds.'

Thom, Gabby and Bret entered the office right after Zeke returned to it.

"There's sixteen more gold bars back there in his bedroom," Zeke said in way of greeting.

Bret had got a cart at the freight office and it was at the foot of the stairs. It took several trips down the stairs to carry all the contents of the safe and wardrobe to the cart. After the first trip, Zeke stayed with the cart, guarding its contents. A few curious onlookers peered through the doorways leading into the saloon and dining room but none of them ventured into the hallway.

As they pushed the loaded cart out of the hotel Zeke said, "Be watchful now, no telling what may happen between here and the Elkhorn."

They were about halfway to the Elkhorn when Spirit suddenly appeared, stood crossways on the boardwalk and emitted a low, short growl. Zeke stopped and scrutinized the area more closely. Then he saw the reflection of moonlight glinting off of a gun barrel as it moved. It came from the rooftop of a building across the street.

Zeke quietly said, "On the roof across from us," as he stepped back with one foot and spun sideways.

The rifle on the rooftop roared a split second before Zeke's gun barked a reply. The slug from the rifle splintered a hole into the boardwalk at the spot Zeke had just vacated. The man with the rifle tumbled from the roof and landed with a thud.

With his six-gun pointing the way, Zeke crossed the street. The man had landed hard and was lying on his stomach … dead.

Zeke reached down and rolled the carcass over to get a look at his face. It was the gunsmith. As he studied him Zeke ejected the spent cartridge from his gun and replaced it with a fresh one. Suddenly he remembered where he had seen the gunsmith before. The night the stagecoach stopped early, this man was at that station. He walked back across the street as he pondered on what his recollection meant.

When he got to the other side Bret said, "Zeke I've never seen anyone step back, spin sideways and shoot like you just did. Where did you learn to shoot like that?"

"I don't know," Zeke replied, "it just seemed to be the natural way for me to draw and shoot."

"I reckon it serves you well, you're the fastest I've ever seen. Do you know who the shooter is?"

"He's the gunsmith, except I'm not so sure that's what he really was," Zeke responded. "The night before the stagecoach wreck he was at the station that we stopped at overnight. I didn't think anything of it at the time, but he left in a bit of a hurry when the other passengers and I came into the station. I figured that he was in a hurry to get somewhere."

"Do you suppose that he had anything to do with that wreck," Thom asked.

"I don't know," Zeke said, "and he sure ain't going to tell us."

A small crowd started gathering by the dead gunman.

Zeke said to Bret, Thom and Gabby, "I don't think that there will be anymore trouble for awhile. If you three can get this gold on down to the Elkhorn, I'll take care of things here and join you there in a bit."

Spirit stayed in the shadow of the buildings as Zeke crossed the street and the other three pushed the cart towards the Elkhorn.

When Zeke got to the gathering crowd he said, "One of you men fetch the undertaker. Do any of you know who this man was?"

A man in the crowd replied, "I'm the one what does the burying here. I've seen him around town off and on but don't rightly know his name."

Zeke knelt beside the body and starting searching the dead man's pockets, in an attempt to learn who he was. All he found was twenty-seven dollars and sixteen cents in coin, a room key, bag of tobacco, a packet of rolling papers and a few wooden matches. He did not find anything to indicate the man's name.

"Here's what money that he had, reckon that'll get him buried," Zeke said as he held it towards the undertaker.

With a crafty look in his eyes, the undertaker took the money and replied, "I normally get thirty-five and their belongings for burying his kind."

Zeke studied the undertaker before responding. He saw a short man that stood about five and a half feet tall, heavyset, a luxurious handle bar mustache and wearing the apparel of a barber. "I take it that you are the barber as well?"

As he twirled one end of his mustache between the fingers of his right hand the man said, "That's right ... I am Claudio Kanaris the barber, dentist and undertaker."

"I see," Zeke replied, "how much do you charge for a haircut?"

"I charge five cents."

"How much do you get for a shave?"

"I get two cents for a shave."

"You charge the same for a haircut or a shave as everybody in this part of the country does. In most places, getting a man buried costs less than fifteen dollars. Maybe you can make an exception this time," Zeke said.

"My price for burying a man is thirty-five dollars," Claudio smugly replied.

Zeke's eyes hardened as he said, "There are a few types of people that I have no use for. Being a greedy nit-wit is one of them."

The sound of snickering came from the bystanders as Zeke continued, "I know full well that you don't normally get that much for burying a man. You will be paid your going rate and not a penny more."

Zeke raised his voice and asked, “Does anyone here know what Claudio normally charges for burying?”

“Twelve dollars,” a voice called out.

“That’s right,” another said.

Turning his attention back to Claudio Zeke said, “Reckon you should have taken what you were offered. You’ll get another dollar for displaying him in front of your shop for three days. He went by the name of Curly … maybe somebody will recognize him and know his full name. You take thirteen dollars from what I just gave you and give the rest back to me.”

Claudio sheepishly complied as he said, “You can’t blame a man for trying, can you Marshal?”

Zeke just looked at him in disgust, then turned and headed for the Elkhorn.

Chapter Fifteen

When Zeke entered the Elkhorn, he went straight to Bret's office. He entered the office just as Bret shut the door to the safe and locked it.

"I reckon that it'll be quite for the rest of the night," Zeke said as he entered the room. "Bret I'll take you up on your offer of a room. I'd like to get an early start in the morning and I'll get back here just as quick as I can. I'll get a saddle for Blaze in Carson City and ride him back here."

"You can have the room next to mine. It is the second one at the top of the stairs," Bret replied a he opened his desk drawer and removed a key. Handing the key to Zeke he said, "Here's the key to the door."

Zeke took the key and turned towards the door as he said, "Thanks, I'm going to go get Angel then I'll be back."

As Zeke walked up the boardwalk to Roberts' office, Blaze once again joined him. There were a few small groups of people gathered along the way. They grew silent as Zeke approached and after he passed them, they broke into excited whispering.

Zeke carefully observed his surroundings as he walked, on the alert for more trouble. He paid particular attention to the rooftops.

Zeke decided to stop at the Top Hat and get some milk from Big Red for Angel. When he entered, he saw Mike and Andy standing at the bar, dripping wet. Seated at a table near the staircase, was the girl that they had been fighting over.

Zeke stopped beside Andy and Mike, "You two smell kind of ripe and you're all wet. What happened? I thought you had a way to settle the argument of who gets the girl first."

Andy answered, "When we got outside we stepped around to the alley side of the building. Mike scratched a line in the dirt about five feet from the wall with his boot heel. He said we would stand with our toes touching the line and the one that pees the highest on the wall wins."

"Would've worked too, if'n you hadn't cheated," Mike exclaimed.

Zeke asked, "Just how did he cheat?"

"I was peeing farther up the wall than him so he moved closer to it." Mike replied. "So I moved closer than him, then he moved closer and I did too. First thing you know we're standing right next to the wall."

"He made his pee splash onto my head," Andy retorted.

"That ain't true Marshall, 'twas his own piss splashing on him. Then he peed on me a' purpose so I naturally gave him some 'o mine. First thing, you know we are both soaking wet from each other's piss, and we still don't know who is a 'gonna get her first."

With a smile tugging at his lips Zeke asked, "Have you thought about just asking her which one of you she wants to be with first?" Then he continued, "You two are not going to be worth anything until this is settled. I'll go ask her for you."

Mike and Andy stared at each other with their mouths hanging open as Zeke walked to the table where the girl was sitting.

Zeke stopped at the table and got his first close up look at her. She appeared to be in her mid to late twenties. Her hair was dirty blond … she was not a beautiful woman but she was not totally unattractive. She stood about five feet two inches and had the weary look about her of a woman well used for many years.

"Sit down marshal," the girl invited when Zeke stopped at her table.

Zeke sat down, cleared his throat and said, "I'm not here for me, it's those two brothers standing over there. They have been fighting over which one gets to have you first. I told them that I would settle it for them. Which one do you want to take first?"

"Tonight Marshal, I don't want either one, I can smell the stink on them from over here. Tomorrow if they take a bath and put on some clean clothes, I'll consider taking one of them first."

Zeke asked, "Which one?"

"It doesn't rightly matter," she replied. "One's the same as another."

"In that case," Zeke responded, "how about the oldest one first?"

"That's fine with me," she said. "I may be just another whore but they have to take a bath first."

Zeke went back to Mike and Andy, "Which ever one of you is the oldest gets to go first … tomorrow and after you take a bath."

Mike and Andy looked at each other, then Mike said, "That won't work Marshal, we ain't got nary an idea which of us is the oldest … we're twins."

Andy said, "If'n that's the way she feels about it, you can have her all to yourself Mike. I'll get me another gal."

Mike replied, "I don't think that I want her either. Let's go over to the bathhouse, get clean, come back here and get us a couple of other whores tonight. Don't know what I seen in her anyway."

"Me neither let's go," Andy said as he turned towards the door.

Zeke watched them leave and shook his head as he thought, 'All of that fighting and now neither one wants her. He turned his attention to the bartender and asked for tequila. As the bartender poured the tequila, Big Red approached him.

"I haven't heard a shot lately ... does that mean the shooting is over with for now?"

"I think that you're right," Zeke replied. "I certainly hope so, I want to get a good nights rest before leaving in the morning. This brings me to why I'm here. I am hoping to get some milk for tomorrow, if possible."

"Of course," Big Red said, "There's some left over from this evening's milking and she'll be milked again shortly after sunup tomorrow."

"I hope to be well on our way by then," Zeke replied. "I need to get Angel to her family and get back here as quickly as I can."

"I'll get you what I have in the back," Big Red said as she turned and started for her office.

She came back with a whiskey bottle filled with milk in each hand. As she handed the bottles to Zeke Big Red said, "If your looking for a place to stay you can stay here ... with me. A man has his needs and I will take good care of you."

Zeke looked at her and said, "Red you are a right handsome woman and I appreciate the offer. But I am a happily married man with a family."

"They would never know," Big Red persisted.

"You're right, if I gave in to temptation they may never know … but I would. I'll be your friend Red, but I'll not be sharing your bed. The only woman that I share a bed with is my wife, Little Doe."

"Well Zeke you can't blame me for trying."

Zeke said, "Maybe some day I will tell you how I met Little Doe … when and how I knew that she is the only woman for me."

Big Red watched Zeke leave and thought, 'If I had met a man such as him years ago my life might have been different.'

Arriving at Roberts' office without incident, Zeke went inside to get Angel.

Roberts was in his office and in way of greeting said "I heard more gunshots. Do I need to attend to anyone?"

"No Doc," Zeke replied, "the last shots you heard was someone taking a shot at me. He'll not be needing to be patched up … he's dead. I'm certain that he was one of the Lisping Bandit's men. There's probably one or two more of his men still in town but I doubt that there will be any more trouble 'til Cameron gets here … that's his real name. I had a little run-in with him at Fort Lowell a few years ago. He was a Major in the cavalry then and he blames me for getting him thrown out. He's due to arrive here in about four days and I'll be back before then."

"If he shows up here with all of his gang, it's going to take more than just you to stop him. I doubt that you will get much help from the people here." Then Roberts continued, "I'm no gun-hand, but I can shoot a rifle and there's Bret Stevens over at the Elkhorn. I suppose Thom and Gabby will help, outside of that I don't believe that you can count on any one else around here."

"I've been thinking along those same lines Doc and I agree that it is going to take a few more men than what we have here. When I am in Carson City, I will try to round up a posse. Cameron's wanted here in the State of Nevada as well as the Arizona Territory. He held up his first stagecoach between Tucson and El Paso about three months after the cavalry kicked him out. About a month later, he held up two more at the same spot. Then he held up four on the road to Yuma from Tucson. He was alone on the first hold up but after that, he had more men with him. He disappeared from southern Arizona about a year after he held up his first stagecoach. First, there were rumors that he was dead and then there were several reports of him operating in northern Arizona and southern Nevada. I came to believe that he has a hideout in the badlands of northern Arizona."

Zeke continued, "From what Thom was told, I know that the stagecoach wreck was more than an attempt at robbery. It appears that Cameron is trying to kill me. I don't know yet just how he knew that I was on that coach. Was it just a coincidence that Cameron's man was at that stage stop?"

Roberts said, "My question would be why you were even on that stage. From all the stories I've heard about you, you ride Blaze accompanied by Spirit and a packhorse."

"Usually that's true, Blaze and the buckskin that I use as a packhorse both have plenty of stamina and can cover a lot of ground in a day," Zeke replied. With the weather being rainy and cold, I figured that traveling by stagecoach, I could stay dry, a bit warmer and I would get there in about the same amount of time. Turns out I was wrong."

Zeke continued, "The question of how Cameron knew that I was on that stagecoach keeps nagging at me. The more I think on it, the more I disbelieve that it was coincidence. I'll get it figured out sooner or later, but for now, I need to gather up Angel and turn in for the night. I'm staying at the Elkhorn and we'll be pulling out early in the morning."

Zeke picked his pack up off the floor and shrugged it onto his back. Then he put the carrying pouch around his neck, over his right shoulder and slung under his left. When Zeke entered the living quarters to get Angel, she spotted him and started waving her arms as she gurgled with happiness.

After placing Angel in the sling, Zeke left Roberts' place and headed back to the Elkhorn.

Chapter Sixteen

Zeke slept well and was up before daybreak. The room that Bret provided for him was actually two rooms, one with a bed, washbasin on a stand, and a water pitcher. There was also a mirror hanging on the wall above the stand and a chair close to the bed. The other room contained two overstuffed chairs, a small table and three straight back chairs. A large pitcher full of water was on the tabletop. A small stove was by the wall separating the two rooms. A box of firewood was at the side of the stove.

Zeke put some firewood into the stove and lit it. He opened his pack, removed the coffee pot and coffee. After putting a handful of coffee into the pot, he filled it with water and set it on the stove. Then he got the smaller of the cooking pots, filled it half-full of water and put it on the stove beside the coffee pot. He got one of the whiskey bottles full of milk and placed it in the pot of water to warm.

While he waited for the coffee to boil, Zeke went through his backpack and removed all of the diapers he had for Angel. He placed his clothing in the bottom of the satchel and put the diapers on top.

As he placed what he would need for the next couple of days in the bag, Zeke thought, 'Bret said I could have these rooms for as long as I need them. I'll just leave what I won't need here.'

When the smell of coffee started permeating the room, Zeke checked the milk. It was warm … Zeke poured some into Angel's bottle and set it on the table. Then he went to the bed and got Angel. He held her as he poured himself a cup of coffee. Then he sat at the table still holding her while she drank her milk and he drank his coffee. After Angel drank her fill and went back to sleep he laid her on one of the stuffed chairs and finished packing what he figured he would need.

He wrapped the warm whiskey bottle of milk in a diaper and placed it on the table. Then he filled one of his canteens with coffee and the other one with water. The small pot and coffeepot were the last items to go into the satchel. He slung the pouch around his neck and over his left shoulder, picked up Angel and placed her in the pouch. He put her bottle and the warm bottle of milk in the pouch with her. He picked up the rifle and slung it on his shoulder and then he picked up the satchel, left the Elkhorn and went to the livery stable.

When he entered the stable both Blaze and Spirit greeted Zeke. He leaned his rifle against one of the closed stall gates, then propped Angel, who was awake, in a sitting position against a stack of hay.

Spirit went to Angel and cocked his head to one side then the other as he checked her out. Then he lay down beside her and Angel waved her tiny arms in the air, gurgling with happiness.

Zeke watched the two of them as he got some grain for Blaze and thought, 'I sure am going to miss her. But she needs to be with her kin, I wonder what they are like. I sure hate having to tell them that their daughter Marjorie is dead. At least they won't have to wonder what became of her and then there's Angel … she will surely be a solace to them.'

Thom entered the stable about ten minutes after Zeke got there. They prepared the buggy and left town as a faint glimmer of light began showing on the eastern horizon. Blaze and Spirit ran alongside of the buggy for a while then raced ahead.

"Why are those two racing ahead of us," Thom asked. "Do they sense something up ahead?"

"They're just playing," Zeke replied with a chuckle. "They'll run a mile or two then stop and wait for us. After we pass them they'll do it again."

It was about mid-morning when they arrived at the junction leading in a northerly direction to Carson City. The other trail went in a southeasterly direction to the Mormon settlement at Las Vegas.

They stopped at the junction to rest the horses. Spirit was sitting on his haunches beside Zeke when he suddenly jumped to his feet and ran down the trail to the southeast.

"What do you suppose caused him to take off like that," Thom asked.

"Reckon we'll know soon enough," Zeke responded. "There's someone or something that he figures he needs to check. We need to take cover as a just in case. Blaze is also aware of something, his standing still with his head up and ears twitched forward like that means he hears a noise in the distance."

There were several large boulders just off of the trail. Zeke grabbed the rifle from where he put it in the buggy as they hurried to the boulders. A few minutes later, they heard the distant sound of hoof beats.

"Sounds like three horses moving at a pretty good pace," Zeke said. "We'll know who they are shortly."

It wasn't long before the horses came into view in the distance.

"Looks like two riders and a pack horse," Zeke commented. As he watched them get closer he said, "I can't make out for sure who they are but those riders sit their saddles like Lance and Lefty do."

The riders were still in the distance when Zeke stepped out from behind the boulder. With a note of relief in his voice he said, "It is them … its Lance and Lefty."

Zeke and Thom walked back to the buggy and waited. Spirit raced ahead of the riders and stopped beside Zeke. Lance and Lefty galloped up to them shortly thereafter.

In way of greeting Zeke said, "I surely am happy to see you two … but what are you doing here?"

Lance and Lefty quickly told him about the telegram from Bob. They also told him what Little Doe had said about him being okay now. Lance finished up by saying, "We didn't have much to do so we decided to come out here just in case you needed a hand."

"As a matter of fact," Zeke responded, "I can use a couple more guns. But before we get into that, how did you know where I am?"

Lefty said, "Little Doe said you were in the mountains close to a place that was warmer than the surrounding area. Then I recalled what a miner over at the McClury mine said about working a mine in these parts that had hot springs around it and we figured that's where you were. She also said that a baby and another man would soon join you, but she didn't say that the man was Thom."

Zeke replied, "I didn't meet up with Thom 'til yesterday. She probably meant Gabby."

Then Zeke told them, in detail, what had happened since the stagecoach wreck. How he found Angel and her dead mother. How he met Gabby at the bridge and all that had happened in Agua Caliente.

He then said, "I am starting to believe that the wreck was an attempt to kill me. We know that Cameron was behind it, but I can't figure how he knew that I was on that stage. One of his men was at the way station that we stopped at overnight. He left when we came in … but was he there by chance or was he waiting to be sure that I was on that stage?"

Zeke continued, "We'll get that all sorted out eventually. Right now, I need to get Angel to her family in Carson City. My mind will sure rest a lot easier knowing that the two of you are in Agua Caliente. You should get there around mid-day. When you get there go to the Elkhorn and find Bret Stevens, he's the owner. Tell him who you are and that you met up with us along the trail. You also need to find Gabby, besides those two and the doctor, I don't know who you can trust. If no one besides Bret, Gabby and the doctor know who you are, you may be able to learn something. A woman that goes by the name of Big Red has a whorehouse there and something is not quite right about her. She was helpful in some of the information she gave me, but something about her story just doesn't ring true. I should be back sometime tomorrow or the next day at the latest."

Lance went to the packhorse while Zeke was talking, got Blaze's tack and placed it in the back of the buggy saying, "Reckon you'll need this."

They talked for a few more minutes before parting company. Zeke and Thom headed for Carson City … Lance and Lefty towards Agua Caliente.

It was mid-afternoon when Zeke, Thom and Angel arrived in Carson City. Spirit disappeared as they approached the edge of town.

Thom said, "I have nothing of a pressing nature to do … I believe I'll get a horse here and go back to Agua Caliente with you. I saw a fine looking animal at the stable when I rented this buggy. He's a gelding and stands about as tall as Blaze."

"That's fine with me Thom," Zeke replied. "We can get back a little quicker on horseback."

They rode directly to the livery stable where Thom had rented the buggy. Thom paid the liveryman for the use of the buggy and bought the gelding along with a bridle, saddle and saddle blanket. The five-year-old horse was a dappled grey and stood just short of Blaze's seventeen hands.

While there, Zeke arranged for a stall for Blaze. After taking Angel's diapers and the remaining milk from the satchel, he placed them in the pouch with Angel. He also took the wanted fliers, folded them and put them in his shirt pocket. Leaving the rest of their belongings in the stable, they left to find Angel's family.

"I saw the sheriff's office as we came into town," Zeke stated. "Reckon we ought to start there, he'll more than likely know where the Catesby place is."

As they neared the sheriff's office, a man came out turned and started walking toward them … it was the sheriff.

The sheriff was lean, stood at five feet eight inches tall walked with the assurance of a man that knows what he is doing.

When they drew close to each other Zeke said, "Afternoon Sheriff we were just on our way to see you. I am Zeke Cooper and this gent is Thom Langely."

"Pleased to make your acquaintance, I am Marc Hansen. Zeke Cooper … is that as in Marshal Zeke Cooper?"

Zeke looked down to where his badge should be and realized that the sling over his shoulder covered it. "Yes it is. I need to talk to you about a couple of matters, the first being the whereabouts of the Catesby family. This tyke here in the pouch is their granddaughter."

"What about Marjorie? Where is she," Marc asked.

"She's dead," Zeke replied. "I buried her."

Then Zeke told Marc how he found Angel and her dead mother and the location. He also told him about Bart McHune.

"How did Marjorie die," Marc asked.

"When I found her she probably hadn't been dead more than a day or so. Her face was puffy and she had several broken bones. I would say that she was beaten to death."

Marc said, "That's a shame about Marjorie I sure hate to hear it. Do you know that there is a thousand dollar reward out for McHune? … Speaking of rewards Henry Catesby posted a five hundred dollar reward for Marjorie."

"Yes I know about the rewards, McHune had these fliers on his person," Zeke said as he took them from his pocket.

"Henry has the mercantile just up the street there," Marc said as he pointed to a sign on the other side that read Catesby Mercantile. "After you finish with him come and see me. I'll be back in the office in about an hour and I'll get you your reward money."

"I don't take reward money for myself. I'll take the money on McHune and put it in the bank here for Angel. We'll be back after I deliver Angel to her family," Zeke said.

Zeke, Angel and Thom crossed the street and proceeded to the mercantile. When they entered the store, there was one customer at the counter paying for his purchases. The man behind the counter was about six feet tall, with thinning hair. He was slim and wore a pair of spectacles clamped onto his nose.

A woman entered from the rear of the building carrying a bolt of cloth.

As the customer finished paying and turned to leave, the man behind the counter removed his spectacles and said, "Put that over here on the counter, Martha."

Then he turned to Zeke saying, "What can I do for you two?"

"I am looking for Henry Catesby," Zeke said.

"I am Henry Catesby and this is my wife Martha. What business do you have with us?"

"It's about your daughter Marjorie," Zeke replied.

Martha's right hand flew to her throat as her face paled. Then she asked, "Where is she? Is she all right?"

"I'm afraid I have some bad news concerning Marjorie," Zeke replied. Then he told them how he found Marjorie and Angel. Where he buried Marjorie and placed a marker on her grave. He also told them about Bart McHune.

He lifted Angel from her pouch and held her out to Martha saying, "This is your granddaughter. I don't know what Marjorie named her but I call her Angel."

Martha reached out to take Angel but stopped when Henry sharply said, "Martha!"

Then Henry turned to Zeke saying, "If what you say about Marjorie is true, I thank you for burying her. But you'll not be saddling us with that bastard child."

Zeke was seething with anger as he calmly said, "I do not take kindly to being called a liar. Just what would you have me do with her? She is your granddaughter and of your blood. Your daughter would probably have wanted her to be with you."

"I don't give a whit what Marjorie would have wanted or what you do with her." Then he continued self-righteously, "I am a deeply religious man and I'll not have a bastard child in my home."

Zeke's eyes were black with fury and with an icy cold, hard voice said, "I am not a man taken to profanity, but in your case I'll make an exception. You are without a doubt the most no-good, self-righteous god-damned son-of-a-bitch I have ever come across. This is your granddaughter and she had no control over the circumstance of her birth."

"Matters not what you say, you'll not be leaving her here. Do with her as you will, but I'll not be raising her in my house," Henry piously retorted.

Martha said, "But Henry ..."

"Shut up Martha, you stay out of this. I'll not be having that bastard child in my house," Henry self-righteously stated.

Zeke calmly handed Angel to Thom then turned his attention back to Henry. He pulled his right arm back and closed his hand into a fist. He hit Henry, knocking out two teeth, breaking his nose and knocking him out.

As Henry lay unconscious on the floor, bleeding profusely from his broken nose and busted mouth, Zeke turned his attention to Martha Catesby. "I am sorry missus Catesby ... I don't normally resort to what I just did. I'll be taking Angel with me. If you ever want to see your granddaughter, the sheriff will know where she is."

Zeke then turned to Thom, took Angel from him, placed her in the pouch and walked out of the store with Thom right behind him.

Chapter Seventeen

After leaving the store, they walked in silence for several minutes before Zeke spoke, "You've been here before Thom, where's a good place to stay for the night?"

"There's the Carson City Hotel back the other direction, I've stayed there a couple of times. It's pretty clean and their dining room has decent food."

Zeke said, "Okay then, we'll go there and get quarters for the night. Then I need to find the sheriff, as there are still a couple of matters I need to discuss with him. I also need to send a telegram to Bob in Sacramento."

"The telegraph office is right across the street from the hotel," Thom replied.

They turned around and went back up the street to the hotel where Zeke arranged for a suite with two bedrooms. Then they went across the street to the telegraph office.

When they entered the office, Zeke crossed to the counter, picked up a pencil, got a sheet of paper and wrote:

Bob Douglas

Sacramento House

Sacramento, California

Am held up with problems at Agua Caliente, Nevada

Do you still need me there?

Staying at the Carson City hotel will be here till tomorrow

Zeke Cooper

Zeke handed the message to the telegrapher, showed him his badge and said, "I want this to go out at the highest priority. When you get an answer, would you see that I get it right away? I'm staying at the hotel."

The telegrapher took the message, read it and turned to the telegraph keys. He tapped out the message, listened to a reply from the other end then turned back to Zeke and said, "It's done Marshal. I'll send a boy with your reply soon as it comes in."

They left the telegraph office and Zeke said, "Reckon we should find the sheriff now. Maybe he's back in his office."

Sheriff Marc Hansen arrived at his office at the same time as Zeke and Thom did.

In way of greeting Marc said, "I see you still have the baby with you, did you find Catesby?"

"We found him alright," Zeke replied. Then he briefly told Marc what had happened with Catesby.

"He is kind of a miserable cuss most of the time," Marc responded. "There are a lot of folks around here that would like to do what you did. After Marjorie disappeared, he got worse than he already was."

Then Marc continued, "We can go to the bank now, before it closes and get the reward money for you."

Zeke replied, "Speaking of the reward money I wasn't going to collect the money that Catesby posted for Marjorie. But as things turned out, I reckon that I might as well collect it. Is there an orphanage around here?"

"The Reverend Boleyn and his wife run a home about four miles east of town. You can't miss the place, it is a large two story house that sits back about five hundred feet from the road. They are a kindly couple and she will receive good care there."

After they finished at the bank, Zeke told Marc about Agua Caliente and its outlaw element.

Zeke continued, "Right now I have three men in the hoosegow there. One of them being Sam Forrester, there's a federal death warrant out on him. Another of the three is Jared Witherspoon. He is the one that killed the sheriff in Virginia City about six years ago. The third man goes by the name of Blackie, I don't know much about him … yet. We need to get a circuit judge to Agua Caliente soon as possible. Agua Caliente also needs a sheriff. I have reason to believe that the Lisping Bandit will show up there in three or four days. There are at least twelve to fifteen men in his gang … probably more."

"I am the sheriff of Carson City … my jurisdiction doesn't extend that far," Marc stated. "We can go over to the courthouse and find out about getting a circuit judge down to Agua Caliente. George Lashley is the federal marshal here … his office is also at the courthouse. There are five or six men here that would probably be willing to go to Agua Caliente with him."

"That's a good thought and I appreciate it," Zeke replied, "but I don't believe that we will need any more gun-hands. Counting myself, we have four that are right handy with a gun and another four that know how to use one. Then there's the townspeople, if they don't want to help defend their town maybe it ain't worth saving."

They entered the courthouse and went to the circuit judge's office first. Judge Randolph Morrison was standing beside a large bookcase containing law books, when they entered the office. He stood just over six feet tall and weighed around two hundred twenty pounds. His hair was brown, a bit curly and well trimmed. He had blue eyes with a kindly glint to them. Except for a handlebar mustache drooping a little past his chin from his upper lip, he was clean-shaven. He appeared to be in his early forties. "What can I do for you gentlemen," he brusquely asked.

Zeke replied, "I am Deputy United States Marshal Zeke Cooper and we need a judge in Agua Caliente soon as possible." He then told Morrison who he had in jail and why they were there.

"It'll take about three days for me to clear my calendar," Morrison responded, "I can be there within four or five days."

"Maybe you should make it five days," Zeke said. "I'm kind of expecting the Lisping Bandit to attack the town within four days from today. If so I reckon that we'll have more prisoners for you to judge."

"In that case I'll be there in five days … or before." Morrison continued, "Bob Douglas has told me a lot about you. I use to be a deputy marshal, working for Bob. I haven't seen him for a couple years now, how is he doing?"

"He's doing fine," Zeke replied. "I'll tell him that you asked after him."

Zeke then stated, "I need to get to the marshal's office and get a copy of the death warrant on Forrester."

"The marshal's up around Virginia City," Morrison replied. "He won't be back for a couple of days. If you leave before he gets back, I'll bring the warrant with me."

As Zeke, Thom and Marc left the courthouse Marc said, "I need to get back to my office. If there is any thing else I can do, just let me know."

"Thanks Marc you have been a big help to us," Zeke replied.

Blaze met them in front of the courthouse and walked beside Zeke and Thom as they went to the stable.

At the stable, they saddled their horses and rode out of town towards the Boleyn place. Spirit joined them about a half mile outside of town. They rode at an easy lope in silence until Thom stated, "Angel seems to like riding in her pouch with you. I don't believe that I have heard her cry at all since we met up."

"Believe me," Zeke responded, "she has a healthy set of lungs … her crying is how I found her. Come to think on it, I've only heard her cry twice, when I first found her and then again when McHune stripped her naked and left her in a snow bank. She seems happy enough and I know that she likes riding in her pouch. Whenever she wants something, she lets me know by making different sounds."

Dusk was approaching as they rode up the drive to the Boleyn place. It was a very large two-story house resembling a large hotel. A large porch ran the full length of the house. There were several rocking chairs of various sizes on the porch as well as two wooden benches with backs. A hammock hung between two of the porch columns at the left end. It had a large well-kept yard with flowers planted close to the house. The implements of child-hood were scattered throughout the rest of the yard. Large trees surrounded the house and yard, one very large tree was in the center of the yard with a swing hanging from one of its limbs. A hitching rail was on the left side of the three steps leading up to the porch.

The happy sounds of children at play permeated the air. A woman sat on one of the rocking chairs holding a baby as she slowly rocked back and forth and watched the children at play. Seven girls and six boys ranging in age from about four to ten years old played in the yard. Some of them gathered at the swing while some more were at a teeter-totter and others were chasing each other in a game of tag.

As Zeke and Thom rode towards the hitching rail, the children quit their various activities and started gathering at the steps to the porch.

The woman that was sitting in the rocker arose and handed the baby she was holding to a girl that had just came out of the house to the porch.

"Good evening gentlemen," the woman said, as Zeke and Thom stopped at the hitching rail, "I am Thelma Boleyn."

Zeke replied, "I am Zeke Cooper and this is Thom Langely. We've come to talk with Reverend Boleyn."

Thelma turned to the girl that had taken the baby and said, "Katherine will you please tell the Reverend that there are two gentlemen here to see him."

Katherine disappeared back into the house carrying the baby. Thelma then turned her attention to the children and said, "It is time for supper, you children go wash up before you sit down at the table."

Thelma then said, "Mister Cooper you and Mister Langely dismount and come up onto the porch to wait for the Reverend. He will be here shortly."

Thelma had an expression of curiosity on her face as she watched them dismount and climb the three steps onto the porch.

Reverend Boleyn came out of the house about the same time as Zeke and Thom stepped onto the porch. Boleyn was a big man, standing just over six feet tall, large boned and well proportioned. He appeared to be in his mid to late thirties. The hair at his temple had signs of gray and he wore no facial hair. His hazel colored eyes had a twinkle of friendliness to them.

His deep voice boomed as he said, "Howdy gentlemen, I am Reverend Boleyn. Most folks call me Thunder … reckon it's on account of my voice. Katherine said that two men with a baby were out here and wanted to see me. What can I do for you?"

"The baby's name is Angel," Zeke replied. "I am Zeke Cooper and this is Thom Langely."

Zeke then told Thunder and Thelma that Angel's mother was Marjorie Catesby and how he found her. He ended his narration with, "I took Angel to Henry Catesby and his wife Martha. Catesby does not want her in his house because as he put it, she is a bastard child. I'm afraid I lost my temper when he called her that and I hit him, knocking him unconscious. That basically is why we are here."

"She certainly is welcome here," Thunder said. "She is one of God's children and you can rest assured she will be well cared for. I've known Henry Catesby for several years. As long as I've known him, he has interpreted the good book to his own liking and after Marjorie disappeared, he got even worse. I'll have a talk with Henry and explain to him that the term bastard in the good book does not refer to a father here on earth. I doubt that it will make any difference to Henry, but I will try. In fact I'll make that the subject of this Sunday's sermon."

"Angel is only part of the reason that we are here," Zeke stated. "I collected the five hundred dollar reward for Marjorie and the thousand for McHune … I never keep reward money and thought that you might be able to use it. As for Angel, I don't intend on leaving her here permanently. There's a matter in Agua Caliente that I need to tend to and would like to leave her here, in your care while I do so. It shouldn't be for more than a couple of weeks … if that. If Catesby doesn't change his mind by then, I will take her with me to Silver Wolf, that's my ranch in Arizona. Little Doe and I will raise her as one of ours."

Thelma's right hand flew to her throat as she exclaimed, "Goodness, I know who you are. I thought that your names were familiar, you are Marshal Zeke Cooper." Then she turned to Thom saying, "And you are the writer that writes about Zeke. You must come in and take supper with us. I must say that we do enjoy your stories … the older children read them to the younger ones. Your stories are among their favorites. Just listen to me blabber on … you must think that I'm a blithering idiot. Give me that child and you two go around back to the pump and get washed up for supper."

Zeke and Thom went around back and washed before entering the house. The dining area was a very large room measuring about thirty feet in length and twenty feet wide. There were two long tables in the room. Thelma and the younger children were sitting at one. Thunder and the older ones were sitting at the other. The low murmur of conversation and a little bit of laughter filled the room.

The room grew quiet when Zeke and Thom entered.

"Zeke you and Thom sit here with me," Thunder's voice resounded through the room as he indicated two chairs.

Thunder sat at the head of the table, Zeke and Thom seated themselves on the chairs on either side of him. Three older children came from the kitchen carrying bowls and platters filled with food. A woman in her mid to late thirties who also carried food followed them. They placed the food on one of the tables, disappeared back into the kitchen and came back with food for the other table.

The food was plain, but plentiful consisting of boiled potatoes, green beans, elk roast, biscuits and pitchers of milk. As they ate Zeke took stock of the room, not including Angel, he counted seventeen children and three adults. They all appeared to be happy and content with their surroundings.

Zeke looked at Thunder saying, "You have quite a few children here Thunder, it must keep you scrambling just to care for them. Are they all from around here?"

"We farm just over a hundred acres and grow most of what we eat." Thunder responded. "We also have two milk cows, some chickens and several pigs. What we don't need for ourselves we sell in town. Also there is plenty of game in the surrounding area."

Thunder continued, "All of the children are not here, three of the older boys and one girl are in town. Two of the boys are seventeen the other boy and the girl are both eighteen. I reckon that they will be staying here with us until they find a place of their own to put down roots. Two of the boys work for the freight company hauling freight. The other boy works at the bank and the girl works at the courthouse. They work in town and help with some of the expenses around here."

"Some of the children are from around here. Some are from the east where they round up orphans and instead of caring for them send all over the age of five packing west. Mei-Ling, the girl holding Angel, is from China ... her parents sold her at the age of four to a wealthy merchant by the name of Chan. He brought her and many others to San Francisco. She lived there as one of his servants until two years ago. While cleaning one of his rooms she dropped a heavy vase and broke it. This angered Chan and the next day he sold her to a man by the name of Leighton. He runs a traveling brothel that makes regular rounds to the mining camps."

"But," Zeke protested at what he was hearing, "she's no more than a child. He surly didn't use her as a whore."

"Actually she turned eleven last month," Thunder said. "Mei-Ling ran away from Leighton when he stopped in Carson City just over a year ago and hid in the surrounding area for four days. She was picking food from one of our fields when we discovered her. She was very frightened and tried to run but we caught her. I was a missionary in China for five years before I came here. I learned to speak Chinese while I was there but it was a different dialect than what she spoke. Fortunately, she could speak a little bit of English. Between her broken English and my garbled Chinese, we managed to communicate. She has become quite fluent in English during this past year."

When Zeke first heard the name Leighton, he thought, 'surely it can't be him.' "This man Leighton, do you know anything about him or where he came from?"

"All I know," Thunder responded, "is that his given name's Luke. Judging by his speech, I figure that he came here from one of the southern states. He comes through these parts about every six months. Reckon that he's due most any day now and he'll be looking for Mei-Ling. He is offering two hundred dollars to any one that will tell him where she is. The folks that know she is here won't tell him. Marc Hansen, the sheriff, knows she's here and lets me know when Leighton is in the area. But I'm fearful that someone that would tell him, may find out that she's here."

"If this Luke Leighton is who I think he is, you won't have to worry about it," Zeke said. "About ten years ago Luke and his brother Jebediah were sentenced to twenty years in prison. Five years ago, six inmates tried to escape. They killed two guards and Luke is the only one that made it. The other five, including Jebediah, died in their attempt. When we get back to town, I'll talk to the sheriff and let him know who this Leighton might be."

Night had long fallen by the time Zeke and Thom left the Boleyn's house. As they mounted their horses, Spirit appeared out of the darkness.

When they got to town, they stopped at the sheriff's office. Sheriff Hansen was there.

"Sure am glad to catch you here Marc," Zeke stated. "We just come from the Reverend Boleyn's place. While there, I learned of a whoremonger by the name of Leighton … Luke Leighton. If he is who I believe him to be, he is an escaped convict. He escaped from the federal prison in Virginia about five years ago."

Zeke then told Marc what he knew about Leighton.

When Zeke finished telling him about Leighton Marc responded, "I know who you are talking about Zeke. I haven't seen any fliers on him or I would have him locked him up by now. I'll keep a close eye out for him and arrest him soon as I see him. The first time he was here and I saw little Mei-Ling with him I started asking questions. I know that most women who live that type of life are doing so by their own choice. But Mei-Ling is a child and just not old enough to make that kind of choice. I asked his other girls about her and couldn't find any evidence showing that Leighton used her in that manner."

Marc continued, "She ran away from Leighton the day after he arrived here. He came to me and demanded that I find her and bring her back. I formed a search party of men that I could trust to keep their mouth shut. There was no way that when we found her that I would bring her back to him. We found where she was hiding … it was in an abandoned miners shack about a mile from the Boleyn place. I figured she was as safe there as any place that I could hide her until Leighton left. I rode out there a couple times a day checking on her. I didn't let her know that I knew where she was hiding. I figured that if she did it would scare her into running again. I intended on taking her to Reverend Boleyn after Leighton left the area."

Chapter Eighteen

After leaving the sheriff's office, Zeke and Thom went to the stable and cared for their horses. They then made their way to the hotel.

When they entered the hotel the desk clerk called out, "Mister Cooper I have a telegram for you. It just got here less than an hour ago."

Zeke crossed the lobby to the desk clerk and took the telegram. He opened it and read:

Marshal Zeke Cooper

Carson City Nevada

Do not need you here will catch morning train to Carson City

Will join you there or Agua Caliente

Bob Douglas

Zeke folded the telegram and put it in his shirt pocket. He was a bit relieved that Bob no longer needed him in Sacramento but wondered what it was that was so urgent to begin with.

They climbed the stairs up to their room in silence as Zeke contemplated on the two telegrams. 'It was urgent that I get there, but now I am not needed … it just doesn't make sense.'

After they entered the suite, Zeke opened his valise and removed the first telegram. He held the two telegrams side by side as he studied them, trying to find a clue to the answers of the questions forming in his mind.

Turning to Thom Zeke said, "These telegrams don't make sense. The first one says that it's urgent that I get to Sacramento and the second says that he does not need me there."

Thom asked, "Have you considered the possibility that Bob did not send the first one?"

"I have thought of that," Zeke replied. "Reckon Bob can tell me when he meets up with us."

"We could go to the telegraph office and find out where they were sent from," Thom replied. "Each telegram is marked with letters and a number that tells which station it originated from."

They left the hotel and crossed the street to the telegraph office. As they entered, the telegrapher greeted them with, "Marshal I sent a telegram for you over to the hotel."

"I got it, thanks," Zeke replied. Then he handed the first telegram to him as he asked, "Can you tell me where this originated."

The telegrapher took the proffered telegram, looked at it then said, "It came from here Marshal and I'm the one that sent it out." He pointed at the small letters and number on the bottom left corner of the telegram and continued, "See these initials and number? The initials stand for the telegraphers name and the number is the station that it came from."

"I know that it's been a while since you sent this," Zeke said. "But do you remember anything about the man that had you send it?"

"Actually I do remember him but only because of the way he acted. When he gave me the message to send, I noticed that it read 'here in Sacramento'. I told him that he was in Carson City and not Sacramento. He became very angry and with a bad lisp told me that it was not my job to correct what he wrote."

When Zeke heard about the lisp it confirmed his suspicions but just to be sure, he asked, "Can you describe this man?"

The telegrapher replied, "I sure can, he was about six feet tall, blond hair, a short beard and he had small delicate looking hands with long fingers. He also wore his gun tied in much the same manner as you wear yours. I can't get it out of my mind that he might have been the lisping bandit that we hear about."

Looking at the man behind the counter Zeke said, "I would say that you are right, you have been a big help and I give you my thanks."

Zeke and Thom left the telegraph office and went back to the hotel, each lost in their own thoughts.

After they entered their room Zeke broke the silence, "I reckon that Cameron has a bigger hate for me than I realized. At the time of his dismissal from the cavalry he blamed me as the cause. He appears to be an intelligent man and I would have thought that by now he would have realized that it was his own actions that got him tossed. It is strange to me that some people can't accept the consequences of their own actions but have to blame others for the misery they bring upon themselves."

They talked awhile longer then turned in for the night.

They were up early the next morning and readied themselves to leave Carson City. In the dim light of predawn, they made their way to the stable where both Spirit and Blaze greeted them. As they left the stable, dawn was beginning to show itself with a faint glimmer of light on the eastern horizon.

Blaze was lifted his feet high, prancing sideways as they rode through town.

"Blaze wants to run," Zeke commented. "When we reach the edge of town I'll give him his head and let him go. Your horse is a fine looking animal and of a good size but if we outrun you, I'll stop and wait for you after Blaze settles in."

When they reached the edge of town, Zeke slacked off on the reins and Blaze took off at a full gallop. Thom's grey made a valiant effort at keeping up. The grey was fast but he steadily lost ground to Blaze from the beginning. After about a mile Thom pulled the grey back to a canter as he watched Zeke and Blaze disappear into the distance.

Thom thought, 'I always knew that Blaze is one fast horse but I never figured that he's that fast. This grey is fast, probably the fastest I've ever ridden, but he sure can't hold a candle to Blaze.'

About thirty minutes later he found Zeke standing under a tree alongside the trail, waiting for him. He had a small fire going and just finished preparing a pot of coffee. Blaze was cropping some grass nearby. Spirit was sitting on his haunches near Zeke, with one side of his lip slightly curled up as if he were laughing.

Thom dismounted saying, "I'd swear that Spirit is laughing at me."

"He ain't laughing at you Thom, he's just showing that he enjoyed the run. Coffee will be ready soon, sure am glad that Lance and Lefty thought to put the coffeepot and coffee in my saddlebags. Have some jerky in the bags too, not much of a breakfast but reckon that it'll do till something better comes along."

"I'll walk my grey and cool him down a bit while we wait for the coffee," Thom replied.

They were soon chewing on jerky and washing it down with coffee. After another thirty minutes they broke camp, and rode on towards Agua Caliente.

Blaze settled into his ground-covering canter and the grey was able to keep up with him. They rode that way for about an hour then Zeke pulled Blaze to a trot for a few minutes and then a walk for about ten minutes. Then they went back to a trot and then a canter. They repeated that cycle about every hour … walk, trot, canter, trot and walk.

They had been riding about three and a half hours when Zeke spotted a stand of trees ahead and said, "From the looks of those trees up ahead I'd say that there's water there."

When they got to the trees, they saw a small stream running through the middle of the stand. Grass was showing itself between patches of snow.

Thom asked, "Just how did you know there would be water here?"

"There are many things that indicate nearby water," Zeke replied. "These trees are cottonwood and they are a thirsty tree. Where there's more than one or two you can count on finding water nearby."

"But how did you know that they were cottonwood trees from way back there?"

"By the size and shape of the stand," Zeke replied. "During the warmer months you can tell by the leaves. If the leaves are dark green it means that there is an ample water supply. If they get water, only when it rains the leaves would be a pale green. That holds true for most trees … the darker green the leaf the more ample its supply of water."

They dismounted, loosened the saddles on the horses and let them graze on the grass. After letting the horses rest for about an hour, they continued their journey toward Agua Caliente.

Whenever Zeke was on the trail Spirit would run ahead on a zigzag course as though he was searching out any dangers on the trail. They were about seven miles from Agua Caliente when Spirit suddenly appeared in front of them standing cross ways on the trail.

Zeke pulled Blaze to a stop as he said, "There's something wrong up ahead."

"How do you know that," Thom asked.

"Whenever Spirit stands crossways to the trail like that he either wants me to follow him or there is something out of place ahead," Zeke replied.

About a half-mile ahead, the trail made a sharp turn to the right before cresting a small hill. Just before the bend, there were several large boulders and a thick stand of trees. Spirit led them on an oblique course away from the trail. When the stand of trees and boulders were between them and the trail, he turned and headed towards the trees.

"We'll soon know what's bothering Spirit," Zeke commented. "Once we get to those trees, stay in the stand or behind one of those boulders until we learn what is out there. For the last couple of hours we have been following the tracks of a single horse with a loose shoe. Whoever is riding that horse may be of a mind to bushwhack us."

When they reached the trees, Zeke got the binoculars from his saddlebag and pulled his rifle from its scabbard as he dismounted. Thom dismounted and stayed well inside the stand of trees as Zeke made his way to the edge alongside the trail. From the concealment of the trees, Zeke looked through his binoculars and slowly scanned the area ahead of him. He spotted a single horse a little less than a quarter of a mile ahead, tied to a tree alongside the trail. Not seeing the horse's rider Zeke thought that maybe the rider was behind the tree.

Zeke stayed focused on the tree and searched for a sign that the rider was there. Not spotting anything, he started slowly scanning the side of the snow-covered hill on the opposite side of the trail. He saw a slight movement behind a small brushy tree about three hundred yards away.

Zeke focused on the tree and saw a man sitting on a large rock next to the tree. From Zeke's vantage point, he could plainly see the man. Then Zeke realized that the man was not watching the trail but rather something farther down the slope of the hill.

Scanning down the slope Zeke spotted two heads silhouetted above a large boulder. They were about three hundred feet from the man behind the tree and appeared to be watching the trail.

Zeke slowly scanned the rest of the hillside but found nothing else of interest. He carefully made his way back to Thom. He noted that Spirit had disappeared once again.

"There are three men on the hillside on the other side of the trail," Zeke stated when he reached Thom. "Two of the men are together behind a large boulder and watching the trail. They are more'n likely waiting for us. The third man is higher up than the other two. He's sitting on a large rock beneath a tree and watching the two behind the boulder instead of the trail."

Zeke continued, "I figure that if I call out to them they'll let us know what their intentions are." He handed the binoculars to Thom as he continued, “You watch the man by the tree farther up the hill when I call out. I have a feeling that he is not of any danger to us, but we need to be certain.”

Chapter Nineteen

When they reached the edge of the trees, Zeke pointed out the two positions of the three men.

Thom focused on the two men behind the boulder then started to sweep towards the other man. He had moved the glasses a short distance from the two behind the boulder and suddenly stopped. "I'll be doggoned," he quietly stated, "Spirit is crouching in a large patch of snow just above the boulder looking straight at those two. He blends so well with the snow I almost didn't see him."

"Yeah, I wondered if you'd see him there," Zeke replied.

Thom focused on the man at the tree as Zeke called out, "This is Zeke Cooper, are you waiting for me?"

Two rapidly fired rifle shots answered his question. The shots were so close together that it almost sounded like one. On the heels of the two shots another rifle spoke, followed by a terrified scream.

Thom handed the binoculars to Zeke saying, "Take a look, the man by the tree shot one of them behind the boulder. Spirit has the other one on the ground beside the boulder."

Zeke looked first at the man by the tree. The man held his rifle in one hand as he held his arms up into the air. Then Zeke focused on the boulder and saw that

Spirit did indeed have one man down with his massive jaws clamped around his throat.

Zeke walked from the tree line into the open and motioned to the man by the tree to come down. He turned to Thom saying, "Keep an eye on him, I'm going to check on our two friends over there"

When Zeke got to the boulder, he saw that both men were alive. The one was shot in the right shoulder … it appeared to be shattered and was bleeding profusely. The other one was lying on his back, pasty faced and staring at Spirit's head with big terrified eyes.

Zeke kicked their rifles out of reach, took their revolvers from their holsters, and tossed them.

Zeke said to the one with the shattered shoulder, "Stuff your bandana into that hole in your shoulder. Don't want you to cheat the hangman by bleeding to death."

"Go to blazes," the man retorted, "if'n your going to hang me anyways, I'd just as soon bleed out."

"Can't let you do that," Zeke replied, "either you use your bandana to stop that bleeding or I will stop it. Rest assured you'll not enjoy the way I'll do it."

Zeke turned his attention to the man that Spirit had pinned to the ground. He snapped his fingers saying, "Okay Spirit, let go."

Spirit released his grip around the man's throat, snarled and slobbered on his face then sat back on his haunches about three feet away.

Zeke looked the man over and outside of being terrified he seemed to be uninjured … if you didn't count the very large wet spot that was on the front of his pants and the horrible stench that was emanating from his body.

"Get up from there, go behind that boulder get your britches off and clean yourself," Zeke harshly stated.

"Th … Tha … That wolf," the man stuttered.

"He ain't going to hurt you so long as you do like you're told. Now get over there and get yourself cleaned or I'll let him have you."

With his eyes riveted on Spirit, the man warily got to his feet and headed behind the boulder, with Spirit trailing behind.

Thom and the other man arrived just then. The man stood right at six feet tall, maybe a little less. He was slim of build, red headed, blue eyed and a smattering of freckles scattered across his face. He wore his six-shooter tied to his upper right thigh. His posture was that of a man that was sure of himself and his capabilities.

"Howdy," the stranger said, "names Roebuck … James Roebuck but most folk's call me Buddy."

"Pleased to meet you Buddy," Zeke responded. "Reckon we owe you our thanks for stepping in like you did. I'm Zeke Cooper and this is Thom Langely."

"Happy to be of help, I knew that those two were up to no good."

"How did you happen to be here," Zeke asked.

"Well I hadn't planned on it," Buddy stated. "My horse has a loose shoe and I was heading to Agua Caliente, hoping to get it replaced there. I was walking my horse when I heard those two coming. I've heard that Agua Caliente is an outlaw friendly town and not wanting any trouble, I ducked behind some trees till they passed. They didn't see me and were talking kind 'a loud. I heard one of them say, 'That's a good spot over there behind them boulders. We can bushwhack him before he knows what hit him. He should come by here sometime today, if not we'll stay till he does.' That just plain got my curiosity up and I decided to settle in, watch and take a hand if need be."

"That was a pretty fair shot you made from up there," Zeke stated. "That and the way you wear your six-shooter, I figure that you know how to use both. The question that's in my mind is which side of the law are you on?"

With a slight chuckle Buddy replied, "I am on which ever side is right." Then he continued, "I was a deputy in Cheyenne for a little better than a year and I decided to continue my journey west."

"You have something waiting for you when you get to where you're going," Thom asked.

"Don't know, but I reckon I'll know what I'm looking for when I find it."

Zeke asked, "What if you don't find it?"

"If I don't find it in the west, I'll go back to the east."

"I take it that you are a traveling man," Zeke replied. "Good luck on your journeys and hopefully you will find that which you search for."

The outlaw with the shattered shoulder had sat up. He groaned in pain and cussed as he stuffed his bandana into his shoulder wound.

"I know who he is," Thom exclaimed. "He goes by the name of Concho … I saw him in the saloon at Witherspoon's hotel.

The other outlaw came out from behind the boulder with Spirit stalking close behind him.

"That one there is called Pete." Thom continued, "He slops drinks behind the bar at Witherspoon's."

"I reckon they're tied in with Cameron," Zeke stated. Then he turned his attention to Concho saying, "How about it Concho, are you two some of Cameron's men?"

"None of your business who we are," Concho retorted.

"Normally you'd be right," Zeke stated, "but when you tried to bushwhack us that made you my business. I'm short on patience with the likes of you. Tell me why you were out here laying for us?"

Concho replied, "I said it ain't any of your dam ..."

The butt of Zeke's rifle connected with Conchos left jaw. It made a whacking sound, rendering him unconscious.

Zeke then looked at Pete saying, "Why were the two of you trying to kill us?"

Pete licked his lips as his eyes darted to Spirit and then back to Zeke as he stammered, "I ... I ... I ... We were after the reward money."

Reward money," Zeke stated. "What reward money?"

With his head hanging down and eyes fixed on Spirit, Pete quietly replied, "Big Red is offering ten thousand dollars to anyone that kills you."

Zeke asked, "Are the two of you part of Cameron's bunch?"

"No we both just work for Witherspoon. Concho deals cards and takes care of business when Witherspoon ain't there and I usually tend to the drinks in the saloon."

"Okay," Zeke stated. "Where're your horses?"

Pointing at a stand of trees about a hundred feet away Pete said, "They're in the trees over there."

"I'll go fetch them," Buddy said as he started walking to the trees.

Concho moaned as he began to come out of his unconscious state. He struggled to a sitting position as he rubbed the large lump on the side of his jaw. He spat a broken, bloody tooth onto the snow. “Damn you, you knocked out my tooth. You had no call to do that.”

“Reckon that when you set up your little ambush, it gave me the right. Now get to your feet and behave yourself else I’ll do it again,” Zeke replied with a cold, hard edge to his voice.

Buddy arrived with the two horses saying, “Here’re their horses. As I said, my horse has a loose shoe and I’m going to walk him into town. Reckon I’ll be seeing you there.”

Buddy turned and started walking to his horse.

Zeke whistled and Blaze came from the trees and trotted towards them with Thom’s horse coming along with him.

“Hold on Buddy, Zeke called out,” there’s no need for you to walk into town. You take one of their horses, whichever one it belongs to can walk, leading yours into town.”

One of the horses was a sorrel and the other one a large buckskin. Buddy chose the buckskin.

“That’s my horse,” Concho exclaimed.

“Then I reckon that you’re the one that’s going to be walking to town,” Zeke replied. “Let’s get mounted and we’ll pick up Buddy’s horse as we go by there.”

“I ain’t a doing’ no walking,” Concho belligerently stated. Then with his good arm, he grabbed at Pete as he started to mount, jerking him onto the ground.

Zeke’s rifle butt struck Concho on the right jaw. Once again, Concho was unconscious. But at least both jaws were now the same, as they each had a very large lump.

Zeke went to Pete's horse and cut the right-hand rein from the bridle. It was a strip of leather about three-quarters of an inch wide and six feet long. Carrying the rein, he went back to Concho and lashed his hands together in front of him.

Saying, "I reckon that he is going to get his wish and ride into town," Zeke reached down and grabbing the unconscious Concho under his good arm and heaved him to his feet. "Buddy grab the other side of him and we'll toss him over the saddle of Pete's horse."

They tossed Concho over the saddle belly down. Then Zeke got the lariat hanging from the saddle and cut a length about ten feet long. He tied one end around the lashed hands of Concho, tossed the rope under the horse and walked to the other side. Picking up the rope, he looped it around Concho's ankles, pulled it tight and tied it. Then he took the remaining piece of lariat and tied it to the right-hand side of the bridle. He cut the remaining rein from the bridle and used it to tie Pete's hands.

"Okay Pete, you get up on that horse behind Concho," Zeke said.

With some difficulty, Pete managed to get on the horse. Zeke then pulled Pete's hands forward stretching his arms over Concho's body and tied them tightly to the saddle horn.

"I can't ride like this," Pete protested.

"You can ride like that or fall off and be dragged. If you don't want to be dragged I suggest that you do your best to stay on there," Zeke retorted.

Zeke took hold of the rope tied to the bridle, walked to Blaze and mounted. Thom and Buddy mounted their horses they all rode up the hill with Zeke leading the horse carrying Concho and Pete.

When they got to Buddy's horse, Buddy untied it and tied the reins to his saddle.

As they rode towards Agua Caliente Zeke told Buddy all that happened since his arrival there. Finishing with, "If you're of a mind to stick around we can use your help."

"Thanks for the invite," Buddy replied. "Reckon that I'll do just that."

There were several people on the boardwalk and they all turned and stared at them as the rode down the street. Blaze pranced sideways lifting his legs high, in way of showing off to the people on the boardwalk.

"How did you teach him to do that," Buddy asked.

"I didn't," Zeke replied. "He knows that he's a fine looking animal and just plain likes to show off every chance he gets."

They rode past the Top Hat on their way to the sheriff's office. Lance and Lefty were lounging on the bench that was in front of the place. Zeke started to call out to them but Lance slightly shook his head from side to side before he could.

Zeke quietly said to Thom and Buddy, "Something's up, Lance indicated that I shouldn't speak to him."

When they got to the sheriff's office, Zeke obliquely looked back at Lance and Lefty … they went into the Top Hat.

Zeke, with the help of Thom and Buddy got first Pete and then Concho off the horse. Then they prodded them into the office and into the remaining empty cell in the back while Gabby watched from where he sat behind the desk.

When they re-entered the office, Gabby said, "Boy am I glad to see you, there's a couple of gunslingers in town that I don't recollect ever seeing before. I ain't knowing for sure but I think that they might be part of the Lisping Bandit's bunch. They got here same day as you left and went straight to the Top Hat. Not that there's anything wrong with going there but that's where they went. I see you got Concho and Pete there. What'd they do?"

As Gabby was talking, Zeke thought, 'He's probably talking about Lance and Lefty. I told them that they could trust Gabby along with Bret and Doc Robert's … wonder what happened that they didn't talk to them.' Then he replied to Gabby, "I'll check those gunslingers out in a little bit. Concho and Pete tried to bushwhack Thom and me about five miles or so out of town. Buddy here jumped in and helped us out. He's going to be staying on to give us a hand when Cameron shows up with his bunch. Is everything else okay? What about those three in the back, did they give you any trouble?"

"Witherspoon and them other two been squabbling amongst themselves. I finally went back there to shut them up and told Witherspoon that he looked ridiculous, sitting there naked as a jay bird."

Zeke asked, "Are you saying that Witherspoon still doesn't have his clothes?"

"No I gave them to him," Gabby replied. "After I told him that he looked ridiculous, he cussed till the air turned blue. He cussed me with words that I never heard before … fact is I think he made up some of them words. I made him apologize for calling me all those nasty names, and then I kicked his clothes into his cell. After he got his clothes on, he offered me five thousand dollars to unlock the cell doors. I said that I couldn't do that and he started cussing again. I told him that if he kept cussing me I would take his clothes away from him again and burn them. He said that he weren't cussing me … he was cussing you. He told me what all he was going to do to you and he was going to dance on your bones. Then he said that he'd give me ten thousand dollars to let him out."

"Ten thousand dollars is a lot of money," Zeke replied.

"I reckon that it is," Gabby said. "But then I'd have to see myself every time I looked in a mirror. I'd still be a miserable cuss after the money's long gone. In my way of thinking, it just ain't worth it. If'n I'd taken that money it'd be the same as me stealing it from the folks that they stole it from."

"Can't argue with you there Gabby," Zeke said. "Thom, Buddy and I need to get on down to the stable and look after our horses. Then I'll look up those two gunslingers and see what they have on their minds. If you don't mind you might get the doc to come and take a look at Concho's shoulder."

When they got to the stable Zeke, Thom and Buddy busied themselves with taking care of their horses. Zeke had just put down a measure of grain for Blaze when Lance slipped into the stable through the rear.

"Sure glad that you didn't give us away," Lance greeted them. "You're right about Big Red … she has more going on than she wants to be known."

"What's happened since you and Lefty got here," Zeke asked. "Gabby thinks that you two are gunslingers."

Lance gave a short chuckle, "Big Red thinks that we are too. In fact she jumped to the belief that we are part of Cameron's gang … we just sort of let her believe that."

Then Lance continued, "When Lefty and I rode into town, we decided to wash the dust out of their throats and stopped at the Top Hat. As we were standing at the bar enjoying a drink a woman asked us to sit at a table with her. Not wanting to offend a lady, we did as she asked.

After we sat down at a table away from the others, she asked, "What news do you bring from Ryan?"

Lance and Lefty both knew that the Lisping Bandit's name is Ryan Cameron and realized that she thought that they were his men. Lance decided to play along and see where it would lead … he looked at Lefty and then replied, "We don't know you lady. Just who are you and why should we tell you anything?"

Seething at the rebuff she replied, "I am Ryan's cousin Barbra and known as Big Red. Now you tell me what you know about the Major."

"Since you put it that way I guess I can tell you," Lance responded. "We got word to meet him here."

"That's better," Big Red said. "When will he be here?"

"Don't know for sure," Lance replied. "Figure that it could be any day now."

"While you are here, you can have a room at the hotel. When you go there, you need to talk to a man that goes by the name of Concho, tell him that I sent you. Keep out of sight as much as possible, there's a United States Marshal nosing around. He's already put three of our men in jail."

"We didn't see any marshal when we came into town," Lefty said. "Just who is he and where is he at?"

Before Big Red could reply, Lance said, "That's right just who and where is he? We'll take care of him."

Big Red replied, "He left for Carson City this morning and should be back in a couple of days. His name is Zeke Cooper."

"Zeke Cooper," Lefty exclaimed. "We left Arizona on account of him. It's gonna take a heap of doing to do him in."

"You're right," Lance said, "I suppose that we could set up an ambush. But what about that wolf that's always with him? I understand that he's warned Cooper of ambushes that were set for him."

"I suppose that we could kill the wolf first," Lefty responded.

"I don't know about that," Lance replied, "other people have tried and died for their efforts. The Indians consider the silver wolf to be sacred, that he has mystical powers and that great harm will come to anyone that tries to kill him."

"That's a bunch of rubbish," Big Red said. "The wolf is just a wolf and Zeke Cooper is just a man ... they can both be killed."

"Rubbish it may be," Lance said, "but I've seen and heard things that says differently. I think that our only chance to get Cooper is to watch him for a day or two and learn when and where he goes. That way we will be able to set an ambush for him ... inside a building when the wolf ain't around to warn him."

"You can setup an ambush right here," Big Red said. "It'll be easy, he's just another man and I'll entice him up to my room. You two be there waiting for him and catch him by surprise."

"That just might work," Lance answered. "In the meantime we'll get familiar with the town, as a just in case."

Lance and Lefty left Big Red sitting at the table after telling her that they would be back later.

They untied their horses and led them down the street towards the stable.

"Do you think that she believes us," Lefty asked.

"I'm sure that she does, she was looking pretty smug and feeling good about herself when we left," Lance answered. "I'm thinking that maybe we shouldn't let Gabby, Bret and the Doc know who we are just yet. I know Zeke said that we can trust them and if he says that we can, we can. But there just might be others still in town that are in cahoots with Cameron and we don't want them to see us with any of those three."

"I'm of the same mind as you," Lefty responded. "It was plain good luck that Big Red mistook us for what we ain't. She's sure gonna be madder than an old wet hen when she finds out who we really are."

Lance chuckled and said, "I do believe you're right.

When they got to the stable, they arranged for a stall and took care of the horses. Then with rifles in one hand and saddlebags over their shoulder, they walked to the hotel, found Concho and arranged for a room.

Lance finished his narration by saying, "We haven't talked to Bret, Gabby or Doc Roberts because of the way Big Red reacted to us. We figured that the wrong person might see us talking with them. We know that a man what goes by the name of Concho at the hotel is one of them."

"You're right," Zeke agreed. "You will be able to find out more of what's going on if they believe that you are what they think you are. As for Concho, he is one of the men that we brought in with us. He and the other one that calls his self Pete tried to bushwhack us about five miles from town."

Then Zeke told Lance what had happened and Buddy's part in it finishing with, "I'll let Bret and the others know who you are and what you are doing. I'll take a turn around town in a little bit and let my presence be known. When I run into you and Lefty I'll brace you as if I believed you to be a couple of hard cases."

The three of them talked a bit more then Lance left the stable the same way that he had come in. He went back to the Top Hat keeping the buildings between him and the main street. When he got there, he and Lefty sat at a table away from everyone. Lance told Lefty about the conversation that he and Zeke had. He also told him what Zeke was going to do when he ran into them.

Chapter Twenty

After Lance left the stable Zeke said, "I figured that there was more to Big Red than what she presented herself to be. But I never would have thought that she is Cameron's cousin."

"That is a bit of a surprise," Thom replied.

Buddy talked to the blacksmith about shoeing his horse. Then the three of them left the stable walking towards the Elkhorn. They each carried a rifle in their left hand and their saddlebags tossed across the right shoulder.

When they entered the Elkhorn Zeke said, "You two go on and get yourselves a drink … I'm going to find Bret."

Thom and Buddy went to the bar, as Zeke headed to Bret's office. The door to the office was open and Bret was sitting behind a desk. He looked up, saw Zeke approaching and motioned for him to come in as he said, "Come in Zeke and close the door … I have a couple of things to tell you about."

Zeke entered the office and closed the door. He crossed the room to a chair facing the desk and sat down.

With a slight smile Zeke said, "I have a couple of things to tell you as well."

"First off," Bret said, "how did things go in Carson City? I don't see Angel so I take it that you found her family. They were probably sad to hear about their daughter but at least they have Angel."

"Yes and no," Zeke replied. "I found Marjorie's folks, her mother wanted to take Angel but her father refused to have what he called a bastard child in his house. Right now Angel is with a preacher and his wife, who run an orphanage outside of Carson City. When things are finished here, I'll go get her and take her to Silver Wolf with me."

"I can't imagine not wanting your own grandchild," Bret stated. "You'd think that with their daughter gone they'd be happy to have their granddaughter with them."

"Regrettably there are some men like Catesby," Zeke replied. "They have their own notions about things and no amount of facts or reasoning will change what they falsely believe to be true."

"I agree with that," Bret said. "They are to be pitied. Luckily Angel has you."

Zeke changed the subject saying, "We ran into an ambush about five miles outside of town." Then he told Bret about the ambush and Buddy, finishing with, "Concho and Pete are sitting in jail now."

"Sounds like you've already learned about the ten thousand dollar bounty Big Red put on your head," Bret responded. "There are two hard cases in town and they wear their six-guns as if they know how to use them. They showed up here the same day that you left for Carson City. I have never seen them before and I don't know what their game is, but they'll bear watching."

"Actually," Zeke replied, "I know who they are. They are my partners, they came here looking for me."

Zeke then told Bret about how they had met up at the road junction. He told Bret that when Lance and Lefty came to town they just happened to go into the

Top Hat for a drink. She mistakenly believed that they rode with Cameron and they decided to let her believe that what she thought was true.

Zeke continued, "Cameron and his men will be showing up in the next two or three days. When I leave here, I'm going to take a turn around town and see what I can shake out. I believe there may be more outlaws here and it's time to round them up … before Cameron gets here."

Bret stood up behind the desk as he said, "If you don't mind, I'll just come along and keep you company."

"Glad to have you," Zeke replied as he too stood up from the chair that he was sitting on.

They left the office and crossed to the bar where Thom and Buddy were standing. When they got there Bret motioned to the bartender … he brought a bottle of tequila and two glasses sitting them in front of Zeke and Bret.

Bret poured tequila in both the glasses. As they sipped on their drinks, Zeke told Thom and Buddy what they were getting ready to do and that they would all meet at the jail later.

"If you don't mind," Buddy replied, "I'll just kind 'a shadow you from the other side of the street."

"Sounds like a good idea, I'm coming along with Buddy," Thom stated.

"Okay," Zeke responded, "but when we go into the Top Hat wait outside for us and keep an eye on whoever comes out."

When they left the Elkhorn, the sun had slipped about halfway behind the mountain to the west.

"Looks like we have about two hours worth of light left," Bret commented.

Outside of meeting some of the townspeople on the boardwalk, they got to the Top Hat without incident. Just before they got there, Zeke saw Lefty, who had been sitting on the bench in front of the place, stand and go inside.

When Zeke and Bret entered the Top Hat there were two men sitting at a table with two of Big Red's girls. Two more men were standing at about the halfway point of the bar. Four girls were sitting at a table near the stairway leading to the rooms upstairs. Big Red was behind the bar serving a drink to one of the two men standing there. Zeke quickly looked around the room for Lance and Lefty … they were not there. He walked to the far end of the bar with Bret beside him. When they got there, Zeke positioned himself so that he had a clear view of the room and the door leading outside.

Zeke detected a hint of nervousness in Big Red as she walked toward them.

When she got to where they were standing, she greeted them with, "Hello Zeke I see that you made it back safely. Did you locate Angel's family?"

Without waiting for a reply she turned her attention to Bret saying, "Good to see you Bret, what brings you to my establishment?"

"I was just out stretching my legs when I ran into Zeke here and decided to mosey along with him," Bret replied.

Keeping her eyes averted from Zeke she continued, "I know Zeke drinks tequila but I have no idea what you drink."

"I'll have the same as Zeke … tequila."

Zeke watched Big Red closely as she turned to get two glasses and a bottle of tequila. He thought, 'She sure is nervous about something, probably getting ready to make her play. I'm sure that she knows about the failed ambush by now.'

Big Red set a glass in front of each of them and poured tequila into them saying, "The drinks are on me."

Just then, the man at the bar who she had not served earlier tapped his empty glass on the bar and indicated that he wanted another drink. Big Red looked at him and without a word, turned and walked to the two men, took the empty glass and filled it. After serving the beer, she talked to the two for a minute or two.

While Big Red busied herself with the two men Zeke turned to Bret saying, "She's getting more nervous by the minute. Don't know what she's up to but reckon we'll soon find out. Lefty came in here just before we got here but I don't see him, or Lance either. They are more'n likely upstairs waiting for me. Big Red plans on getting me up there so they can ambush me. Reckon she's going to be a mite surprised when she finds out who they really are."

"I believe you're right," Bret replied. "She's up to something all right. I'd say that she's telling those two no-goods to watch me while she takes you upstairs. Don't worry about them, if she does make her play to get you upstairs I'll take care of them. The two men sitting at the table over there are locals and nothing to be concerned about."

Big Red left the two outlaws and slowly walked back to where Zeke and Bret were standing at the bar. Keeping her eyes averted from Zeke's she nervously said, "Zeke I have something upstairs in my room that you need to see. I think that it is important. Could you come and take a look at it?"

Zeke quickly looked at Bret who gave him a knowing nod. Then he replied to her, "Well sure, let's go take a look at what you have."

With a barely audible sigh of relief, Big Red came out from behind the bar. She and Zeke headed to the stairway leading to the balcony and rooms upstairs. When they got near the table with the four girls Big Red turned her attention to one of them and said, "Heather I will be upstairs with the marshal for a few minutes and I need you to tend to the bar while I am gone."

Without waiting for a reply from Heather, Big Red continued to the stairs with Zeke. At the top of the stairs, they stepped onto the balcony and proceeded towards the hallway at the far end of the balcony leading to the rooms. At the end of that hallway was a door and just before getting to the door, another hallway led to the right. When they got there, Zeke looked down the hallway and saw doors leading to rooms on both the left and right-hand sides.

Her voice had a slight quiver as Big Red broke the silence, "This is the door to my rooms," she said as she indicated the door in front of them.

The door was not locked she opened it and gestured for Zeke to go in first.

Zeke thought, 'I know Lance and Lefty are inside waiting for me. Big Red believes that they are going to ambush and kill me. She's in for a surprise but the question is, did she put another gunman in there with them?'

Zeke placed his left hand on Big Red's right elbow. With a flourish he motioned with his right hand while putting pressure on her right arm, propelling her into the open doorway saying, "Ladies first."

Big Red went through the doorway, immediately turned and ran toward the far right hand corner as she shrieked, "He's right behind me, kill him."

The sound of two gunshots simultaneously roared followed by the thudding of a body hitting the floor. Two more shots echoed from downstairs.

Chapter Twenty One

Zeke dove through the doorway with gun in hand. He landed on the floor on his left side. With his six-gun covering the room, he surveyed his surroundings.

Lefty was standing in a doorway at the left rear corner of the room replacing the cartridge that he had just fired. Lance was about center of the far wall putting a fresh cartridge in his gun. Big Red, or Barbra, was standing in the far right hand corner. She was ashen faced and her right hand was clutching at her throat. A body with a very large hole in the center of his chest lay on the floor in front of her. The man was obviously dead.

Zeke quickly got to his feet and holstered his gun. "Nice little welcome you arranged for me … Barbra." Then he gestured first towards Lance and then Lefty, "Meet my partners Lance and Lefty."

Barbra didn't answer as her legs gave way and she slid down the corner of the wall to the floor. Her head slumped forward onto her chest and her body trembled as she hysterically sobbed.

Zeke looked more closely around the room. The outside wall had a good-sized window providing a view of the street below. A wingback chair was beside the window with a table about three feet in diameter beside it. A drop-leaf table sat about center of the room. Three wingback chairs were scattered about the room.

A settee, matching the chairs, sat about mid-way along the inner wall. A liquor cabinet stood at the far end of the settee. On top of the cabinet a half dozen glasses sat on a silver tray. The door of the cabinet consisted of small panes of glass divided by a latticework of wood. The cabinet contained three bottles of fine brandy, one of which was about half full, two bottles of whiskey and four bottles of wine.

There was an arched doorway in the far wall where it met with the outside wall. Each wall had several paintings hung on them, all mounted in very ornate frames. Three hung on the left hand wall as you entered the room. A brass sconce centered in the space between each of them held a partially burned candle. The outside wall held two paintings each centered halfway between the window and the left and right-hand walls. The inside wall held four paintings with a brass sconce placed between each of them. A very large painting with a brass sconce on each side hung centered on the far wall.

Four of the paintings were landscapes … two mountain scenes and two of rugged canyons. Three were of a young nude woman in three different poses. The model for the painting was unmistakably Barbra, during her younger years. One painting was a scene of a harbor with many ships at anchor. A brass plate mounted on the bottom of the frame said San Francisco Harbour and below that in smaller letters eighteen sixty three. One painting was of a city. This painting too had a brass plate mounted to its frame and simply stated Boston.

The painting centered on the far wall was of a clipper ship. The ship was under full sail with three square-rigged masts and a spinnaker. The brass plate on the frame identified it as the California Clipper.

As Zeke studied the room he thought, 'Something here is not right. But what is it.' He continued pondering on his surroundings. He looked at Barbra who was still slumped in the corner and now convulsively sobbing.

Zeke pointed to the liquor cabinet and said, "Lance there's brandy in that cabinet. Pour her some, maybe it'll quieten her enough so that we can get a few answers from her."

Lance filled a glass with brandy and took it to Barbra. She gulped half of the brandy and her sobbing became a little quieter. She continued sipping on the brandy between sobs.

Zeke continued pondering on what was wrong. His eyes wandered around the room as he contemplated on the puzzle. He looked at the furniture and saw nothing out of place. Then he studied each painting in turn. He looked at the California Clipper and started to look at the next painting. His eyes snapped back to the painting of the ship. He thought, 'That's it, this painting and the one of the harbor do not belong here. Everything in this room is of a feminine nature except these two paintings … they are that which a man would hang. They either mean something to her or there is a man somewhere.'

Zeke went to the arched doorway and stepped through it as Lefty stepped to the side. The room was a little larger than the other room. It was her bedroom and it too was garishly furnished. Several paintings hung on the walls of the bedroom. All but one of the paintings was of the same woman in various stages of undress. One painting was totally out of place … it was of a boy about twelve standing beside a horse. The boy in the painting looked vaguely familiar.

Zeke took stock of the room. A glass paned door mid-way along the outside wall opened onto a balcony that ran the full length of the building. A large four-poster bed stood in the center of the room close to the rear wall. The bed had a canopy of pink silk. Curtains made of pink gauze surrounded the bed hanging from the canopy to the floor. A large wardrobe made of white oak stood in the front right-hand corner. It measured about eight feet in height, six feet in width and about four feet deep. A folding dressing screen was beside the wardrobe. The screen consisted of three panels. The panels covered with gold brocade had raised figures of sea horses. The sea horses on each panel were of different colors. On one panel, all of them were blue, one all red and the other all green. In the far right corner of the room was a table about three feet high and three feet in diameter. On top of the table, a large porcelain washbowl sat to one side. A porcelain pitcher sat on a porcelain tray beside the bowl. A vanity with gilded carved decorations stood along the outside wall between the door and far corner. A large mirror, separate from the vanity, filled the space between the vanity and far corner of the wall. The frame of the mirror had the same decorations as the vanity.

Zeke walked back into the main room. Barbra was now lying in a fetal position on her left side facing toward the wall. She whimpered as she sucked the thumb of her right hand.

Zeke looked at Barbra and stated, "I don't reckon that we'll be getting any answers from her anytime soon." Then he pointed to the dead outlaw and asked, "Do either of you know who he is?"

"He went by the name of Slim, came in here about an hour ago." Lefty responded. "He and Barbra went into her office soon as he got here. When they came out she told us that Slim would be helping us to kill you."

Lance spoke up saying, “I told her that we didn’t need help from anyone and especially from someone that we didn’t know. She said, ‘Slim is very good with a gun and has a lot of experience in such matters.’ We didn’t have much of a choice than to let him come with us. While we were waiting, he strutted around and bragged about what he had done with a gun in the past. Had he actually done everything he claimed he had he’d have to be well over a hundred years old. When Lefty came in here to let us know that you were coming, he crouched behind that liquor cabinet with both of his guns drawn and pointing at the door. When Barbra came through the door she was in his line of fire, he stood and stepped away from the cabinet so he could get a shot at you.”

“Sure glad the two of you were in here,” Zeke responded. Then he continued, “I need to get downstairs and see how Bret is doing. Keep an eye on Barbra while I’m gone, no telling what she’ll try next. If you go through Slims’ pockets, we might learn more about him. Search these two rooms and see what you can find.”

Chapter Twenty Two

Zeke left the room and headed toward the stairway. He looked down to the barroom from the balcony as he walked. The two outlaws that had been standing at the bar when he left were now sitting on the floor with there backs against the bar. One of them was clutching his bloody right wrist … blood was also leaking out of his right foot. Both of their guns were on the floor about ten feet from where they sat. Bret was sitting at a nearby table holding his six-gun on top of it, pointed at the two outlaws. Thom and Buddy were standing one on each side of the door by the outside wall. The two locals were still sitting at the table with two of the girls. The girl named Heather was behind the bar and the other three were still sitting at their table. Three more girls were sitting at a table next to them.

Zeke descended the stairs and walked to where Bret was sitting. "Looks like you have things under control here," he said in way of greeting. "I heard two shots … what happened?"

"Soon as you left the room these two fixed their eyes on me," Bret replied. Then he continued, "I stepped away from the bar so I would have a clearer view of them. When they heard the shots from upstairs they went for their guns."

Bret indicated the one that was bleeding and continued, "Sanchez there is the faster of the two so I shot his wrist to dissuade him from shooting me. His gun was half-drawn when his wrist shattered and he shot himself in the foot. After he shot his foot, he fell to the floor where he is sitting now. When his partner Ramón saw my gun firing, he threw his hands in the air while yelling, 'don't shoot … don't shoot.' I defanged him and told him to sit beside his partner."

"I take it that you know who these two are," Zeke said. "Are they part of Cameron's gang?"

"I don't believe that they are," Bret responded. "From what I understand they used work the mines here. When the mines started to play out, they turned to the other side of the law. They've been wintering here for the last four or five years. I would guess that Big Red offered them something to shoot me."

Zeke turned to the two outlaws and asked, "Is that right Ramón? Did Big Red offer you something to shoot Bret?"

Ramón sullenly stared at Zeke and didn't answer.

"How about you Sanchez," Zeke asked. "What did Big Red offer you?"

Sanchez gave Zeke a defiant sullen look and spit on the floor. Zeke's gun found his hand and roared. The floor between Sanchez's thighs splintered.

With his gun, pointing toward Sanchez Zeke barked, "Answer me else the next shot will be a bit higher."

Sanchez's face blanched, his eyes bulged, his mouth opened and closed as though he was trying to talk, but no sound came out.

Zeke swung the barrel of his six-shooter towards Ramón saying, "Do you want to tell us what we want to know? Or should I just shoot you instead of Sanchez and be done with it?"

Ramón started talking and Sanchez soon found his voice and contributed to the conversation. Big Red offered them five thousand dollars to kill Bret. They were to wait until they heard shots from upstairs. Bret was right in his belief that they were not part of the Lisping Bandits gang. They rode the trails between Carson City and Virginia City and from there to Sacramento. They held up and robbed small unsuspecting groups of travelers during most of the year. When the weather turned cold, they would come to Agua Caliente for the winter.

Heather was still behind the bar and Zeke turned his attention to her saying, "You won't be needed behind there Heather go back to the table where you were."

He then went to the table where the two locals were sitting. "This establishment is closed for now." Zeke pointed at one of them saying, "You go to Doc Roberts' office and tell him we need him here." Pointing at the other one he said, "You go to the barber shop and tell Claudio that his services are needed here."

The two men left and Zeke asked the girls, "Who else is here? Are there more upstairs and if so how many?"

One of the girls replied, "Mary Jo and April are upstairs. Mary Jo's with Mike and Andy's with April."

"Then there are eleven of you girls that work here," Zeke asked.

"Yes that's right," she replied.

Zeke went back to where Bret was and called Thom and Buddy over.

When Thom and Buddy got to them Zeke said, "We need to get over to Witherspoon's hotel and round up any outlaws that may be there. Thom I want you to go upstairs and tell Lance and Lefty to come down here.

Then I want you to stay there and watch Barbra. Buddy you wait here for the doc. When Roberts is finished take Sanchez and Ramón to the sheriff's office and lock them up. Be sure and search them before you put them into a cell. Then come back here and check all the rooms upstairs. Bring anyone you find down and keep them here till we get back."

A few minutes after Thom went upstairs Lance and Lefty came down. Zeke asked, "Did you find anything of interest? … How's Barbra doing … is she in any shape to talk yet?"

"It'll be awhile before she's able to tell us anything," Lefty replied. "We gave her some more brandy and put her in her bed. She was falling asleep when we left."

Lance said, "When we were putting her in the bed my foot hit something on the floor beneath it. It turned out to be a strongbox. I think that you will find the contents interesting."

"Right now we need to get over to Witherspoon's hotel," Zeke replied. "There are probably a few outlaws still there that we need to round up. We'll look at it when we get back from there."

As Zeke, Lance, Lefty and Bret left the Top Hat they met Doctor Roberts coming in.

"I was told you need me here," Roberts said in way of greeting. "When I heard the shooting I figured that I'd be sent for."

"It wasn't me that did the shooting this time," Zeke replied. "Bret here had to shoot Sanchez who in turn shot himself in the foot. There's also a dead outlaw in Big Red's room upstairs. While you're here, you might take a look at Barbra … she put a bounty on me and is kinda upset that I'm still alive. Thom's up there with her and can fill you in on what's happening."

Roberts went into the Top Hat … Zeke and the other three proceeded on to Witherspoon's hotel.

The lobby was empty when they entered. They looked in the saloon and it too was empty. When they checked the dining room they saw two men sitting at one table, three at another and one sitting by himself at a third table. The rest of the tables were empty.

"The three men sitting together are townspeople. The one sitting by himself goes by the name of Juan … he works for Witherspoon. The two of them showed up here together. He's probably running things now that his boss is in the hoosegow. The other two have been coming here for two years now … they stay the winter and haven't caused any trouble. They have a small mine up in the mountains about twenty miles from here. I've seen Gabby with them on occasion … he can probably tell you more about them."

"Who does he have working the kitchen," Zeke asked.

"A couple of Chinese men were running the kitchen when Witherspoon bought the place. He kept them on, but they won't give us any trouble," Bret said.

"Okay," Zeke responded, "Juan knows we're here and has been eyeing us … let's go ease his mind as to why we are here. Lance you and Lefty lock the entry doors then check upstairs. If anyone is up there bring them down to the lobby."

Lance turned and headed to the entry doors as Zeke and Bret stepped into the dining room.

When they were about twenty feet from Juan, he sprang to his feet. He wore a six-gun tied to each thigh with their pearl handles pointed in … he was a cross drawer. He wore a vest with Mexican silver dollars as buttons … his holsters were also decorated with silver dollars. As he came to his feet Juan's right arm crossed over his left as he grabbed for the handles of his shooters. His right-hand gun had almost cleared leather and his left was almost as far out of its holster when Zeke's gun roared.

The bullet from Zeke's gun found its mark shattering Juan's right wrist and then hit his left arm just above the wrist. After breaking the bone and taking a chunk out of his left arm, it punched a hole in Juan's left side just below the rib cage where it came to rest.

With a stunned look on his face, Juan slumped back onto the chair he had been sitting on.

With his gun still trained on Juan, Zeke walked to him, took his left-hand gun from its holster and tossed it to one side. The right one was on the floor where it fell when Juan dropped it … Zeke kicked it farther away.

"Juan who else is here," Zeke asked. "Is there anyone else that works for Witherspoon?"

Juan glared at Zeke with his mouth turned down and hatred showing in his eyes but did not answer.

Zeke stepped closer to Juan and placed the muzzle of his gun against Juan's left ear. He coldly and calmly said, "I have no patience with the likes of you … answer my questions else I'll connect your ears."

Juan's face blanched and he replied, "No savvy."

Zeke cocked the hammer of his gun and spoke in the Mexican language, "Answer my questions or I will do as I said."

Juan's eyes bulged out as they rolled upward, slobbers appeared around his mouth he farted mightily and passed out.

As Zeke replaced the spent cartridge in his gun, he noted the two Chinese cooks peering into the dining room from the doorway into the kitchen. Holstering his gun, he said to Bret, "Reckon we ought to bind his arms and stuff something in the hole in his side to keep him from bleeding to death."

"I'll have the cooks bring some rags from the kitchen," Bret replied.

Zeke turned his attention to the other five people in the dining room and announced, "Gentlemen I am Zeke Cooper … deputy United States Marshal. Tonight we are in the process of rounding up the known outlaws that are here. We expect the Lisping Bandit to attack Agua Caliente within the next few days. Those of you, who are willing to defend your town, be at the sheriff's office in the morning. The rest of you stay indoors and out of the way."

The cooks soon came into the dining room with a handful of rags and a pail of water. Zeke watched as they used two of the rags as tourniquets, one on each of Juan's upper arms. They wadded up a smaller rag and stuffed it into the hole in his left side. Then wetting another rag, they bathed the blood off of Juan's wrists and side. They gathered the unused rags after completing their task, picked up the pail of water and started to leave.

"I'll take that," Zeke said as he took hold of the pail with the now bloody water.

Zeke dumped the water on Juan's head. Juan gasped as he regained consciousness.

Speaking in Mexican Zeke asked, "Who else is here … is anyone else here that works for Witherspoon?"

Juan answered in English, "I am the only one here. You have everyone else locked up."

"What about the Lisping Bandit," Zeke asked. "Are any of his men here?"

"No," Juan replied. "You killed the only one that stayed when the others left town. They will be back and this time they will make sure you are dead."

Zeke turned his attention to Bret saying, "Take this cockroach out to the lobby. I'm going to take a look in the kitchen."

Bret herded Juan to the lobby as Zeke went to the kitchen. The two Chinese cooks were the only ones there.

Zeke went back to the dining room then turned toward the door and walked to the lobby. Lance and Lefty were back from upstairs and reported that all of the rooms were empty.

Zeke turned to Bret and asked, "Is there any other place in town that an outlaw might be?"

"Not unless they are hiding somewhere," Bret replied. "They usually hang around the hotel here or at the Top Hat."

"Then it might be a good idea to sweep the town and be sure. I'll go finish at the Top Hat while the three of you drop Juan off at the jail and then search the town."

Lance spoke up saying, "If there are any outlaws hiding out, they may circle behind us and come to the hotel here. It might be a good idea to have someone here as a just in case."

"That's a good point," Zeke replied. "You all wait here while I go to the Top Hat. I'll have Buddy come over here to watch the hotel."

Chapter Twenty Three

When Zeke entered the Top Hat, he saw that it was much the same as he had left it. Except now, Mike and Andy Ballard were sitting at a table with Mary Jo and April. A man was slumped at a table with his elbows resting on the tabletop and his head propped up by his hands.

Buddy was sitting at a table that gave him a full command of the room as well as a clear view of the doorway. Zeke stopped in front of Buddy and asked, "Did you get everyone down from upstairs?"

"Only Mike, Andy and their two girls were up there," Buddy replied. Then he gestured toward the man slumped at the table, "That one sitting over there claims to be a member of the town committee. He came in not more'n ten or fifteen minutes ago and got a might upset when I wouldn't let him leave before you got here. He says his name's Jake Quigley."

Zeke took a harder look at the man and said, "That's who he is alright. I'll go see what he's doing here."

Zeke went to the table where Quigley was sitting.

"Quigley why are you here," Zeke asked.

Quigley looked up at Zeke and nervously replied, "I heard the shooting and came to see if I could be of help."

"I don't believe you," Zeke said with a cold, flat voice. "You are not the type to offer help in matters such as this. I do not like to be lied to and I suggest that you tell me the true reason you came here."

After about thirty seconds of silence Quigley quietly said, "I'm sorry Marshal … I won't lie to you again. After I heard the shooting, I waited as long as I could but when I hadn't heard anything I came to see if Iris was okay."

"Who is Iris," Zeke asked.

Quigley pointed at a table where some of the girls sat, "She's the one wearing the green dress at that table over there."

Zeke looked at Iris and saw a woman that appeared to be in her early thirties. She had long brown hair, makeup heavily caked on her face and her lips painted a very bright red. She was not an attractive woman at all … she was just this side of plain ugly.

Zeke asked, "If you're so concerned about her welfare why are you not sitting with her? What is she to you?"

"She's the one I come to when my wife won't take care of my needs," Quigley whined. "I'm a married man and can't be seen in public with her."

"Get out of here and go home," Zeke said in disgust. "On your way home you might think about your wedding vows and what they mean."

Zeke watched Quigley stand up from the table and dejectedly walk out of the saloon with his head hanging.

Zeke went back to Buddy and told him what happened at the hotel. He finished by saying, "I need you to go to the hotel and watch things there. If anyone comes in find out who he is and why he's there. Stop at Doctor Roberts' on your way to the hotel, and tell him that he has another patient at the jail."

After Buddy left, Zeke closed and locked the door. Then he crossed the room to the table where Mike, Andy and the two girls were sitting.

"Andy I want you and Mike to watch things down here while I go upstairs," Zeke said. "If anyone insists on coming in, come and get me." Then he turned his attention to the girls and asked, "What about the back door, is it kept locked?"

"It usually is," one of them replied. "It should be closed with a bar dropped across it."

"I'll go check it and make sure," Mike said.

Zeke turned and went upstairs to Barbra's rooms. When he entered the room, Thom stood from the chair that he had been sitting in by the window.

"How's Barbra," Zeke asked in way of greeting. "Is she able to talk yet?"

"She's sleeping," Thom replied. "She woke up once after Roberts left but went right back to sleep after I gave her some more brandy."

Zeke saw a strongbox sitting on top of the drop-leaf table. The box measured about two and a half feet long, one and a half foot wide and as deep. Carved on the lid was a square-rigged ship with three masts under full sail. A brass plate fastened to the lid beneath the carving had the words California Clipper etched on it. The box had a handle on each end and two latches securing the lid shut.

Zeke flipped the latches down and swung the lid open. There were three items inside the box. One was a newspaper called The San Francisco Miner. It was dated December eleven eighteen sixty-two. The headline on the front page blared: California Clipper ~ Ship of Doom.

Zeke read the news account below the headline. The California Clipper left Boston Harbour June sixth eighteen sixty-two. It took about six months to complete the first leg of its voyage to China. The vessel had not yet cleared the harbor when the first mate discovered three stowaways. Two of them were whipped and tossed over the side where they promptly drowned. The third one a lad of about fourteen known only by the name of Bob remained aboard and served as the Captain's boy. The second tragedy that befell the ship was the disappearance of Mister Wilson, her second mate. They were in a storm tossed sea just before entering the Magellan Straits when he was lost. The morning after the California Clipper tied up at the waterfront here the first mate found the Captain with his throat cut and a knife sticking from his chest. The motive was apparently robbery as the ships strongbox and the Captains log are missing. A search of the ship, the docks and surrounding area for the cabin boy was fruitless. He left the ship the evening before to take the captains' laundry to one of the many laundries on the waterfront. Many fear that he too is a victim. Beneath a sketch of Bob at the end of the article, it asked Have You Seen Him.

Zeke refolded the paper and placed it on the table. Then he took the captains logbook from the box. The book measured about seven inches wide, a foot tall and about one and a half inches thick. The front and back covers were made of leather. It had four evenly spaced holes along the left-hand edge and bound together with twine, allowing the insertion of more pages as needed. Lettered on the front cover at the top was Clipper Ship California. Lettered near the bottom it read Ships Master and below that the name Captain Ian McIntyre.

In the center at the top of the first page was the date June sixth eighteen sixty-two. The first entry neatly lettered below the date read; the day is clear and visibility is about twenty miles. We got underway on the swift morning tide at eight bells and twenty-two. My cabin boy took sick and could not make the voyage. Mister Wilson discovered three stowaways while inspecting the cargo. I kept the youngest, a lad of about fourteen as my cabin boy. The other two we tossed overboard after giving each of them fifteen lashes. Unfortunately, they were unable to swim ashore and drowned.

Zeke quickly scanned the following entries. Except for four entries, they dealt with the weather, unusual events of the day and the distance covered. The first of the four was dated June nine eighteen sixty-two. The first part of the entry was much the same as the others. The last part of the entry read; I have discovered that my cabin boy is not a boy, but a very well endowed lass. We have a long and difficult voyage ahead of us and I should put her ashore as quickly as possible … perhaps at the colony on New Providence Island.

The second of the four entries read June twelve eighteen sixty-two. The last portion of the entry read; I succumbed to temptation last night and took the lass to my bed. She fought me at first but soon accepted her fate. Even though she was a virgin and unwilling at first, she was quite comforting. We joined four times last night and each time she seemed to be a bit more eager.

The third of the four entries read July ten eighteen sixty-two. The last portion of the entry once again was about the girl. It has been a little over a month since I took the lass to my bed. She has been in my bed every night since then. The lass quickly learned how to treat a man and I believe her to be a natural born harlot. I believe she now looks forward to our nightly trysts as much as I do. She is such a comfort to me during the lonely nights at sea and I cannot put her ashore just yet.

I have decided to keep her with me until our return to San Francisco from China.

The fourth entry of the four read August thirty eighteen sixty-two. The weather is foul and stormy and the waves are breaking at about twenty feet. We are making very little headway against the oncoming sea. Once we get into the Magellan straits, it should be a little easier going. We lost Mister Wilson sometime last night. Presumably, one of the many waves cascading onto our decks washed him overboard.

Zeke put the log on the table alongside the newspaper. Then he took the remaining item from the strongbox … it was an oilskin pouch containing several sheets of paper. Most of the papers had to do with the cargo the ship was carrying. One of the papers was a copy of a receipt for gold coin in the amount of twenty thousand dollars and signed by Captain Ian McIntyre.

The pouch also contained a lock of hair tied together with a thread. The hair was very fine and appeared to be that of a baby.

Zeke put the pouch with its papers and lock of hair back into the strongbox. Then with a thoughtful expression on his face, he picked up the newspaper and went into the bedroom. Comparing the picture in the paper to Barbra's face, he concluded that she was the one pictured in the newspaper. The picture was some sixteen years old but except for her long hair, her facial appearance had not changed much.

Walking back to Thom, Zeke handed the paper to him saying, "What do you think Thom? Is that drawing in the paper of Barbra?"

Thom took the paper and studied the picture. Then he too walked into the bedroom and compared the picture to Barbra. Upon his return he placed the paper back on the table as he stated, "There sure is a strong resemblance. The article says that they are looking for a boy, maybe it's her brother."

Zeke picked up the Captain's logbook and held it out to Thom saying, "Read this and see what conclusion you come to."

Thom took the logbook and began reading. When he finished reading, he laid the book on the table, picked up the newspaper and once again looked at the picture. "I'm of the same mind as you. The so-called lad in this picture is probably her. Which brings up the question … did she kill Captain McIntyre?"

"My thoughts exactly," Zeke replied. "Also why did she assume the Captains name? Only she can tell us … how long has she been in that deep sleep?"

"I reckon that it's been close to an hour now. She drank most of that bottle of brandy," Thom replied. "When Roberts was here he said that the brandy was as good as anything that he had to give her."

Zeke responded, "I believe it's time to wake her up and get some answers"

When they reentered the bedroom, Zeke pointed at the painting of the boy and horse, "Doesn't that boy look similar to the one in the paper?"

"It sure does," Thom responded. "Maybe it's Barbra when she was younger."

"Maybe so," Zeke replied dubiously. "But for some reason I don't think so. Only Barbra can tell us."

Zeke crossed the room to the washstand and picked up the pitcher, which was almost full of water. He took it to the side of the bed and dumped about half of the contents on Barbra's head.

Barbra let out a mighty groan and both arms flailed at the air. "Wh … Wha … What," she spluttered as she regained consciousness.

Zeke noted with satisfaction that Barbra was groggy and therefore would be more forthcoming with answers to his questions.

The first question Zeke asked was, "Barbra did you arrive in San Francisco from Boston aboard the California Clipper?"

Barbra sought to sort things out in her groggy mind as she thought, 'He can't know that, how could he?'

Zeke saw that she was trying to clear her mind and barked, "Barbra answer my question."

With her mind in a state of confusion Barbra replied, "Ye … yes that is how I got to San Francisco."

"Why did you kill Captain McIntyre," Zeke asked with a cold flat voice.

"I … I," Barbra stammered, "He killed two of my brothers and turned me into a whore."

Sensing that she was ready to open up Zeke said, "I reckon that's reason enough." Then in a soft tone of voice he asked, "What about Wilson the second mate, did you have anything to do with his going overboard?"

In her confused groggy mind, Barbra mistakenly believed that she had an ally in Zeke and answered, "He killed my father … I slit his throat and shoved him overboard."

"Who is the boy with the horse in the painting," Zeke asked.

"That is my son, Ian," Barbra replied.

"Where is Ian?"

"He's in San Francisco."

"Why isn't he with you?"

"He doesn't know about me. Right after he was born I left him on the steps of a church with the name Ian McIntyre pinned to his blanket."

"He appears to be about twelve in the painting. How did you get it?"

"I hired a Pinkerton man to find him and then had him commission an artist to paint a picture of Ian," Barbra replied.

Then it was as though a floodgate opened and Barbra started talking. She told Zeke and Thom her whole sordid story. Her mother's sister was Ryan Cameron's mother. She told how she had run into her cousin in Virginia City. She also revealed that she had killed seven men all told, counting the Captain and second mate of the California Clipper.

She finished telling her story. Then with a combination of a whimper and a sigh she said, "I suppose I'll be hanged for what I've done. After it is done will you find my son and give him what I leave?"

Zeke replied, "I don't know if you'll be hanged or not. This part of the country has a lot of violent men and at times, the law is beyond reach. It's at those times that a person does what he must do. Perhaps you were justified in killing the men that you did. It will be up to a court of law to decide if you hang or not. A judge by the name of Randolph Morrison will be here in a few days. I don't know him very well but I believe him to be a just and honorable man. I would say that the least that will happen is that you will go to prison. Your activities with your cousin, the lisping bandit, don't speak well for you. If hanging is your fate I'll make sure your son receives that which is rightfully yours."

Zeke said to Thom, "I don't know what I am going do with her yet. We can't keep her here with the window and door opening to the outside and we can't put her in jail. You stay here and guard her … I'm going down and look around her office."

Chapter Twenty Four

Zeke left Barbra's rooms and headed toward the stairway. As he walked, he pondered on what to do with Barbra. He thought 'If she were a man it would be simple I could just stuff her in the jail … or shackle her in the livery stable. If I leave her where she is, she will be able to escape through the window or door. If only her rooms didn't open to the outside …. Wait a minute, that's it … the inside rooms don't have any windows or doors leading out … I can put her in one of them and have the blacksmith fashion a way to lock it from the outside.'

When Zeke entered the barroom Mike said, "The rear door is locked up tighter 'n a drum Marshal. Andy and I want to help any way that we can."

"That's right," Andy said, "we ain't too good with a leg-iron but we're accurate with a rifle."

"Good," Zeke replied, "I reckon we can use your guns when Cameron shows up with his gang. I need one of you to fetch the blacksmith, if he isn't at the livery find him. I need him as soon as he can get here."

"I'll get him," Mike stated. "If he ain't at the stable I know where he lives."

Mike left to get the blacksmith and Zeke went to Barbra's office.

The office was about fifteen feet in each direction. The doorway was at the left hand corner of the room, a desk sat near the far corner. A safe standing about three feet high and three feet square occupied the near right-hand corner. A large cabinet standing about seven feet high and one and a half foot deep occupied about ten feet of the space between the doorway and safe. The only chair in the room was behind the desk. Zeke opened the doors to the cabinet and saw that it contained several bottles of liquor, bar glasses and other bar supplies.

Zeke went behind the desk and sat down. The desktop had nothing on it. The desk had three drawers on each side and one drawer below the top, between the side drawers. He opened the drawers one after the other but found nothing of interest. As he searched the drawers, he thought 'the combination to that safe should be here somewhere.' The combination was not in the drawers. He pulled each drawer all the way out of the desk and looked on the bottom side of each of them … he did not find the combination. Zeke stood, went to the cabinet and carefully searched each shelf … he found nothing. He was standing beside the safe when he finished searching the cabinet.

Looking down he saw some writing on top of the safe … in faded ink was the date August twenty-nine eighteen sixty-two. Zeke thought 'that date seems familiar to me.' He pondered on the significance of the date and realized that it was the date that Barbra avenged her father's murder.

Thinking that that could be the combination, Zeke knelt in front of the safe. He spun the dial and then twisted the dial first to twenty-nine then eighteen and sixty-two in succession … it remained locked.

Zeke thought 'August is the eighth month I'll try eight first.' He once again twisted the dial back and forth stopping at eight and the rest of the numbers in turn.

When the safe once again remained locked, Zeke thought, 'guess that ain't the combination.' He stood up from his squatting position in front of the safe. He paced around the room as he pondered on where the combination could be. He had a nagging feeling that he had the combination, yet the numbers he tried did not work. Suddenly he stopped pacing as a thought came to him. He rushed back to the safe and once again squatted in front of it.

He spun the dial a couple of times to the right. Then twisting the dial back and forth, first to the left then to the right he stopped at the numbers in reverse order. Zeke twisted the handle on the door and it swung open.

Inside the safe, he found, two ledgers, a Virginia City bankbook and a medium sixed metal box. Zeke opened the box and saw that it contained gold and silver coins. He dumped the coins onto the top of the safe and counted them back into the box. It came to five hundred sixty three dollars and eighty-two cents.

Putting the box back into the safe Zeke removed the two ledgers and the bankbook. He crossed the room and placed them on top of the desk. He first opened the bankbook and saw that the last entry was six days ago. It was a deposit of two thousand five hundred dollars and brought the total amount in the account to ninety-six thousand four hundred dollars. He then opened one of the ledgers. It was a simple business ledger, each page divided into four columns. At the top of the left-hand column, it read item, the next column read income and the third one read expense. The right-hand column did not have a label. It obviously was a running tally of the difference between income and expense.

Zeke looked through the remainder of the ledger and found each page to be the same. He closed it, sat it aside and opened the second ledger.

Some of the pages were full, some only partially and others were blank. The name of a different girl headed each of the used pages. Each line had a date and a monetary amount. Some lines had a single dollar amount and others had multiple amounts.

As Zeke looked through the ledger, he saw that some girls had multiple pages while others had only one. As he leafed through it, something kept nagging at him. 'Something ain't right here,' he thought. 'This is nothing more than a ledger keeping track of a whore's earnings … but something is wrong.' He scrutinized the ledger more closely and it suddenly dawned on him. He opened the first ledger alongside the second one. The handwriting in the second ledger was that of a woman and the writing in the first was a masculine scrawl.

Zeke pondered on the meaning of the two different handwritings. 'The writing in the ledger with the girl's earnings is more than likely that of Barbra's. The handwriting in the business ledger is undoubtedly that of a man. Does she have a partner or has she hired a bookkeeper?'

Standing up from where he was sitting Zeke walked to the door and looked out into the barroom. He saw Heather and called for her to come into the office.

When she got there Zeke asked, "Heather who does Barbra leave in charge when she isn't here?"

"If Slim isn't here she leaves me in charge," Heather replied.

"Then maybe you can tell me who does her account book?"

Heather responded, "Slim does the accounting and orders all the supplies that we need. We used to run out of things before Slim started doing it."

"Who is this Slim, did he come here with Big Red?"

"He came here about a year after I got here," Heather replied. Then she continued, "I think he used to ride with the Major."

Zeke asked, "The Major? Do you mean the Lisping Bandit?"

Heather responded, "Yes but he doesn't like that name and Big Red told us to never call him that."

"Why do you think Slim used to ride with him?"

Heather replied, "Because the first time I saw him was when he came in here with the Major and several other outlaws. When the Major and the others left Slim stayed here. At first, he stayed with Big Red but now he has his own room next to hers."

"What does Slim do besides the account book and ordering?"

"He takes care of anyone that gives us a problem and he goes to Virginia City for Big Red every couple of months."

"I take it that you have been here for a long time," Zeke said. Then he asked, "Did you know Big Red before you came here?"

"No," Heather answered, "I met her when I got here. I heard about the hot springs here and decided to come here because it's warmer in the winter. Big Red opened this place for business the same day I arrived. I went to work here that night and have been here ever since. I know that she is in a lot of trouble but I want you to know that she treats us girls better than any other place that I have worked. Do you have any idea about what's going to happen to her?"

"That's going to be up to a judge to decide," Zeke replied. "But I would say that the least that will happen to her is that she will go to prison for the rest of her life. She has admitted that she's killed seven people and depending on the circumstances of those killings, she could very well be hanged."

"I hope that they don't hang her," Heather said. "What is to become of this place when she is gone? She has a son someplace … I think he's in San Francisco."

"Yes I know," Zeke replied. "Unless she requests otherwise everything that is rightfully hers will go to him."

"I could run this place until everything is settled," Heather offered. Then continued, "Slim taught me how to order and keep track of everything."

"I'll talk to Big Red about your offer. If it is alright with her you can run this place till things are settled."

Heather asked, "Does that mean we can reopen now?"

"Maybe tomorrow," Zeke said. "You go on back out there for now. You can serve drinks to anyone that's already here. But the doors are to remain locked for tonight."

Heather returned to the bar as Zeke placed the ledgers and bankbook back into the safe. He closed and locked the safe's door, left the office and walked towards the stairway. Before he reached the foot of the stairs, the front door opened and Andy came in with the blacksmith. "Marshal, this here is Clive Baxter, the blacksmith."

"Glad you could get here Clive," Zeke stated. "Come upstairs with me and I'll show you what is needed."

As they climbed the stairway to the rooms upstairs, Zeke explained what he had in mind to Clive.

They checked the doors to the inside rooms. The third door they checked was unlocked. Zeke swung the door open and looked inside … it obviously was not in use. The room was about fifteen feet in each direction and sparsely furnished. A small bed that looked well used stood with the head about center of the far wall. A chamber pot was on the floor at the edge of the bed. A porcelain basin sat on a small washstand in the corner, a water pitcher on the floor beside it. A cracked mirror hung on the wall above the washstand. A wooden chair, that turned out to be quite rickety, was at the foot of the bed. A kerosene lantern hung from a hook on the wall next to the door.

Zeke turned to Clive saying, "This room will do if you can secure the door from the outside."

Clive carefully examined the frame and door, then he said, "This is a good strong door and it will be no problem to fashion a couple of hooks and a bar to secure it. I'll go back to my shop and get what I need. It won't take long to fix this door the way you need it.

Clive left to get what he needed and Zeke went to Big Red's rooms. Thom was sitting in the chair beside the window when Zeke entered.

"Have you learned anymore since I left," Zeke asked.

"No," Thom replied, "I tried talking to her but it's like talking to the wall. She just lays there on her back staring at the ceiling."

Zeke walked into the bedroom and just as Thom said, she was lying on her back staring at the ceiling. "Big Red there are a couple of things we need to discuss."

Big Red continued staring at the ceiling as though she did not know Zeke was there.

"Big Red," he firmly said, "we need to talk."

She continued to stare at the ceiling, ignoring him.

Zeke moved to the side of the bed at which he sat the water pitcher earlier. He picked-up the pitcher and dumped the remaining water on her head. Big Red let out a high-pitched screech as she sat up in bed.

"Why'd you dump that water on me," she snarled.

"As I said, we need to discuss a couple of things and I'll not be ignored when I talk to you," Zeke replied.

Big Red stared at Zeke for a minute and decided that he meant what he said. "What do you want to know," she quietly but sullenly asked.

"Tell me about Slim," Zeke replied. "I know he did your account book and ordered your supplies. Where did he come from and what else did he do for you?"

"He came here from Texas where he owned a bordello. He got into a gunfight with a quarrelsome drunk one night and killed him. The sheriff of the town tried to arrest him and he shot and killed him too. He left Texas and eventually hooked up with the Major. He rode with him for about six months before he came here. When the Major and the other men left he stayed with me as my business advisor and lover."

"I understand that when neither you nor Slim are here you leave Heather in charge," Zeke stated. Then he asked, "Do you want her to keep this place open until things are settled?"

Big Red lay back down and dejectedly whispered, "It doesn't matter."

A pounding noise came from the hallway and Big Red sat back up in the bed as she exclaimed, "What's that noise?"

"That would be the blacksmith," Zeke replied. "He is working on a door to a room across the hall. When he is finished it will be securable from the outside and that will be your new home till the judge gets here."

With panic stricken eyes Big Red protested, "Why can't I stay here? I promise I won't try to escape."

With a hard edge to his voice Zeke responded, "I don't trust you and I certainly don't believe anything you say. You put up ten thousand dollars for anyone that could kill me and you tried setting up an ambush right here in your room. Now you want me to trust you. You have proved yourself to be a liar and by your own admission, you have killed seven times." Then he continued, "The only reason that I'm going to keep you in a room here instead of at the jail, is the kindness you showed by providing milk for Angel. Now get out of that bed and gather up anything you want to take with you."

Big Red got out of bed and gathered a few articles of clothing and her toiletry items.

Zeke watched her closely as she chose what she was going to take with her. She went to the wardrobe and with a furtive glance over her shoulder, placed her body so it blocked his view of what she was getting.

She put everything on the bed and bundled them together in a blanket.

When she completed tying the bundle Zeke said, "Before we leave here I'm going to search you for any weapons. Take off your clothes and lay them on the bed."

Big Red's eyes showed fear as she said, "I'm not going to undress in front of you."

"No you're not," Zeke retorted. "Step behind that dressing screen and get your clothes off."

With a slight glimmer of hope in her eyes, Big Red went behind the screen and began undressing. As she removed each garment, she laid it across the top of the screen.

Zeke took each piece of clothing and after inspecting it tossed it onto the bed.

After Zeke inspected the last article of clothing, Big Red said, with a false sense of bravado and a tinge of sarcasm, "Did you find anything? Give me my clothes so I can get redressed."

Zeke thought, 'I know she took something out of the wardrobe that she didn't want me to see.' He picked the clothing up from the bed and went to the front of the screen. He held the clothing up to the top of the screen as if to hand them to Big Red.

She reached over the top of the screen to take the clothing. Instead of handing her the clothes, Zeke dropped them to the floor and with one swift motion toppled the screen.

Big Red stood there with her arms outstretched and naked except for two items. Strapped about midway on the inside of her left thigh was a holstered derringer. Strapped to the inside of her right thigh was a dagger in a sealskin sheath.

Her hands dropped and she grabbed at the derringer. Zeke's six-gun appeared in his hand and he pressed the end of the barrel underneath her chin. The pressure under her chin forced her head to tilt back and she stared at the ceiling, scratching at the derringer with her right hand.

Maintaining the pressure against her chin, Zeke reached down with his left hand and took the derringer from her. He tossed it on the bed and then removed the dagger from her right thigh. The blade of the dagger was six inches long. Both sides of the blade were sharp and tapered to a very sharp point. He re-holstered his gun as he stepped back and said, "You can get dressed now."

Zeke watched as a crestfallen Big Red picked the screen up from the top of her clothing and quietly but sullenly redressed.

When she once again was dressed Zeke said, "I reckon the blacksmith is about finished with fixing the door to where you are going to be staying. It's time to move you over there."

Silently Big Red reached for the bundle on the bed.

Zeke stopped her saying, "Leave that bundle right where it is. After what you just tried, it is clear to me that I'm going to have to search it before you can have it. I'll look at it later and if you haven't hid something in there I'll bring it to you."

Big Red stared blankly at Zeke then meekly walked to the door. They left the bedroom and crossed the room where Thom was. They entered the hallway and Zeke led her to the room that would be her home until her trial.

Clive had finished his work and was picking up his tools as Zeke and Big Red approached the room.

"Just finished Marshal," Clive stated. Then he handed Zeke a one-inch square iron bar about three and a half feet in length. He gestured at two brackets fastened to the door saying, "Once you drop the bar across the door here it'll be as secure as a jail cell."

Zeke told Big Red to go into the room as he looked at the bar and examined the door. Clive had fashioned four u-shaped brackets and attached one on each edge of the door about three feet from the floor. He fastened the other two brackets to the doorframe, one on each side.

Big Red entered the room and flopped down on the chair at the end of the bed. The rickety chair wobbled and collapsed under her weight. She landed on her back with a loud thud and a screech resembling that of an owl. Her hands formed into fists as she waved them in the air and pounded the floor with her heels.

Zeke looked at Clive saying, "I don't reckon that she's ain't any too happy." He closed and locked the door, then dropped the bar in place.

Zeke continued, "In case you haven't heard, we're expecting the Lisping Bandit and his gang to attack the town in the next three or four days. A meeting with several of the townspeople, me and my partners will be held at the sheriff's office in the morning."

"I'll be there Marshal," Clive said as he finished gathering his tools and left.

On his way downstairs Zeke stopped at the rooms that Big Red had occupied. When he entered the room Thom was sitting in one of the wingback chairs writing on a tablet.

Thom paused his writing and looked at Zeke, "I'm just jotting down some notes on what has happened in the last few days. Of all the books that I've written about you, this will be the first one that I can write with first hand knowledge."

With a slight chuckle Zeke replied, "It ain't over yet." Then as he walked towards Big Red's bedroom he continued, "Big Red put a bundle of necessities together. I told her that I needed to check it for any weapons before she can have it."

Zeke walked to the bed and untied the bundle that was sitting on top of it. He searched each piece of clothing, item by item and placed them on the bed beside the bundle. He found nothing hidden in the clothing, the only items left in the bundle was a hand-held mirror and a hairbrush. He picked up the hairbrush, examined it and seeing nothing out of the ordinary tossed it onto the pile of clothing.

Then he picked up the mirror. The mirror portion was square, about six inches in each direction and encased in silver. The handle was also made of silver and just over twelve inches long. Squiggly scrollwork ornamented both the frame and handle. Zeke looked at the front and the back of the mirror and as he started to lay it down, he noticed something not quite right with the handle.

He scrutinized the mirror handle. About four inches from the end was a very thin line. About half of a squiggle was on each side of the line and would not have been noticeable, except the two halves did not match. Zeke turned the mirror over and the backside of the handle was the same.

Grasping the bottom portion of the handle with his right hand and the top with his left Zeke pulled the handle apart. The bottom portion of the mirror handle was actually the handle to a dagger. The blade was much the same as the dagger he took from Big Red earlier … six inches long, sharp on both edges and tapered to a very sharp point.

With a grim expression on his face, Zeke tossed the mirror and dagger onto the top of the pile of clothing and went to the room where Thom was.

Seeing the expression on Zeke's face Thom said, "I take it that you found a weapon or two in her bundle."

Zeke nodded his head once and said, "She's one very dangerous woman."

The two of them left Big Red's quarters and went downstairs. Heather was behind the bar and everyone that was there when Zeke went upstairs was still sitting in groups of two and three at various tables.

Zeke walked to the bar and said to Heather, "I talked to Big Red and as far as she's concerned you can run this place until things are settled. But as I said earlier, you will stay closed for tonight."

"Okay Marshal I'll open it tomorrow," Heather replied. "What about Big Red? Can I go up and see her?"

"Not tonight," Zeke said. "You can see her tomorrow and then only if one of us is with you."

Zeke then turned and faced the tables where the Ballard twins and the rest of the girls were sitting. Raising his voice so they could all hear him he said, "Big Red is locked in a room upstairs any of you that want to see her can do so tomorrow … but no one is to go to that room unless one of us is with you."

Zeke and Thom left the Top Hat and headed to the sheriff's office. When they stepped out into the stillness of the night a light drizzle with a little bit of snow mixed in was falling. The snow melted as soon as it hit the ground. When they entered the office Lance, Lefty, and Gabby were there.

"It's pretty quiet out there," Zeke said in way of greeting. "Did you find any more outlaws when you made your sweep through town?"

"Nope, it's quieter than a graveyard," Lance replied.

"Gabby says when it gets this quiet it's getting ready to snow," Lefty said.

"You can bet your last penny on it," Gabby said. "When it gets this quiet it's gonna snow and snow hard. Course it won't be nary as bad here as up on the mountain. Why I remember one time a few years ago, it got so quiet that you could hear the footsteps of a cougar a half mile away. It started snowing that day and kept snowing for nigh unto two weeks. Yes sir it dropped so much snow that it plumb covered up the smaller trees and some o' the mid-sized ones too."

Gabby continued, "Now if'n I recollect correctly it were about this time of year, maybe a bit earlier. That's the time them sugar foots bound for California got themselves snowbound trying to get through that pass. If'n they'd a had a guide worth his salt they would of went around the mountain stead of trying to go over it. Must have been a right miserable time for them, they had no shelter except for their wagons and they burned them to keep warm. When they run out of food, they killed and ate their horses and mules. After they ate all of the horses and mules, they commenced to eat each other. When they started out there were close to a hundred of them by the time they were rescued 'twas only 'bout half that many. Now mind you, they was there for about three months and I don't know when they ran out of food but even so, I don't believe that I could eat another person. No sir there's plenty of animals and critters out there to eat … ain't nary a need to eat another person."

"Speaking of food," Lefty said, "my belly's telling me that it's past time to put something in it."

"I agree with you," Zeke said, "let's go over to Bret's and eat. Have the prisoners back there had anything to eat?"

"I gave them coffee, a piece of bread and some bacon this morning," Gabby replied.

"In that case they are probably getting a bit hungry. You can bring something back for them after we eat."

They all left the sheriff's office locking the door behind them. The snow mixed rain was falling a little heavier now than it was when Zeke and Thom left the Top Hat.

Chapter Twenty Five

Zeke slept fitfully that night awakening several times. Each time he awoke, he was thinking about the events of the last few days and what was yet to come. He finally gave up on sleeping and got out of bed about three-thirty in the morning. He lit a lantern, dressed and left his room. Carrying the lantern, he made his way downstairs and to the door leading outside. He extinguished the lantern and placed it on a table near the door.

Zeke stepped outside closing the door behind him. He stood still on the covered boardwalk waiting for his eyes to adjust to the eerily quiet darkness. After his eyes adjusted, he turned and headed to the stable. A light snow without rain was now falling and there was close to a half-inch covering the roadway. When he entered the stable both Blaze and Spirit met him near the door. Blaze softly nickered in way of greeting and Spirit rubbed his head on his leg.

Zeke lit a match, located the lantern hanging on a nail beside the door and lit it. The stable was about one hundred feet deep and half that wide. A hayloft was above the first thirty feet of the building. Stalls covered the entire length of the right-hand side. The stalls were about fifteen feet deep and six feet wide. A manger with a feed trough built to the side of it was at the head of each stall. Identical stalls also covered the last half of the other side. Wooden posts about eight inches square supported the roof structure. The posts placed at twenty-foot intervals, ran down the center the full length of the building. Attached horizontally to each post were two boards four inches square and seven feet long. Each four by four protruded an equal distance from the post in each direction. They were about three and a half feet above the floor with each end fastened to the top of a four by four post. Some of them held tack while others were empty.

Zeke carried the lit lantern to Blaze's stall and set it on the floor. He put some grain in the feed trough and then put fresh hay in the manger. Blaze started eating and Zeke walked to the back door of the stable with Spirit at his side.

Attached to the rear of the stable was a corral two hundred feet deep. The only way in or out of the corral was through the stable. A water trough and a hay bin were located on the left-hand side off the corral close to the rear wall of the stable. The corral was empty … snow covered the ground as far as he could see.

Spirit sat on his haunches beside Zeke as they both looked out through the doorway. He lifted his nose and sniffed at the air then he stood and slowly moved his head from side to side while sniffing at the air. His head stopped with his nose pointed slightly to the left. His ears cocked forward, he sniffed again and then took off, running in the direction that his nose had been pointing.

'Reckon he's going after his breakfast,' Zeke thought. 'I wonder if Gabby has any coffee going at the jail.' With that thought in mind, he went to Blaze's stall and picked up the lantern. He patted Blaze on the rump and walked to the door. He hung the lantern back on its nail, blew out the flame and walked out the door. He stood still once again waiting for his eyes to adjust to the dark. After his eyes adjusted to the darkness, he walked to the sheriff's office.

A glimmer of light showed through a crack of the window shutters. Figuring Gabby had the door locked, he looked through the crack of the shutters and saw him setting at the desk, sipping on a cup of coffee … his rifle lay across the desk close to his left hand. Zeke tapped on the window to get Gabby's attention.

Gabby's left hand grabbed the rifle as he put the cup of coffee down and his right hand found the trigger guard with his finger resting on the trigger. He stood with his rifle pointed at the window and called out, "Whose there?"

"It's Zeke, open the door … let me in."

Gabby laid his rifle back onto the desktop, walked to the door and opened it. "Coffee's on the stove, just made it," Gabby said in way of greeting.

Zeke got one of the tin cups hanging from the wall, went to the stove and filled the cup with coffee. He took a sip of coffee then asked, "How long do you suppose this snow's gonna last?"

"Hard telling," Gabby replied. "It'll be light afore long and we can take a gander at the clouds to see how dark they are. From the looks o' what I saw yesterday it's gonna be a long lasting storm. Probably last three maybe four days. Depends on which direction it's coming from. Yesterday it looked like it was coming from the north. Mind you now if'n twere 'a coming from the west or south it'd blow itself out in a day or less. Come light we can take a look-see and figure out how long she's gonna be around."

Thinking about the pending arrival of Cameron and his gang Zeke asked, "If the storm's coming from the north how much snow will we get here? Will the road to the east be passable?"

"Possibly," Gabby replied, "it depends on how long the storm lasts. I'd say that you could use the road today and maybe tomorrow. If it snows longer than two or three days it'll have to be cleared first."

Zeke pondered on what the snowstorm meant to them. "Could you get back to your place if this storm lasts for a few days?"

"Couldn't get back there now," Gabby replied. "Probably couldn't get as far as the bridge. The Ballard's will be here for a spell too. The only way in or out of here now is to the east."

Zeke fell silent as he mulled over what he knew of the area. Agua Caliente is in a hollow on the lower eastern side of the Sierra Nevada Mountains. On three sides, the mountain is very steep. The northern side is too steep for any kind of trail. The western and southern sides both have a trail that are a bit treacherous in the best of weather. With a heavy snowfall, they would become impassable. That leaves the road to the east the only way in or out. The road gently rises for about five miles before it crests and starts down the other side.

Zeke asked, "How long after the snow quits will the road become passable?"

"Shouldn't be more'n a day or two," Gabby replied. "There's that contraption over by the freight office. They use it to clear snow from the road if'n it gets too deep for their wagons or the stagecoach to get through."

"How often does the stage come here?"

"Once a week," Gabby replied. "Believe it'll be here tomorrow. Elmer over at the freight office can tell you for sure. That's where the stage stops, it usually gets here around mid-afternoon but this snow may hold 'er up a bit."

About five-thirty Zeke and Gabby left the sheriff's office, locked the door behind them and went to the Elkhorn. There was activity in the kitchen when they entered and the smell of coffee filled the air. Bret emerged from the kitchen carrying two steaming cups of coffee. He walked to a nearby table that had a full cup of coffee setting on it. He set the two cups on the table saying, "Come and join me here, I was just telling Miguel what I want for breakfast and saw you come in."

As they sat down a woman appeared from the kitchen and came to the table. She appeared to be in her late twenties, her long black hair was braided on each side.

When she stopped at the table Bret said, "This is Consuela, she and her husband Miguel do the cooking for us here." Then he continued as he pointed towards Zeke, "Consuela this is Zeke Cooper and you already know Gabby."

"Senor Cooper," a beaming Consuela said, "I have heard many things about you and greet you with great pleasure. I hope you give the banditos here what they deserve."

With a slight chuckle Zeke replied, "We certainly intend on doing just that."

"Good," Consuela stated, "but now you must eat. We have eggs, bacon, ham and beefsteak."

Zeke ordered beefsteak and eggs. Gabby ordered ham and eggs.

Consuela disappeared back into the kitchen. She returned about twenty minutes later carrying two platters. Miguel followed her with two more platters, one of them covered with a white cloth.

Consuela sat one of the platters that she had on the table in front of Zeke and the other in front of Bret. They each contained a large steak, four eggs and beans.

Miguel sat one of his platters in front of Gabby and the other in the center of the table. Gabby's contained the same as the other two except his had a large, thick slice of fried ham instead of a steak. The covered platter had several hot tortillas about four inches in diameter.

As they started to eat, Lance and Lefty came down from upstairs. "Pull a table up to this one and join us," Zeke greeted them. They had just finished joining the two tables together when Thom and Buddy walked in the door.

Consuela came from the kitchen as the four new arrivals sat down. She carried two steaming cups of coffee in each hand and placed one in front of each of them. Then she took their breakfast orders and went back to the kitchen.

As they ate, they discussed what needed done before the Lisping Bandit showed up.

"We don't know yet how many of the townspeople are going to help defend their town when the outlaws show up," Zeke stated. Then he continued, "We can put the ones that do show up on the roofs with long guns. I understand from what Gabby has told me the only way into town will be from the east. A lookout at the crest of the hill will be able to spot any riders long before they get here."

"I spotted you and Thom almost an hour before you got to the ambush," Buddy stated. Then he continued, "With a set of binoculars you could probably see to the junction from the crest of the hill."

"When it gets light I'm going to take a ride out there and have a look see," Zeke said.

"I'll ride along with you," Lance said.

"I am just going to scout out a position for a lookout," Zeke replied. "Before our meeting this morning I need you and Lefty to look the town over to determine which rooftops will give the best advantage for the men with rifles. If you're of a mind too, check on Big Red and have one of the girls fix her some food."

Buddy asked, "What about me … is there anything in particular that you want me to do?"

"Yes," Zeke responded, "familiarize your self with the town. While you are doing that keep an eye out for anything that we can use to barricade the road at the entrance to town."

When they finished eating Zeke arranged for Bret to furnish food for the prisoners.

"What kind of food do you want to feed them," Bret asked.

"If we feed them too good they may not want to leave," Zeke wryly replied. "There's eight of them for now … I reckon a bucket of beans ought to take care of them. Gabby can give them coffee to wash the beans down."

Bret chuckled and said, "I like the way you think … nothing too good for our guests."

Gabby waited for the bucket of beans and the rest of them left the Elkhorn. They stepped out into the dim twilight of early morning. The snow was still falling but as Zeke walked to the stable, it abruptly stopped.

After saddling Blaze, Zeke rode out of town towards the crest. Spirit joined them about a quarter of a mile outside of Agua Caliente. He ran alongside of them for a while then disappeared as he ran ahead. The snow gradually became deeper as they climbed the hill … the deepest part was just above Blaze's fetlocks.

They were about five hundred feet short of the crest when Spirit reappeared, standing cross ways in the road. Blaze stopped and then Spirit led them diagonally to the northeast. He led them on a twisted course around trees and a few large boulders. As they crested the hill, Zeke smelled smoke. Spirit led them to some large boulders just over the crest and stopped.

Zeke dismounted and surveyed his surroundings. They were in a small clearing outlined by five large boulders. He walked to a boulder on the easterly edge of the clearing and warily looked around it. He spotted a thin column of smoke about three hundred feet away. It was climbing into the air from the far side of a very large boulder to the east of his position. Another large boulder was to the south of the first one, a gap of about four feet separated them as they formed a right angle. Then he spotted two horses amongst some trees about fifty feet to the southeast of the camp, each of them picketed with a lead rope about ten feet long.

Cautiously Zeke worked his way closer to the campsite, keeping himself concealed by trees and boulders. As he got closer to the camp, he could hear two angry voices arguing. From behind a large tree about fifty feet from the boulders, he looked through the gap between them. He saw two men, one of which was sitting on a small boulder and the other squatting by the fire and complaining. "We ain't got any coffee," he angrily stated. "I still say that we should go into town and get some."

"If you hadn't been such a pig and drunk it all last night we'd still have some," the other one angrily retorted. "We ain't going to town; we are staying right here till the rest of them get here."

"Dam-it Segundo they ain't the ones out here freezing their hind-ends off … we are! If'n you weren't such an ornery dang fool idiot we'd be at the Top Hat right now, where one o' Big Red's whores could warm us up."

"I'm telling you we ain't going to town just yet!"

"But I'm cold and I'm hungry! Those beans you cooked up last night ain't worth spitting on ... I told you that the bacon you put in them was rancid and no good but you used it anyway. Even a halfway-starved coyote wouldn't eat them. You stay here and freeze ... I'm gonna go to town, get something to eat and get warm."

Segundo jumped to his feet, with his right-hand resting on the handle of his pistol he snarled, "You ain't gonna go nowhere. You're staying right here till the others gets here."

The other outlaw jumped to his feet saying, "You best find your self some help if'n you think you're gonna stop me."

They both drew their guns and started shooting at each other. After they emptied their six-shooters, the one that was complaining had a gaping hole where six shots entered his belly. He dropped his gun, clutched his stomach with both hands and fell to his knees. "You kill't me," he said as he toppled onto the ground face down.

Segundo holstered his gun as he pressed his left hand to his right side, just below his ribs where a bullet hit him ... that was the only wound he had. "Reckon you can argue with the devil now," he sardonically stated.

Zeke hurried to the opening between the boulders and stepped through with the muzzle of his gun leading the way. When Zeke came into the campsite, Segundo had his back turned towards him.

"You've already been shot once today," Zeke stated with a flat tone to his voice. "Unbuckle your gun-belt and drop it or I'll just naturally have to shoot you again. Besides, we both know your gun's empty."

Segundo dropped his gun-belt then turned to face Zeke. Segundo's mouth dropped open as he bewilderedly tried to sort through what confronted him. He saw a man staring at him with flint hard eyes and pointing a gun in his direction. A very large wolf sat on his haunches beside the man. The wolf was intently staring at him with drool dripping from his mouth as he licked his chops. When he finally realized who the man with the wolf was, his face blanched, his knees buckled, he wet his pants as he fell to the ground and rolled onto his left side.

After Segundo hit the ground, Spirit came to where he lay. Segundo watched with a fear etched face and bulging eyes as the wolf snarled and sniffed at his crotch. Then Spirit straddled Segundo's body and while continuously snarling, slobbered on his face … with a high-pitched tone to his voice Segundo whimpered, "Mommy" and passed out.

Zeke holstered his gun and whistled for Blaze. Blaze trotted into the camp a couple of minutes later. Spirit was now sitting about five feet from the unconscious body.

Zeke got a set of arm shackles from one of his saddlebags and then went to Segundo. Using his foot, Zeke rolled him onto his stomach and shackled his arms behind him. Then he rolled the outlaw onto his back. Using his knife, he cut the outlaws shirt away from his wound. It was a clean shot in as much as it did not hit any bones or vitals. However, it did take a small chunk out of his side. Zeke cut a piece off the shirt and pressed it to the wound to staunch the flow of blood. He held the rag there for several minutes, until the flow of blood slowed and the rag was stuck to the wound.

Zeke picked up Segundo's gun-belt and removed four cartridges. He pried the lead slug from each cartridge and emptied the gunpowder onto the rag that was stuck to the wound. Then he went to the campfire and got an ember, which he used to ignite the gunpowder.

When Zeke lit the powder, it flashed and the smell of gunpowder mixed with the stench of seared flesh filled the air. Segundo's body jerked and he let out a wailing high-pitched scream that sounded like an animal in great pain.

'Must have regained consciousness,' Zeke thought, 'looks like he fainted again though.'

Zeke went and got one of the two horses and led it back to the camp. Two saddles with bridles draped over their horn and two sets of saddlebags were on the ground between the campfire and the boulders. He saddled the horse, then picked up the dead outlaw and laid him belly down across the saddle. Using the lariat that was hanging from the saddle, he tied the outlaw's hands together with one end of it. Then he tossed the rope under the horse to the other side. After walking around the horse, he looped the rope around the outlaw's ankles. Then he pulled the rope tight and tied it, securing the body to the horse. He led the horse to a nearby tree and tied the end of its lead rope to a branch.

Zeke got the other horse, led him back to the campsite, and saddled it. After saddling the horse, he checked on Segundo … he was still unconscious. There were two canteens on the ground by the fire. Zeke picked up one of them and shook it. It felt like it was close to full. He pulled the cork from the mouth of the canteen and poured the contents on Segundo's head.

Segundo spluttered to consciousness and he wildly jerked his head from side to side, as he frantically searched his surroundings with wide-open fear filled eyes. He spotted Spirit sitting on his haunches about five feet away … Spirit stood, licked his chops, growled and stepped closer to Segundo.

Segundo made a strange high-pitched wailing noise as he stared at Spirit. When Spirit took another step towards him, he wailed once more and then fainted … again.

Zeke looked at Segundo and then at Spirit. Spirit cocked his head at Zeke with the lip on one side of his mouth curled up, as though he was laughing.

With a chuckle Zeke said, "Spirit you keep doing that and we'll never get done with what we came here to do." Then he dragged the unconscious Segundo to the horse and tossed him across the saddle. He then tied him to the horse the same as he did the dead outlaw's body.

After tying Segundo to the horse, Zeke went to the saddlebags and checked their contents. The only thing he found of importance was eight hundred thirty-seven dollars in one of the bags. One hundred thirty seven dollars was silver coin, three hundred in gold coin and four hundred in paper. He secured the bag with the money to Blaze's saddle as he wondered where the money came from.

Zeke looked down the slope to the east, thinking this might be a good spot to have a lookout. He could see the trail between Carson City and the Mormon settlement to the south but not the road leading to Agua Caliente. After extinguishing the campfire, Zeke cut a small branch off a tree on the west side of the boulders. Using the branch, he brushed out all signs of the camp having been there.

Blaze and Spirit followed Zeke as he led the outlaw's horses through the trees. When he got to the road leading to Agua Caliente, he tied the lead rope of Segundo's horse to the saddle on the dead outlaw's horse. Then he tied the lead rope of that one to the saddle on Blaze.

Zeke stepped up onto Blaze's saddle and rode to the boulders where Concho and Pete had waited to ambush him. Looking to the east Zeke had a good view of the road all the way down to the junction. He also noted that the clouds were breaking up and the sun was trying to make its presence known. Satisfied that this was a good spot for a lookout, Zeke headed back to Agua Caliente.

They were about halfway to town when Zeke heard Segundo moan loudly. Three retching sounds followed the moan as he puked up beans and chunks of bacon.

It was past mid-morning when they arrived in Agua Caliente. As he rode through town to the sheriff's office, Zeke noted the lack of activity in the town.

Chapter Twenty Six

Zeke stopped in front of the Sheriff's office, dismounted and went inside. Gabby was the only person there.

"Where is everybody," Zeke asked in way of greeting. "Didn't anyone show up for the meeting?"

"They sure did," Gabby responded. "Dang near the whole town showed up. There were too many to fit in here, so Bret took them to his place. I stayed here so as I could tell you where they are. Did you find a likely spot for a lookout?"

"Sure did Gabby," Zeke answered. Then he continued, "I have a prisoner and a dead man outside. We need to take care of them before going to the meeting."

Gabby followed Zeke out to the horses. "Which one o' them is alive?"

"This one here," Zeke said as he went to the horse carrying Segundo and started untying him. Segundo was conscious and groaning as they pulled him from the saddle.

When Gabby saw Segundo's face he blurted, "Good Lord man do you know who this is?"

"I reckon his name's Segundo, that's what the dead one there called him before they shot each other."

"That's what they call him alright," Gabby said. "He's the Lisping Bandit's right hand man.

"Segundo means second and I kinda figured that was the case," Zeke responded.

Segundo clutched at the wound on his left side and swayed a bit on his feet as he groggily looked around. He had the appearance of a man who had been through an unimaginable experience, His face was ashen, his jaws were slack and his mouth hung open. His eyes were bulged and had a wild look in them as they came to rest on Zeke. He tried to talk but only babble came from his mouth and sounded much like that of a pig rooting for food.

"He's scared plumb stupid," Gabby exclaimed. "What'd you do to him?"

"I don't think it was me," Zeke replied. "He emptied his six-shooter into his partner's gut then he turned around and saw me and Spirit … I think Spirit might've scared him."

Zeke gripped the stupefied Segundo by the right arm and led him inside.

After locking Segundo into one of the already crowded cells Zeke and Gabby left the sheriff's office, locked the door and headed toward the Elkhorn.

"What about that dead feller? We just gonna leave him there," Gabby asked.

"I don't reckon he's going to complain any and it's cold enough to keep him from stinking for awhile," Zeke replied. "After the meeting I'll have Claudio take care of him."

When they entered the Elkhorn, fifty-three men were sitting in groups at different tables and talking loudly amongst themselves. Bret, Lance, Lefty, Thom, Buddy, the Ballard twins and Doctor Roberts were all standing in a group close to the end of the bar. The room became quiet as Zeke and Gabby made their way to them.

When Zeke stopped beside the group Bret asked, "Did you find a good spot to place a lookout?"

"Sure did," Zeke replied, "managed to bring in a couple of outlaws too … one alive and one dead." Then he quickly told them what happened, finishing with "Segundo is in a stupefied state of mind right now. Hopefully he'll come around in a little while and we can get some answers out of him. Doc, you might take a look at him after the meeting."

Then Zeke turned his attention to the men sitting at the tables and raised his voice as he addressed them. "Some of you know why we are gathered here. For those of you who do not, we expect the Lisping Bandit to attack your town within the next day or two. We don't know for sure just how many men he'll have with him … but we have reason to believe that it will be a sizeable number. We need volunteers to help defend your town."

"Why should we volunteer to be shot or killed," Jake Quigley demanded. "Things were pretty good here before you came along and ruined it."

"Jake, you're a sniveling jackass," Bret loudly proclaimed. "Maybe you should shut up and listen before you start running your mouth."

"You can't talk to me like that," Jake protested. "I'm a member of the town committee and it is my duty as such to voice my concerns."

"We all know the only thing you're concerned about is the amount of money you can make." Bret retorted. Then he added, "That and the whore over at the Top Hat."

The room erupted into loud laughter. A red-faced Quigley jumped up from where he was sitting and stomped to the door. Before going out, he turned back to the room and shouted, "You're all going to be sorry if you listen to Cooper. He's gonna get most of you killed if you do." Then he turned around, opened the door and stormed out.

The laughter in the room died down and Lance said, "Do you reckon that means he ain't volunteering."

There was murmuring among the men and Zeke waited for it to quit before saying, "I know you're all concerned about what's going to happen and how we should prepare. Unless someone comes up with a better plan, we will barricade the entry to town … that will take the brunt of their attack. Most outlaws will attack only when the odds are in their favor and we can limit the amount of bloodshed if we have enough men to show a strong defense. Nine of us standing here will be at the barricade and Doc will be doing whatever he needs to do. We need men on the rooftops armed with rifles. There will be a lookout just over the crest of the hill east of town. He'll be able to see the junction leading to Carson City and will have ample time to get back here to warn us that they are coming."

Zeke continued, "I know some of you are unable to help, there is no shame in that and I understand."

A man sitting about center of the room stood up exclaiming, "By jeez Marshal you can count me in! My name's Jackson I ain't had cause to shoot at another man since I lost my leg in the second battle of Bull Run. I'm still a right good shot with a long gun and I'm ready to put a slug in a few of them outlaws. I say 'tis 'bout time we rid ourselves of them for good."

"Me too Marshal," Clive stated, as he stood up.

The room became very quiet as some of the men looked shamefully around the room and others hung their heads staring at the tabletop in front of them.

Zeke let the silence build for a couple of minutes and then said, "As I said earlier, if you are unable to help defend your town there is no shame in not volunteering.

But there are fifty-three of you in this room and I find it hard to believe that only two of you are able-bodied and willing."

Bret stepped away from the bar saying, "All of you have known me for several years and I know all of you. I also know that only three of you are unable to help. Maybe the rest of you just need a little time to think it over. Think it over, talk it over between yourselves and decide."

Bret paused and looked questioningly at Zeke. Zeke nodded at him to continue. "While you are thinking and talking it over, remember how it was when the outlaws had their way with this town. Remember the drunken brawls, the random shootings at all hours of the day and night and the taking of whatever they wanted."

"What about Sheriff Tucker," a man sitting at one of the tables called out. "You're telling us to remember what it was like. I remember that he stopped all of that."

"Yes he did," Bret responded, "and at what cost?"

"Didn't cost me nary a dime," the man smugly replied.

"That's where your thinking is wrong." Bret retorted. "You evidently haven't yet heard that Tucker's real name is Forrester. Witherspoon and Forrester were in cahoots, not only here but also in other towns before coming here. Witherspoon cooked up a scheme to extort money from every business in town. Forrester collected the money and they called it a tax. You are paying that so-called tax on everything you buy. The two of them are now sitting in jail and waiting for the hangman's rope. When I asked you at what cost, I did not mean the cost that you pay with money, I was referring to your self worth."

The man had no more to say and once again, the room fell silent.

Doctor Roberts broke the silence, “Each and every one of you are going to have to decide if you have the courage to fight for your town or not. You will decide if you are man enough to stand up and protect that, which is yours. On the other hand, you can decide that you will let other men do the fighting for you. Every man feels fear to one degree or another in a situation such as this. He can swallow that fear and do what he must do, or he can give in to it and run. For those of you who are able-bodied and decide not to fight … I say you are a coward. When you decide to leave this town running from your cowardice, which you will do, remember that you will be taking yourself with you. For the rest of your life you will remember this day and regret your decision to become a coward.”

“I couldn’t have put it better Doc,” Zeke stated. Then he addressed the men in the room, “Clive, you and Jackson come by the sheriff’s office after dinner tonight. For those of you that do decide to help, come by the sheriff’s office and let us know. As for those of you who decide that you cannot or will not help, I suggest that you stay inside and keep out of our way.”

Men furtively glanced at each other as they silently got to their feet. The room started emptying as some of them hurriedly left and others sheepishly walked out.

As the room emptied Zeke asked Bret, “How many more do you reckon will volunteer?”

“I would say that all of them that will already have,” Bret responded.

“That’s pretty much what I think. We don’t really need them but I kinda figured that they would take pride in the fact that they had a hand in getting rid of the outlaws, which would make it easier for your next sheriff.” Zeke stated.

The meeting broke up … Gabby and Roberts went to the jail. Lance and Buddy went to the stable to get their horses … they were taking the first watch as lookouts. Lefty, Lance, Thom and the Ballard twins went to gather items suitable for use as a barricade.

Zeke watched as everybody left then turned to Bret saying, "This town is going to need a strong sheriff to prevent the outlaws from taking over again."

"I've been thinking along that same line," Bret replied. "What do you know about Buddy? He seems pretty comfortable with himself and appears to be a man that can handle a situation."

"Don't know much about him, he was a deputy up in Cheyenne till recently. From what I've seen, I'd say he would be a good sheriff."

Zeke turned to leave as Bret said, "Reckon I'll have a talk with him when he gets back."

Zeke left the Elkhorn and went to the sheriff's office.

Doctor Roberts had just finished examining Segundo as Zeke entered the office. "You may as well put him back in a cell Gabby. There's nothing more that I can do for him."

Gabby gripped Segundo's arm and urged him up from the chair that he was sitting on.

Segundo got to his feet … fear etched his slack-jawed face as his unblinking, terror-filled eyes darted around the room. Slobber ran down his chin as he slowly and repeatedly twisted his head from one side to the other.

Zeke watched as Gabby led the shuffling Segundo back to a cell. "What do you think Doc? Do you think he'll be able to tell us anything before long?"

"I don't rightly know, something scared him mighty bad," Roberts replied. "Right now I'd say that he's living in his own private hell. I've read of cases like this but this is the first that I've seen. Do you know what scared him?"

"Not for sure Doc, but I think that it might've been Spirit. What if Spirit confronted him again … would that shock him back to reality?"

"Once again I really don't know," Roberts replied, "from what I've read I would think not. If confronted by Spirit again he quite possibly would react like a cornered rabbit." Then he continued, "As you know, if you corner a rabbit and clap your hands real loud, it'll fall over dead more than half the time. He may eventually come back to his senses on his own."

Gabby returned from the back in time to hear what Roberts just said. "I doubt that he'll ever get his senses back. I 'member when I was just a sapling back home in Tennessee a man got scared plumb stupid and he died that 'a way. He came from up north somewhere to be our schoolmaster. He thought himself to be a right smart man and anything he didn't know he claimed he did. Just about, everyone in town warned him not to go into the woods by his self, because of the bears. Nonetheless, he knew more than anyone else did and one day he went into the woods by himself. We found him 'bout three days later. He was holding a bunch of wildflowers in his hand and babbling crazily about a bear. We brung him back to town and all he did after that was wonder about town, holding a bunch of wildflowers and babbling about a bear. He became the village idiot and died about five years later still babbling about that bear. I reckon Segundo's gonna be the same way if'n he gets his speech back."

The door leading outside abruptly swung open and Mike Ballard, rushed in. "Marshal," he breathlessly gasped, "you best come quick, I think Big Red is dead."

Zeke said, "Mike you sit down here and catch your breath." Then he looked at Roberts and said, "Let's go take a look at her."

Chapter Twenty Seven

When Zeke and Roberts entered the Top Hat Heather wailed, "She's dead Marshal, I think she killed herself."

Zeke and Roberts went up the stairs to the make-shift cell that held Big Red. Andy was standing guard at the closed door to the room. He opened the door for them saying, "I think she's dead."

Big Red's grotesquely distorted body lay on the bed, her swollen tongue hung from the left corner of her wide-open froth covered mouth … her face twisted as though she was in great pain. Her eyes were wide-open as they vacantly stared at the ceiling. A pint-sized bottle with a skull and cross bones molded onto its side lay on the floor beside the bed. The bottle's contents was better than half-gone. The washbowl was on the floor beside the washstand, a bottle of ink, a pen, and two envelopes were on top of the stand.

Roberts walked to the bed, lifted her right hand and examined her fingernails … the skin under the nails was a deep purple. Then he bent over and sniffed at her mouth. He detected the odor of bitter almonds. "She died from poison, smells like cyanide."

Zeke picked the bottle up from the floor, held it to his nose and then handed it to Roberts. "Reckon you're right about the cyanide Doc … that's what was in this bottle. But the question is how did she get hold of it?"

"Cyanide is pretty common," Roberts replied. "She could have gotten it most anywhere."

"That's not what I meant. When I locked her in here I searched what she brought with her and she didn't have that bottle then," Zeke said. Then looking towards the door he called for Andy to come in.

Andy entered the room and Zeke asked, "Andy do you know how Big Red got the writing materials and this bottle?"

Andy replied, "She must have got it this morning after I took her to the outhouse. When we came back inside, she asked me if she could go to her office and get some things with which to write. I didn't see any harm in that so I brought her to the office and watched as she gathered what she needed. I saw her pick up that bottle but I didn't pay no never mind to it 'cause I was watching for weapons. I'm sorry Marshal reckon I should've paid more attention to what she was gathering."

"Don't worry about it Andy," Zeke said. "Go get the undertaker, be sure to tell him to bring some help to carry her out of here."

Andy left to get Claudio and Zeke picked up the two envelopes on top of the washstand. One envelope had the name Ian McIntyre wrote on it and appeared to contain several sheets of folded paper. The other one had Zeke Cooper written on it.

Zeke laid the envelope addressed to Ian back on the stand then opened the one addressed to him. It contained two sheets of paper. One sheet had only the name and address of the detective agency that had found Big Red's son for her.

Zeke read the other sheet of paper.

Zeke Cooper,

I believe you to be a man of honor and I am sorry for that which I am about to do. When the details of the killings I have done come out, I will surely be hanged or at the very least sent to prison for the rest of my life. Neither of which do I wish to endure. I feel that justice was served when I killed Captain McIntyre … he was the cause of two of my brothers drowning and he turned me into a whore. Mister Wilson killed my father and I believe myself to be justified in sticking a dagger in his throat before I pushed him over the side into the storming sea. One of the other five men that I killed knew that I killed Captain McIntyre … I killed him to keep him quiet. I killed the other four because it seemed like the thing to do at the time and I wanted their money.

Although I may deserve hanging or imprisoned, I will not have my life ending in that manner. When I finish this, I am going to drink the bottle of cyanide I took from my office earlier. You said that when it's all over that you would see to it that my son Ian would receive that which is mine. There is money and a bankbook in the safe in my office. The numbers scratched on the top of the safe is the combination to the safe in reverse order. I pray that you do as you said you would.

I wrote a separate letter for my son Ian and I trust that you will see that he gets it. For Ian's sake, please bury me under the name Barbra McIntyre.

I thank you and goodbye

Barbra

Zeke refolded the sheets of paper, put them back into the envelope and put it in his pocket. "Reckon she didn't want to be hanged, Doc."

"I'm not sure but what hanging would've been less painful," Roberts replied. "Judging by the way her body and face are contorted she suffered a great deal of pain before dying."

Zeke looked around the room and then said, "Don't reckon there's anything else here that needs our attention, we may as well get out of here."

Roberts left and went to his office. Zeke picked up the letter on top of the stand and went to Big Red's living quarters. When he got there, he opened the strongbox from the California Clipper, placed the letter to Ian in it and then went downstairs.

As he entered the barroom, Heather greeted him. "Marshal we want to give Big Red a decent funeral and burial."

"Fine," Zeke replied, "Andy went to get Claudio, talk to him when he gets here."

Zeke walked to the far end of the bar and had Heather serve him a glass of tequila. He slowly sipped the tequila as he watched the door and pondered on the events since his first arrival in Agua Caliente … and that which was yet to come. Something at the back of his mind kept nagging at him. 'Something ain't right,' he thought. 'I just can't figure what it is, but I reckon it will come to me afore long.'

Andy entered the bar and walked to where Zeke was standing. "Claudio said he'll be here soon as he can round up a couple of men to help him."

About a half-hour later, Claudio entered the bar followed by two men. The two men were carrying what looked like a tabletop with a handle protruding from each corner … it was about two and a half feet wide, six feet long and looked like it had seen better days. Claudio crossed the room to where Zeke was standing.

"Who's gonna pay me Marshal," Claudio demanded, "Big Red is a big woman and I should get more than my standard fee."

Zeke looked at Claudio and thought, 'I really don't like this money hungry little weasel.' "Talk to Heather, she and the other girls want to give Big Red a good funeral."

"Another thing," Claudio continued, "when you had that meeting earlier, you said a large number of outlaws will be attacking the town. How many coffins do you think I will need when it's over?"

With hard, cold eyes touched with a bit of anger, Zeke coldly replied, "You mean the meeting you didn't come to? Are you trying to figure out how much money you can gouge from the town for your services? I would hope that there ain't gonna be a need for any coffins. Of course, if there is a large number of outlaws killed we might just form a burial detail and put all of them in a common grave. If we do that, you won't need a single coffin."

"You can't fault a man for making a living," Claudio whined.

"I don't," Zeke replied, "I find fault with any man that takes advantage of a situation to charge two to three times what he normally gets for the same job."

Claudio turned as if to leave but stopped and turned back when Zeke stated in a low tone of voice, "Just a minute you little piss-ant, I have a couple more things to say to you. First off, I absolutely do not like you. You are nothing more than a greedy little weasel and I believe people like you are nothing more than a boil on the backside of decent folks. Secondly, when you talk to Heather and the other girls it will behoove you to give them a fair price."

Heather was behind the bar at the opposite end, three of the girls were sitting at a near-by table. Zeke watched as Claudio went to Heather and the girls.

Claudio talked with Heather and the three girls for about five minutes … all the while furtively glancing at Zeke. He finished talking to them, motioned for the two men that came with him to go upstairs and then followed them.

Soon after they went upstairs there was a thudding sound followed by very loud cussing. Heather exclaimed, "What was that?"

Zeke responded, "Sounded like their rotten board broke and Big Red landed on the floor."

One of Claudio's men ran down the stairs and out the door. He returned within minutes pushing a one-wheeled cart. He turned the cart around and dragged it up the stairs.

The cart was about two and a half feet wide and five feet long. Except for the wheel, it was made of wood. The spoked wheel was made of iron, about eighteen inches in diameter and attached to the center of the cart at one end. The opposite end of the cart had two handles about three feet long.

Claudio appeared on the upstairs landing followed by his men, one of them pushing the cart. Big Red's body was on the cart, her head at the same end as the wheel and her legs hanging over the other end. They stopped at the edge of the landing and got into a heated discussion about how to get the cart down the stairs.

After a lot of wild gesturing, Claudio started down the stairs. One of the men stood on the first step of the stairs and put his hands against the wheeled end of the cart. With him pushing against the weight of the cart, they eased it onto the first step. As the man in front of the cart took a step backwards to the next step he lost his footing. Falling backwards, he struck Claudio knocking him off his feet. The two of them tumbled to the bottom of the stairs and lay there with their legs and arms tangled together. The other man did his best to hold the cart back but he lost his grip. The cart bounced onto the second step and tipped end over end. Big Red's carcass flew off the cart and somersaulted to the bottom. She landed with a thud on top of the tangled bodies at the foot of the stairs. After tipping end over end, the cart slid, with its wheel pointed up, the rest of the way down the stairway and came to rest against the pile of bodies at the base. The man that lost his grip ran down the stairs and pulled Big Red's body off Claudio and the other one. After they managed to get untangled and to their feet Claudio held his right forearm with his left hand and whined, "My arm's broken."

Heather, horrified at the spectacle that took place before her eyes, reached under the bar and grabbed hold of the six-shooter that was there. Pointing the gun towards Claudio she screeched, "You son-of-a-bitch, you're going to have more than a broken arm." She pulled the trigger and there was a very loud roar. She missed Claudio and the slug imbedded itself in the wall behind him.

Claudio's eyes bulged with terror as his face drained of all color. Holding his broken arm, he ran out the door and down the middle of the road. As he ran, he started yelling for help with a high-pitched voice.

Heather ran from behind the bar with the gun in hand and out the door after Claudio. Soon as she got to the center of the road, she gripped the gun with both hands and took another shot at him. She missed him once again … he jumped into the air and ran faster. She shot four more times stopping only because the gun was empty. The last shot hit him in his left thigh, he let go of his broken arm and grabbed at his thigh as he fell to the ground.

The three girls that were at the table run out behind Heather, one of them grabbed a broom on the way out. The four of them ran to where Claudio lay screaming for help. The girl with the broom whacked him repeatedly, until the broom handle broke. Then all four girls commenced kicking him.

Everybody that was in the bar followed Heather and the three girls. Zeke was the last one out and had intended on taking the gun from Heather but everybody trying to get through the door at the same time slowed him down. By the time he got to Heather, she had thrown the empty gun at Claudio.

As the girls ran toward Claudio, Zeke slowly walked behind them thinking, 'They'll probably whack on him a few times with that broom. It won't hurt him much more and the girls will get their rage out of their system.' By the time he got there, a large crowd had gathered on each side of the road. The girls yelled profanities at Claudio as they repeatedly kicked him. The cheering crowd started betting on which girl would stop first.

One man in the crowd was foolishly brave enough to try to pull one of the girls off Claudio. She stopped kicking, turned around and balled her right hand as she cocked her arm. She kneed his groin and then as he doubled forward she let her fist fly. She hit him square on the jaw and he stumbled backwards. His feet couldn't keep up with his body … he fell onto his butt. She kicked him onto his back and then turned her attention back to Claudio.

Zeke decided it was time to stop the girls, he drew his gun intending on firing it into the air to get their attention. Before he fired, he spotted two three-gallon buckets sitting beside a water-trough. He went to the trough and filled one of the buckets with water.

Doctor Roberts was in front of the crowd close to the trough and as Zeke filled the bucket Roberts said, “I was wondering how you were going to stop them.”

“I don’t consider myself stupid enough to step into that fray,” Zeke replied. “I figure the water might cool them down a bit. There’s another bucket there if you want to help. We can throw water on them from each side at the same time.”

Roberts filled the bucket as he asked, “Do you think we should run after we douse them?”

Zeke replied with a chuckle, “Might be a good idea Doc, but then again those girls can run pretty fast.”

After tossing the water onto the girls, they both took a step back. The cold water shocked them out of their rage and they stopped administering their brand of justice.

Roberts knelt beside Claudio and examined him. He stood back up saying, “Outside of his broken arm he isn’t hurt bad. He has a lot of bruises and the gunshot is no more than a graze. A little salve will take care of that.” Then he bent down, gripped Claudio’s good arm and helped him to his feet as he said, “Get on your feet Claudio and come to my office. I’ll take care of that arm and give you some salve for that bullet burn.”

Claudio struggled to his feet, once again held his right arm with his left hand and whined, “Marshal you have to arrest them, you saw what they did to me.”

“I saw them give you pretty much what you deserved,” Zeke replied.

Claudio spluttered, "What about Heather? She shot me in the leg and I insist that you arrest her."

"Yeah there's that," Zeke said. "But then again that leg wound is no more than a burn from the bullet. It's no worse than an ember burn from your stove."

"You are the only law here," Claudio persisted. "I demand that you arrest all of them."

With a humorous glint in his eyes, Zeke replied, "Seeing that you insist I reckon I'll have to arrest them." Then he turned to Heather saying, "Heather being that he insists that I arrest the four of you I'm going to have to do just that. As he said, I am the only law here at this time and I do have to arrest you. Now tell me, were you trying to hit him or just scare him a little bit?"

"Marshal I was trying to hit that son-of-bitch, but he kept running."

Zeke responded. "In that case your fine will be one dollar for shooting at Claudio and one dollar for missing him. I am suspending both fines for one year, if you shoot at anyone else during that year you will have to pay the fine. As for you other three you're fined one dollar each and those fines are also suspended for one year under the same terms."

The crowd that had gathered around roared into laughter when they heard what Zeke said. Claudio got so mad that all he could do was splutter spit from his mouth while making incoherent noises.

Doctor Roberts took Claudio's left arm and led him towards his office. As the crowd began breaking up, Zeke heard the pounding hooves of a single horse in the distance. Looking up the road to the east, he saw a horse and rider galloping towards town.

Chapter Twenty Eight

As Zeke watched the horseman he thought, 'Probably Lance or Buddy coming to see what the shooting was about.' The rider was soon close enough that he recognized him by the way he sat his saddle …it was Lance.

Zeke turned to go to the Elkhorn and saw Bret standing at the edge of the road, watching the approaching rider. He walked over to Bret.

When Zeke stopped beside him, Bret commented, "That must be Lance or Buddy coming in to see what the shooting was about."

"It's Lance," Zeke replied.

"From this distance he looks like any other rider to me," Bret said. He then asked, "How can you tell from this far?"

"By the way he sits his saddle," Zeke replied. "He was shot in his left shoulder and right side a few years ago and he started riding again before his wounds fully healed. He rode bent to the right as if to ease the pain from the wound on his side. We rode hard and covered a lot of territory before he should've been on a horse again. Now out of habit he rides canted a bit to the right."

Lance slowed his horse as he entered town and dismounted beside Zeke and Bret … Lefty and Thom joined them.

"We heard the shots," Lance stated. "I came to see if we are needed."

"It was just one of Big Red's girls shooting at the undertaker," Zeke responded. Then added, "Big Red killed herself and when Claudio and his men were taking the body out they kind of dropped it down the stairs. Heather got a little mad about that and she took a few shots at him."

Lance drew his six-shooter and fired two rapid shots into the air. "I'm not going back to the lookout today and that was to let Buddy know there's no need for concern."

"I have a nagging feeling that something ain't as it seems," Zeke said. "Lets go to the Elkhorn and talk through what we know, maybe that will jog loose what's bothering me."

"I'll be there soon as I get my horse taken care of," Lance stated as he started walking his horse toward the stable.

Zeke and the rest of them went to the Elkhorn ... Lance joined them about twenty minutes later.

Zeke, Lance, Lefty, Thom and Bret sat at a table in the Elkhorn and began discussing what they knew.

Zeke began the discussion, "We know that this town was under the control of Witherspoon and Forrester for the last couple of years. Under their control, it was outlaw-friendly and among the outlaws that come here is ex-cavalry Major Ryan Cameron ... also known as the Lisping Bandit."

"This town was outlaw ridden for several years before Witherspoon got here," Bret interjected. "The Lisping Bandit and his gang were some of the outlaws that came here long before Witherspoon and Forrester took control of the town. I don't think there is any connection between them."

Zeke asked, "What about Blackie? He referred to Cameron as the boss, but he was working in Witherspoon's hotel."

"Sometimes," Bret replied, "when one or two of the outlaws that come here on a regular basis run out of money, Witherspoon lets them work in the hotel. He doesn't pay them anything but room, board and a few drinks. The only paid help that he has are Ramón and the two Chinese cooks in his restaurant."

"That makes sense now," Zeke stated. Then he continued, "We have nine men in jail, two of them are members of Cameron's gang. We don't know how many men are in his gang, maybe when Segundo comes to his senses he'll tell us. At least six of his gang left town when they found out I was alive and here. Three of his men, Slim, Curly, and the one that Segundo shot, are dead."

Lance asked, "How do we know that the Lisping Bandit is going to attack this town?"

Zeke looked at Lance for about thirty seconds then exclaimed, "That's it, that's what's been nagging at the back of my mind. We don't really know … we have been going on what some of the outlaws that are in jail said. There is no way that they could know what he is going to do. But if he's not going to attack, who was Segundo and the one he killed waiting for?"

They talked awhile longer, going over what they knew and making detailed plans for when the attack happens.

Zeke ended the discussion saying, "We may very well be getting loaded for bear and nothing but a mouse will appear. I'm not so sure that the Lisping Bandit is going to attack the town … but then again who was Segundo waiting for." Then he added, "I'm going to the jail, maybe he can talk sense now."

"Reckon me and Thom will get something to eat then go relieve Buddy," Lefty stated.

When Zeke and Lance left the Elkhorn, the sun had set but dusk had not yet given way to the approaching darkness. Gabby was sitting at the desk when they entered the sheriff's office.

"That sure were some show them gals put on," Gabby said in way of greeting. "Last time I saw a show that good was at the opera house up in Virginia City."

"That was some show alright," Zeke replied with a wry grin. Then he asked, "How's Segundo, has he come to his senses yet?"

"He was still blabbering when I looked in on 'em 'bout an hour ago," Gabby stated. "I think he was trying to say wolf."

"I'll check on him," Zeke replied. "You go on down to the Elkhorn and get the prisoners their evening meal. You may as well eat while you're there."

"Reckon I'll do just that," Gabby said as he got to his feet and headed for the door.

With Lance following, Zeke went to the cells in back, removing the key ring from its hook by the door as he went. Zeke stopped in front of the cell holding Segundo. Segundo was standing by the bars staring out with terror-filled eyes, his tongue licking at the slobber running down his chin. He was making a sound that sounded much like a wounded animal whimpering.

'Don't think that he will be able to talk anytime soon,' Zeke thought. Witherspoon and Concho were in the same cell as Segundo. Unlocking the cell door Zeke commanded, "Witherspoon get out here."

As he came through the door, Witherspoon complained, "About time you got me out of there. You can't keep all of us packed in here like this. There's plenty of room at my hotel, you could lock us in some of the rooms there."

"I have a few questions to ask you," Zeke responded, "maybe I'll consider moving some of you after you give me some answers."

They returned to the office, Zeke pointed at a chair in front of the desk and told Witherspoon to sit down.

Zeke settled himself onto the chair behind the desk. He drew his six-shooter and gripping the handle with his right-hand rested it on top of the desk pointing at Witherspoon. "The last time we talked you weren't very forth-coming." He cocked the hammer of the gun as he said, "For your sake I hope you're more talkative this time."

Witherspoon's eyes opened wide as he nervously licked his lips. With a slight tremor to his voice he asked, "Wha … What do you want to know?"

"If you recall I asked you about your ledgers," Zeke replied. "I know that one of the ledgers records the dates and amounts of money you and Forrester forced the businessmen of this town to pay to you. I know that you collected tribute from the outlaws that came here. Tell me about the ledger that records your dealings with the outlaws."

Once again, Witherspoon nervously licked his lips before answering. "It shows how much they paid to stay here, the date they arrived and the date they left. For each fifty dollars paid they could stay in town for up to five days."

"In other words," Zeke said, "You charged them ten dollars a day."

"No that's not how it worked," Witherspoon stated. "Each gang of outlaws paid ten percent of the amount they had stolen since their last visit. The fee covered every member of that particular gang, if they all came at the same time. However, if some came on one day and some more of the same gang came on another day then both groups had to pay the fee."

"I know that you don't trust them to be honest with you," Zeke said. Then he asked, "How do you know how much a particular gang stole since the last time they were here."

"We get a lot of circulars and fliers at the sheriff's office," Witherspoon responded. "That and the outlaws like talking about other outlaws. When I hear about a holdup, I keep the information in a ledger with the outlaws name, where he did the holdup, the date and how much he got from the robbery. I also mark it on one of my maps."

"On the Arizona Territory map you put a circle around an area that's marked with an x," Zeke stated. "What does that circled x mean?"

"That's where I think the Major has his main hideout," Witherspoon replied.

The door to the outside opened and Gabby entered carrying a bucket of beans and some flour tortillas for the prisoners.

"Put Witherspoon back in his cell," Zeke said. "After they've ate we'll move some of them from here."

Witherspoon stood up from where he was sitting and went back to the cells with Gabby right behind him.

Zeke heard horses outside and got up to investigate. He opened the door and saw Buddy, Lefty and Thom dismounting their horses with their guns pointed at two men that were still sitting on theirs. After getting both feet on the ground, Buddy said, "Okay, the two of you climb down off them horses."

Zeke stepped back as Buddy, Lefty and Thom herded the two men into the sheriff's office.

Zeke asked, "Who are these men?"

"They belong to the Lisping Bandit's gang," Buddy replied. "They just rode up to me as pretty as you please, thinking that I was with Segundo. They planned on meeting up with Segundo and Smokey … Smokey's the one that Segundo shot. They were a bit disappointed when I told them that Segundo and Smokey were already in town." Then pointing at the biggest of the two men he said, "They call him Shorty and this other one is Rio."

Zeke studied the two men as he listened to Buddy. The one called Shorty stood about six feet five inches tall and had a hard packed muscular body. Rio stood right at six feet tall and also had a muscular build.

Buddy continued his narration, "We decided to ride to town together. I had figured on bringing them to the sheriff's office before arresting them. When we met up with Lefty and Thom about halfway I decided it was time to arrest them."

"What about Smokey," Rio demanded. "How bad is he shot?"

"He's dead," Zeke replied. "Segundo filled his belly full of lead."

"I'll kill him for what he did to my brother," Rio exclaimed.

Zeke thought to himself, 'Rio's pretty upset about his brother. He just might be mad enough to give me a straight answer to any question I ask him.' Then he looked at Buddy and said, "Take Shorty to a cell in back." He looked at Rio and pointed at the chair in front of the desk, "You sit down there Rio we're going to have a little talk."

"I want you to know," Zeke began, "I'm sorry about your brother. I was there and saw what happened … Segundo killed him over nothing. They argued about not having any coffee and Smokey wanted to go to town and get some. Segundo killed him to keep him from going."

"Smokey was a might headstrong," Rio responded, "but that weren't no reason to kill him. It was a mighty sorry day when we hooked up with the Major. If we hadn't of done that Smokey wouldn't of been alone with Segundo."

"Why was he alone with him," Zeke asked. "Why weren't you with them?"

"We were close to Carson City when my horse threw a shoe," Rio replied. "I needed to get my horse re-shod and Segundo thought it would be best if all four of us didn't ride there together. Shorty came with me while Smokey and Segundo came on here. We were going to meet close to where we ran into Buddy."

"Where had you been before your horse threw a shoe?"

Rio answered, "We held up the bank in Virginia City. After robbing the bank, a posse came after us. We headed north and lost them in the mountains then we circled back to the south. We were about five miles east of Carson City when my horse threw its shoe."

"Segundo had eight hundred thirty seven dollars in his saddlebag," Zeke stated. Then he asked, "Is that what you got from the Virginia City bank?"

"Yeah, that's what we got," Rio replied. "That damn Segundo just couldn't wait to get here and spend his share on the whores. We had to come here because he wouldn't divvy up the money 'til we got here. I wanted to go back to Post Cameron, get the money the Major owed us and move on."

"Post Cameron," Zeke said, "I've never heard of that … where is it?"

"Post Cameron's located in the mountains sort'a east of Lee's ferry. It ain't an army post but the Major runs it like one. He used to be in the cavalry and he named it after his self. He's the Lisping Bandit but he gets really mad if you call him that," Rio stated.

"How many men are at Post Cameron," Zeke asked.

Rio replied, "I don't rightly know, was only there for a little over three weeks. I'd say the most I've seen is about forty or so at one time, but then I understand that not all of them belong to that lisping idiot's gang."

Zeke asked, "If you believe him to be an idiot why are you with him?" Then he added, "Tell me about Post Cameron."

Rio appeared eager to talk and readily answered, "I don't know the name of the mountains it's in, but they're kind of a light vermillion in color. Post Cameron is in what looks like a box canyon, but it ain't. The mouth of the canyon is about an eighth of a mile wide and is located on the southeasterly side of the mountain. The canyon runs from the southeast to the northwest, it's about three quarters of a mile long and about half that wide. The canyon walls on three sides are steep and about six hundred feet high. Except for where it's been cleared for building, the canyon floor is covered with trees and brush."

Rio continued his narrative, "There's a slot canyon a little better than half-way up the canyon on the easterly side. I just happened to stumble onto it, a thick stand of trees and scrub brush hide it. It runs into the side of the mountain at an angle to the west for about twenty-five feet, and then makes a turn to the north. It starts out about two and a half feet wide then after the turn it widens to fifteen feet or so. About the last hundred-fifty to two hundred feet going to the north, it narrows a mite and then turns into a tunnel. The tunnel's plenty wide enough for a man to ride his horse through with no trouble at all. The northern end of the tunnel is behind a waterfall and the mountain is right near vertical at that point. The top of the waterfall is crescent shaped and juts out about ten to twelve feet."

"Does anyone besides you know about the slot canyon," Zeke asked.

"I don't believe so," Rio responded, "just me 'n Shorty. The floor of the canyon is sandy … snakes and rodents made the only tracks I saw. Everybody I talked to think that they are in a box canyon with just one way in. I don't think that that lisping peacock knows about it either. He has men guarding the mouth of the canyon but nowhere else."

Zeke asked a few more questions and learned that Rio, Shorty, and Rio's brother Smokey had been in southeastern Arizona, where they rustled fifty-two head of cattle. They planned to drive them to Oregon and sell them there. Segundo and five other outlaws rode up on them about ten miles from the Vermillion Mountains. Segundo convinced them that it would be in their best interest to sell the cattle to Cameron and join the gang.

Deciding that he had learned all that he was going to from Rio he turned to Gabby saying, "Take him to the back and give him something to eat. No need to cram him into a cell just let him sit on the floor back there. We're going to be moving some of them in a little bit."

As Gabby took Rio to the back Lance stated, "I've been in that country that he talked about and it's pretty wild. The closest I've been to the Vermillion Mountains is about fifteen to twenty miles. It's about a hard day's ride this side of the painted desert." Then he asked, "Where do you figure on moving some of the prisoners to?"

Zeke replied, "I figure we can shackle them to the posts down at the livery stable. We'll leave Segundo and three of the wounded here."

After the prisoners finished eating, Zeke had all of them except Segundo, Juan, Sanchez and Concho come out of their cells.

After putting leg irons on the seven prisoners Zeke, Lance, Lefty and Buddy herded them outside and to the middle of the road. It was dark when they left the sheriffs office but they could see where they were going by the faint illumination from the light that spilled from the buildings on each side of the road.

When they turned toward the stables Witherspoon stated, "You're going the wrong way … my hotel's the other direction."

Zeke answered him, "You're not going to your hotel … your days of comfort are over. After the judge gets here, some of you will hang and the rest of you will go to prison. In your case Witherspoon, I reckon you'll meet the hangman's rope."

When they reached the stable, Zeke stepped through the doorway, removed the lantern from the hook that it was hanging on and lit it. He led the outlaws to the center-most post and told them to sit around it. He set the lantern on the horizontal beam attached to the post. Then using the extra shackle that he brought with him, he shackled them together … closing the circle.

Buddy stated, "After I go get some grub in me, I'll take whatever watch you want me too."

"We won't need to stand guard over them," Zeke stated. "They won't be going anywhere and they'll be well guarded." Then he raised his voice and called "Spirit!"

Spirit bounded into the stable through the rear door and came to Zeke. He looked up at Zeke then he went to the prisoners and started sniffing at them. He started at Witherspoon, sniffed him then hiked his leg and marked him. He did the same with each of the outlaws in turn … except for Rio and Shorty; he sniffed at them but did not mark them. Then he sat on his haunches about five feet from the nearest outlaw. He snarled at him, licked his lips and with slobber dripping from his mouth emitted a low growl. He then moved to the other side of the circle and did the same.

Zeke noticed that Spirit didn't mark Rio or Shorty but instead lightly nuzzled one of their legs. He thought that's strange and made a mental note to question them further.

With a serious expression on his face Lance asked, "Do you think it'll be safe to leave them here with that wolf?"

"Well sure," Zeke replied, "they're shackled to the post … they ain't going anywhere."

"I wasn't thinking about them escaping," Lance persisted with a slight smile. "I was thinking about that time down in Sonora when Spirit killed a man and ate most of him."

Zeke noted Lance's smile and caught on that he was having a little fun at the outlaws' expense. "It was just that one time and it was several years ago. He hasn't even killed anyone since then … I think they'll be okay."

"Well maybe so," Lance replied, "but I'm still kinda concerned about 'em. Reckon we'll know in the morning." Then looking down at the outlaws sitting around the post he said, "If you stay real still and don't talk too loud he might not bother you."

A white-faced Witherspoon stammered, "Yo ... Yo ... You can't leave that wolf in here with us."

"Reckon I can," Zeke replied as he picked up the lantern and turned the wick down. "The lantern feels like it's about full of oil and with the wick turned down it'll probably burn for three maybe four hours. It'll give enough light so as you can watch Spirit watch you."

Zeke and the others then turned, left the stable and went to the Elkhorn to get their supper.

Bret was in his office when they entered the Elkhorn ... he left the office and joined them for their evening meal.

As they ate, they talked about the events of the past few days and the improbability of the Lisping Bandit attacking the town.

"We need to keep our vigilance," Zeke stated. "I don't think there is a need to post a watch outside of town tonight. We can use the rooms Big Red was living in. The balcony outside the rooms provide a good view of the road coming into town. It looks like it'll be a cloudless night and even though there won't be a moon tonight there will be enough starlight to see to the crest."

"That'll sure be a whole lot more comfortable," Lefty commented. "Me, Lance, Thom and Buddy can take care of that."

Lance, Thom and Buddy nodded their heads in agreement and Lance said, "Even if it clouds up we will be able to hear any approaching horses from a long distance after the town noise dies down."

They finished their dinner and each had a drink as they continued their discussion. After finishing their drinks, Lance stood up saying, "Reckon we ought a' get on over to the Top Hat."

As the other three got up from the table to leave, Zeke got to his feet saying, "I'll walk as far as the jail with you ... Clive and Jackson are probably there."

Chapter Twenty Nine

Zeke finally got to bed and in that twilight zone between wakefulness and sleep, he thought, 'It's not like Spirit to pass up a chance to pee on an outlaw. Why did he nuzzle Rio and Shorty instead of marking them? … I'll find out more about them in the morning.' Then his thoughts turned to Angel as he drifted into a light sleep.

About three-thirty a noise awakened Zeke and he sat up in bed listening. Then he heard it again … it was a slight creaking sound. As he intently listened he heard it once more, but this time he also heard the soft shuffle of horse hooves. He sprang from the bed and hurried to the window. He saw the back of a carriage pulled by a team of horses headed east out of town.

Zeke hurriedly got dressed and went to the Top Hat … instead of going in the door he climbed the outside stairs to the balcony. Lance was standing next to a chair watching the carriage making its way to the east.

"Did you see who's in the carriage," Zeke asked.

"It was the store keeper Jake Quigley and one of the whores," Lance replied. Then he continued, "I heard the door downstairs open and close but I couldn't see who it was from here. I waited a few minutes and then I saw the carriage coming from behind Quigley's store. He stopped in front of here, got out of the carriage and went to whoever it was that had come outside.

They talked for a couple of minutes but all I could hear was a low murmur. Then Quigley came from the boardwalk carrying two good-sized bags with the whore close behind him."

"Do you know which whore it was?"

"I don't recall her name … I believe it was some kind of a flower. From what I've seen of her I'd say that she is one of the least popular ones."

"Reckon that would be Iris," Zeke stated.

"Yep, I believe that's her name."

"I wonder if he took Iris on a business trip with him," Zeke said. Then he asked, "Or did Quigley run off with a whore? Reckon we'll find out which soon enough."

They both fell silent as they watched the carriage. When it was about a mile out of town the carriage sped up and they could hear the horses' hoof beats.

Lance stepped inside and came back with two steaming cups of coffee. They sipped their coffee in silence as they watched the dark outline of the buggy climb the hill.

After the buggy disappeared over the crest, Zeke broke the silence, "The way Spirit reacted to Rio and Shorty has me a bit puzzled."

"I noticed that too," Lance replied, "it just ain't like him. He probably senses something about them and doesn't associate them with the others."

"I've been thinking along that line myself," Zeke stated. Then he continued, "I won't be able to go back to bed now and I reckon that this is as good a time as any to question them."

Zeke left and went to the stable, when he opened the door Spirit and the soft nickering of Blaze greeted him as he stepped inside. The lantern on the beam above the outlaws was still burning. He walked to the lantern and turned the wick up to give more light.

Witherspoon whined, “About time you came to get us out of here. It’s cold and that damn wolf won’t let us sleep.”

“I didn’t come to get you out of here,” Zeke retorted. Then he added with a cold, flat voice, “As for that damn wolf, his name is Spirit and I suggest you remember it.”

Zeke reached into his pocket and got the shackle key saying, “Rio I’m going to take you and Shorty back to the jail. The rest of you stay seated while I release them from the circle.”

After telling Rio and Shorty to stand, Zeke unlocked the shackle connecting Rio to Ramón leaving the loose end connected to Ramón. Then he moved to unlock the one between Shorty and Witherspoon. When he squatted down to unlock the shackle, Ramón clambered to a crouching position. With the loose end of the shackle swinging in his hand Ramón leaned towards Zeke, Rio kicked him in the groin at the same time Spirit clamped his jaws on his arm. Ramón screamed and fell to the ground. When Ramón hit the ground, Spirit released his arm and clamped his massive jaws firmly around his neck. Ramón’s eyes opened wide with terror, just before he passed out.

Zeke had heard Ramón behind him and he fell sideways as he twisted around with his six-gun in his fist. He saw Rio and Spirit put Ramón down and held his fire. He stood up and holstered his gun as he stepped to the unconscious Ramón.

“Okay Spirit you can let go of him, he ain’t going anywhere,” Zeke said.

Spirit released his hold on Ramón’s neck and sat back on his haunches.

Zeke looked at Rio and said, "I appreciate what you did."

"It seemed like the thing to do," Rio replied. "But as it turned out you and Spirit had things under control, I don't think that I was really needed."

"Even so, I don't forget those kinds of actions."

Zeke went back to Shorty and unlocked his shackle at Witherspoon's leg. Then he had the five remaining outlaws tighten the circle so he could shackle Witherspoon to Ramón.

Zeke handed the key to Rio saying, "Go ahead and unlock your shackles while I take a look at Ramón's arm."

Zeke cut Ramón's shirtsleeve off his bleeding arm and used it as a tourniquet and bandage.

Then he stood and said, "That ought 'a take care of him till the doc looks at his arm later."

Rio unlocked the shackles' and threw them in a heap about ten feet away.

Zeke noted the position of the shackles then said, "We're going to the sheriff's office, I have a few questions I need you to answer."

As they stepped through the doorway to the road, the lantern flickered and went out. Witherspoon cried out, "You can't leave us here in the dark." Spirit emitted several low-pitched menacing growls. The only sound following the growls was a couple of whinnies from Blaze.

After their eyes adjusted to the darkness of the night, Zeke had Rio and Shorty walk ahead of him to the sheriff's office. They were about halfway there when the door of the office swung open and light spilled through the doorway as Gabby came outside carrying his rifle.

Gabby heard their footsteps on the boardwalk but couldn't make out who it was in the dark. He stepped backwards out of the light as he called out, "Who's there."

"It's Zeke and two of the prisoners," Zeke replied.

Recognizing Zeke's voice, Gabby stepped back into the light saying, "I put a fresh pot of coffee on a while ago, reckon it's 'bout ready."

After they all got in the office, Gabby said, "Miguel probably has the kitchen at the Elkhorn fired up by now. If'n you don't need me here I'm gonna wonder on down there and get me some vittles. I'll be back soon as I can"

"That'll be fine Gabby. Ain't any need to hurry, take your time."

Gabby asked, "You want me to feed the prisoners down at the stable?"

"Not till after daylight," Zeke responded. "You can feed these here at the jail any time you're of a mind to."

Zeke got a cup, filled it with coffee and told Rio and Shorty that if they wanted some to go ahead and help themselves. Then he told them to sit in a chair in front of the desk as he went behind it and sat down.

After they all sat down Zeke said, "When I talked to you earlier I thought that the reason you readily answered my questions was because of what happened to your brother. When I saw how Spirit acted towards you, it puzzled me, as he usually takes every opportunity he gets to mark an outlaw. I want to know where you came from and more about your dealings with the Lisping Bandit."

They talked close to an hour, with Zeke interrupting a few times to ask a question. Rio and Smokey were originally from west Texas and raised there on a small ranch close to the New Mexico border. Their father joined the confederate army when the war started and came home with his left leg blown off before it was over. Their mother died about a year after their father came home. Their father wasn't worth much after he came back from the war … he drank every cent he could get hold of. He died about three years after their mother did. Shorty's parents, which had the neighboring ranch took Rio and Smokey in and finished raising them.

A train killed Shorty's parents when it hit their wagon. After they buried Shorty's parents the three of them rounded up about one hundred fifty head of cattle and started driving them west. They figured on driving them until they found a good spot to start another ranch.

They were just west of the New Mexico, Arizona line when a group of about twenty-five riders surrounded them. Their leader wore a sheriff's badge and accused them of being free rangers. When they protested that they were just moving their cattle west in search of land for a ranch, the sheriff said that the judge would decide that. The sheriff and half of his men took them to a small settlement called Reeves … the rest stayed with the cattle.

After about five miles of riding, they saw a small settlement ahead. Thirty minutes later, they rode into Reeves, Arizona. The settlement consisted of a small two-story hotel, a saloon, livery stable, stagecoach office, sheriff's office and jail. There were also ten to twelve dwellings. All the buildings were weather worn and neglected to the point of being dilapidated.

They stopped in front of the sheriff's office, which had a four-cell jail behind it. As the sheriff locked them into three separate cells, he told them that the judge would see them in the morning.

Early the next morning the judge held court in the saloon and charged them with free ranging. He lectured them about stealing other people's grass and then without hearing what they had to say he pronounced them guilty. He fined them one hundred fifty head of cattle and sentenced them to ninety days of hard labor.

While serving their sentence they learned that five Reeves brothers owned the town and a five thousand acre ranch that surrounded it. After serving the ninety days, the sheriff and five men escorted them to the west boundary line of the ranch. He threw their unloaded weapons onto the ground and ordered them to leave the territory.

Rio, Smokey and Shorty rode west until they were out of sight of the sheriff. They found a secluded area and waited for nightfall. That night, aided by the light from a quarter-moon, they searched for their cattle. They only had about five hours of moonlight that night and found no sign of their cattle. They searched the following four nights with the same result … no sign.

On the sixth night, after deciding that their own cattle were long gone, they rounded up what they could of the other cattle. By daybreak, they were pushing fifty-one head of cattle toward the mountains to the northwest. They pushed them hard that first day and managed to pick up another four head along the way. That evening they reached the foothills of the mountain range. They found a small canyon and drove the cattle into it.

That night the wind picked up and daybreak showed a sky full of low hanging, ominous black clouds. The cattle were restless, sensing that which would soon be unleashed. Rio, Smokey and Shorty discussed staying put until the coming storm was over.

Suddenly bolts of lightning traced through the angry looking clouds. With a very loud clap of thunder, the sky opened up and started pouring rain down upon them. Fearing that the canyon would become flooded, they decided that it would be best to push on. They drove the restless cattle westward in the heavy downpour of rain. After its initial fury, the rain let up a little bit, occasionally slowing to a light drizzle. Around mid afternoon, the rain stopped and the sky began to clear. They turned the cattle into a more northerly direction and started them up the side of the mountain.

Two days later, they were on the Mogollon Plateau. From their vantage point atop the plateau, they could see a vast desert lay to the north. The sands of which were many different hues of red ... from a dark vermillion to a light pink.

After descending from the plateau, they turned westward and stayed close to the foot of the mountain, where there was food and water for the cattle. A few days later, they ran into Segundo and his men.

Rio finished the narration saying, "Our cattle were stole from us and we were put in jail on trumped up charges. Now here we are in jail again."

The room fell silent filled for about thirty seconds. Zeke broke the silence saying, "You said that you rounded up fifty five head of cattle, yet when you ran into Segundo you had fifty two. What happened to the other three head?"

"The day after we came down off the mountain we ran into an Indian hunting party," Rio replied. "They hadn't had any luck finding any game and we gave them three head."

"You've certainly had your share of bad luck," Zeke said. Then he added, "I figure you were justified in rustling the cattle, but you'll have to stand trial for robbing the bank. Was anyone shot during the robbery?"

"No, nobody was shot," Rio replied. "We couldn't have shot anyone even if we were of a mind to. Segundo had the only loaded gun and our bullets were in his saddlebag."

"Why were your guns empty," Zeke asked.

"When we first met up with Segundo he took our guns and emptied them," Rio answered. "He told us that we would get our bullets back when we leave Post Cameron. He didn't give them back to us until the posse from Virginia City was chasing us."

Zeke was silent while he pondered on what all he had learned from Rio and Shorty. He finally broke the silence, "Give me your word that you won't try to leave town and I'll not lock you back up for now. A judge will be getting here most any time now and after he hears your story, it'll be up to him as to what happens to you. He was a United States Marshal before he became a judge and I believe him to be a fair minded man."

"You have our word on it," Rio said ... Shorty nodded his head in agreement.

"When Gabby gets back we'll head over to the Elkhorn and get breakfast," Zeke said. "While we're there I'll talk to Bret and arrange for a room and grub for you two until your trial.

Chapter Thirty

Zeke waited until Gabby came back to the jail then he, Rio and Shorty left and went to the Elkhorn. A faint glimmer of light was beginning to show on the eastern horizon.

After he ate breakfast, Zeke went to the stable to feed Blaze and check on the prisoners. Both Blaze and Spirit met him at the door when he entered the stable.

From the dark interior of the stable the complaining voice of Witherspoon also greeted him, "Is that you Cooper? It's about time you came to let us out 'o here. We're not animals and you can't keep us here like this."

"You're right Witherspoon," Zeke replied. "You are not animals … you're nothing more than a blight on the backside of humanity."

"You have to at least turn us loose so we can do our morning business," Witherspoon whined.

"Reckon I can do that," Zeke responded. "Wouldn't want you to crap your pants and stink the place up all day."

Zeke unlocked one end of the shackle between Ramón and Witherspoon. He had them move away from the post and lay on the ground in a circle. Then he squatted and relocked the shackle.

Zeke stood back up saying, "You can go do your business now."

"How do you expect us to go anywhere locked together like this," Witherspoon complained.

"Reckon you'll figure it out when you have to go bad enough," Zeke replied.

With a higher pitched voice, Witherspoon asked, "Where're we supposed to go? We can't just do it right here."

"You can go down to the far end of the corral," Zeke stated with a flat voice.

"What're we gonna use to wipe ourselves?"

Zeke looked at Witherspoon for a couple of seconds and then with a cold measured voice said, "There're plenty of horse turds out there. Now get out of here before I change my mind and lock you back around that post."

The outlaws shuffled, cussed and stumbled in one direction then the other. They finally figured out that if they moved in a circle they could drift in the direction they wanted to go. As the outlaws made their way to the far end of the corral, Spirit followed about ten feet behind them.

Lance and Lefty entered the stable and saw the outlaws shuffling and stumbling in a circle.

Lefty asked, "Is that some kind 'a new dance you got them doing?"

With a chuckle Zeke replied, "Yeah it's called the 'gotta go waltz'. They said they had to go and I was of no mind to escort them one at a time. I figure they can't get into any mischief shackled together like they are."

The three of them started caring for their horses. They fed each of them a bucket of grain and put down some fresh hay. Then as their horses ate, they curried them.

Zeke saddled Blaze saying, “After I get that bunch out there shackled back around that post I’m gonna take Blaze out for a good run.”

“You can go ahead and go now if you want too,” Lance said. “We’ll lock them back around the post when they finish out there.”

Zeke handed the shackle key to Lance saying, “I’ll take you up on that offer. Gabby should be here ‘afore long with some food for them.”

Zeke looked to the far end of the corral before he left. Spirit was no longer out there, ‘probably gone to find his breakfast’ he thought.

Lance and Lefty also looked out at the outlaws and Lance busted out laughing. “Look at them,” he said, “the way they’re squatting there they look like a bunch of turkey buzzards circled around their prey.”

Chuckling, Zeke replied, “Well they are vultures.” Then he turned and walked out of the stable with Blaze following him.

Zeke mounted Blaze when they got outside and they headed east at a fast trot. At the edge of town, he let Blaze have his head … Blaze jumped into a full gallop. About two miles out of town, Spirit appeared and raced alongside of them.

As they raced along the roadway towards the crest, Zeke became lost in his thoughts. He pondered on everything that had happened since the stagecoach wreck. The Lisping Bandit came to mind and he thought, ‘That time he challenged me to a duel I should have killed him. Instead, I made him out to be a fool. He ain’t a stupid man, yet he blames me for the consequences of his actions. He’s already killed seven people trying to get me. Looks like I’m going to have to hunt him down and kill him before he kills any more.’

Then his thoughts turned to the outlaws that killed his father in an ambush a little over ten years ago. He remembered the rage and thirst for vengeance that he felt at that time. He also remembered the night in the mountains outside of Prescott, when his burning rage for vengeance died and the embers of justice flamed in its place. 'That night I vowed to use my gun on the side of justice,' Zeke thought. 'I can't hunt him down to kill him, but I will find him and bring him to justice.'

Blaze ran at a full gallop for about a mile then settled into his fast ground-covering gait. Zeke continued pondering on recent events. An image of Angel appeared in his mind, 'At least I found Angel in time to save her. I sure miss that little tyke. As things have turned out I could've kept her with me.'

Suddenly Blaze's gait changed and he came to a stop. They were about five miles east of the stand of trees at the crest. A carriage was lying on its side at the edge of the roadway. There was a body in the road and one on the other side of the carriage. A team of horses still harnessed and dragging their traces was grazing about a hundred yards away.

Zeke dismounted and went to the body in the roadway. It was the whore Iris, her neck was broken and she was dead. Then he checked the other body … it was Quigley. Quigley was still alive … he was busted up pretty bad and unconscious. Then he inspected the carriage and as he suspected the linchpin was missing. "That idiot Quigley was probably in too much of a hurry to secure the linchpin and it worked its way out," he muttered.

He walked back up the road searching for the missing linchpin. He found it in the center of the roadway about fifty yards from the wreck. He picked up the linchpin and examined it. There was nothing wrong with it … it just hadn't been secured properly. He walked back to the wagon dropped the linchpin on the ground then mounted Blaze. He took the coil of rope hanging from the saddle and threw a loop over one of the wagon wheels. Then he wrapped the rope around his saddle horn, turned Blaze around and urged him forward, pulling the wagon back onto its wheels.

Zeke released the rope from the wagon wheel, coiled it and hung it back on his saddle. Then he retrieved the team of horses … outside of a few scratches from being dragged the double yoke was in good condition and still fastened to the end of the traces. After getting the team into position, he used the linchpin to fasten the double yoke to the wagon. On the ground were several pieces of luggage and the wagon's necessity box. Opening the box, he found a large washer and cotter pin, which he used to secure the linchpin in place.

Zeke picked up that which had spilled from the wagon and put it back into it. Going to Iris's body, he picked her up and placed her in the back of the wagon. Then he picked up the still unconscious Quigley and laid him alongside of Iris. He then climbed to the driver's seat, turned the wagon around and headed back to town. Once he got the team moving he gave them their head and they settled into a fast trot with Blaze and Spirit running alongside. When they reached the edge of town, Spirit disappeared.

Quigley was regaining consciousness and moaning loudly by the time they pulled up in front of Doctor Roberts' office.

Roberts heard the wagon pull up in front of his office and stepped outside just as Zeke climbed down from the driver's seat.

"I've got Quigley and Iris in the back of the wagon Doc," Zeke stated in way of greeting. "I found them on the road about ten miles out. Their wagon turned over when the linchpin worked its way out. I believe Iris is dead but Quigley's still alive."

Roberts examined Quigley and Iris then said, "She's dead alright and Quigley is almost there. Help me get him inside and I'll do what I can for him."

Together they pulled Quigley from the wagon, carried him inside and laid him on the examination table. As Roberts began to examine Quigley, Zeke said, "If you don't need my help Doc, I'm going to take Iris to the undertaker. Then I'll stop at Quigley's and tell his wife that he's here."

Roberts replied, "That'll be fine Zeke, when you talk to her tell her that I don't think he'll make it."

Zeke started to the door then paused and said, "By the way Doc there's an outlaw at the livery that could use your attention. It ain't anything dire, Spirit bit his arm last night and I bound the wound to stop the bleeding."

Roberts looked at Zeke and said, "Okay when I finish with Quigley I'll go down and take a look at him."

"Don't go by yourself, one of us will go with you," Zeke said as he continued to the door.

Zeke drove the wagon to Claudio's barbershop and funeral parlor, climbed down from the wagon and went inside. Claudio was sitting on a bench with his wounded leg resting on a three-legged stool.

"You shoot someone else Marshal," Claudio sarcastically asked.

"No," Zeke good naturedly replied, "this one died from a broken neck. She's in the back of the wagon."

"As you very well know I've been shot in the leg and I can't get around too well. She'll just have to wait till I get some help," Claudio replied in a sullen voice. "Who's gonna pay me?"

Zeke took a deep breath then with deliberate and measured words slowly said, "Claudio you ain't wounded, and that bullet just barely grazed you. The burn it left isn't as bad as an ember from your stove would make. It will behoove you to stop feeling sorry for yourself, quit your whining and do your job."

"Who's gonna pay me," Claudio demanded.

"If she doesn't have the money for you to bury her, the town will pay you," Zeke replied. "Now you stop being ridiculous, get out there and get that woman."

Claudio got to his feet and forgetting to fake a limp silently went through a doorway to the back. He reappeared with a cart and went out to the wagon. Zeke helped him take Iris's body from the wagon and put it on the cart.

Zeke then walked to Quigley's store, leading the team and wagon. When he went inside, a woman was behind the counter and she had just finished with a customer. The only other person in the store was a boy in his early teens, dusting the stock on the shelves with a feather duster.

The woman appeared to be in her early thirties and stood about five feet tall. She was very petite, with red hair and striking green eyes. While not a raving beauty, she was quite handsome. Zeke wondered why Quigley left this woman and ran off with the whore Iris. When he approached the counter, she spoke with a soft voice that had a slight Irish brogue. "If I am not mistaken you are Marshal Zeke Cooper, I am Veronica Quigley. My father named me after Saint Veronica and I insist people call me Veronica. The boy over there is my son Patrick."

"Yes I am Zeke Cooper," Zeke replied. "I'm afraid I have some bad news about your husband. I found him about ten miles out of town, his wagon was on its side and he was unconscious. I brought him to Doctor Roberts' and the doc doesn't think he'll make it. Your team and wagon with what he had with him is out front."

Veronica remained silent for about thirty seconds as she absorbed what Zeke had just told her. Then she nodded her head and said, "Thank you for bringing the horses and wagon home. Was that whore with him?"

"Yes she was," Zeke replied. "She's dead … her neck was broken when the wagon rolled over."

"I can't for the life of me understand what he saw in her. Whatever it was, it destroyed our marriage. It's been nothing but a sham since he took up with her." Veronica continued, "I suppose that I should go see about him, although I really don't give a whit whether he dies or not. He snuck out of here in the middle of the night and I didn't expect him to come back. Except for the few dollars that I have hidden, he took all of the money we had."

"I picked every thing up at the wreck that I could find and put it in the back of the wagon," Zeke stated. "The money is probably in one of his bags."

"Some of it might be in his bag," Veronica said. "He also carries a large amount of cash in a money belt." Then she raised her voice and called to Patrick, "Patrick go out front, get the bags out of the wagon and bring them in here. I want you to mind the store while I go to Doctor Roberts' office with Marshal Cooper."

As they walked to Robert's office, Veronica said, "It was hard for me to make a home for my son after Patrick's father died. Mister Quigley pursued me and promised me a good home for me and my son if I married him. I don't want to seem cold and uncaring about Mister Quigley, but truth is he killed any feeling I may have had for him. We've only been married just short of five years. The first two years were good but then he started coming home late at night. I became suspicious and after asking questions, I finally learned about him and his whore. That was about three years ago … I kicked him out of my bed and made him sleep in a different room altogether."

Zeke asked, "What happened to Patrick's father?"

"He was killed using dynamite, we had a small claim about a mile out of town," Veronica responded. "He was blasting a new shaft off of the main tunnel … the blast collapsed the roof and it buried him. He was dead by the time we got him dug out. I sold the mine to one of the men that worked for us and moved into town. The money I sold the mine for lasted me for a while but I had to find work. Mister Quigley hired me to work in his store and we married about a year later."

They soon arrived at Roberts' office … Zeke opened the door, Veronica stepped inside and he followed her. Roberts looked at Veronica from where he was standing by the examination table. "Hello Veronica, I'm sorry but Jake died a couple minutes ago." Then he looked at Zeke and said, "He never fully regained consciousness."

"Doctor Roberts I'm sure that you did all that was possible for him," Veronica stated. "I don't believe his dying is a loss to anyone, least of all to me. Still I suppose it's my Christian duty as his wife to bury him. I'll stop by Claudio's on my way back to the store and make the arrangements."

"I can do that for you," Roberts protested.

"I'll do it myself," Veronica replied, "I have something special in mind for him. Right now I am more interested in the money belt he was wearing."

Roberts pointed at his desk as he said, "It's over there on the desk along with his watch and change purse."

Veronica walked to the desk, picked the change purse up and opened it. It contained three silver dollars and some change. "Doctor Roberts how much do I owe you for what you have done?"

"A dollar will be plenty," Roberts responded.

Veronica gave him a silver dollar from the change purse and then put the purse in a pocket on her dress. She picked up the money belt and told Roberts he could have the watch and anything else that Quigley had. Then she turned and started walking towards the door.

"That money belt looks pretty fat," Zeke remarked. "I'll walk with you back to the store."

They stopped at Claudio's on the way to the store and Veronica arranged to have Quigley buried.

Veronica stated to Claudio, "Jake Quigley is dead and his body is at Doctor Roberts' office. I want you to go get him and bury him. I also want you to put that whore Iris in the same box with him. Before you put either one in the box, you are to remove every stitch of clothing from both. They cavorted naked in life, so they may as well be naked in death. Then I want you to make a headstone with these words on it:

Here lies Jake Quigley and Iris the whore
He betrayed his faithful wife for the ugliest whore in Nevada
Now they can rot together in each other's arms for all eternity

Veronica then told Claudio that after he figured out how much it all would cost to come to the store.

As they continued on to the store Zeke asked, "Are you going to stay here and run the store?"

"Yes," Veronica replied, "Jake did very little around the store for the past two years and I have learned to run it quite well."

Chapter Thirty One

After escorting Veronica to her store, Zeke went to the Top Hat … Heather was behind the bar when he entered. "Marshal Cooper," she called out, "Iris is gone. I think maybe she left with Quigley."

"You're right Heather," Zeke replied. "She did leave with Quigley, he wrecked his wagon about ten miles out of town and they're both dead."

Heather's right hand flew to the base of her throat as she uttered, "Oh no, that's terrible." Then she continued, "I don't, for the life of me, know what he saw in her. The only time she had any work was when we were crowded and every other girl was busy, or when Quigley came in."

Zeke told Heather what he knew about the two deaths and that Veronica Quigley was taking care of the burial.

Some of the other girls started gathering around and while Heather told them about Iris, Zeke left.

Zeke started to the jail but changed his mind when he saw Lance and Roberts going towards the livery stable … he went there instead.

When Zeke entered the stable, Ramón was standing and Roberts was removing the bandage from his arm.

After removing the bandage, the wound started bleeding again. Using his finger Roberts probed and poked the wound on Ramón's arm. He shook his head saying, "This is a very nasty wound and it goes to the bone on both sides. It needs sterilized and then cauterized to stop the bleeding. But on the other hand if he's one of the outlaws that's going to be hanged we can just bind it tightly ... he'll probably last long enough to get his neck stretched."

Zeke responded, "I don't believe that Ramón is going to hang Doc, but he'll go to prison for a few years."

"In that case I suppose we should do what we can for him," Roberts said as he tied the bandage around Ramón's upper arm as a tourniquet. Then he reached into his bag and took a bottle of mescal from it, "I'm out of alcohol but this'll work just as well. If one of you will build a small fire, I can heat my cauterizing iron."

"Instead of building a fire," Zeke said, "we can get the same results with gunpowder."

"Yes that will work just as well," Roberts replied. He should be lying down when we do this, wish we had a table to put him on."

Pointing towards the grain bin in the front corner of the stable Lance said, "We could put him on top of that bin over there."

They unshackled Ramón from the circle of outlaws, took him to the grain bin and sat him on top of it.

Roberts handed the bottle of mescal to Ramón as he said, "You best take a good swig of this ... it's going to sting pretty bad when I pour it on your arm."

Ramón took the bottle, put it to his lips and gulped down a large mouthful and then another before lying down. Roberts took the bottle back and waited a couple minutes for the alcohol to take effect. Then he slowly poured the remaining contents of the bottle on Ramón's arm, thoroughly washing the wound.

Ramón yelped and winced with pain a few times, as Roberts cleaned the wound.

When Roberts finished cleaning the wound, Zeke had already removed the slugs from four cartridges. "Here's the gunpowder Doc, I figure there's enough powder in two cartridges to do one side of his arm."

"You've done this before but I haven't," Roberts replied. "I'll just help Lance hold him while I observe."

Roberts held Ramón down by pressing his shoulders tight against the top of the grain bin. Lance held the injured arm straight out with one side of the wound on top. Zeke removed a match from his pocket and then poured the powder from two cartridges onto the wound. He scratched the match into flame and held it to the gunpowder.

The powder flared and the acrid smell of gunpowder and the stench of burnt flesh filled the air. Ramón let out an ear-piercing scream, lost control of his bladder and passed out.

Lance turned the arm over and with a wry smile said, "I thought outlaws were tough. Look at him, he screamed like a baby, wet his self and passed out."

With a slight chuckle Zeke replied, "They are tough in their own minds Lance just ask any one of them." Then he poured the powder from the remaining cartridges on the wound and lit it. Once again, the pungent smell of gunpowder and the stench of burned flesh filled the air.

Roberts examined the wound and said, "Gunpowder is certainly an effective method of cauterizing." Then he removed the tourniquet, applied some salve to the wounds on Ramón's arm and wrapped a clean bandage around them.

Zeke and Lance carried the unconscious Ramón back to the other outlaws and shackled him back into the circle.

The sky was darkening when they left the stable … ominous black clouds were quickly painting over what had earlier been a clear, blue sky. The menacing clouds obscured the top of the mountain north of town as they roiled on their journey to the south … promising a heavy winter storm. About ten minutes later, a cold, harsh wind roared through the hollow bringing a copious amount of snow with it. The raging storm lasted into late afternoon, at times limiting visibility to no more than four feet.

As the storm raged outside, the saloon at the Elkhorn began filling up. Bret looked over the bar area and saw Clive Baxter, one of the three remaining members of the town committee.

Bret approached the table where Clive was sitting and said, "Clive we need to call a meeting of the town committee. We have some pressing business to take care of. Jake Quigley is dead and Witherspoon is in the calaboose … that leaves you, Roberts, and me. Soon as this storm lets up we'll get the doc down here and decide what's to be done."

The cold, howling wind stopped as abruptly as it had started. The snowfall began to slacken and finally stopped. The sky began sweeping the clouds away as the storm continued its journey to the south. The storm left about two feet of snow on the road running through town. Snowdrifts ranging from three to five feet were alongside the structures of the town.

After the storm moved on Clive went to Roberts' office and the two of them entered the Elkhorn about ten minutes later.

Bret met them as they came in saying, "Let's go to my office, it'll be a little quieter there." Then he added, "We probably ought to ask Zeke Cooper to join us ... he may be able too give us some insight on a couple of matters."

After Zeke joined them in the office, Bret stated, "We are two members short and we need to have a town meeting to elect their replacements. However, two things are more pressing than that ... we need a sheriff and we need to decide where to hang at least two men. We can hang them from the crossbeams at the livery stable or we can hang them from a tree. Zeke knows more on these matters than we do and I believe he can guide us on how to go about what we have to do." Then he turned to Zeke and asked, "How many men do you think will be hanged and how do you figure we should do what needs doing?"

"First of all," Zeke responded, "Forrester already has a death warrant on his head and Witherspoon will most likely hang alongside of him. Judge Randolph Morrison is coming from Carson City to hold court. I don't know much about this judge except he used to be a federal marshal. I only met him once but I figure him to be a man that will judge according to law and on an individual basis."

Zeke continued, "As for where they should be hanged, I would say build a gallows outside the entrance to town where all who come here can see it. You can be certain that word has not yet got around that you will no longer tolerate outlaws. After the hanging leave the gallows standing as a statement to all outlaws that are of a mind to come here. Also those that are sentenced to hang should be hanged the next morning ... unless the judge says differently."

"But we don't know who will be hanged until after their trials," Clive stated. Then asked, "How are we going to know how big to make the gallows?"

Zeke responded, "We know with certainty that Forrester and Witherspoon will be hanged. Two more outlaws will probably go to the gallows and there's a chance of maybe one or two more. I suggest that you build a gallows large enough to handle six to eight men. A gallows is a gruesome sight and the larger the gallows the more gruesome it is. The more gruesome it is the better it will serve its secondary purpose of dissuading any outlaw that comes this way."

After very little discussion, they agreed to build a gallows about a quarter of a mile from the town entrance.

Clive stated, "The old Cascade mine has a large stockpile of lumber that we can use to build the gallows. I'll round up a couple of men and we'll get the gallows built."

Then the discussion turned to hiring a sheriff and Clive remarked, "The sheriff in Carson City can probably recommend someone that we can hire,"

"Zeke, what about Buddy," Bret asked. "What do you know about him and do you think that he'll take the job?"

"All I know about him," Zeke responded, "is that he bought into a fight that wasn't his because he felt it was the right thing to do. He served as a deputy sheriff in Cheyenne for better than a year. I believe that he would make a good sheriff for you. But you'll have to ask him if he wants the job."

"Actually," Bret said, "I have talked to Buddy and I believe that he will take the job if we offer it to him. Being that there's only three of us on the town committee we must all agree whether or not to offer him the job."

After a very short discussion, the committee decided to offer the job as sheriff to Buddy.

Zeke told them that he would find Buddy and send him to them.

Lance, Lefty and Thom joined Zeke as he left the Elkhorn to find Buddy. When they stepped outside and saw the blanket of snow covering the town Zeke remarked, "I don't know about you two but I've seen enough snow here lately to last me a lifetime."

"I agree with you," Lefty replied. "Once we get out of here I don't care if I never see another flake of snow."

"Well, I disagree with both of you," Lance commented. "I kinda like to see a little snow on the mountain peaks … as long as I don't have to be near it."

The sheriff's office was the first place they stopped … Buddy and Gabby were sitting at the table playing a game of checkers. They watched as Gabby cornered and captured Buddy's last checker.

"Buddy," Zeke said, "the town committee wants to talk to you. They're in Bret's office at the Elkhorn waiting for you."

Buddy responded, "They're going to offer me the sheriff's job, aren't they?"

"That's exactly what they have in mind," Zeke replied.

"Bret talked with me a while ago," Buddy said, "and I kinda thought that's what he had in mind. I've pondered a bit on what I would do if they did ask me to be sheriff. I could do worse, but it'll have to be with the understanding that I will be moving on when I figure it's time to do so."

"Every town needs a good, strong sheriff ... especially Agua Caliente," Zeke replied. "Outlaws have had their way here for several years. It'll take a considerable amount of time before they learn that they are no longer welcome here."

"I agree with you on that count," Buddy stated. "Guess I should tell you the reason I left Cheyenne. A gunslinger that had a reputation of being a fast gun killed a man in the street for getting in his way. When I tried to arrest him he attempted to draw on me ... he wasn't fast enough. Then it started, every so often a gunslinger would show up and call me out in an attempt at building his reputation. Instead, my reputation as a fast gun spread and the flow of gunslingers increased. It doesn't bother me much to kill a man that needs killing, but the senseless killing that happens when called out for no other reason than building a reputation got to me. I left Cheyenne to get away from those seeking me out. I told the sheriff that I was leaving and my reason for doing so. He said that he was sorry to see me go but that he understood and wrote me a letter of recommendation." Then he said, "Zeke you are well known for your prowess with a gun. Why don't these wannabe's seek you out?"

Zeke replied, "I used to wonder about that myself and have come to two conclusions. One is I usually shoot to maim rather than kill, no gunslinger wants his career ended by having his shooting hand or arm crippled. That brings us to the second reason ... reputation for not killing."

"I can draw fast and hit a man in the chest," Buddy replied. "But I don't think I could be fast and hit just his hand or arm."

"With practice you can," Zeke responded. "I suggest that you go out somewhere by yourself and practice every day. Forget about speed and concentrate on accuracy. Pick smaller and smaller targets as you become proficient in hitting where you aim. Then when you can consistently hit an object the size of a silver dollar, practice your accuracy with speed."

"I'll take your advice Zeke," Buddy said. "I reckon I'll go meet with the town committee, I'll probably accept the job but they'll have to hire Gabby as my deputy."

"Hold on there Buddy," Gabby exclaimed. "I for darn sure ain't no lawman, besides I got my own place that'll need taking care of come spring."

"You can give it a try until then," Buddy replied as he walked out the door.

After Buddy left Gabby grumbled, "I ain't got no knowledge on how to be a deputy."

Zeke replied, "Gabby you've been acting pretty much like a deputy ever since we started rounding up these outlaws. About the only thing, that you haven't been doing is patrolling the town, watching for anything amiss and getting paid.

Gabby responded, "You mean that I can just kind 'a sit around all day and when I get tired of sitting, wonder around town and say howdy to all the folks. Why I can do that, I thought there was a whole lot more to being a deputy. That's pretty near what I been a doing all my life, but it weren't no job and I never got paid for doing it."

"There's a little more to it than that Gabby," Zeke said. "I reckon Buddy will tell you what he needs a deputy to do."

Buddy returned to the sheriff's office about forty-five minutes after he left to meet with the town committee. In way of greeting he announced, "I've just been sworn in as the town sheriff and they agreed to my having a deputy."

Then he walked to the desk, pulled the center drawer open and took out two badges in the shape of a five-pointed star. One of them had the word sheriff engraved on it, which he pinned to his vest on the left hand side. The other one read deputy. "Hold up your right hand Gabby and I'll swear you in as a deputy."

"Not so fast there mister sheriff," Gabby protested. "When you met with them feller's on that town committee, did they tell you that you will be the sheriff? Or did they ask you to be?"

"They asked me," Buddy replied.

"Well nobody ever asked me to be a deputy," Gabby declared.

Buddy looked at Gabby for about five seconds and realized that he had just assumed that he would want to be a deputy. Then with an apologetic smile said, "I'm sorry Gabby you have been doing such a good job of taking care of things around here, I thought that you'd want to be a deputy. Will you take the job of being my deputy?"

With a big smile on his face Gabby threw up his right hand as he said, "Your darn tootin' I will."

Buddy swore Gabby in as deputy, handed him his badge as he said, "Besides your pay as a deputy the town is paying for your room and board at the Elkhorn."

Zeke started towards the door as he said, "I reckon the two of you have a lot to discuss right now, so we'll get out of here and leave you to it." Lance, Lefty and Thom followed Zeke outside.

"Reckon we ought to go check on things at the Top Hat," Zeke said as he headed in that direction.

When they entered the top Hat Heather was behind the bar dispensing drinks. The Ballard twins were sitting at a table, drinks in front of them and they each had one of the girls sitting on their lap. There were seven other men in the room, two standing at the bar, sipping drinks and talking to Heather. The other five were sitting at a table across the room from the bar, playing cards. Zeke recognized all of the people in the room as some that he had seen before.

They stepped to the bar and ordered a drink. Zeke asked Heather if there were any problems and she assured him that all was well. They finished their drinks and then went to the stable. Someone had filled the lantern with oil and hung it back on its peg by the door.

Zeke lit the lantern and then they took care of their horses before checking on the prisoners. Ramón was conscious and complaining about his arm. The other prisoners complained about being there.

"I realize that you are bored sitting here with nothing to do," Zeke stated as he sat the lantern on the beam above their heads. "Cheer up … I reckon Spirit will be here before long to entertain you."

Chapter Thirty Two

Zeke and the other three left the stable, went to the Elkhorn, and ate supper. Bret saw them when they came in and joined them at their table. After eating Lance, Lefty and Thom went to the Top Hat, too renew their vigil of the night before.

"From what Gabby has told me," Zeke said, "the stage from Carson City will probably be here tomorrow. Do you reckon it'll be able to get through all this snow that got dumped on us?"

Bret chuckled then replied, "Actually I believe it will for two reasons. If you were to go outside and feel the ground beneath the snow, you will find it to be warm. The snow in town, except for some of the deeper drifts, will turn to mud by morning. The other reason is that in the morning Elmer will take his snowplow out and scrap the snow to the side of the road."

"It's a long ways to the junction to Carson City," Zeke stated. "How can he get that distance cleared before the stage gets here?"

"He can't, but he won't need to clear to the junction," Bret replied. The snow on this side of the crest will likely be twice as deep as it is here in town. It probably left no more than a quarter as much on the other side. If the stagecoach is on schedule it'll be here shortly after mid-afternoon tomorrow."

They discussed the phenomenon of the hot springs and the warmth they gave the town. They soon talked of other matters and after about two hours, Zeke called it a night.

After Zeke entered his room, he picked up the rifles he had there and laid them on the table. Then he laid his six-shooter on the table and did his nightly ritual of unloading each gun before taking them apart. He cleaned and oiled each of the guns and then re-assembled them. He carefully examined each cartridge before re-loading the guns. After he finished cleaning and loading his guns, he extinguished the lamp and went to bed.

As he lay in bed his thoughts turned to Angel and then to Little Doe. 'I know Little Doe doesn't show any favoritism among the children but I kinda think that Angel will change that. All of the children have spoiled Zachry and I can just imagine what they'll do with Angel.' As he drifted into that twilight zone between wakefulness and sleep, these thoughts were in his mind.

On the blackboard of his mind, he saw Little Doe surrounded with children with her arms outstretched as though she was reaching for something. Then he saw a man place Angel in Little Doe's arms. Zeke knew he wasn't the man handing Angel to Little Doe but couldn't see who it was. There was a young girl standing by the man but he could not see her face.

Zeke awoke with a start, listened for any strange noises and hearing none decided it was his vision that had awakened him. He lay there and pondered on the meaning of the vision but came to no conclusion. Then he thought, 'I reckon that it'll all become clear to me eventually. At least I know that Angel safely got to Little Doe.'

As he drifted towards sleep, he had another vision. This time he was riding towards a red mountain range. There were five other riders with him but he could not tell who they were. Then he turned his head as if to speak to the rider alongside of him … it was Rio. Rio pointed in an oblique direction toward the mountains. They rode in the direction that Rio pointed and were soon splashing upstream in a shallow river. They came to a waterfall that fed the river. Riding through the waterfall, they entered a large tunnel. The tunnel took them to a slot canyon. They rode through the slot canyon, which gave them entrance into a canyon. The light was murky but Zeke could see several buildings in the distance.

The vision ended and Zeke fell into a deep sleep. When he awoke the next morning, he got out of bed and went to the window. There was a glimmer of light in the east announcing the approaching sunrise. He dressed and headed downstairs in search of coffee. Miguel and Consuela had just arrived and it would be awhile before they had any coffee ready. He knew that Lance and Lefty would have a pot of coffee at the Top Hat and decided to go there.

Blaze nickered a greeting when Zeke stepped out onto the boardwalk. He looked around to see if Spirit was nearby … he wasn't. He noted that snow no longer covered the now muddy road and started to the Top Hat with Blaze walking beside him. When he got there, he used the outside stairs to climb to the balcony.

There was two chairs on the balcony and Lefty was sitting on one with a cup of coffee in his hand.

"That coffee sure smells good," Zeke said in way of greeting. Without waiting for a response from Lefty, he went inside and came back out with a steaming cupful for himself.

Zeke leaned against the wooden railing at the edge of the balcony. As he sipped on the hot coffee, he told Lefty about his visions. Then he said, "I've came to some conclusions about what I saw. What do you suppose it means?"

Lefty was quiet for about a minute as he pondered on what Zeke had just told him. He finally broke the silence, "We know that when you have these visions they pretty much tell you what is about to happen. The mountain that you saw sounds like the one where Rio said Cameron has his hideout. I would say that two of the riders you saw with you are Lance and me. You saw Rio and the other two would be his partner Shorty and maybe Thom."

"That's pretty much the way I see it, I do intend on bringing Cameron in. I don't think that one of the riders is Thom however. He can shoot and if asked would probably ride with us, but he's not a gun-hand. Bob will probably be with us, the telegram I got from him said that he's going to meet us here. My main question about that vision is why are Rio and Shorty with us? I figured that they would be going to prison for their part in that bank robbery."

"Maybe the judge won't see their part in the robbery the way you do," Lefty stated.

"Could be," Zeke replied, "if it was up to me, after hearing their story I would've gave them their horses and told them to ride on. This badge that I carry now and then gets a bit heavy at times, but it does serve its purpose." Then he continued, "What is perplexing about the visions is the one that showed a man handing Angel to Little Doe. After we finish up here, I plan on going to Carson City, get Angel and take home to Little Doe. Then round up a small posse and go get Cameron. The question on my mind is if another man takes Angel to Little Doe, where am I?"

"There could be many explanations to that," Lefty replied.

"Yeah I reckon you're right," Zeke said. "Fretting over it ain't going to do any good."

The sun was just peeking over the mountain to the east of town when they heard the rattle of trace chains. Looking to see where the noise came from they saw Elmer just leaving the freight depot with a four-horse team pulling his snowplow.

As they watched Elmer make his way out of town, Lance appeared with a cup in one hand and the coffee-pot in the other. "Figured that you might be ready for a refill," he stated.

Zeke and Lefty held out their cups so Lance could pour the coffee.

Where's Thom," Zeke asked.

"He's inside sleeping," Lance replied. "He was up all night writing until about two hours ago. Reckon he'll sleep for awhile."

They finished drinking their coffee, left the balcony and headed to the stable to care for their horses. Blaze joined them at the foot of the balcony stairs and walked alongside of Zeke. Just before they got to the stable they met Gabby, he came from the stable where he had tried to give the prisoners their breakfast. He had an empty pail in one hand and in the other a pail full of beans.

Gabby was laughing but he finally managed to say, "Them fellers in there sure don't like you very much and they really don't like Spirit."

"Why do you say that," Zeke asked.

"Well sir," Gabby laughingly said as he tried to compose himself. "Last night it was late when I gave them their supper. I didn't want to wait until they finished eating so I could take the utensils back. Instead of taking plates and spoons, I had Miguel roll the beans into some tortillas and I took ten of them along with a pot of coffee. I poured each of them a cup of coffee, sat the tortillas filled with beans where they could reach them and left."

Gabby's narration was broken up with guffaws but he managed to finish. "When I brought them their breakfast they yelled, 'Get them damn beans out of here.' Going by what they said, Spirit showed up right after I left last night. While they were drinking on their coffee, he ate the tortillas and beans. Reckon them beans gave him gas 'cause not long after he ate them he started emitting some very foul odors. They said after he ate he sat on his haunches, stared at them, licked his chops and growled. All of a sudden, he stood up, came closer to Witherspoon, turned his backside towards him and let out a very long, loud fart. After farting, he turned around, faced them and sat on his haunches, once more staring and growling at them while waiting for another one to build up. When he had another one ready, he went to a different outlaw, turned his backside to him and farted again. He repeated that all night long, giving each outlaw in turn a first hand smell. Some of the farts were long and loud and some were not, but they all had a very foul smell. The obnoxious odor permeated the air and got so bad that Blaze reared up on his hind legs, pawed at the air and whistled shrilly through his nostrils. When he came down on all four legs, he trotted out of the stable."

Gabby paused then continued, "I'd swear that while them fellers in there was telling me about last night, Spirit sat on his haunches listening and he had a very pleased grin on his face … it was almost like a smirk."

After getting his laughter under control Zeke asked, "Is Spirit still in there?"

"He sure is," Gabby replied. "He's having too much fun aggravating them outlaws to leave."

"Spirit does enjoy toying with outlaws," Zeke stated. "Reckon we ought to get in there and take care of our horses."

They started on to the stable and instead of walking beside Zeke, Blaze dropped back behind them. When they entered the stable, Blaze stopped just short of the doorway and neighed very low … it sounded almost like a growl. He stuck his head inside the stable with his nose up and sniffed at the air. Then he whinnied and walked on in.

As Zeke came into the stable Spirit, with his lips curled into a cocky grin, came to greet him. Then he went back to the outlaws, growled at them, turned and went out the rear door.

Witherspoon saw Zeke come in and whined, "You can't keep us in here like this. That wolf of yours has kept us awake every night since we've been here. Do you know what he did last night?"

Zeke dryly replied, "Yeah, I heard. Didn't I tell you that he would entertain you?"

"It's not funny," Witherspoon snapped. "You're treating us like rabid animals. We aren't animals we're men and should be treated as such."

With a flinty hard voice Zeke said, "Witherspoon you need to get a few things straight. I don't consider you animals … I consider you as nothing more than vermin that we'll be well rid of once you're gone. You have led a life that can end in only one way … by hanging. Up until now, when found out you managed to scurry away into the darkness … like the cockroach that you are. A judge will be here any day now and twelve honest men of this town will sit on a jury. They will judge you and we both know what that verdict will be. Justice will be done when you swing right alongside of Forrester. Instead of complaining to me about what you call inhumane treatment, the time you have left on this good earth will be better spent thinking about what you are going to say to God … you'll be meeting him soon."

Zeke paused and then addressing the other prisoners stated, "All of you miscreants will be judged according to your misdeeds. Some of you will be meeting the hangman's rope and some of you will be going to prison. Have no doubt about it, justice will prevail and it will be swift and sure."

Without waiting for a response, Zeke turned and walked away from them.

After tending to the horses Zeke, Lance and Lefty went to the Elkhorn and had breakfast.

It was close to noon when Elmer returned from clearing the snow from the road to the crest.

Evidently, the word of mouth telegraph had done its job well. Thom who was sitting on the balcony at the Top Hat spotted a group of seven riders as they came over the crest. He quickly found Zeke, Lance and Lefty talking with Bret at the Elkhorn and informed them of the approaching riders.

"Maybe Cameron's going to attack after all," Zeke stated. "There's only seven of them, reckon we can handle them, no need to alarm the town."

They left the Elkhorn and started walking to the entrance to town. As they passed the sheriff's office Zeke turned to Thom saying, "Thom step in there and tell Buddy about the riders."

Buddy and Gabby caught up to them just before they got to the town entrance. The Riders were now no more than half a mile away.

As he observed the riders Zeke commented, "They're riding too easy to be intent on attacking this town."

"I think you're right," Bret replied. "Still that big man in front looks a bit familiar, maybe when they get closer I'll know who he is."

"I know who he is," Lance stated. "That's Matt Braddock … we sold him that horse he's riding about two years ago. It's one that Blaze sired with Scar."

The riders pulled to a stop in front of Zeke and the others as Matt called out, "Howdy Zeke … Lance … Lefty, you too Bret. Heard you're getting ready to have a little dust-off with a bunch of outlaws. We're here to join you in the dance."

"Your help is appreciated Matt," Zeke replied. "But I'm afraid you come for nothing, we no longer believe that Cameron is going to attack the town."

"Now that is a shame," Matt said as he and his men dismounted. "I was kinda hoping that we would be getting rid of them critters once and for all."

"We are going to be rid of some of them," Bret stated. "Three of them are already dead and another eleven are fixing to be tried soon as the judge gets here from Carson City. Expect three or four will get their necks stretched and the rest will be busting rocks for a while."

Matt replied, "We'll just stick around for the trial and hangings." Then he turned to one of his men and said, "You hear that Ned, you skedaddle back to the ranch and bring back the buckboard."

Ned stated, "It's gonna be way after dark afore I can get back here. Can't I wait until first light to go?"

"I reckon that you're right," Matt responded. "But you best be sure that you are out of here by first light. Being that you're going tomorrow, you can spread the word of what's happening here. Also, bring missus Braddock back with you." Then he said to Zeke, "My wife is a sister to the Doc's wife … White Wing. Reckon they can enjoy a visit while we're here."

They talked a little more while standing at the town's entrance. Buddy was introduced to Braddock as the new sheriff and Gabby as his deputy. Some of the townspeople began gathering in small clusters as word of the riders at the town entrance spread.

Braddock stated, "Looks like some of your folks are wondering who we are. Maybe we ought 'a go on down to the Elkhorn and set their minds at ease. Bret if I recollect correctly you have some mighty fine sipping whiskey there."

Braddock and his men led their horses as they all walked down to the Elkhorn. Most of the people that they passed on the way recognized Braddock and waved to him as he went by. At the Elkhorn, they tied the horses to the hitching rail in front and went inside. After having a drink or two, Braddock's riders started drifting out stating that they were going to look around the town.

As his riders left the Elkhorn Braddock stated, "Reckon I know where those boys are headed. I doubt that they have more than a dollar between them. Guess I better go talk with Big Red and arrange for them to have their fun."

"You'll need to see Heather," Zeke stated. "Big Red is dead and Heather is running the place … at least until we locate her son."

Zeke then told Braddock how Big Red died and why she killed herself.

Braddock shook his head as he said, "Well I'll be danged, I always felt that there was more to her than she let on. I never dreamed that it would be something like that. She always seemed nice but then it's been a spell since we stopped coming here." Then he explained, "One of Witherspoon's bartenders that goes by the name of Concho shot and killed one of my men 'bout two years ago. Nobody admitted to having seen the shooting and Concho claimed self-defense. I know better, the boy packed a shooter but he was no gun-hand. When I went to Sheriff Tucker, he said that it was self-defense and claimed there was nothing he could do about it. After that we started going to Carson City for our supplies … the trip takes two more days, but no one else is going to die for no reason."

Chapter Thirty Three

It was right at four that afternoon when the pounding of hooves announced the arrival of the stagecoach from Carson City. It clattered through town and stopped at the freight depot.

Zeke was among the crowd waiting to see who got off of the stage. The first one off was a young man that resembled the Ballard twins. He reached back into the coach and helped a young lady out. It later turned out that he indeed was Billy Ballard and the young woman was his new bride.

The next one off was Bob Douglas. Zeke started forward to greet him but Bob reached up and helped a young girl out of the coach. Zeke stopped in his tracks as he thought, 'that's Mei-Ling … what is she doing here?' Then Bob reached up to the coach again and someone handed him a baby.

"Angel," Zeke exclaimed as he rushed to her.

When Angel heard Zeke's voice, she turned her head towards him. Her eyes lit up, she gurgled with happiness and her arms pumped at the air as she reached toward him.

Zeke's heart filled with joy as he took Angel from Bob and held her to him. "Don't get me wrong Bob, I'm happy that you brought Angel but I'm wondering why."

"Randy and I thought would be best to bring Angel and Mei-Ling with us," Bob stated. "We have a bit of catching up to do, let's get inside somewhere and wet our throats while we're at it."

Judge Randolph Morrison was the next and last person to step off the stage. Zeke greeted the judge and then suggested that they go to the Elkhorn.

They went to the Elkhorn after Bob arranged to have their belongings brought there. When they entered, Zeke led them to a table in the dining area.

After they were all seated at the table Zeke commented, "Judge Morrison I didn't expect you for another day or two."

"Unless we are in court call me Randy," Morrison replied. "I had planned on being here tomorrow, I'll let Bob fill you in as to why we came today instead."

Bob cleared his throat then said, "First off I got your telegram stating that you were coming to Sacramento. When you didn't show up, I telegraphed Tucson inquiring as to your whereabouts. Then about a month later, you sent me a telegram from Carson City. Why were you coming to Sacramento?"

Zeke responded, "I received a telegram that I believed was from you. It stated that you needed me in Sacramento as soon as I could get there. I've learned since then that it was sent from Carson City and not by you." Then Zeke told him about the stagecoach wreck and the highlights of what happened since. He finished by saying, "We no longer believe that Cameron is going to attack the town but we do have eleven prisoners to be judged."

Bob listened to Zeke's narrative and then said, "Sounds like the Lisping Bandit has a mighty big hate for you. After we finish with the business here we'll hunt him down."

Angel had went to sleep in Zeke's arms and Mei-Ling had her head resting on her arms on top of the table … she wasn't sleeping but she was close to it.

Zeke stood as he said, "Reckon I'd best get these girls upstairs and to bed." He took them to his rooms and returned about fifteen minutes later.

"Reckon the trip tuckered them out," Bob stated when Zeke returned. Then he continued, "I arrived in Carson City a few hours after you and Thom left. When I visited with Randy, he told me what you're doing here and that he planned to come here tomorrow. I told him that I would hang around Carson City until he was ready to leave, figuring that we could rent a buggy and come together. I spent the time visiting with the different folks that I know there. I ran into the sheriff, Marc Hansen, as he was leaving the telegraph office … he didn't look very happy. When I asked him what was troubling him he told me about Mei-Ling. He also told me that the whoremonger Luke Leighton arrived in Carson City the day before. Right after Leighton arrived in town he went to the sheriff's office. He stated that he knew where Mei-Ling was at, demanded that Marc go get her and return her to him. Instead of going to get Mei-ling Marc arrested Leighton on the charge of being an escaped convict. He sent a telegram to the federal authorities in Virginia informing them that he had Luke Leighton. Then he handed me the telegram that he had just received. It informed him that they had recaptured Luke Leighton about four years ago and hanged him for his part in killing the guards during the escape."

Bob paused, took a sip of the whiskey in front of him and then continued, "Marc and I talked over what could be done. We decided that he would keep Leighton locked up until I could get Mei-Ling away from there. I rented a buggy and went out to the Boleyn's place.

When I saw Mei-Ling and Angel together, I instinctively felt that I should bring them both with me. When I got back to Carson City, I left Mei-Ling and Angel in my hotel room and went to see Randy. I told him that I had Mei-Ling and Angel with me and why."

Randy interrupted Bob saying, "Legally Mei-Ling belongs to Leighton and the law recognizes his right to take her. As a judge, I stand for and enforce the law. However, the reason I became a judge is that too many times I saw the letter of the law enforced in an unjust manner. The letter of the law is harsh and has no compassion, but the man sitting in judgment must consider each case on its own merit, judge accordingly and bend the law when facts dictate. I figure it will only be a matter of time before Leighton files papers in a court of law to claim Mei-Ling. Once he does that, it will give me legal notice of his claim on her and I would have to find in his favor. Without having received legal notice, I am able to ignore that bit of unjust law and do what I consider best for the child."

They discussed the merits of the law for a while then the subject turned to the prisoners. After consulting with Bret, they decided that the largest room in town was the barroom at the Top Hat. Zeke, Bob and Randy left the Elkhorn after Randy stated that he wanted to look at the barroom.

When they entered the Top Hat, Heather was behind the bar and talking with Braddock as he sipped on the drink in front of him. The Ballard twins were sitting at a table with two girls. Two girls seated at another table were vacuously staring around the room. The rest of the girls were upstairs taking care of their customers needs.

Zeke informed Heather as to the reason they were there. Randy looked around the room and then walked up onto the stage. He stood there, nodded his head a couple of times and said, "This room will work quite well. We will need to rig something to serve as a desk."

"There's a desk in the office," Zeke responded. "We can place it anywhere you're of a mind to have it."

"Good, we'll set this place up as a court of law in the morning," Randy replied. "Court will start at ten sharp, at which time a jury will be selected. We also need someone to record the proceedings."

Zeke talked to Heather and told her that during the court proceedings she had to close. He then asked her if she would take notes of the court proceedings and she readily agreed.

The sun had been in the sky for about an hour the next morning when Clive and four men left town. They had a wagon loaded with timber and lumber that they had taken from the stockpile at the defunct Cascade mine.

About eight-thirty, Judge Randolph Morrison walked into the Top Hat and supervised the task of turning the barroom into a courtroom.

They took the desk from Big Red's office and placed it on the stage. After trying several locations for the desk, Randy settled on having it centered at the front edge of the stage. An area to his right, next to the bar was set up for the jurors. After removing all the tables from the barroom, they scavenged up more chairs to fill in the vacant spots.

The room started filling up with the townspeople around nine-thirty and some of them helped where they could. As the room filled, it became loud and boisterous.

Zeke and Randy had already discussed the prisoners, what they had done and the order in which they would proceed into court. At Ten O'clock Judge Randolph Morrison, with a six-gun strapped to his right hip, mounted the steps onto the stage and stood behind the desk. He had placed a gavel on the desk earlier, which he now picked up and rapped it on the desktop bringing the room to silence.

After the room fell silent, Judge Morrison took about thirty seconds and looked around the room, locking eyes with several of the men there. Then he pulled his six-gun from its holster and held it at his side as he said, "Gentlemen my name is Judge Randolph Morrison and even though this establishment is a whorehouse, this room is now a federal courtroom and you will give it the respect it demands. I will tolerate no outbursts, profane language or disrespect of any kind against the court or the prisoners." Then he laid his gun onto the desktop saying, "Before I became a judge, I was a deputy United States Marshal. I assure you that I do know how to handle this gun and will do so if I deem it necessary."

Morrison let the silence build in the room and then broke it saying, "The first order of business will be to pick a jury. Bret Stevens, do you believe that you can judge a man with an open, impartial mind?"

"Yes your honor I believe that I can," Bret replied.

"Very well," Morrison said. "You are now the foreman of the jury and as such you will pick eleven honest men to sit in judgment with you."

As Bret started picking eleven men, Morrison motioned Zeke and Bob to his side. "Zeke you and I are the only federal officials here and normally I would appoint you as the prosecutor. Because you have more knowledge than anyone here does about what each of the outlaws has done, you'll have to testify against each of them." Then he looked at Bob and said, "If you'll do it, I need you as the prosecutor."

Bob replied that he would serve as prosecutor. Morrison then told Zeke to bring in the first of the prisoners.

The first into court would be Rio and Shorty … they were waiting at the sheriff's office. Zeke walked off the stage and to where Buddy was standing. He gave Buddy the order in which the outlaws would appear. Then Buddy left to get Rio and Shorty.

Bret had just completed choosing the jury when Buddy returned with Rio and Shorty.

Rio and Shorty stood before the judge as Bob stated that the charge against them was robbing the bank in Virginia City. When asked how they pled they both answered guilty.

"Being that both of you have pled guilty, the only thing left for me to do is to give you your sentence," Judge Morrison stated. "This court sentences you to five …."

Zeke interrupted, "Just a minute your honor, before you sentence them I believe there to be extenuating circumstances in their case that you should hear first."

Judge Morrison gave Zeke a hard look as he asked, "Just what are those circumstances Marshal Cooper?"

Zeke narrated what Rio and Shorty told him had happened to them since they left Texas.

Judge Morrison listened intently and after Zeke finished he looked at Rio and Shorty asking, "Is what he said on your behalf the way it is?"

Both of them replied that what Zeke said was pretty much the way it happened. Morrison banged his gavel on the desktop and said "Court is in recess for thirty minutes. Marshal Cooper I'll see you in Big Red's office.

After they entered the office, Morrison shut the door behind them. Then he asked, "Zeke why did you not tell me about Rio and Shorty before we came to court?"

"Well Randy," Zeke replied, "I have two reasons for not telling you. One is that I did not want to influence your judgment of them. The second is that I wanted to see if they would accept the responsibility for their actions with out making excuses."

"I was going to sentence them to five years at hard labor," Randy said, "but now I have something else in mind. It appears that you, Shorty and Rio have an enemy in common. They know exactly where the Lisping Bandit's hideout is and could lead you there. If you want to use them for that purpose, I'll place them in your custody."

After Zeke stated that he would accept custody of them, Morrison said, "If you don't have any more surprises for me let's get back to the courtroom."

They went back to the courtroom and Morrison sat down behind the desk. He ordered Rio and Shorty to stand once again.

They stood and Morrison stated, "I was going to sentence you to five years at hard labor. Due to your circumstances as to why you were there, I am sentencing you to two years of hard labor. However, I am suspending that sentence and placing you in Marshal Cooper's custody on the condition that you lead him to the Lisping Bandit's hideout. When I am notified that the Lisping Bandit has been brought to justice your sentence will be vacated and all records of these proceedings will be destroyed."

Rio and Shorty looked at each other in disbelief, then Shorty said, "Me and Rio will certainly live up to our end of that bargain your honor."

Chapter Thirty Four

The next prisoners brought in were Ramón and Sanchez. They pled not guilty but the jury found them guilty of attempted murder. Morrison considered their past and sentenced them to fifteen years at hard labor.

Zeke watched as Buddy brought Segundo in and escorted him to where he would stand before the judge.

As Zeke observed Segundo shuffling across the floor, he noted that his shuffle was not quite the same as it had been and he thought, 'He's faking it, he's regained his senses.' Then looking at Segundo's eyes he saw that they were no longer filled with terror … they had more of a crafty look as he darted them from one side to the other. His slack-jawed slobbering had also stopped.

Bob stated, "Segundo is charged with murder and is also second in command to the Lisping Bandit."

When asked how he pled, Segundo gestured wildly around the room and uttered, "Wu … Wu … wooooof."

"What is he trying to say," Judge Morrison demanded.

"He's faking that he's trying to say wolf," Zeke responded. "He was scared senseless awhile back but I believe he has come back to reality and that he is just pretending to be crazy.

Morrison asked, "How do you know that he's just pretending to be crazy?"

Zeke responded, "When he actually was scared senseless his eyes were terror filled, he was slack-jawed and he slobbered drool all over himself. Now his eyes are no longer terror filled … they have a crafty look about them. He is not slack-jawed now nor is he slobbering."

Judge Morrison nodded his head then looking at Roberts said, "How about it Doctor Roberts, is what Marshall Cooper said possible?"

"Well your honor," Roberts replied, "I know that when Segundo was brought in he was a babbling idiot. He looks saner now than he did a couple of days ago. I would need to observe him for a day or two in order to say with any certainty one way or the other."

Zeke closely watched the expression on Segundo's face as Roberts spoke. He saw the right corner of his mouth twitch.

"Your honor," Zeke called out, "I can prove right now that he is faking it."

Judge Morrison asked, "Just how will you do that?"

"Spirit is the wolf that scared him senseless I can call him in here an …"

"No," Segundo blurted and then threw his left hand over his mouth as he realized what he had just done.

With a slight smile toying at his lips Judge Morrison stated, "Marshall Cooper it appears that you just proved Segundo to be faking." Then he looked back to Segundo and stated, "You are charged with murder. How do you plead?"

With a half-hearted attempt at a snarl Segundo replied, "You ain't gonna be able to prove a thing on me."

Morrison banged his gavel on the desktop and said, "Seat the prisoner and call the first witness."

Segundo sat down on the chair that Buddy led him to as Bob called for Zeke to take the stand.

"Marshal Cooper," Bob said, "tell us where you first saw Segundo and what you witnessed?"

Zeke told the court where he first saw Segundo and what he witnessed.

Segundo yelled out, "That were self-defense, he was a gonna shoot me!"

"Is that right Marshal," Bob asked. "Was it self-defense?"

"In my opinion no," Zeke responded. "Segundo goaded Smokey into drawing on him."

After Zeke completed testifying, five more people testified against Segundo. Their testimony accused Segundo of six murders that they had witnessed on different occasions.

The jury, after deliberating for two and a half minutes, found Segundo guilty of seven killings.

Morrison rapped his gavel and stated, "The prisoner will stand." Segundo got to his feet and Morrison stated, "Segundo you have been found guilty of seven murders. At sunrise three days hence, you will hang by your neck until you are dead." He then announced that the court would be in recess for one hour.

Zeke, Randy, Bob, Bret, Lefty and Lance headed for the Elkhorn, intending to get something to eat.

When they left the Top Hat, Zeke commented, "It appears that there's a lot more people in town now than there was earlier. I reckon Braddock's rider spread the word of what is going on here."

Ned, Matt Braddock's rider, left town an hour before daybreak. As he rode to the ranch, he spread the news of what was going on in Agua Caliente. He arrived back just before mid-day, driving a buckboard with Mrs. Braddock on the seat beside him. Three men on horseback rode alongside of the buckboard. The cowboy telegraph was in good working order and people began drifting into town.

"Agua Caliente will be crowded by the time this business is over and done with," Randy stated. "By setting the hanging date three days from now it'll give time for word of a hanging to spread and people will start showing up to watch. It is my belief that a well witnessed hanging is as effective as a gun in enforcing the law."

"I believe you're right," Zeke replied. "However I do believe that it will serve us well to know who is coming into town. We should post a couple of men at the town entrance to learn who they are."

Lance spoke up saying, "You don't need Lefty and me in the courtroom … we'll do it."

"Actually that'd be one of the sheriff's duties," Zeke stated. "Best talk to him about it first. Also, if someone like Gabby or maybe one of the Ballard boys was with you it will make it a lot easier as they will know a lot of the people coming in."

They entered the Elkhorn … Buddy sat with them. As they ate their late lunch, they discussed the wisdom of posting a couple of men at the town entrance to check out any newcomers. They decided that Lance, Lefty and Gabby would greet every one coming into town.

After Judge Morrison called the court back into session, Juan was brought in tried and found guilty of murdering at least three men that the witnesses could testify to … he was sentenced to hang.

Pete and Concho were called next … they too were found guilty of multiple murders and sentenced to hang.

The next and last to be called in were Witherspoon and Forester. The charge against Witherspoon was robbery and murder. When asked how he pled, Witherspoon pompously responded, “Your Honor these scurrilous accusations against me are entirely untrue. I am a well-respected businessman in this community and also the head of the town committee here. The unscrupulous actions of Marshal Cooper since he arrived here is outrageous. He locked up Sheriff Tucker claiming that he was someone by the name of Forrester. Sheriff Tucker is a good, honest man. Outlaws infested this town when he became sheriff and he brought them under control. After Cooper falsely arrested Sheriff Tucker and locked him in jail, he intimidated the entire town for his own evil purpose. I demand that you release us immediately and place Cooper under arrest.”

An explosion of laughter erupted when Witherspoon finished speaking and the judge banged his gavel on the desktop to silence the courtroom.

The courtroom finally fell silent and Judge Morrison stated, “I’ll take that as a not guilty plea.” Then as he gestured towards the defendants chair added, “Now you sit in that chair while we proceed.”

“Bu … Bu … But,” Witherspoon sputtered.

Judge Morrison banged the gavel, silencing Witherspoon and said, “But nothing, sit down on that chair as you were told.” Then he looked at Forrester and said, “State your name.”

“It’s Sam Forrester your honor.”

“Are you aware that there is a death warrant on your head and you will be hanged,” Morrison asked.

"Yes sir," Forrester replied. "I am ready to accept what I am due."

Morrison instructed Forrester to sit on the witness chair and Bob asked, "How long have you and Witherspoon been partners?"

"Ever since we deserted from the army," Forrester replied. "Reckon that's been ten maybe twelve years ago."

Witherspoon jumped to his feet shouting, "That's a lie!"

Morrison pointed a finger at Witherspoon and sternly stated, "Sit down … I will not tolerate outbursts like that in my court." Then he continued, "Sheriff if he disrupts this court again you stuff a rag in his mouth and if that doesn't work, whack him alongside the head."

Witherspoon meekly sat back down and Bob continued, "Were you coerced into giving evidence against Witherspoon?"

I don't rightly know what that word korst means," Forrester replied.

"I'll ask you in a different way," Bob said. "Why are you testifying against Witherspoon?"

"I kind 'a figure that me and him been partners for so long that we should swing together," Forrester stated. "Besides most o' the stealing and killings were his ideas. He told me that with his brains and my gun we would get rich."

With a few questions from Bob, the jury heard about the life of crime that Sam Forrester and Jared Witherspoon lived. The only murder that Witherspoon actually committed himself was the killing of the sheriff in Virginia City.

The jury, after deliberating for less time than they did with Segundo, declared Witherspoon guilty of murder, robbery and numerous other crimes both known and unknown.

Upon hearing the verdict, the crowd in the courtroom broke into raucous approval.

Morrison banged his gavel on the desk many times before the crowd fell silent.

Then he commanded Witherspoon to stand. "Jared Witherspoon you have been found guilty of murder, robbery and other crimes … at sunrise three days hence, you will hang by your neck until you are dead."

"Nooooo," Witherspoon wailed, "you can't hang me."

Judge Morrison stated, "Actually I can … you will hang. I also declare that all of your property, real and personal, now belong to the town of Agua Caliente. Sheriff, get Witherspoon and Forrester out of here."

As Buddy escorted Witherspoon and Forrester out of the courtroom, the voices of the spectators began to fill the room. Judge Morrison rapped on the desktop with his gavel until once again there was silence.

"This court is still in session," Morison declared. "We have the matter of Ryan Cameron who is known as the Lisping Bandit to consider. We are going to try him and unknown others in absentia … Marshal Cooper take the stand and tell us what you know about the stagecoach wreck that he caused."

Zeke took the stand and started his testimony. "I received a telegram that said I was urgently needed in Sacramento … I believed it had been sent by Bob Douglas. I have since learned that Bob didn't send the telegram and that it was actually sent by Cameron from Carson City."

Zeke told them about the man that left the way station in a big hurry the evening before the wreck. He described the scene of the wreck and that he saw the backs of seven men walking away from the edge of the cliff that he was laying at the bottom of.

"You saw the backs of seven men," Bob stated. "Could there have been more?"

"I only saw the seven as they walked away from the cliff's edge," Zeke stated. "I can't say for sure, but as they rode their horses away from there it seemed like there were more."

"How many people were killed in the wreck," Bo asked.

"Seven people were killed and I buried them there," Zeke responded.

With Bob asking questions, the court heard the string of events leading up to Zeke getting to Aqua Caliente and his recovery from temporary amnesia. He told of the events pertaining to Cameron that happened since his arrival.

Zeke completed his testimony and Bob called Thom Langley to the stand. He had Thom state his name and then asked, "What brought you to Agua Caliente?"

Thom replied, "I am a writer of short stories and novels, I also send news reports to several newspapers back east. I was in Carson City gathering background for a book when a man told me that Zeke Cooper died in a stagecoach wreck. When I asked him where the wreck happened he said he wasn't sure, but that he heard about it here in Agua Caliente. So I came here hoping to learn more about it." He then narrated what he had learned from members of the Lisping Bandit's gang.

Thom finished his testimony and Judge Morrison turned to the jury and said, "You are sitting in judgment of Ryan Cameron and men unknown. Even though they are not here your judgment is just as final and binding as if they were."

The jury deliberated for just under ten minutes and found Ryan Cameron and unknown others guilty of at least seven murders.

Upon hearing the verdict, Morrison pronounced their sentence. "Ryan Cameron and unknown others having been judged and found guilty of murder in open court and in absentia are hereby sentenced to death by hanging."

Then he banged the gavel and declared the court closed. The desk was taken back to the office, the extra chairs removed and the tables placed back into there positions. The courtroom was once again a barroom in a whorehouse.

It was dusk when Zeke, Bret, Bob and Randy left the Top Hat … the piano started playing as they walked out the door.

As they stepped out onto the boardwalk, five riders dismounted and tied their horses to the hitch-rail in front of the Top Hat.

Bret looked up and down the road running through town and said, "By the time we get the hanging done this town is going to be bursting at the seams."

"That will be good," Randy stated. "That means there will be a large audience to witness the hangings. Each time someone tells the story of what they saw here it'll be stretched a bit more. I'd wager that two years from now when you hear the story you won't recognize it."

"Judging by the number of horses tied at the hitching-rails," Zeke said, "I'd say that there are at least thirty more people in town now than there were this morning. I reckon we're going to have to move the prisoners from the stable. I'll meet up with you later at the Elkhorn …

I'm going to the sheriff's office and talk to Buddy about where to move them."

Buddy was sitting behind his desk, sorting through some fliers when Zeke entered. He looked up and stated, "That was the fastest court proceedings I ever witnessed. Eleven men tried and convicted … all in less than a day. Reckon that's what you'd call swift justice."

"I doubt that you could find any one in this town that hasn't witnessed the shooting, killing or maiming of someone by one or more of those tried," Zeke responded. Then he continued, "With all the people that will be coming to town we are going to need to move the prisoners from the livery stable back to the jail."

Zeke and Buddy went to the stable and brought the prisoners back to the jail. They put Forrester in the cell with Segundo, Blackie with Juan and Ramón with Sanchez. Witherspoon, Pete and Concho shared the fourth cell. After locking the prisoners in their cells, Zeke and Buddy went back to the office.

As Zeke started toward the door leading outside he stated, "I plan on leaving soon as the hangings are done with. The way this town's filling up, I reckon that you may be needing help. If so, you can count on me, Bob, Lance and Lefty at anytime."

"I'll keep that in mind," Buddy replied.

Zeke left the sheriff's office and went to the Elkhorn. When he got there, he joined Bret, Bob and Randy in Bret's office. The maps that came from Witherspoon's office were lying on top of the desk and Randy was holding one of the ledgers. They were comparing the ledger's entries to the locations marked on the maps.

In way of greeting Zeke as he entered the office, Bret stated, "By using these maps and Witherspoon's ledgers we figure that we can return about half of the money that he had to its rightful owners."

"What do you figure on doing with the hotel and the rest of the money," Zeke asked.

"That'll be up to the town committee, but we're going to have to elect two more members before that can be decided," Bret replied. "Randy thinks we should incorporate and become a proper town. We'll have an election after the town quiets down and the townspeople can decide if they want to incorporate."

Zeke changed the subject, "I want to leave to go after Cameron soon as the hangings are over. I reckon I can get Doc Roberts to watch over Angel and Mei-Ling while I'm gone."

"No need to ask him," Bret said, "Angel and Mei-Ling are in the kitchen with Consuela right now. She has been mothering them since they got here and I'm certain that she'll be happy to continue watching over them until you return."

"Now that we have that settled," Bob said, "I'll find a horse and come with you.

Zeke stated, "Let's go eat supper and then we'll round up a horse for you."

Before they left the office Randy said, "Zeke I am going to issue a death warrant with Ryan Cameron's name on it. Since we don't know for sure just how many men were with him, I am also issuing twelve John Doe death warrants. Before you execute any of the John Doe warrants, you must be certain that they were there when that stage was wrecked."

Then he turned to Bob saying, "Bob being that you are going with Zeke I am temporarily reinstating you as a federal marshal. When you capture Cameron and whoever else was involved in wrecking that coach, you both must agree that you have the right one's before you hang them."

The four of them left the office and went to the dining area where they joined Lance, Lefty and Thom.

"I'm leaving right after the hangings to go after the Lisping Bandit," Zeke declared as he sat down.

"Lefty and I are going with you," Lance stated. "How about you Bob, are you coming with us?"

"If I can round up a horse I am. Going to see what I can find after we finish eating," Bob replied.

"You can take my horse," Thom stated. "I'm not a gun-hand so I'll not be going with you. I figure I'll go to Tucson after I gather a little more background material here. Instead of riding my horse, I'll take the next southbound stage to Ehrenberg and catch the paddlewheel from there to Yuma. Then I'll take the stage from Yuma to Tucson."

Then he added, "Zeke if you would like for me too I'll take Angel and Mei-ling with me and deliver them to Little Doe."

"That's a good idea Thom," Zeke replied. "Mei-Ling needs to get out of Nevada as quickly as possible … once she's at Silver Wolf she'll be safe."

Chapter Thirty Five

The town took on a carnival-like atmosphere over the next two days as it filled with people. They arrived by horseback, buckboard, wagon, and carriage. They arrived individually, in groups and entire families. By evening of the first day after the trial, there was not a room available. Some of the townspeople rented out rooms in their residence. A temporary camp appeared just outside of town.

George Lashley, the marshal from Carson City, came into town with a prison wagon mid-afternoon of the day before the hangings. He stopped at the sheriff's office told Buddy who he was and that he brought a prison wagon just in case there were any prisoners to transport.

Another wagon rolled into town right behind the marshal's prison wagon. The wagon, completely closed in served as living quarters for the driver. The driver climbed down from his seat on the wagon, removed the duster that he was wearing and tossed it onto the driver's seat. He stood just over six feet tall and had an angular body. He was wearing a black top hat, a black coat with long tails and a black bow tie. He stood on the boardwalk beside his wagon, chewing on a cigar butt as he observed the bustling all around him. He turned, tossed his cigar butt onto the ground and then with a wry grin on his face he entered the sheriff's office.

When he entered the sheriff's office, he looked at Buddy and then with his left hand removed his top hat with a flourish. He bent his angular frame forward in a bow and held his right arm out as he said, "My dear sir I am Quincy Nathanael Montgomery." Then he straightened up and said, "I am a hangman extraordinaire and it is my understanding that you are in need of my services."

Buddy thought about his first day in Cheyenne … there was a hanging that night and Quincy was the hangman. The two outlaws he hanged that night had robbed the bank and killed a bank customer in the process. Quincy entertained the crowd gathered at the gallows for about two hours before the hanging.

"I know who you are Quincy, I saw you in Cheyenne a while back," Buddy stated. Then he asked, "How did you know that we are going to have a hanging?"

"Well sir," Quincy replied, "there are possibly three explanations to that … maybe more. First off, I have a nose for this sort of thing. Second, you can't keep a multiple hanging quiet. Then there's the third reason, the marshal here told me up in Carson City that you might be in need of my services."

With a slight chuckle Buddy replied, "However you heard about it, we are going to have a hanging. How much is a hanging worth?"

"Well now that all depends on several things," Quincy replied. "If you want a number one deluxe, first class hanging it'll cost you twenty dollars a head. Those twenty dollars includes a hood and new rope. If you want preaching and gospel singing before hand, it'll cost you two bits a head more. If the person that's getting hanged fights it, it could cost as much as another five dollars … depending on whether or not I have to knock him out first. Now mind you that doesn't happen very often but it does happen now and then."

Buddy replied, "I'll have to talk to the town committee about your fee. I don't rightly know how much the town is willing to pay for a hanging."

"I saw your gallows outside of town … it's a fine looking one and big too. Quincy stated. Tell me, just how many men are you figuring on hanging?"

"Seven," Buddy replied.

"Seven men," Quincy exclaimed. Then he rubbed the stubble of beard on his jaw with his right hand and said, "Seven men huh … tell you what I'll do. I'll hang the lot of them for a hundred dollars even and throw in two hours of preaching and gospel singing. Mind you now, if I have to conk any one over the head to get him to hold still it'll still cost you extra."

"Quincy you have yourself a job," Buddy stated. "I'll have to run it past the town committee but I'm sure they'll okay a hundred dollars. The hanging is at sunrise tomorrow morning … maybe you should check the gallows and make sure that it's in proper working order. If anything is wrong with it, talk to Clive at the livery stable."

"I'll do just that," Quincy replied. "But first I'd like to talk to the ones that I'm going hang."

Buddy led Quincy to the cells in the back. He pointed to the cell that held Ramón and Sanchez and said, "Except for those two everyone in here will be hanged." Then Buddy left and went back to the office, leaving Quincy to talk to the prisoners.

Quincy spent about fifteen minutes with the prisoners asking each one how he felt about being hanged.

When he came back to the office he said, "Well, they all except for one seem to have accepted their fate and will go peaceably. There's that one in the cell with two others that started blubbering like a baby, when I asked him how he felt about his upcoming hanging. I just might have a bit of a problem with getting him to hold still. I'm going to go check the gallows now and get it ready for in the morning. I like for those that are going to hang to be there for the preaching and gospels singing … I sort'a feel like it puts their soul to rest somewhat."

As he started towards the door Quincy said, "I'll talk to you later sheriff and let you know if I need anything."

When Quincy got outside, he climbed to the driver's seat of his wagon, turned it around and drove to the gallows. The gallows was on the north side of the road and about an eighth of a mile from town. There were at least thirty-five different campsites on the south side of the road starting at the edge of town and spreading to the south and the east. Music and the laughter of children at play came from the campsites.

Quincy stopped his wagon at the gallows and climbed down from the seat. He slowly walked around the gallows, inspecting the construction of it. It measured thirty feet long and fifteen feet wide. A post at each corner and at the center of each side supported the structure. Each of the posts rose eighteen feet into the air and was twelve inches square. The posts were cross-braced with eight-inch square timbers and the beams on top off the posts were twelve-inch square timber. The deck of the gallows was made of twelve-inch planks one inch thick. Centered at the southern end a flight of steps ten feet wide, led up to the deck.

Quincy climbed the thirteen steps to the topside of the deck … a railing three feet high enclosed the deck. Two feet in from the western edge and evenly spaced were eight trap doors measuring three feet in each direction. Centered eight feet above the trap doors was a twelve-inch beam supported by twelve-inch posts. Close to the railing on the south end, a lever made of iron jutted up about three feet. Iron brackets attached to the bottom side of the deck held a one and a half inch square iron bar and a clevis attached the lever to the bar. The bar ran the length of the gallows about two inches from the eastern edge of the trap doors. Tongues of iron attached to the bar at each of the hinged trap doors held them closed.

After he examined everything, Quincy descended the stairs and went to his wagon. He climbed into the wagon and came back out carrying a two hundred foot coil of one and a half inch rope. He cut seven pieces from the coil, each twenty feet long. Then he carried the seven lengths of rope up to the gallows deck where he fashioned a hangman's noose on one end of each rope and a slipknot on the other. Then he tossed one of the ropes over the beam above each trap door. He opened the slipknot into a loop, passed the noose through that loop and pulled the rope tight around the beam.

Quincy noticed a small crowd gathering at the foot of the gallows as he worked. He paused from what he was doing and announced, "Folks the hanging is going to be at sunrise tomorrow morning. Two hours before then we are going to have some preaching and gospel singing. I'd appreciate it if you would spread the word to your neighbors."

After he finished preparing the gallows and without saying any more to the crowd, he descended from platform, climbed onto his wagon and went to the sheriff's office.

Buddy was coming out of his office when Quincy pulled up and asked, “Is the gallows okay?”

“Sheriff that’s a mighty fine gallows,” Quincy replied. “Stout too, unless you tear it down it ought to last for many years.”

“We figure on leaving it there as a deterrent to any outlaws that might be of a mind to come into our town,” Buddy stated. Then he asked, “Is there anything else that you need?”

“Well yes as a matter of fact there is. I’m going to need enough firewood for a bonfire that’ll last for a couple of hours,” Quincy answered. Then he said “I reckon the prisoners should be there about two hours before sunrise so as they can hear the preaching and gospel music. It’ll also give the crowd a chance to look them over before they’re hanged.”

“I’ll see that a load of fire wood is brought to the gallows,” Buddy stated. “I’ll have the prisoners there about two hours ahead of the hanging. Is that all you need?”

“One more thing,” Quincy stated, “where’s the best place to eat?”

Buddy pointed down the road to the Elkhorn as he said, “That’d be the Elkhorn.”

When Quincy entered the Elkhorn, he spotted Randy Morrison seated at a table along with Zeke, Bob, Lance, Lefty and Thom. He walked over to the table, stopped and said, “Evening Judge it’s good seeing you again.”

“Sit down here Quincy,” Randy replied. “We were just talking about you.”

“That’s mighty kind of you Judge,” Quincy said as he pulled out a chair and sat down. “What can I do for you?”

"As you know," Randy began, "the more gruesome an event is the more it will be talked about. Over time as people talk about it, the more ghastly it will become. Agua Caliente has been a haven for outlaws and we want the word to spread that they are not welcome here anymore. That's where you come in … it is a normal practice when you hang a man to put a hood over his face and tie his legs together. Both the hood over the head and tying of the legs is for the benefit of the on-lookers. I want you to not put a hood over their heads or tie their legs together. If the crowd sees the grotesque contortions of their faces and the wildly kicking legs, they will talk about the hanging more often. With each telling of the story, it will grow and eventually, in a few years exaggerated to the point that it's almost unrecognizable. The story of the hangings will act as a deterrent to any outlaws that are of a mind to come here."

Chapter Thirty Six

Quincy parked his wagon at the campsite across the road from the gallows. The majority of the people camped there knew each other and took the occasion as an opportunity to visit with friends that they hadn't seen for many months. He visited each camp telling them that there will be preaching and gospel singing for two hours leading up to the hanging at sunrise.

About three hours before sunrise, Quincy started stacking a large amount of wood for a bon-fire. When the stack was finished, he reached in his pocket and got a match. He struck the match to life and held the flame to the stack of wood. Then he stood back and watched as the small flame licked at the wood and spread throughout the stack. After the bon-fire started burning well, he walked to the gallows, reached into an inside pocket of his coat and brought out a harmonica. Quincy sat down on the third step of the gallows, put the harmonica to his lips and began playing a mournful tune.

Soon after Quincy started playing his harmonica, people from the campsites started wandering over to the bon-fire. The crowd grew as the townspeople started showing up.

Quincy ignored the crowd as he played one mournful tune after another as he waited. When he saw the wagon bearing the seven condemned men, he quit playing the harmonica, returned it to his pocket and climbed the steps to the gallows deck.

Gabby drove the wagon and Buddy was standing with one knee resting on the seat as he faced the shackled prisoners in the back. Buddy held a shotgun with his right hand, finger on the trigger and the barrel of the gun rested across the crook of his left arm.

Zeke, Lance and Lefty rode their horses on the left side of the wagon and Bob, Shorty and Rio did likewise on the right side as they escorted it to the gallows. Gabby stopped the wagon close to the gallows steps. Buddy kept the shotgun trained on the prisoners as he and Gabby dismounted the wagon and walked to the rear of it. Lance, Lefty, Shorty and Rio helped the shackled prisoners out of the wagon.

All of the prisoners except for Witherspoon willingly got out of the wagon and climbed the thirteen steps to the gallows deck. When they got there, Quincy took hold of the right arm of each in turn, led him to a trapdoor and instructed him to stand on it.

Witherspoon sat cowering in the far corner of the wagon. He was sobbing loudly and wailing like a baby between sobs. Zeke and Bob each grabbed one of his legs and dragged him from the wagon. After they got him out of the wagon, they stood him on his feet. His legs buckled and he crumbled to the ground, still loudly sobbing and wailing. There was a very foul stench emanating from his body and his pants were sopping wet.

With Zeke on one side of the sobbing and wailing Witherspoon and Bob on the other they half carried and half drug him up the steps to the deck.

Quincy stated, "I kind of figured that he was going to act like this and I'm ready for him." He had them place Witherspoon on the trapdoor nearest the release lever where he had earlier tied a small rope over the beam.

"You just hold him upright there, while I rig this rope on him," Quincy stated.

Zeke and Bob held Witherspoon in a standing position as Quincy wrapped the rope around his chest and under his armpits. He tied it there with a slipknot that would release with a tug on the rope. The rope was long enough for him to wrap it around the railing by the lever.

Zeke and Bob removed the shackles from the each of the prisoners and tied their hands behind their backs. Then they went back down the steps and stood slightly away from the crowd.

Quincy stood at the center of the front railing as he attempted to lead the crowd in singing some hymns, but the loud sobbing and wailing coming from Witherspoon drowned him out.

After three attempts at singing, Quincy turned his back to the crowd and went to Witherspoon. He stood beside him, reached beneath his coat and brought out a wooden club wrapped in leather. The club was about twelve inches long and one inch in diameter. He raised the club into the air and whacked him behind the right ear … rendering him unconscious.

The rope tied around Witherspoon's chest held him in a more or less upright position. Quincy walked back to where he was at the railing and led the crowd in the singing of three hymns.

When they finished the third hymn, Quincy cleared his throat and began preaching. He preached about the wages of a misspent life and what a terrible thing it is to have it end by hanging. He preached for about twenty minutes and then they sang some more hymns. He alternated between singing and preaching until it was time for the hanging.

A faint light on the eastern horizon announced the approaching sunrise. Quincy noticed Judge Morrison who had arrived about a half hour before, standing with Zeke and Bob.

Quincy left where he was standing and continued preaching as he walked to the lever. He put his right hand on the lever and held the rope in his left. Watching Judge Morrison, he led the crowd in saying the Lord's Prayer. About half way through the Lord's Prayer, Witherspoon regained consciousness and once again began to sob and wail.

The leading edge of the sun peeked over the hill and Judge Morrison nodded. Quincy pulled the lever and the end of the rope at the same time.

The crowd became silent as the trapdoors opened. The only sounds heard were a high-pitched aieeee from Witherspoon and a mournful wolf howl in the near distance. Seven bodies dropped and stopped with a thud. Each of the seven ran in the air as though they were trying to run from the noose around their neck.

Their faces, grotesquely twisted out of shape all turned a shade of purple. Their eyes bulged out and their tongues lolled out of their gaping mouths as they did the hangman's jig at the end of their rope. They all danced for several minutes then one after another, they slowly became still. Witherspoon fought the hardest and was the last one to hang limply.

The crowd stared at the grisly spectacle in front of them and many of them turned away in horror … some of them lost what the had in their stomachs while others had dry heaves. They all were silent as they slowly left, some going back to their camps and the others back to town.

The bodies remained hanging where they dropped until the next morning when were cut down the next morning.

There was a discussion about burying the now hanged men the day after their sentencing. The decision was too bury them in a mass grave with a single large monument. The words on the monument to read:

Here lie seven murderers and thieves
Their names are not worth mentioning
They thought to control our town ~ they were wrong
Let this be fair warning to any of the same notion

Claudio hired two men to dig the mass grave just to the east and north of the gallows.

Zeke, Lance, Lefty, Bob, Rio and Shorty said their goodbyes to Randy, Thom, Bret and the rest, mounted their horses and left.

Chapter Thirty Seven

They stopped at the junction to rest the horses and brew some coffee. They ate some of the cooked meat and tortillas that Miguel had insisted that they take with them.

When they left the junction, Rio led them south towards the Mormon settlement at Las Vegas. About halfway between the junction to Agua Caliente and Las Vegas a very large boulder was on the east side of the road with several smaller boulders on each side of it. Rio turned off the road at the boulders and circled around to the other side of them. The boulders, trees and brush screened a well-defined trail from the road … they stopped and rested the horses there. When they continued in a southeasterly direction, they rode two abreast.

They rode hard for three hours and then stopped to rest the horses. The first rest stop after leaving the road was on a long slope leading down into a valley. A large mountain range was in the far distance. As they continued their journey, the terrain opened up into larger flat expanses. Scattered through the valley were gigantic columns of rock reaching high into the sky as they stood sentry over their domain. There also were mesas and small mountain ranges with tooth-like jagged peaks. The stark blackness of the small mountains forebodingly stood out against the muddy red hue of the valley. The terrain was dry and except for a few scrubby bushes scattered intermittently there was no vegetation.

During one of their rest stops late in the afternoon Rio pointed towards the large mountain range they were riding towards and said, “We’re not gonna make it to that mountain afore dark.” Then he pointed to one of the smaller mountains, “There’s a good spot, with water over there to camp.”

The mountain that he pointed at had a grayish hue to it instead of the stark blackness of the others and the top of it was rounded rather than jagged. After their rest, they rode in a slightly more southerly direction. They got to the mountain just before dusk. Rio led them to the mouth of a small canyon and a campsite fifty feet into the canyon. There was a rock fire-ring about three feet in diameter. The ring had a large flat rock in the center of it. It was obvious that people used the campsite many times in the past. There was an ample supply off forage for the horses and a water tanque located about a hundred feet into the canyon supplied them with water. Small trees dotted the canyon floor and the steep slopes of its walls.

They unsaddled their horses and Zeke removed the pack from the buckskin. Lance and Lefty quickly gathered deadwood and built a fire as Zeke opened the pack. Bob took the bean and coffee pots from the pack to the water tanque and filled them with water.

When Bob returned with the water Zeke threw a couple handfuls of beans into the pot along with some chunks of salt pork. He then placed the pot of beans on the flat rock in the center of the fire-ring. He threw a handful of coffee into the coffeepot and placed it at the edge of the fire. After the coffee boiled a few minutes, they sipped on the hot coffee while waiting for the beans to cook. The beans were done and ready to eat about an hour later. After they ate all they wanted, Zeke added water, a handful of beans and a couple chunks of salt pork to the pot.

Rio asked about posting a watch for the night. Zeke told him that there was no need to do so, that Spirit and Blaze would let them know in ample time should anyone come around.

A sound awoke Zeke just after four the next morning. He quickly looked towards the sound and saw Lance putting wood on the glowing embers of the campfire.

Zeke got up from where he was laying and walked over to Lance. Lance stated, "Didn't mean to wake you up, I was just getting the fire going again to make some coffee."

"That's alright," Zeke replied, "reckon that it's about time to be moving about anyway."

The coffee was boiling when Lefty joined them. They were sipping on their first cup of the day when Bob joined them and then a couple of minutes later Rio and Shorty did the same. A full moon just past halfway on its journey to the west bathed the area with light.

They ate the beans that cooked overnight, saddled their horses and broke camp. They rode just south of due east as the headed toward the mountain range. Just as the day before they stopped about every three hours to rest the horses. Also just as he always did, Spirit scouted to each side and ahead, rejoining them when they stopped to rest.

They got to the foot of the mountain range just before mid-morning and Rio stated, "Probably ought to rest our horses here afore we start up. It's gonna be a bit rough getting to the top of this mountain. The only time I've been across here was when Segundo took us to Virginia City. There's a nice game trail on the other side but we had to pick our way around boulders and such coming down this side … it took us nigh unto three hours."

Spirit disappeared while they rested the horses. After a fifteen-minute rest, they mounted their horses and started to climb the side of the mountain. Suddenly Spirit appeared in front of them standing sideways.

"What's that wolf doing," Rio asked.

"He doesn't want us to go this way," Zeke replied. Then as Spirit twisted around in a circle he added, "He wants us to follow him."

Spirit led them south about a mile to a wide wash gently sloping up the side of the mountain in a south-easterly direction. The bottom of the wash was sandy until they got a little better than three-fourths of the way to the top. The bottom of the wash from that point to the top was intermittently bedrock and sand.

The horses easily traversed the wash to the top … it took just under an hour. When they reached the top, they stopped to get their bearings. There were many game trails leading down the eastern slope of the mountain. Just past the foot of the mountain to the east was a well-traveled road leading from the north to the south. Beyond the road lay a vast desert, dotted with mesas, small plateaus, and buttes. Some of the mesas rose one thousand feet and better above the floor of the desert. Thin pinnacles reached up into the sky, some solitary in their vigil over the desert floor and others in groups of three and four. Many dunes dispersed throughout the desert gave the impression of an undulating sea, with the structures of the desert being ships making their way through the passage of time. In the far distance, they could see the Rocky Mountain range stretching from north to south as far as the eye could see in either direction.

To the north, they could see a good-sized lake with a large settlement beside it. Verdant fields radiated out from three sides of the settlement. The Mormons who had settled there turned the dry desert into fertile fields by irrigating the parched desert. Farther to the north, they saw a train puffing smoke into the cloudless sky as it made its way eastward on the transcontinental railroad.

More desert, small mountains and the Colorado River lay to the south. There were three small settlements and several farms between them and the river.

Rio pointed to a spot just before the beginning of the Grand Canyon and stated, "Lee's ferry is right about there … that's where we can get across the river."

Following a well-defined game trail, they descended the mountain. When they reached the road, they turned their horses south and rode hard and fast stopping to rest about every three hours. Nightfall was quickly approaching when they arrived at Lee's ferry. Zeke paid the ferryman extra to cross the river in the dark and they made camp on the other side.

They were up well before daybreak the next morning and they rode eastward at the first glimmer of light. The sun had been up a little more than an hour when Rio pointed at the top of a vermillion colored mountain in the distance and said, "There, that's the mountain where we're headed."

The mountain was east and a little south of them. They turned the horses to the southeast and rode on. Just before midday, they were due west of the mountain and they turned to the east. About an hour later, they came to a stream that ran in a southwesterly direction. Rio stated that the stream was coming from the vermilion colored mountain to the northeast of where they were. They turned to the northeast and followed the stream, which had small trees, grass and scrub brush growing on each side. By mid-afternoon, they were about five miles from their destination.

They stopped to rest the horses and Zeke said, "Reckon we should make camp here for about an hour or so. We'll build a small, hot fire and if anyone spotted our dust they'll think that we're an Indian hunting party."

The campsite was on level ground covered with grass and surrounded by several oak trees and scrub brush. They ate and rested for an hour and a half in which time Zeke questioned Rio and Shorty about Post Cameron.

Zeke asked, "How many men does Cameron have guarding the canyon?"

"When we came into his canyon there were two men on each side of the mouth leading in," Shorty replied. "But when we left there was only one man on each side."

"What about the buildings," Zeke asked, "how many are there and what are they used for?"

Rio pulled the grass from a small area and using a short stick drew the layout of Post Cameron on the bared ground. He drew six rectangular buildings laid out in a circle. A square building was in the center of the circle. Away from the group of buildings, he drew a large oblong building with a circular enclosure at one end of it and stated that it was the stable and corral.

The square building was Cameron's quarters. Four of the six rectangular buildings were bunkhouses that would hold fifteen men each. One was the kitchen and dining hall. The sixth building had no use … it was just there.

They broke camp about an hour later and followed the stream northwest to the mountain. They rode at a slower pace so as not to stir up any dust. When they got to the foot of the mountain, it was as Rio had described it.

They had to ride through brush, around a large tree and three large boulders to get to the edge of the waterfall. There was a level area about twelve feet wide between the waterfall and the vertical side of the mountain. They rode single file behind the waterfall and entered the tunnel with Rio leading the way. After they left the tunnel and entered the slot canyon, they rode two abreast with Zeke and Rio in the lead.

The sides of the slot-canyon had horizontal stripes of many different colors and hues. Its sides were mostly vertical except for three separate places that curved outward and over. At those places, the opening at the top of the canyon was no more than two feet wide.

When they got to where the canyon turned south and narrowed to about two and a half feet, they dismounted, pulled their rifles from their scabbards and went the rest of the way on foot. When they emerged from the slot canyon, they were in a large stand of trees with a heavy undergrowth of brush. They cautiously made their way to the edge of the trees. Staying just inside the tree line, they had a good vantage point to observe the camp. The ground gently sloped for about five hundred feet to the floor of the canyon. The near edge of the camp was another five hundred feet beyond the slope.

Zeke had brought his binoculars with him … he panned the canyon that lay before them. After searching the canyon, he focused on the camp and studied each building in turn. He observed six horses and two large mules in the corral. Beside the stable was a wagon with sideboards about three feet high. As he watched, two men came out of the square building, walked to the stable and disappeared inside it. They reappeared in the corral, each carrying a bridle. After they each bridled a horse they led them into the stable and about five minutes later they rode from the stable toward the mouth of the canyon.

Zeke lowered his binoculars saying, "I reckon they are going to the mouth of the canyon to stand guard."

Shorty replied, "Probably are, it's that time of day. When it gets dark enough, you'll see the campfires that the idiots build. That's something I never did understand … how can you guard something at night if you build a fire and announce where you are?"

With a chuckle Lance said, "Don't be so hard on them Shorty, maybe they're scared of the dark."

"Could be," Shorty replied with a grin, "I'll guarantee you that they'll build a fire big enough to scare off any critters within five miles."

Lefty and Rio joined the good-humored bantering about the lack of braveness and the cowardice of the men guarding the canyon.

Zeke turned to Bob saying, "The shadows are getting pretty long … when dusk gets here we'll slip down there and see what we can see."

As they watched and waited for dusk, two riders came in from the mouth of the canyon. They rode to the stable, dismounted and led their horses inside. A few minutes later two horses entered the corral from the stable. When the two men left the stable, they went to the square building in the center of the compound.

They saw no more movement and shortly after dusk, they moved down the slope. The stable was the first building they came to … they quickly and quietly slipped inside. The stable was about seventy-five feet in width and twice that long. There were four rows of stalls … one row along the length of each sidewall and a double row down the center. One stall contained a large white stallion, the rest were empty.

Zeke stated, "That stallion looks like one of the horses that I saw when the stagecoach was wrecked."

"That horse belongs to the Major," Shorty replied.

"There are six more horses and two mules in the corral," Zeke said.

"The mules are used to pull the wagon," Rio stated.

"Then I reckon that means there are nine outlaws here counting Cameron," Zeke responded. "We know that at least two men are in Cameron's quarters. Assuming that Cameron is there with them that makes three there and the two guarding the mouth of the canyon makes five. We need to find the other four before we make our play."

Two of the bunkhouses each had light spilling from a window. They quietly slipped to the open window of the nearest one and crouched down beside it. Zeke stealthily stood and peered inside. There were three men sitting at one end of a large oblong table playing with a deck of cards. A liquor bottle, which was almost empty, sat on the table in front of them. They were talking loud enough that Zeke and the rest of them could plainly hear every word.

One of the outlaws said, "We're dang near out of whiskey, we only got two bottles left. How long do you suppose the major is gonna keep us here afore we head south?"

"Dunno," another answered, "All I know is that Segundo and those other three should be back here any day now. Those that were in Agua Caliente should be here already. The major said that when they get back we're gonna go south down around Tucson."

"I say something just ain't right," the third outlaw said. "I'd feel a whole lot easier if'n we knew for sure that we killed Cooper in that wreck. We should a' climbed down there just to be sure about it."

"You worry too much," retorted the first one. "There ain't nobody can live through a wreck like that. Besides, even if he did live through the wreck he would have been so broken up that he couldn't go anywhere. On top of that there was a blizzard coming shortly after we left that mountain and their bodies ain't gonna be found till after spring thaw."

Zeke stepped away from the window and motioned for the others to follow him. He led them to the other bunkhouse that had light inside. Standing at the side of that window Zeke peered inside. It looked much the same as the first one, except there was just one outlaw inside. He was lying on a bunk and appeared to be asleep.

Zeke squatted down below the window and quietly told the rest of them that there was only one man inside and he appeared to be sleeping. Suddenly they saw an oblong shaped light spill from the doorway of the building in the center.

Two men came out through the doorway and closed the door behind them. They came toward the building where Zeke, Bob and the rest of them were.

As the two outlaws got nearer Zeke was able to hear what they were saying. One of them said, "I think it's time that we get out of here. The Major's crazier than a loony bird and he's gonna get us all killed. 'Twas bad enough that we went along with killing that Marshal Cooper and on account o' that we're going to have every lawman in the country looking for us. Now he wants to go and take over Cooper's ranch."

The other one replied, "I think you're right. I say we skedaddle down to Mexico for awhile and the sooner the better."

"Okay," the first one said, "we'll wait till the Major's asleep and then slip outta here. Let's get our horses ready and soon as he's asleep we'll go."

The two outlaws turned to a more direct route to the stable and did not see Zeke and the others pressed against the bunkhouse wall, as they passed some hundred feet from them.

Soon as the outlaws passed them, Zeke and Lance each with gun in hand, quietly and swiftly closed the distance between them. Using their guns, they each struck an outlaw a hard blow to the head … rendering them unconscious. Bob, Lefty, Shorty and Rio quickly joined them and they carried the limp bodies into the stable.

Chapter Thirty Eight

When they got inside the stable, Shorty found a lantern and lit it. They found a coil of rope and cut off two lengths long enough to tie the outlaw's hands behind their backs. Then they dragged their bodies to a post about five feet away. They lashed them to the post in a sitting position back to back. Then they used the bandanas from each of the outlaws' neck as a gag.

When he was satisfied, that both outlaws were gagged and securely tied Zeke said, "Let's get the one that's asleep in that second bunkhouse we looked in. Gather all the rope that you can find and bring it with you."

When they left the stable, each was carrying a coil of rope. They slipped into the bunkhouse and approached the bed occupied by the outlaw. Zeke drew his gun and whacked the sleeping figure along side his head, making sure that he would not be waking up any time soon. He then took a sock from one of the outlaw's feet wadded it up and stuffed it into his mouth as a gag. He removed the bandana from the outlaw's neck and tied it tightly across his mouth, holding the sock in place. Zeke then rolled the outlaw's unconscious body onto the floor as he said, "I'm going to show you how to tie an outlaw in a way that he can't get loose and cause any trouble."

Then using one of the coils of rope, he tightly bound the outlaw's hands behind his back. He wrapped the rope twice around his ankles and pulled it tight, bringing his ankles to his wrists and tied it. After tying the wrists and ankles together, he made a small loop in the tag end next to the ankles. Then he ran the rope around the neck of the outlaw, back through the loop, grabbed a handful of hair and pulled his head back. He pulled most of the slack from the rope and tied it around the bound ankles. Then he rolled the trussed body onto its side saying, "You need to leave a little bit of slack in the rope around the neck so he doesn't choke. With him tied in this manner he'll be so busy keeping slack in the rope that he won't have time to get into any mischief."

"We need to take care of those three in the other bunkhouse before we go to Cameron's quarters," Zeke stated. "Hopefully we can do it without firing a shot and alerting him."

"I have an idea," Shorty said. "Me and Rio can go in the bunkhouse first, they're sort of expecting us and won't think anything's wrong. If you wait a bit afore you come in we can get the drop on them before they know what's happening."

"Good idea Shorty," Zeke responded. "Reckon that's what we'll do."

They left the bunkhouse and stealthily approached the one with the three outlaws inside. When they got there, Zeke, Lance, Bob and Lefty stood to the side of the door where they would not be in the light when the door opened. Rio and Shorty opened the door and walked inside, leaving the door open. The three outlaws were still sitting at the table, one at the end facing the door and the other two on either side of him. The one on the end looked up to see who came in. "Its 'bout time you got back. Where're the rest of them?"

Shorty and Rio continued walking to where the outlaws sat … Shorty on one side of the table and Rio on the other. They each stopped behind an outlaw and Shorty replied, "Reckon they're still in Agua Caliente."

"What're they doing there," the outlaw demanded. "Segundo knows that we're heading south when they get back here. We're dang near outta whiskey and they're in Agua Caliente drinking all they want. I've of a mind to shoot him when he gets here."

Shorty stated, "Guess you can shoot him if you want to but he won't be back here anytime soon. The last time we seen 'em he was dancing at the end of a rope."

Zeke and the rest of them rushed through the door with their guns drawn. The outlaws started to get to their feet as they reached for their guns. Shorty and Rio each drew their gun and whacked the side of the head of the outlaw in front of him.

"Sit back down and be quiet," Zeke barked at the outlaw that was still conscious.

The outlaw's face blanched to white as he realized who had just told him to sit down … his jaw flopped open, his eyes opened wide, his knees buckled and he dropped back onto the chair.

Shorty, with his gun raised high into the air turned to the outlaw and with a swift sharp blow to the side of his head caused him too lose consciousness. They quickly tied the outlaws in the same manner as Zeke had trussed the last one.

They left the trussed outlaws on the floor of the bunkhouse and silently made their way to Cameron's quarters. Zeke looked through the window and a feeling of extreme contempt swept over him as he observed Cameron pacing the floor. The room was twenty feet long and fifteen feet wide. A table about ten feet long and four feet wide was in the center of the room. Twelve chairs surrounded the table and a large candelabrum hung over the center of it. Instead of candleholders, it had twelve hooks with small glass oil lanterns hanging from each. The candelabrum was about four feet in diameter and suspended at the end of a small rope, which ran through a pulley attached to the ceiling. The rope, tied to a hook fastened to the wall on the far side provided a means to lower the candelabrum.

The wall opposite the window had four large maps pinned to it, one each of California, Nevada, Utah and the Territory of Arizona. The wall opposite the entry door had a doorway in the center … the door was closed. The wall on each side of the door had two oil paintings hung on each. The paintings were of the surrounding countryside and similar to the ones that were hanging in Big Red's quarters.

A gun-belt with a gun in its holster hung from a wooden peg on the left side of the doorway. A military saber in its scabbard was lying on the far corner of the table end closest to the closed door.

Zeke backed away from the window and motioned for the others to follow him. He led them about fifty feet from the building and then quietly said, "Cameron's in there by himself, I'm going in there to get him. I want two of you to check the back of the building to see if there is a back way out, the other three needs to go to the trail leading to the mouth of the canyon. If there's gunfire those two out there will probably come to see what it's about."

Bob asked, "Are you sure that you want to go in there alone? If we all bust in there probably won't be any gunfire."

"You're right Bob," Zeke replied with a hard edge to his voice, "but when he killed seven people while trying to kill me he made it personal. Now he thinks I'm dead and that he's going to take over our operations. Thanks for the offer of help but I'll do this myself."

Zeke turned and headed back to the building. Bob and Lance walked with him to the door and then made their way around the building. Lefty, Rio and Shorty went to watch the trail.

Zeke gave Bob and Lance time to get around the building then kicked the door open. Cameron's back was towards him when he stepped inside.

Cameron spun around to see who the intruder was. He recognized Zeke standing just inside the doorway. With a very pronounced lisp he shrieked "You … You're supposed be dead."

Then with a high-pitched wail, Cameron spun around again and ran to the corner of the table where the saber lay. He grabbed the saber scabbard with his left hand and drew the saber with his right. Holding the saber into the air over his head, he swung it wildly in a circular motion. He dropped the scabbard, uttered a roar much like that of an enraged bull and ran towards Zeke. As he ran towards Zeke, the wildly swinging saber hit and severed the rope securing the candelabrum. The candelabrum crashed onto the tabletop shattering the glass oil lanterns. Oil spread across the table and ran onto floor, with the flames from the lanterns licking at it in close pursuit. The building was made of wood and was very dry … it didn't take long for the fire to spread to the walls and up the side of them.

At the same time as Cameron cut the rope Zeke's gun found his fist and roared to life. It spit a slug that found its mark … shattering Cameron's right shoulder.

Cameron dropped the saber, turned around and wailing like an injured baby ran towards the gun hanging on the wall. He pulled the gun from its holster with his left hand, spun around and tried to train it on Zeke.

He wasn't quite fast enough and Zeke's gun barked again … before Cameron pulled his trigger. The second slug also found its mark and shattered Cameron's left shoulder.

Flame covered both walls of the room and the fire was making its way across the ceiling. The fire, which separated the two, was too intense for Zeke to get to Cameron.

Zeke shouted, "Cameron get to the window and I'll pull you through." Then he turned and rushed outside and around to the window. Once again, he called for Cameron to get to the window.

Cameron responded with high-pitched shrieking, wailing and badly lisped cuss words … but he did not move.

In very little time, the fire totally engulfed the building in flame. They could hear Cameron's high-pitched wailing above the sound of the roaring fire. The wailing soon became a whimper and then they heard only the sound of the fire and the distant pounding of hooves. Zeke and the other five stepped away from the firelight, stood in the darkness and waited for the riders to arrive.

The two outlaws that were guarding the mouth of the canyon arrived a few minutes later. They stopped their horses about twenty feet from the burning building. As they dismounted, they saw the group of men standing in the darkness and assumed they were Cameron and the other outlaws. One of them said, "We heard the gunshots and then saw the fire so we figured we should come in. What's going on?"

"It's Zeke Cooper," Zeke answered.

"What do you mean Zeke Cooper? We killed him," the other outlaw exclaimed.

"No he wasn't killed," Zeke replied. "In fact you're looking at him and it would be a very good idea if you were to unbuckle your gun-belts and drop them."

The two outlaws looked at each other and attempted to draw their guns.

Six six-guns roared to life before the outlaws completed their draw. Gun-smoke and the acrid smell of burned gunpowder permeated the air as the two outlaws dropped to the ground … dead.

Lance started towards the two horses that the dead men rode in on as he said, "I'm going to take one off their horses and go get ours."

"I'll go with you," Shorty stated.

As Lance and Shorty rode into the darkness Zeke said, "Reckon we ought a check on our prisoners and put them all in the same building."

"What are we going to do with those two dead ones," Rio asked.

"Leave them where they are," Zeke replied. "Tomorrow a couple of the prisoners can bury them." Then he wryly added, "If they haven't been eaten by critters before then"

They all chuckled at the last comment and headed to the stable. Spirit appeared out of the darkness as they started to the stable and walked beside Zeke. When they got there, Spirit stopped just outside the entry to the stable. The lantern was still burning when they entered and the two outlaws were now conscious.

Zeke removed the gag from each of them and one demanded, "Who are you? Why did you tie us up?"

"I am the man that you tried too kill when you wrecked that stagecoach," Zeke replied.

"It weren't our idea," the other outlaw whined. "It was the Major's idea, that's who you want."

Zeke looked at him with disgust, "That's the trouble with vermin like you, you're big and brave until caught. Then as the cowardly curs that you are, you try to place blame for your actions on someone else. The Major is dead and you will be visiting him soon. Now shut up or I'll crack you across the head again."

They untied the two outlaws and herded them out of the stable. The outlaws saw Spirit as they left the stable and with a high-pitched voice one of them yelped, "There's a wolf there."

"That's right," Zeke responded, "his name's Spirit and he'll be keeping you company tonight."

They proceeded to the bunkhouse, which had one man inside. The trussed outlaw was still unconscious and laying just as they had left him. Zeke directed the two outlaws to pick him up and carry him to the bunkhouse where the other three outlaws were. As they carried the trussed outlaw, he started moaning his way to consciousness. When they got to the bunkhouse, they laid him on the floor.

Zeke stated, "Spirit will keep them company tonight … there's no need to truss these two like we did the others."

They tied the two with their hands behind their back and their ankles bound together. Then they untied the four trussed up outlaws, removed their gags and retied them in the same manner as they had just tied the other two. They placed the six outlaws in a sitting position side by side against the wall.

Spirit found a corner of the room outside the circle of lamplight and sat on his haunches. He watched the room from the dimness of the corner where he sat.

The outlaws started moaning and groaning their way to consciousness. After they regained consciousness, three of the four recognized Zeke and quietly uttered some very unflattering cuss words. The fourth one did not know who was standing in front of them, but they all knew that they were in deep trouble.

"Now that you have all woke up from your naps," Zeke stated, "we're going to have a little talk. I believe that you all know who I am but just in case you don't, I am Zeke Cooper. I am going to ask you a few questions and just so you know I do have a way to determine if you're lying."

Zeke snapped his fingers and Spirit came from the corner. As the six outlaws cowered in fear and tried to push their way through the wall, he sniffed at and marked each one in turn. After he marked all of them, he went to Zeke and sat on his haunches beside him.

"This is Spirit," Zeke stated. "He helps me learn the truth, if I don't believe what you tell me I'll snap my fingers once. If I do that, he will grab the last one that spoke by the neck and shake him. If I feel that you lied to me again, I'll snap my fingers twice and he'll separate you from your manhood."

Zeke let the room fill with silence for about a minute. As the room filled with silence, Spirit slowly looked at each outlaw, moving his head slowly from left to right. As he looked at each one he slobbered drool onto the floor, broke the silence with a snarl and then did the same with the next one.

Zeke pointed at the outlaw on the left end and asked, "Was you with Cameron when he caused the stagecoach to wreck?"

The outlaw licked his lips, swallowed a couple of times and whispered, "Yes."

"Speak up I can't hear you," Zeke snapped.

With a loud, trembling voice the outlaw stammered, "Ye … Yes I was there."

"How many of you were there," Zeke asked.

"Nine … ten counting the Major," came the reply.

Zeke thought there's only nine accounted for here. Then he asked, "You're one, where're the other eight?"

"You got six of us right here and two are at the entrance to the canyon."

"Counting Cameron you've accounted for nine men," Zeke stated. Then he demanded, "Where's the tenth man?"

"He's dead," the outlaw replied. Then he added, "When we was coming off that mountain, his horse spooked and threw him. He landed on his head and broke his neck."

Zeke turned to Bob, Lefty and Rio saying, "I reckon that's all we need to know for now. We'll decide what to do with them in the morning"

They left the outlaws tied and propped against the wall. As they went out the door Zeke looked back, saw Spirit once again sniffing at the outlaws and stated, "They're all yours Spirit."

Chapter Thirty Nine

After leaving the bunkhouse, they went to the building that was the dining room and kitchen. When they entered, Rio removed a lantern from a hook just inside the doorway, lit it and hung it back on the hook.

The kitchen occupied the far end of the building, a pile of firewood was on one side of a large cook stove and a large water-barrel was on the other. A doorway near the left corner of the kitchen led to the larder. Long wooden tables with bench seats occupied the rest of the building. Oil lanterns hung from hooks spaced about fifteen feet apart along each sidewall. They lit four more lanterns on their way to the kitchen. Several pots and pans of various sizes hung on hooks attached to the wall near the stove. A large coffee pot sat on top of the stove near the edge. Hot coals were in the firebox to which they added some of the firewood. A small table near the stove and about four feet from the wall had a coffee grinder attached to one of its corners. The crank of the grinder was on the side nearest the wall. An assortment of knives, cooking spoons and two ladles were also on the tabletop. There were three bags beneath the table, two large and one medium sized. One of the large ones contained coffee beans and the other one flour … both bags were almost empty. The medium sized bag was about half-full of salt.

The larder measured about twenty feet in each direction. The walls were made of wooden planks attached horizontally to vertical beams. The planks were one inch thick and three inches wide and had a space of one inch between them. The construction of the larder was such that it will be cold during the winter and by soaking the slats in the summer, the evaporation of the water will chill it. A side of beef was hanging at one side of the room. Other than the side of beef, all they found in the larder was six small red potatoes, two turnips, three large onions, a half a string of garlic and three dried chili pods. A wooden barrel had about four good-sized handfuls of beans in the bottom. On the floor beside the bean barrel was a large porcelain crock-pot. Inside the pot was a short slab of bacon immersed in lard.

When the rest of them entered the larder, Bob looked in and then turned back to the kitchen. He emptied the stale coffee and grounds from the coffeepot and using the dipper hanging on the side of the water-barrel filled it with water. Then he ground a handful of coffee beans and tossed the ground coffee into the pot. He placed one of the large pots on the stove directly over the firebox and then dipped water into it until it was about half full.

Zeke cut a large piece of meat from the side of beef, carried it to the kitchen and placed it on top of the small table. Then he picked up one of the larger knives and began cutting the beef into two-inch chunks.

As he was cutting the beef, Zeke commented, "By the looks of the larder I'd say that what we heard about Cameron heading south was true. There ain't much back there except for the side of beef. Reckon he was letting his supplies run low so he wouldn't have to haul them."

Lefty and Rio came from the larder carrying all of the vegetables that were there except for the beans.

"Might as well dump those beans back there into a pot with water, they can soak overnight," Zeke stated.

Zeke finished cutting the beef and put the cubes into the pot on the stove. Then he cut the potatoes, the turnips and two of the onions into chucks and tossed them into the pot. He separated the head of garlic into individual cloves and peeled the skin from them. He then used a small knife and sliced the cloves into the pot. Next, he crushed one of the chilies into the pot along with a little salt. By the time he finished the coffee was boiling and ready to drink.

They each found a cup, filled it with coffee and sat at one of the tables. They sipped on the hot coffee as they waited for the stew to cook.

Bob looked at Zeke and asked, "What do you figure on doing with the six that we got tied up?"

"We have the death warrants," Zeke soberly replied, "but I think that you and I should talk to each of them by themselves. Hanging a man is a terrible thing and we must be certain and without any doubt that each of them was there. If we have doubts about the guilt of any one, I reckon that we can take him to Prescott for trial. Any man that was there will get his just reward."

"Why Prescott," Rio asked.

"There's two reasons Rio," Zeke replied. "One is it's more or less on our way home and the second reason is that it is the territorial capital."

"Oh, I thought Tucson was the capital," Rio said.

"It was until last year … that's when it was moved back to Prescott," Bob stated.

They continued talking as they waited. They talked a little bit about the merits of moving the territorial capital from Tucson back to Prescott. The conversation soon turned to subjects that were more mundane. The aroma of the stew cooking on the stove indicated that it was almost ready too eat. As they gathered tin-plates and utensils in preparation of eating they heard the pounding hooves of two horses.

"That's only two horses coming," Zeke stated. "That's not enough horses for it to be Lance and Shorty bringing our horses," Zeke stated. "I reckon that we ought to get out there in the dark and wait for them."

They left the building, went to the stable and waited inside the building in the darkness. They heard the hooves of more horses in the distance … quite a bit behind the first two. As the first two horses grew closer, Zeke recognized the fast-paced gait of Blaze and the buckskin.

"Reckon we're jumping at night shadows," Zeke wryly stated. "Those first two horses are Blaze and the pack-horse."

A few minutes passed and Blaze came into the camp. He stopped, reared onto his hind legs and whinnied as he pawed at the air. When he came back onto all four legs, he lifted his legs high as he trotted obliquely to the stable. The buckskin snorted and trotted behind him.

"Look at that," Zeke commented, "he shows off every chance he gets."

Bob lit the lantern hanging inside the door as Blaze entered the stable. Aided by the light of the lantern they saw the two horses that Lance and Shorty rode to the slot canyon. They had just finished unsaddling and caring for the horses when Lance and Shorty arrived.

They quickly took care of the rest of the horses and went to the dining room. After eating their fill, they went to an empty bunkhouse and found a bed.

Zeke slept fitfully that night as he kept thinking about the outlaws and what was in store for them. About three hours before daybreak, he gave up on sleeping, dressed and silently slipped out of the bunkhouse.

He went to the bunkhouse where the prisoners were. The lamp was still burning and looking through the open door, he saw that all of the outlaws were awake. They were wide-eyed and silently staring at Spirit as he sat on his haunches, licking his lips and staring at them.

As Zeke entered the bunkhouse, Spirit came and greeted him then went outside. Zeke walked closer to the tied outlaws, got hold of the lantern and turned up the wick for more light. Holding the lantern in front of each of them in turn, he silently studied them. All but the last one sullenly stared back at him. As he studied the last one he exclaimed to himself, 'This one is just a boy!' Then he asked the outlaw, "Just how old are you?"

The outlaw hung his head and squirmed as he replied, "I don't know for sure but I think I'm about twelve."

Zeke sat the lantern back on the table, untied the boy's legs, pulled him to a standing position and said, "Come with me."

Zeke and the boy started towards the door and the five remaining outlaws hooted derisively. Spirit darted back into the bunkhouse as they left and the laughter suddenly stopped.

Zeke took the boy to the dining hall and lit a lantern as they entered. They went to the table nearest the stove.

As Zeke lit another lantern he said, "Sit here at this table." Then he went to the stove, took a few pieces of firewood from the wood-box and placed them on the hot coals in the firebox. As the boy silently watched, Zeke ground some coffee, threw it in the coffee pot, added some water to it and sat it on the stove directly above the firebox. The stew that remained from the night before was still warm and he moved it to the edge off the stove away from the firebox. Then he added water to the pot with beans and placed it over the firebox. He chopped up the remaining onion and put it in the bean pot. Then he cut the chili and a head of garlic into small pieces and threw them into the pot along with a bit of salt.

After he finished what he was doing, Zeke turned to the boy and said, "If you give me your word that you won't run I'll cut the rope from your wrists."

"I won't run," the boy replied. "I have no place to run to anyway."

As he cut the rope Zeke asked, "What's your name?"

"Everybody calls me Mickey."

"Mickey … Mickey what," Zeke asked, "What is your last name?"

"I don't know … I was never told," Mickey replied.

"Don't you have any family at all," Zeke prodded.

"I don't think so," Mickey said. Then he seemed to be eager to talk and added, "I remember when I was about four … maybe five I was living with a man and his wife. I guess that she was my aunt 'cause she told me that my mother was her sister. She said that my mother died when I was born and after she died, my father started drinking a lot. One day when I was about six months old, he took me to my aunt and then disappeared. My aunt was real nice to me but her husband didn't like my being there."

The aroma of boiling coffee filled the air and Zeke stood up, got two cups, filled them with coffee, sat one in front of Mickey and sat back down. He noted that the expression on Mickey's face appeared to be open and honest.

Zeke let the room fill with silence and studied Mickey as they sipped on the hot coffee. Mickey's eyes showed gratitude as he began sipping on his coffee … they also showed a sorrowful yearning.

Reflecting on what Mickey had told him Zeke thought, 'The boy seems eager to talk' then he asked, "Where are your aunt and uncle now?"

"He ain't my uncle," Mickey replied in a loud voice. Then after a barely audible sob he continued, with his voice reflecting his hurt, "My aunt died the night of my fifth birthday … I remember that because she baked me a birthday cake. When her husband came home, he got mad about her baking a cake for me and threw it outside. Then he beat my aunt and when I tried to stop him, he pushed me down and broke two of my ribs by kicking me. My aunt died that night and the police arrested him for killing her."

Zeke listened intently as Mickey talked and then he asked, "What happened to your aunt's husband?"

"They put him in prison, but I was told he escaped."

"Mickey, what town did your aunt live in," Zeke asked. "Why are you here with these outlaws?"

"I'm pretty sure that we lived in Chicago," Mickey answered. "After my aunt died I was put into an orphanage and after my ribs healed they put me to work in a slaughter house. There were three more boys my age from the orphanage that worked there. It wasn't too bad except when the boss's didn't think that we were working hard enough, they would tie us to a post and give us at least five lash's with a buggy whip. If we got whipped, we didn't get any dinner that night at the orphanage. I still have a lot of scars on my back and legs from the whippings."

"But how did you get here from Chicago," Zeke gently asked.

Mickey looked at Zeke as tears began forming in his trust filled eyes. He started talking and the tragic story of his young life spilled out.

Chapter Forty

Shortly after his sixth birthday, Mickey and two other orphans ran away from the orphanage. They roamed the streets and docks of Chicago doing what they could to earn a few pennies to feed themselves. Sometimes when they did not earn any money, they filched an apple, a potato or any piece of fruit to feed themselves … yet many nights they slept on an empty stomach. They found shelter at night … sometimes at the stockyards and other times on the wharves between the stacks of cargo.

Chicago had a large number of orphans roaming its streets that survived by begging and stealing. During the winter of eighteen-seventy-two, the citizens of Chicago demanded that the city do something about the street urchins that plagued their fair city. The police swept the streets and rounded up thirty-eight orphans … all of them between the ages of six and twelve. Fourteen of them were girls all between the ages of seven to ten.

The orphans were put aboard a westbound train and the city in its generosity gave each of them one loaf of bread and a bag of nearly rotten fruit. The city hired a man to ride the train with the orphans to make sure that none got off before Kansas.

The railroad telegraphed ahead to their stations that an orphan train was on its way. The stationmasters at all of the stations west of the Kansas state line posted notices that the orphan train was coming. The notices stated the day and time of its expected arrival. Farmers showed up at the different stations when the train was due and some of them took one or two orphans to help work their farms. The oldest and strongest of the orphans were the first to leave the train.

When the train reached Promontory Summit in Utah, eleven orphans remained. Mickey and his two friends were the only boys left. Eight women from Salt Lake City took a girl apiece and a farmer took Mickey's two friends. The man that the city of Chicago hired put Mickey off the train, telling him that he should be able to find something.

A very cold, blustery wind greeted Mickey when he got off the train. Shivering and with a feeling of utter abandonment he wondered what he was going to do as he stood on the station platform and watched the train disappear to the west. The stationmaster looked out his window and saw a skinny, raggedy and forlorn looking six-year-old boy watching the train until it disappeared from sight.

Mickey stood there looking at the now empty tracks for about two minutes before turning away and dejectedly started across the platform.

The stationmaster left his office, stepped out onto the platform and called to Mickey. Mickey turned around and the stationmaster told him to come into his office. When they got back to his warm office he asked, "Was someone supposed to meet you here?"

Mickey replied, "No, I'm one of the orphans from that train." Then with tears welling up in his eyes and spilling down his face he sobbingly added, "All the rest of them found a family to take care of them … I guess nobody wants me."

With a hint of kindliness to his voice the stationmaster said, "I'm sure somebody will want you." Then he asked, "When was the last time you ate?"

"Yesterday," Mickey replied, "I had a little chunk of bread I was saving for today but one of the girls was crying last night 'cause she was so hungry ... so I gave it to her."

The stationmaster reached under his desk, picked up a small basket, and handed it to Mickey. "This is what my missus packed for me to eat today. I'm not really hungry, so you go ahead and eat all of it that you want."

A blue gingham cloth about sixteen inches square covered the food in the basket. Mickey took the basket, removed the checkered cloth and saw what was in it. The basket contained three pieces of fried chicken ... a leg and two thighs. It also had a medium sized baked potato, three biscuits and a small jar of apple butter.

"Gosh mister," Mickey exclaimed, "I've never seen this much food all at one time."

The stationmaster pointed at a small table close by as he said, "You go ahead and sit there and eat all that you want. Mind you now, don't eat it all at once and take your time. My relief man will be here in about three hours and then we'll find a place for you."

Mickey wasn't sure as to what to eat first, he took a bite from the chicken leg then he put some apple butter on a biscuit and tried that. He took a bite from the potato and then finished eating the leg.

Mickey slowly ate for about an hour and a half and all that remained was one biscuit and half a jar of apple butter. For the first time in his life, his stomach was full from eating and he dozed off sitting at the table in the warm room.

The stationmaster's relief arrived and Mickey awoke to the sound of their voices talking about him. He heard the relief man say, "You might try Micah, he doesn't have any boys, all's he got are those two girls and his farm is on your way home."

That's a good idea Ezra I'll try him first. I'd take him myself but I already have young'uns swinging from the rafters."

"How many do you have now Ephraim?"

Ephraim replied, "Seventeen and another one on it's way."

Ephraim and Mickey left the train station and went to a small barn nearby. Ephraim saddled his horse, led it outside and mounted. Then he reached down and helped Mickey swing up behind him. They rode toward Salt Lake City and about five miles from the station Ephraim turned onto a lane that led to a farm house about a quarter mile from the road.

Two barking dogs announced their arrival … a man and two girls came from the barn that was about two hundred feet from the house.

Ephraim rode to where the man and two girls were standing and stopped his horse. "Afternoon Micah," Ephraim greeted the man. "I have someone here that I figure can help you out."

"I don't know about that," Micah replied. "He looks pretty scrawny to me. But step down here and we'll talk it over." Then he turned to the two girls and said, "You two get back in there and finish cleaning them stalls."

The two girls, one twelve years old and the other eleven returned to the barn as Ephraim and Mickey dismounted the horse.

Mickey watched the two girls disappear into the barn wondering what it would be like to stay here.

"Boy you look at me," Micah snapped loudly. "You pay no never mind to them girls, they ain't any of your concern."

"I'm sorry sir I didn't mean any harm, I was just looking at the barn," Mickey responded.

"What's your name boy," Micah asked. "Did you come here on that orphan train?"

My name's Mickey and yes sir I was on the train."

"Working on a farm is hard work," Micah stated. "Have you ever worked on a farm?"

"No sir I haven't," Mickey answered. "But I learn fast and I can work real hard."

"You look pretty runty to me," Micah said and then asked, "Just where have you worked where it was hard?"

"I'm stronger than I look," Mickey responded. "When I was in the orphanage I worked at a slaughter house."

"Humph," Micah retorted and turned to Ephraim saying, "Reckon I can try him for a few days … but mind you if'n he don't work out I'm bringing him back to you."

Ephraim mounted his horse and took his leave. As he rode down the lane to the road he piously thought, 'I did my Christian duty and gave the little ragamuffin food and found shelter for him.' He was full of himself over what he had done with the boy. By the time he reached the road, the feeling of total self-satisfaction overwhelmed him and he joyously sang hymns as he rode home to his family.

When Ephraim re-mounted his horse Micah squeezed Mickey's left shoulder as he said, "Come along boy, I'll show you what needs doing in the barn."

Elated, Mickey entered the barn with Micah while thinking, 'I finally found a family that wants me … I wonder what it's going to be like to have a family and not be hungry any more.'

The barn, one hundred fifty feet long, one hundred feet wide and thirty feet at the highest point of its peaked roof, had large double doors on each end. It had six regular sized stalls and two milking stalls, which were twice as wide. Farming implements, harnesses, and a wagon were neatly in their place.

The girls were busy cleaning the stalls and had already cleaned all but the last two. They were using large square cornered shovels to pick up the manure and place it in a wheelbarrow.

The wheelbarrow was about full and Micah sent the two girls to the house to help their mother prepare supper. Then he told Mickey to wheel the wheelbarrow out and dump it on a pile close to the rear corner of the barn.

They cleaned the stalls in silence, except for when Micah gave instructions to Mickey. It was close to dusk when two cows entered the barn from the rear and each went to one of the milking stalls.

Micah broke the silence saying, "Don't suppose you know how to milk a cow."

"No sir," Mickey replied, "but if you show me how I can do it."

Micah lit a lantern, hung it on a hook in the milk stall and took a milk pail from another hook. He sat down on a three-legged stool and placed the empty pail beneath the milk bag of the cow. He showed Mickey how to pull on the teats to coax the milk out. Mickey caught on fast and was soon milking the cow as if he had been milking cows for years.

Micah watched Mickey milk the first cow, picked up the pail full of milk and said, "There's another pail on the wall in the other stall, you go milk that cow while I take this to the house."

As he happily milked the cow, Mickey thought, 'This ain't as hard as it was at the slaughterhouse and I have a family now too.'

Micah came back to the barn right after Mickey finished milking the second cow. He had a ragged blanket draped over his left shoulder, a tin cup in his left hand and a tin plate in his right.

"Good I see you've finished milking," Micah said as he handed the tin plate to Mickey. "I brought you your supper and a blanket for you to use. You can make yourself a bed in some of the hay in the loft."

A crestfallen Mickey choked back tears as he stammered, "Yo … Yo … You mean I'm not going to live in the house with the rest of the family?"

Micah dipped milk from the bucket with the cup and took a fork from his shirt pocket. He handed the milk and fork to Mickey as he said, "Boy I don't know where you got the notion that you are going to be part of my family. You are no more than a heathen gentile and not worthy of sitting at my table let alone living in my house. You get rid of that notion once and for all … you are not and never will be part of my family."

Micah picked up the pail of milk, turned and left the barn as a brokenhearted Mickey watched him go.

Mickey sat down on the ground with his back against the stall wall. He looked at the plate but could not see what was on it because of the tears flooding out of his eyes. He sat the plate on the ground, drew his knees up to his chest and sobbed broken-heartedly. He cried so hard it made him sick and he vomited. He puked what was left of what he ate earlier and then had dry heaves between sobs. After about thirty minutes, he quit sobbing. As he wiped the tears from his eyes and face, he vowed that he would never cry again.

Mickey went to the water trough just outside the barn and washed his face. Then he went back into the barn and picked up the plate that held his supper. Looking at the plate, he saw a morsel of meat that was no bigger than a half-a bite and a biscuit with watery gravy dumped on top of it. As he looked at the plate, he wondered is this what they are eating at the house. Deciding to find out he went to the house and peeked through a window.

When he saw what they were eating, his stomach felt as if it turned over and he became angry. They were sitting around an oblong table and each had a plate full of food in front of them. On the table were three large platters, one with fried meat piled on it, another had a pile of baked potatoes and the third platter had biscuits. Two large bowls were also on the table, one filled with green beans and the other filled with cooked carrots.

With a feeling of deep sorrow and hatred filling his heart, Mickey slipped back to the barn. Resolving to leave the first chance he got, he ate what little bit of food that Micah had brought him and then climbed the ladder to the loft. It was cold in the loft … he wrapped the ragged blanket around himself and burrowed into the hay in an attempt to keep warm. He slept fitfully and dreamed of a better place to be.

Mickey did what Micah instructed him to do … his days started with milking the cows and they ended the same way … always with a meager portion of food.

Five days later, it was Sunday and when Micah came to the barn to get the milk he said, "Today is Sunday and we do not work on the Sabbath, you are going too have to do all the chores by yourself. I'm taking the family to church after breakfast this morning and won't be back until this afternoon. If you have all your chores finished by the time we get back, you can rest until milking time."

After breakfast, Mickey helped Micah hitch two horses to the wagon. As he watched the wagon disappear from sight Mickey thought, 'this is my chance … I'll go to the house, gather some food to take with me and get out of here.

Soon as the wagon was out of sight, Mickey went to the house. He opened the door, walked inside and went to the kitchen. Three barrels were near the stove, one contained potatoes, one was almost full with turnips and the third one had carrots. On a shelf near the stove, he found an empty flour sack into which he put a few potatoes along with turnips and carrots. He lifted the lid of a large cast iron pot that sat at the edge of the stove … it contained fried chicken.

Mickey pulled a chicken leg from the full pot and started eating it as he looked around for anything else that he might need. A shotgun was leaning against the wall beside the door. He picked it up, decided that it was too big for him, put it back, and continued searching the house. In what appeared to be Micah's bedroom he found a wooden box under the bed. He opened it and saw more money than he thought was possible to see in one place. He took three twenty dollar gold coins and left the rest. He wasn't sure but thought that that would be enough to buy some clothes. Going back to the kitchen, Mickey found a clean cloth large enough to wrap around some chicken. He didn't take all of the chicken … he left two pieces after taking a bite from each. He slung the flour sack over his shoulder, walked out the door and left the farm walking towards the mountains to the east.

Mickey finished telling Zeke his story by saying, "I found Lee's Ferry and they let me stay there and do a few chores now and then for my food. The Major brought me here about a year ago to help around the camp. The first time they let me ride with them was when we wrecked the stagecoach. I thought we were just going to rob it."

Chapter Forty One

Bob came into the dining room right after Mickey started telling Zeke his story, got himself a cup of coffee, sat down close by and silently listened. The other four came in shortly after Bob did. They too got themselves a cup of coffee, sat down and listened to Mickey.

After Mickey finished telling his story, they rustled up some breakfast. As they ate, they discussed what to do with the prisoners.

"The first thing to do is have a couple of them dig a grave for those two bodies out there," Zeke stated. "While that's being done, Bob and I will question each one by himself. We will hang those that admit to being there when they wrecked the stagecoach. If there are any that were not there, we'll take them to Prescott."

Then Zeke looked at Shorty and Rio as he said, "You two have fulfilled your part of our bargain and are free to go. I'll let Judge Morrison know what we have done."

Shorty and Rio looked at each other and then Shorty said, "If it's all the same to you we'd just as soon stay and finish what we've started here."

"Your company's welcome," Zeke replied. "You might also look through the ashes of Cameron's quarters … you might find a strongbox that didn't burn."

They finished breakfast and as they stood up Zeke said, "Mickey you stay here, clean the kitchen and then go take care of our horses."

"Okay," Mickey replied. Then he asked, "What's going to happen to me?"

"Haven't decided yet Mickey," Zeke responded. "It depends on what the other prisoners have to say about you."

When they left the dining room, Rio and Shorty went to the burned rubble that had been Cameron's quarters. The other four went to the bunkhouse where the outlaws were.

When they entered the building, Spirit came to the door to greet them and then he left.

Lance and Lefty picked two of the outlaws, untied them and departed for the stable to find some shovels. Zeke removed the rope from the ankles of the one that did the talking the night before. Then he and Bob took the outlaw to the empty bunkhouse. They sat at the table … Bob reached inside his shirt, removed the packet of the death warrants and placed them on the table in front of him.

"Last night," Zeke began, "you stated that you were with Cameron when the stagecoach was wrecked. How long have you been riding with Cameron?"

"I hooked up with him shortly after he left the cavalry," the outlaw answered.

"What about the rest of them here … how long have they been with Cameron?"

"Except for the kid we all joined up with him 'bout the same time."

"By the kid, you mean Mickey," Zeke asked. "How long has he been here?"

"He's been here a year or so," the outlaw answered. "We seen him hanging around Lee's Ferry for a few years and figured he belonged to one of the families there. About a year ago, the Major found out that he was an orphan and told him that he could come with us."

"What did Cameron want with a twelve year old boy," Zeke asked. "He surely didn't ride with you when you were out robbing people. What did he do around here?"

"Naw he didn't ride with us … hell, he ain't even got a gun," the outlaw replied. "He did chores around the camp that needed doing like cleaning the stable and corral just cleaning up in general. The first time he rode with us was when we went after the stagecoach. The major wanted the boy to see him kill you." Then he mirthlessly laughed and said, "The kid thought that we were just fixing to rob it."

"I've heard enough," Zeke said. Then he looked at Bob and said, "What do you think?"

"All we need is a name that we can write down here," Bob replied.

"The name's Crandle … Mark Crandle. Why're you writing my name down?"

"He's putting your name on a death warrant," Zeke replied. "All of you that caused that stagecoach to wreck were tried in a court of law and found guilty of killing seven people … you will be hanged."

Crandle's face blanched as he protested, "You can't do that … I ain't been in any court room."

"You were tried in absentia, found guilty and sentenced to hang," Zeke replied. "You will all hang before this day is finished."

Zeke and Bob decided to take Crandle to the stable and tie him there while they questioned another prisoner. When they got to the bunkhouse to take one of the outlaws Lance and Lefty were there. They had retied the two outlaws that they had taken earlier.

"I know you haven't dug those graves yet," Zeke stated. "What happened?"

"The only shovel we found was a grain scoop," Lefty said, "and the ground is too dang hard to dig with that."

"Maybe we'll just leave them for the critters," Zeke stated. "Why don't you two go to the kitchen and prepare most of that side of beef to take with us … and anything else you think we might use. Mickey can give you a hand with it."

Zeke and Bob took each of the outlaws, individually, to the empty bunkhouse and questioned them. Each of them told pretty much the same story as Crandle had. Bob wrote their names on a death warrant and then they took them to the stable to await their fate.

Zeke and Bob returned to the dining room after they took the last prisoner to the stable. When they entered, everybody including Mickey was standing by a table, looking at a metal strongbox sitting on it. The box was two feet long, eighteen inches wide, eighteen inches deep and had a lock on it that was holding its hinged lid closed.

"I see you found a strongbox," Zeke said.

"Actually Mickey told us where we could find it," Rio stated. "It was in a hole beneath a large flat rock on the bottom of Cameron's fireplace … couldn't find a key for the lock though."

"It was probably in his pocket," Zeke stated. "Take the box outside and shoot the lock off."

Rio and Shorty each took hold of one of the handles at each end of the box and carried it outside.

As Shorty and Rio walked out the door, Lance asked, "What about the outlaws, are we going to hang all of them?"

"Yes," Zeke replied, "Soon as we get everything together here we'll hang them and be on our way."

A quiet sob came from Mickey, then with a somber face and anxiety filled eyes he asked, "Are you going to hang me too?"

"No Mickey," Zeke replied. "You have done nothing to be hanged for."

Mickey stammered, "Am … Am I going to go to prison?"

Zeke put his hand on Mickey's shoulder, steered him away from the others and said, "Mickey you are not going to prison, you will be going with us to our ranch in Arizona. When we get there you can decide if you want to be part of my family."

Mickey's eyes lit up and with a joyous sob he said, "I'll work real hard … you just wait and see."

"I reckon that you can work hard," Zeke replied. "But first you are going to school."

Rio and Shorty came back with the strongbox and sat it on a table. When they opened the box, they found ten wanted flyers with rewards ranging from one hundred to twelve hundred dollars.

One of the flyers offered a reward of twelve hundred dollars for Cameron also known as The Lisping Bandit. Five of the flyers were for the five awaiting their hanging. One had a reward of one hundred dollars, three flyers each had a one-hundred-fifty dollar reward and the fifth one had a reward of five hundred dollars. Two flyers with a reward of fifty dollars each were for the two that got them-selves killed last night. Mickey identified the man on one of the flyers offering one hundred dollars as the outlaw that was killed as they left the stagecoach wreck. There was a flier for Segundo offering one thousand dollars for his capture.

Five hundred sixty-seven dollars in coin was in the bottom of the box beneath the flyers.

"What are we going to do with all of this," Shorty asked.

"It will be impossible to find the rightful owners of that money," Zeke stated. "Add the money to what the flyers are worth and it comes to four thousand seventeen dollars. That should be enough to get the two of you started again. I'll write on the back of each flier stating that the outlaw is dead. You'll be able to collect the money at any federal marshal's office."

"All that's left to do now is gather what we want to take, hang them varmints in the stable and get out of here," Bob stated.

Zeke turned to Rio and Shorty and asked, "What do the two of you intend on doing? You can come along with us if you'd like."

"We been talking about that," Shorty stated. "We figure on going to California and trying our luck there. First, we're going to have to take care of the cattle we brought here … sure wish we didn't have them to worry about."

"Maybe you don't have too," Zeke replied. "I've been thinking on what to do with the outlaws' bodies after we hang them. I've decided that we can hang them in the stable and after they're dead, we'll set it on fire. The Indians in the area will see the smoke and when they come to investigate they will find the cattle."

They went to the stable to remove the horses and the two mules. Spirit was sitting on his haunches watching the prisoners when they entered.

Shorty, Rio and Mickey picked up some lead ropes and went to the corral to bring out the horses and mules. Zeke, Bob, Lefty and Lance formed a noose in five ropes, tossed them over a rafter, and then placed a horse by each noose. Then they cut the ropes from the ankles of each outlaw, placed a noose around his neck and put him aboard a horse. They wrapped the ends of the ropes around a support post, pulled the slack from each and tied them off. Five horses bolted forward when they received a slap on the rump. Five outlaws dangled from a rope around their neck as they did the hangman's dance. Spirit emitted five mournful howls as though he was alerting the world beyond of the impending arrival of five more misbegotten souls.

They watched the outlaws until they all became still and their bodies were limp at the end of their rope. Then they led all of the animals to the dining hall they tethered all but Blaze and the buckskin packhorse. They carried the bodies of the two outlaws to the stable.

They gathered everything they were going to take and prepared to leave. Shorty and Rio decided to take the two mules with them. They located two canvas tarps and fashioned a pack for each of the mules.

Mickey led the white stallion to where Zeke was and stated that he wanted the Major's horse.

Zeke said, "That's a good sized horse, are you sure that you can handle him?"

"I sure can," Mickey proudly stated. "He likes me and I ride him around here all the time."

They found a suitable saddle for Mickey and put it on the white stallion. Zeke closely watched as the stallion lowered his head and nuzzled Mickey as he softly nickered. It was apparent that the boy and stallion had affection for each other.

They located four containers of coal oil, doused the stable with it and lit it on fire. A small trail of white smoke rose into the air and very quickly turned into a large black column of smoke. They mounted their horses and rode out of the canyon leading the rest of the horses.

After leaving the canyon, they followed a trail leading in a southerly direction. They had ridden about ten miles when they came to a fork in the trail. One fork led to the west and the other turned due south. Rio and Shorty decided to take the westward fork.

Zeke, Lance, Lefty, Bob and Mickey rode south and talked about things to come.